Praise for
THE LEGEND MacKINNON
by Donna Kauffman:

"Adventure, passion, magic and betrayal are the bright threads Donna Kauffman weaves together to create the legend of three bold warriors out of their time." —Nora Roberts

"The characters are captivating, and the love scenes are blistering. . . . [The] balance between tears and laughter . . . makes *The Legend MacKinnon* a truly wonderful read. Enchanting! Donna Kauffman's fantastic!" —*The Literary Times*

"With this captivating story, author Donna Kauffman serves up triple the paranormal fun in a marvelous new novel." —*Romantic Times*

"Intricately woven together with the six main characters each having a different set of problems to unravel. This one kept me spellbound. A terrific read." —*Rendezvous*

"Get ready for some sensuous love stories that will heat up the atmosphere wherever you are and some laughs to tickle your fancy. *The Legend MacKinnon* is pure magic!"

—*Belles & Beaux of Romance Newsletter*

D0288733

LEGEND OF THE SORCERER

DONNA KAUFFMAN

BANTAM BOOKS

New York   Toronto   London
Sydney   Auckland

LEGEND OF THE SORCERER
A Bantam Book / March 2000

ISBN 0-553-57921-5

Published simultaneously in the United States and Canada

Bantam Books are published by Bantam Books, a division of Random
House, Inc. Its trademark, consisting of the words "Bantam Books" and
the portrayal of a rooster, is Registered in U.S. Patent and Trademark
Office and in other countries. Marca Registrada. Bantam Books, 1540
Broadway, New York, New York 10036.

PRINTED IN THE UNITED STATES OF AMERICA

OPM   10   9   8   7   6   5   4   3   2   1

This book is dedicated to my grandmother
You would have loved Alfred, Gagaw.

Also to my mother
I hope I can be for you, everything you were for her.

And to my husband, Mark, who understands quests.

Nadine, thank you for letting me borrow Fish.

LEGEND OF
THE SORCERER

ONE

JORDY DECKER STOPPED for her third Coke in less than two hours. She knew she had a problem, and it wasn't unquenchable thirst.

She looked at Fred, her goldfish, floating upside down in his Tupperware container, on the seat next to her.

"This has turned into the rest stop tour of Florida. And we have four states to go."

Fred swished his deformed tail around the bowl before resuming his belly-up pose.

"Yeah, well, we all can't float through life." She jammed the soda can in the drink holder. "I don't want to go home. There. I've said it. Are you happy now?"

Fred floated, wisely noncommittal.

Home. Warburg, Virginia. Only it didn't feel like home anymore. It had taken two long years to win the court battle against Suzanne. By the time her former business partner was convicted of embezzlement, she was so exhausted that it had been little more than a moral victory for Jordy. She wasn't even angry anymore, she was just numb.

Fighting the battle had cost her everything: her home was gone, her business dismantled, and her former clients didn't trust her, since Suzanne cleverly portrayed herself as the victim. So well, in fact, that her conviction hadn't seemed to change their minds.

But the most devastating consequence by far was that Jordy lost the ability to create the whimsical sculptures that had been her joy in life and her livelihood for the last ten years.

Ten days of lying under the hot Florida Keys sun had given her a great tan, but no answers. It was useless to keep blaming Suzanne for all her misfortunes. If Jordy was feeling unfairly punished, well, she had to let go of that anger and just deal with it. It was over. Done.

She was finally free to get on with her life. Whatever the hell that was going to be.

She pictured herself driving past her old studio, through the neighborhoods of friends who had become clients, and clients who had become friends. She'd drive by the house she'd loved, then walk into the cramped apartment she hated. But it was all she could afford now.

Yes, Suzanne owed her a huge chunk of money from the civil suit, but that was on appeal. Everything her former partner owned was being liquidated, but those proceeds would go to pay off Jordy's legal team. A relief for sure, but she was left to rebuild her business from the ground up. And in order to do that, she had to have a product to sell.

Taking a long sip of her soda, she pulled out the stack of photo envelopes she'd picked up on her way off Mangrove Key. She'd decided to do some painting, watercolors perhaps, as a roundabout way of getting back to sculpting. Something completely different to get the creativity flowing again. She'd taken photos of sunrises, sunsets, palm trees, and mangroves as inspiration.

Forcing enthusiasm, she flipped open the first envelope. Where could she set up an easel in her one-bedroom apartment to catch the best light? She snorted. That was a joke. There was no "best" light. There was no "good" light. Her double-paned windows were perpetually clouded because the seals were broken. She sighed, glanced down . . . and let out a little scream.

Revulsion curled inside her stomach. "Jesus, what in the hell happened to you?"

The stranger in the photo stared silently at her, her face badly beaten.

Who had taken these pictures?

The abuser? Was that twisted or what? And to have them developed at a one-hour photo shop? She slid one picture behind the rest, then another. Maybe this woman was trying to do something about the abuse she'd suffered. Maybe *she'd* had these pictures taken as proof. Why hadn't she gone to the police? Or the hospital? Or maybe she couldn't trust anyone.

Jordy scowled. She knew something about having nowhere to turn. Her gaze was riveted to the tragic, mutilated face. Who was this woman? Had she once been pretty? Her medium-length dark hair was wet, or very dirty, matted as it was to her head. The one eye that wasn't swollen shut continued to stare at her, silently demanding that something be done about this.

Compared to what this woman had been through, Jordy's troubles suddenly seemed trivial.

She could mail them back to the photo shop and hope things would get straightened out. She looked back down at the photos and found herself shaking her head.

Maybe it was because too many people had bailed out on her when she'd counted on them most, but she couldn't just dump these in an envelope and forget about them. Or maybe she was just delaying the inevitable return to Warburg. The return to uncertainty.

She tried to tell herself it was righteousness, not cowardice, that had her turning for the exit going south. She knew it was a little of both.

• • •

IT WAS DUSK when she returned to the Lower Keys. There was a different clerk behind the counter than before, when she finally walked into the ZippySnap. The young woman had unnaturally black hair, which matched her fingernail polish and her lipstick.

"I got these by mistake." Jordy laid the envelope on the counter. "I picked up five envelopes earlier today. Four of them were my pictures. The other one had my name on it, but the pictures aren't mine."

"Did you check the negatives?" she asked, clearly annoyed. The girl only needed a nail file to complete the picture of occupational boredom.

"No negatives in that envelope."

"Can't help you then."

"Where is the young man who helped me earlier today?"

"Jason's gone for good. Parents are making him go back to school." She rolled her eyes, as if Jordy would certainly sympathize with that indignity.

"Okay, then may I see your manager?"

"Sherrill went off with Jason for the rest of the weekend. Sick if you ask me. I mean, she's almost thirty."

Jordy was thirty-one. "Yeah, a real Methuselah complex. About the pictures I got by mistake—"

"Just leave 'em. Probably belong to tourists. Most don't come back, but some call."

Jordy tried a different tack. "Did you deliver any pictures today to someone who looked like they'd been in a fight? A woman?"

"Don't think so."

Just how many black and blue customers do you get? Jordy wanted to ask. "Do you have a policy on pictures that might be, you know, a little out of the norm?"

The clerk frowned suspiciously. "We just print them. If it's about kids or something, we call the cops, but otherwise Sherrill just tells us to shut up and deliver them. Listen, it's time for me to close up. Do you want a refund or a free roll of film?"

"I want you to check the pictures you have here and see if any of them are mine."

Elvira's heavily lined eyes widened. "But that would take, like, forever."

"They might still be here in someone else's envelope. I'm in one shot, so you'll know if you see them."

The clerk slid off her stool and did a half-hearted scan. "Must have been picked up."

Jordy didn't want to just leave the photos, but with her pictures already gone, an easy switch was no longer an option. "I'll be here through tomorrow." She wrote her name and hotel on a blank film envelope. "Call me immediately if they come back in."

She left the store feeling defeated. She glanced through the glass storefront as she kicked her car into gear and jammed it immediately back into park. Elvira had just tossed what looked like her envelope of photos into the trash.

Jordy strode back in. "What did you just throw away?"

The girl looked taken aback. "There were no negatives. They're probably with the other pictures." She shrugged. "They'll just get a new set made."

Jordy hated to admit she had a point, but she wasn't going to pin her hopes on that. She stepped around the end of the counter and fished them out of the trash. "If she comes back with my pictures and wants these, give her my name and the name of my hotel." She glared at the clerk. "*I'll* make sure she gets them."

TWO

MALACAI L'BAAN ANSWERED his fan mail. Grudgingly.

It wasn't that he didn't appreciate the readers who enjoyed his work and took the time to write to him. He loved reading his mail. But couldn't they just be happy reading, or even criticizing, his books? Why the fascination with him personally? He had to be the most boring guy on the planet. He spent most of his time living inside his head, creating his otherworldly stories, and the rest of his time dealing with Alfred.

Responding to fans was an arduous task. He never knew what to say and some of his readers' letters were amazingly . . . graphic. Then again, not responding at all was out of the question.

Alfred, as he so often reminded him, had answered every fan letter he'd ever received, in his own hand. And as the legend he'd become, those letters had been innumerable. His grandson would do no less, even if his handwriting was so much worse.

E-mail had made part of the task easier. Alfred grumbled about the impersonality of it, but as far as Cai was concerned, it was a Very Good Thing. Or it usually was.

Cai frowned as the row of incoming mail scrolled onto his screen. The name was there again.

Margaron. Cai well remembered the spell it had triggered when Alfred had seen the last note. When Alfred went into full rant mode, even Cai couldn't understand the old Welshman's language, but Cai managed to piece together that Margaron was a Welsh name meaning pearl.

He noted the rest of the e-mail address. It was a different provider, but, like the others, it had originated somewhere in the UK. He had fans all over the world, so the location wasn't unusual. It was the tone of the notes that bothered him.

Both of Margaron's previous notes had referenced his new fantasy series, *The Quest for the Dark Pearl*. Part One had been on sale for a little over a week when the first note arrived. He'd responded with the standard thank-you e-mail he used when he deemed the correspondent to be a bit over the edge. Polite, but not inviting further conversation.

The second note had been terse, more emotional, not exactly threatening, but definitely out there. He'd opted to not respond at all, hoping she'd go on to other pursuits. She had rambled on about how the release of *Dark Pearl* had finally proven to her that he was the man meant to guide her future, and that together they were destined for immortal greatness. That had been unnerving, to say the least. But this time she'd gone much farther—and in a very different way.

He read, *Did you pick up the pictures as I instructed? She was quite lovely. Such a pity you didn't respond to my last missive. Perhaps you need the challenge of a good deed, a soul rescued. Yes, I see now that I was wrong in underestimating you.*

I have her here. She loves your work, but she's far from alone, isn't she? Ah, they fantasize about the man who writes of such a powerful and seductive sorcerer. But she sees only the fantasy you

created. I understand the reality. You are the sorcerer. I have
always known this, I alone believed. I have been waiting for your
sign and you have finally given it to me.

Bring me the Dark Pearl, Malacai L'Baan. Surely you don't
want her to suffer for her foolish mortal emotions. Bring me the
Dark Pearl and she will be set free. And we will begin our future
as ordained.

Had some deranged soul out there actually kidnapped
one of his readers? It seemed too ludicrous to even consider.
He'd never received any pictures. What was she talking
about? He scanned the last two notes she'd sent. Neither
spoke of pictures or said anything about abducting anyone.
He closed the file and leaned back in his chair with a deep,
aggravated sigh.

The Dark Pearl series had been inspired by some vaguely
remembered stories Alfred had told him as a child. Cai's
version was entirely fictional, a fantasy involving a magical
dark pearl that his sorcerer hero had already spent some
eight hundred pages searching for, and wouldn't find until
at least book four, if Cai stuck to his outline.

Alfred chose that moment to burst into the office.

"Dilys is heading over to Mangrove to do the marketing. Are you in need of anything?"

Yeah, an e-mail filter, he thought. Cai was careful not to
look at his monitor. Alfred might be in his eighties and
missing more than a few pages from his mental encyclope-
dia, but at times he was very well indexed. Always, it
seemed, when Cai didn't want him to be. "Can't think of
anything."

His grandfather filled the doorway, though his demanding presence was more charisma than physical mass. He
was tall, though less so over the past years. He depended
more and more on his cane, but his wiry frame and
squared, knobby shoulders kept his bearing erect, and there
was an odd grace to his stilted gait. His hair was pure

white and fell to his shoulders in a silvery mane. His goatee and mustache created the look of an Old World scholar and storyteller. Alfred was both.

His color was good today, Cai noted, not as flushed as it had been yesterday. And he hadn't garroted himself shaving. Always a blessing. Cai and Alfred had a longstanding disagreement over the latter's use of a straight razor. It was a battle that, as of yet, Cai hadn't managed to win. A neck undotted with bandages and Kleenex blots was a good sign, but it was the eyes that were the true gauge. They were as clear a turquoise blue as the water that surrounded their home on Crystal Key.

He'd have to be on his toes. No way was Alfred seeing the e-mail. Not after what had happened last time.

"Any good reviews in today's mail?"

"Just fans and the occasional advertisement."

For the most part, Alfred left Cai alone to his work, because he felt that what was in a man's heart and soul was his to transform to the written word alone. But he did enjoy the critical reviews. Cai had caught him snooping through his mail more than once. As any proud grandparent would, he'd say when caught. But Cai knew differently.

Alfred had had a long, and at times outspoken, history with various literary reviewers such as Isolde Morgan. His public battles with her were notorious, and they had cleverly engendered only further review and attention to his work. But while Alfred was still widely considered the definitive Arthurian scholar of the modern era, he'd chosen not to publish anything in the last ten years. He'd said all he had to, was his reasoning for retiring. But Cai knew it was his failing mental faculties that had forced him to end his career.

Alfred had adjusted surprisingly well to his retirement. Of course, it helped that he still spent hours a day holed up writing. He told Cai they were his memoirs and he'd let him in on them when he was good and ready.

Alfred's eyes sparkled. "Any more mail from that Candy's Playhouse website?"

Cai scowled. "No." For a man who resented most things modern, Alfred had taken a perverse shine to certain aspects of the Internet that Cai would just as soon he not know about. "I delete that stuff."

"Of course, but before or after you peruse them?"

"Very funny."

"Just trying to improve your social life." Alfred stepped into the room and Cai shifted to block his computer screen. Alfred's eyesight would do a buzzard proud.

"Trust me, I'll never be that desperate for companionship."

Alfred looked down his narrow nose. "It *has* been a while."

"Why don't we leave that dead horse in the grave today, okay?" When Alfred merely nodded in too-easy acceptance, Cai frowned. "Okay, what's up? When you give me that look I know you've got something up your sleeve."

"I have nothing in my sleeves but my arms." Alfred sniffed indignantly as only a Welshman could.

"Fine. But if Dilys comes home with anything more than boxes of groceries, we're going to have another little chat about blind dates. Understand?" He remembered the blonde lifeguard who'd mysteriously popped up one day during his morning swim to "save him." Alfred had looked so innocent, but Cai hadn't missed the startling resemblance the woman had to Pamela Anderson Lee, nor had he forgotten Alfred's recent fixation with *Baywatch*. Of late, he'd become quite engaged by *Xena, Warrior Princess*. Cai shuddered at the possibilities.

Alfred picked imaginary lint off his pristine white duck shorts saying, "I have had no dealings with Dilys in regards to your dismal social calendar, dear boy." Leaning on his gold griffin-headed cane, Alfred lowered himself to the seat in the corner and elegantly crossed his legs. "Now, why don't we dispense with all this diversionary verbal byplay and you tell me what it is that has you upset. Is it a bad review?"

Cai thought about going with that, but Alfred knew he was rarely put out by negative reviews. "No, nothing like that."

"Eileen?" Alfred said, referring to Cai's editor. "She's not tampering with that bit about the dragon in Book Two, is she? She needs to trust your inner voice." There was only one thing that got Alfred's back up besides "sadly misinformed literary analysts" and that was "frustrated wanna-be writers"—otherwise known as editors.

Cai raised a hand, even as Alfred's gaze shifted to his computer screen. "No, she bagged that revision once I explained how it wouldn't fit in."

"Well, if she'd half a brain in her narrow-minded head, she'd have never questioned—"

"Don't pick on Eileen, you like her, remember?"

"Yes, I do. What is the problem then if it is not the lovely Eileen? Nice Irish lass. A pity she's married. Children, too."

Cai merely tightened his smile. "The only I thing I lust after is her editorial skills." He needed to contact her, he thought, and very possibly the local police. Was someone out there right now, torturing one of his readers? It seemed more fictional than real. But one look at any daily paper proved reality was often stranger than fiction. He just didn't need this wacko to be his reality.

"Well, lust in one's work is always a worthy thing, lad, but you mustn't ignore your more earthly needs. A man can't live in his mind alone. It stunts the imagination, disconnects one from the emotions necessary to bring the words alive on the page."

Cai sighed, knowing he was in for one of Alfred's lengthier speeches on the sins of ignoring the flesh. He didn't need this reality, either. He glanced at the screen, but turned his attention back to Alfred. One problem at a time.

It was often the only way he managed to get through the day.

THREE

❧

JORDY SIPPED HER morning coffee and stared out over the water wafting through the mangroves. Maybe she could do her own investigation and find the woman in the pictures. "Yeah, right," she murmured. Joe Friday she was not.

She focused on the water lapping the mangrove roots. She should start painting here, and use the real thing as inspiration instead of the images from the photos.

Chicken. She should bag this and go home.

Would the police do anything? If no one was pressing charges, maybe they wouldn't care.

Painting. Think about painting. She did some of her best thinking while she worked. In fact, when her mind wandered, the most creative of her creatures emerged from the clay, or from her pen. She usually did a series of ink drawings for new sculptures. Other times she just went directly to the clay and let the creature out. Right this moment however, the only creature begging for release was the haunted woman in the photographs on her dresser.

She headed inside, closing the balcony door behind her. After a hot shower and a talk with the desk clerk, she was on her way to the police. So okay, maybe she was still running. But trying to help someone else felt good. Besides, she honestly had zero interest in water colors.

IT WAS ALMOST lunchtime when Jordy emerged from the Mangrove Key police department. Sgt. Winston had been solicitous and kind, smiling reassuringly as she'd asked several hypothetical questions before getting to her real reason for being there. She realized the officer thought she was the victim herself. His demeanor had undergone a dramatic change when she'd revealed the truth. He explained that the type of assault and battery done to this woman was very serious and indeed a punishable offense that did not require the victim to file charges. The state could do so on its own.

He had her fill out a report and seemed so earnest. She wanted to believe he would do something, even though he'd warned her that it was possible the woman and her abuser were no longer in the vicinity.

Sgt. Winston had thanked her for her concern and told her that she was free to go.

Jordy knew she had done all she could, but she wished that she could have done more. She pulled into the hotel parking lot deep in thought. Then she saw the eye-catching sign. Before she could change her mind, she peeled the hot pink paper off the hotel manager's office window and stepped inside.

She emerged minutes later with a new job as the Mangrove Hotel's arts and crafts camp counselor. The hotel ran a small program for their guests' children, freeing the adults to take fishing excursions and the like. Their regular arts and crafts teacher had taken a sudden leave of absence to tend to a sick family member. So, for the next two weeks, for two hours each day, Jordy would be teaching children to draw, paint, whatever she wanted. The manager showed her to the supply room, which was surprisingly well-stocked, then arranged for her to move to a smaller room in the hotel.

"I know what you're going to say, Fred," she said as she threw her clothes back in her suitcase and collected her toothbrush and shampoo. "Trust me, I know I'm doing the right thing. I'm excited. When was the last time that happened? I know I have to go back and face reality. But the rent is paid for the month. Once I get home, life will just bite me in the butt all over again. And maybe I'm still sore from the last time."

She *would* go back. She'd find new clients, make new friends. She'd come back stronger, and this time she'd take care of her own business. She wouldn't live, eat, and sleep work, either. She'd find balance.

In short, she'd get a life.

She drew in a deep breath and stepped out on the balcony, absorbing the bright sunshine. However, in order to achieve those goals, she had to be able to sculpt, and to do that, she had to rediscover her imagination. Who better to help her than a group of children?

CAI MANAGED TO get the still-lecturing Alfred to accompany him out to the gardens. His grandfather was quite the horticulturist and had created an Eden of their very own behind their home. It was an interesting twist on the delicate tea gardens he remembered with fondness. He'd created a haven that was both serene and whimsical.

Cai often found Alfred out here in the late afternoon talking to his plants, or any one of the pieces of statuary he'd collected over the years. He held forth on a number of subjects, clearly delighted to have a never-tiring audience. At times he'd ask questions, pausing as if hearing a response, answering phantom questions, debating unspoken points.

Many times, Cai would take a seat out of view, and listen as Alfred told the plants his stories of the dark ages and the days of Arthur. Cai marveled over the richness of detail and vast wealth of his grandfather's knowledge. Of course, Alfred would sense when Cai was there, and would suddenly zero in on him with his laser-like blue eyes, firing this question or that, ready for debate. So in touch with reality and yet living in fantasy. As a child, Cai had learned to enjoy his grandfather's oddities. As an adult, he sometimes wished he had the same capacity for unselfconscious whimsy.

He forced a smile now, wishing Alfred would turn to his marble and stone creatures for a speech or two so he could make some phone calls.

Dilys had already left for Mangrove, so she could not help him. Not that he could count on her. Dilys was an eccentric herself with an unswerving loyalty to Alfred.

Their relationship was an odd one. Cai thought she was part Welsh, but her accent was an odd hybrid of English, Scottish, and God only knew what else. She looked to be anywhere from sixty to one hundred sixty. Short, stout-bodied, and stronger than most men, she wore a dour expression that didn't invite conversation. She was a one-woman dynamo. Cai was convinced she'd missed her calling as ruler of a great nation. She could have done that and still had time left over to cook for twelve, run a household of a hundred, and take care of two reclusive men who appreciated her more than the air they breathed. He had no idea why she was so devoted to Alfred, but had stopped trying to discover the answer by his teens. He supposed most would consider her a housekeeper, cook, maid, whatever. Cai thought of her simply as their keeper, period.

The funny thing was that Cai didn't even know what her last name was. She was just Dilys to him.

"I'm in no mood to be coddled by plants and inert statuary, young sire," Alfred started up.

Young sire. Alfred was just winding up, when he'd hoped to wind him down. "It's nice out here, Grandfather. A good breeze today."

"If we must sit outside, then perch there." He pointed to the sanded marble bench beside the koi pond he'd added last year.

"I would love to, but I really have to get to the rest of my revisions. Eileen is expecting them." It was a white lie, but a necessary one.

Alfred grumbled and went right into his Free the Muse speech. Cai left him lecturing the koi on the finer points of protecting one's inner voice from the piranhas of the soul. He sighed wearily as he sat down behind his desk. It was sad. His grandfather's eccentricities had grown to an almost unmanageable level. And Dilys could only be of so much help. Though the woman seemed ageless to him, she was no spring chicken. As unbelievable as it sounded, he'd probably be making some decisions about her care before too long. The idea of Dilys being frail or weak in any way was frightening . . . Lord only knew when the time came, how in the hell he'd handle that.

He turned to his monitor and read the message once again. "And now this."

Cai left a message for Eileen and debated alerting the local police on Mangrove before talking with her. He had no personal lawyer. No agents, publicists, managers, and the like. Only Alfred, Dilys, and Eileen. Fortunately, the publishers had wanted his work badly enough to find a way to deal with the reclusive author. They had portrayed Cai as a man of mystery, which he wasn't keen on, but it allowed him to write and care for Alfred in peace and quiet.

It also helped spawn obsessive fans, determined to find out about the man behind the mystery.

His private line rang and he snatched it up. "L'Baan."

"I just got your message," Eileen said, pausing to inhale. "I thought you quit."

"Only outside my office." Her accent was pure Long Island with enough brass to fill a horn section. "And get off my back already. I've been working seventy-hour weeks. What's this about a letter?"

"You work too hard. I keep telling you, I'll set you and Max up down here in the Keys. You could work at home, be with Lee and Sam. Freelance. Or just work for me."

Eileen's cackle had Cai grinning even as he held the phone an inch from his ear. "I'd die first. New York isn't in my blood, it *is* my blood. And, trust me, Lee and Sam are better off letting Max take care of them. This way they stay alive and I stay out of prison for manslaughter."

"You love those kids."

"Late every evening and most weekends. It's a perfect arrangement for everyone." She sucked another inch of tar into her lungs. "Alfred must be on a real bender today, you're in mother hen mode."

"Speaking of that, be on your toes. He's on his 'editor-as-a-frustrated-wanna-be-writer' kick."

Eileen chuckled. "I'll deal with Alfred on my own." There was a pause, then she grew serious. "You know, Cai, lately Alfred has been a little off, even for him—"

"Listen, I really need to talk to you about this letter."

"Okay, okay." She exhaled loudly. "What about it?"

Cai read it to her. For once, Eileen had no snappy comeback. "Do you think this is legit?" he said finally.

"Good God, I hope to hell not. But we have to play it like it is. Dammit. This isn't the kind of hype we want for the Pearl series."

"This can't leak out, Eileen. Cannot."

Eileen didn't bother to pretend she hadn't thought about it. She might be a good friend, wife to a great guy, and a mother of two delightful daughters, but when it came to his books, she was an editor first, last, and always. "I know, I know. But things like this have a way of taking on a life. I'll do what I can."

"Don't make me regret that I called you before the police."

"Let me talk to legal first, see what our liability is in all this. I'll get back to you."

"Eileen, there is a woman out there, possibly injured, maybe worse. We can't sit around worrying about our legal position on this."

"Yes, we can, and yes, we will. Let me do my job. You do yours. I want those revisions on my desk by Friday."

"Dilys is FedExing them as we speak. Call legal," he instructed. "I agree we need to know how to handle this from a professional angle. But in the meantime, I'm going to figure out what the hell pictures she's talking about, see if I can dig up some leads."

"Leads? Hello. You write fantasy, Cai, not true crime. Besides, you said the e-mails came from the UK. So, what's the point in calling the local guys?"

She had a point. "I'm a good researcher. I'll dig around and see if I can find out who this message came from, where, what provider, and so on. Maybe I can get a name."

"Don't call the police until I get back to you. Agreed?"

"Get back to me quickly, Eileen."

Four

CAI WAS ON the dock when Dilys returned.

He had spent several hours researching on the Internet, but that had proven more frustrating than enlightening. He had learned that international crimes, or threats of crimes, fell under the jurisdiction of the State Department. The magnitude of what he might be dealing with had sunk in.

He was waiting on replies from the service providers about the e-mails, but he wasn't overly optimistic. It was simple enough to open up any number of free e-mail accounts, using any name and address the user felt like providing. That each e-mail had come from a different provider told him the sender had likely figured out an untraceable path. And the service provider wasn't likely to give him any account information on the names, but he asked, nonetheless.

Cai watched as Dilys expertly steered the motorboat against the pilings. She tossed him the lines, which he obediently tied off. He knew better than to offer a helping hand up, and instead jumped into the boat and hefted two cardboard boxes of food and supplies. He also knew it was fruitless to explain that he could do this chore himself, or have the stuff delivered, saving her the trouble altogether.

He did, however, take the heavier of the boxes, knowing Dilys would heave the other two herself, or die trying. They said nothing until they were in the kitchen. Here was Dilys' undisputed domain. Of Alfred's many and varied talents, cooking wasn't one of them. And while Cai could grill a mean shark steak, he humbly accepted his sexist role of landscape pawn and maintainer of all things mechanical, and left the kitchen to the queen.

"Himself asleep?" Dilys asked. She always spoke of Alfred as if he were some sort of past century lord of the manor. And where Alfred's Old World accent ebbed and flowed dependent on the vehemence of his emotions, Dilys' hybrid mix remained as strong as it had been when she and Alfred had moved to Florida twenty-seven years ago.

"About thirty minutes ago," he responded. "He ate the salad you fixed him, said to tell you it was superb."

If there was any pride behind Dilys' curt nod, Cai would never be privy to it. "Are yer whites and darks separated?"

"Yes, ma'am." Cai hid the scowl. He hated wash day. Even as a grown man, he'd always had this ridiculous urge to hide his white BVD's inside his navy blue Dockers. Just to see what she'd do. As yet, he'd never worked up the nerve.

She pulled the mail from one of the boxes and handed it to him. He flipped through the top few, went to toss a piece of junk mail in the trash, then froze. He pulled it back and looked at it, remembering a postcard he'd tossed out over a week ago. A postcard alerting him that his pictures were ready.

"Ye know where to find me then, should you be needin' anythin'," Dilys interrupted, clearly dismissing him.

"Uh, I'm going over to Mangrove for a bit. Shouldn't be gone more than an hour or so."

"I can handle himself if he's to wake," she said with a light sniff. "You go on with yours."

Cai nodded, thankful that she could indeed handle Alfred. Back on the dock, he decided to take the jet boat.

He couldn't recall the exact day the postcard had arrived. Right around the time the second e-mail had shown up, he thought. It had been from some one-hour shop, but he hadn't dropped off film to be developed. He'd thought it was some sort of gimmick, show up and get free film if you become a value member or something. He'd tossed it and not given it another thought.

TEN MINUTES LATER he was docking at the pier behind the storage facility that housed his bike. He ducked into the office. "Hey, you have a copy of the yellow pages I could glance at?"

Dobs, the owner and his occasional fishing partner, looked up from his magazine. "Hey, I heard the snapper are biting. How 'bout it?" He pulled the dog-eared phone book from beneath the counter.

Cai smiled, but shook his head in true regret. "Can't today." Dobs was an older man, a widower closer to Alfred's generation, originally a mailman from Philly.

"How's Alfred? I asked Dilys earlier." He shook his head. "Never get more than a nod out of the old broad."

Cai grinned. Dobs loved to give Dilys a hard time. That act of bravery alone had earned him Cai's awe and respect. "He's doing okay." Cai flipped the book open.

Dobs frowned. "Shame we can't get him out on the water." Fishing was Dobs' cure for everything.

Cai wished it were that simple. "Yeah, me too." He tried to imagine Alfred, holding court with an ocean full of fish and crustaceans and lecturing on young Arthur, Lancelot, and that poor misguided Guinevere. "It would be . . . entertaining." As expected, there weren't many listings for photography shops. "Got some paper and a pen?"

Dobs squinted at what was on the page, then promptly tore it out. "Here ya go."

"Thanks, Dobs. I expect a full report on those snapper next time I come in."

"If I get any extra, I'll drop 'em off."

Cai hid his smile as he turned to the door. Dobs would make sure he had a few "extra." Any excuse to stop off and rile up Dilys. "You're a better man than I."

Dobs' laugh turned into a wheeze. "Nah, just older. She ain't gettin' any younger either. I'll wear her down one of these days."

Cai doubted the United States Marines could wear down Dilys' resolve. But far be it from him to discourage Dobs' fun. "You never know. The world is full of surprises."

CAI HIT PAY dirt at the second shop. There was a stack of postcards on the counter of the ZippySnap that looked like the one he'd received.

"I'm here to pick up some film. Last name is L'Baan."

The woman behind the counter was very blonde and very tan. Her nametag said Sherrill. "Say, do I know you?" she asked with a toothy smile.

"It's possible. I live around here." He nodded toward the file drawers. "I'm kind of in a hurry."

She gave him another lookover, finishing with a direct look that made it clear if they hadn't met before, she was more than willing to remedy that situation. Cai shifted his gaze to the framed pictures on the wall. He heard her sigh, then the sound of the envelopes being flipped through.

"Here you go," she said brightly, putting the thick envelope on the counter.

Cai spun around. "Really?" He looked down at the envelope with a mixture of relief and dread.

The clerk glanced at the envelope. "They were left here almost two weeks ago. We got them done that day."

"I . . . I know. You sent me a postcard, but I didn't get around to picking them up until now. I'm, uh, just glad you still have them."

"We would have called you, but you didn't leave us a number, just your PO Box address."

Cai looked at the handwriting on the envelope. The neatly printed block letters weren't close to his own scrawl. He debated interrogating her, but decided he'd better look at the pictures first.

He sat on his motorcycle and fingered the selfstick flap. Maybe he should just go directly to the police, but maybe this was some sick prank. He tore open the flap and slid out a glossy stack of prints. He wasn't at all prepared for what greeted him.

She was quite lovely.

She had a gamine face with short auburn hair that was lifted by the wind, blowing in soft spikes around her face. Her cheekbones were high and sharp, her mouth small and full. She had a graceful neck, or maybe it was the wispy tendrils that clung to it that made it appear so. She wore a skinny-strapped white tank top and no bra, although there wasn't much there to require one. She looked short, with well-toned arms and a flat, tanned belly, shown off by the baggy khaki shorts slung low on her hips. The heavy leather sandals should have looked like clodhoppers on her feet, instead they made her seem all the more earthy and natural. Her crooked smile was somewhat shy, as if she knew a secret. But there was a twinkle in those eyes, as if it were a secret she was just dying to tell.

It took several seconds before he pulled his gaze from the woman's face and noticed the background. The glass door behind her had the words The Mangrove Hotel stenciled on it. It was a relatively new place, just opened the year before.

So, she was here. Or had been here.

He flipped through the rest of the photos. They were mostly shots of the shore; sunrises, sunsets, narrow focus shots of wildflowers, the occasional manatee or waterfowl. They looked like someone's vacation photos. A chill raced over his skin. Had this nut snatched some innocent vacationer right off the beach?

Then he realized the obvious. The kidnapper didn't have to be in Wales, just have an e-mail account there. She could have been here in the Keys all along. In fact, maybe there was no victim. Maybe the pictures were of Margaron herself and this whole thing was a sick, sick joke.

Oh, how he wanted to believe that. Yet, he thought of the smiling woman in the photo and couldn't imagine that either. He had to go to the police. He'd deal with Eileen later.

The road to the Mangrove PD took him right past the Mangrove Hotel. He found himself turning in. The chances of the woman still being here were slim. But he had to find out.

He swung off his bike and pulled out the photo. "Who are you?" he asked under his breath.

Then he looked up . . . and saw her.

FIVE

J ORDY HAD THAT odd feeling she was being stared at. Tammi Peters finished drawing her dragon with a wild flair of purple flame coming from his mouth, making Jordy smile. "Now, there's a royal dragon if I ever saw one."

She shook off the feeling and looked over the artwork of the other four children.

"What fierce beasts," she exclaimed. "I'm impressed."

"Can we take them to show our parents?" asked Johnny.

Jordy nodded. "Let's clean up. Tomorrow we'll get out the paint." The kids cheered and began noisily gathering up their pastels, crayons, and markers. Jordy watched with great satisfaction as the kids ran to Carol, the head counselor, babbling about the fun they'd had. Taking this job had definitely been the right choice. Working with the kids, seeing their unbridled enthusiasm for even the smallest of projects, watching their eyes spark as their imaginations took over . . . it reminded her of what she'd lost. But in a good way. It made her look at creativity through the eyes of a child, as something fun. Simplified. It gave her hope.

She waved good-bye and returned Carol's thumbs-up.

"Excuse me."

Startled by the deep voice so close by, Jordy whirled around.

"Could I speak to you for a minute?"

His voice was quiet, but there was an underlying intensity that was a bit unnerving.

"I'm sorry, but I'm not a regular member of the staff here. You'll have to go in to the office. They can help you, I'm sure."

"I don't need to speak with the staff. I want to talk to you."

Was he coming on to her? She didn't think so. He wasn't smiling or trying to be charming.

"I'm Malacai L'Baan." He didn't extend his hand. Instead, he studied her closely, too closely, as if looking for some reaction on her part.

Jordy went back to gathering the papers and utensils. "I'm sorry, but I'm in sort of a hurry."

"Maybe these will slow you down." He tossed a glossy photo on top of the stack of paper she'd collected.

It was a picture of her standing in front of the hotel. If he had her pictures, then those photos she'd received were probably his. Was this the man who'd done such horrific damage to that woman? Her gaze was drawn to his hands. Long fingers, not slender, but well formed and unscarred. They didn't look like the hands of a bully. But abusers hands probably came in all shapes and sizes.

"I believe those are mine," she said.

"The envelope had my name on it."

She looked up at him, taking him in for the first time. He was tall, probably just under six feet. Pretty good build, tanned and fit looking, dark hair, attractive. Or maybe he would be if he smiled.

Should she explain about the mix-up? What would she say when he asked for his photos back? What would he do when he found out she'd turned them over to the police?

"What do you know about all this?"

Jordy tensed. "It looks like they stuck the wrong photos in your envelope."

"You looked surprised to see them."

"Well, of course I am. I thought they were lost."

"You're telling me this was a simple mix-up?"

"Yes. What else could it be?" Did he think she was somehow helping the woman he'd beaten up? But why had he taken pictures of her and risked having them developed? None of this made sense.

"Do you work here?" he asked.

"What? Yes. Why?"

"Those look like vacation pictures."

"I'm an artist, they're shots I took as subjects." She sounded too nervous. But he was making her uncomfortable. She should just call Sgt. Winston, not take any chances. She catalogued his features, though she knew she'd never forget a detail. His face was lean planes and hard angles. He'd be challenging to sculpt, she thought, surprised at the sudden itch in her fingertips. She could almost feel the taut skin, the fine bone structure. . . . Her hands tightened on the envelope. And those eyes . . . they'd never come across fully in clay. They needed color. A rich gray, deep and soft like cashmere, and wholly mesmerizing. No, she'd never forget what he looked like.

What was the name he gave her? Mal something. Something unusual, different.

"I really appreciate you dropping these off." She pasted on a smile. "Thank you."

He was still frowning. "You're saying when you went to pick these up they just said they were lost? Wasn't there another envelope somewhere with your name on it?"

"I'm sorry you lost your pictures."

"You don't have them?"

"No." At least she didn't have to lie.

"And you don't know anything else about this. You've never heard of me before."

"No, I've never heard of you," she said, becoming as confused now as he was.

"This makes no sense," he muttered.

"I got the impression the shop wasn't all that well managed. I'd guess this happens to them a lot."

"I don't suppose you'd mind telling me your name?"

"I don't think that's a great idea. Good luck finding your pictures." She laid the envelope on top of the stack of paper and scooped up the pile.

"If this is just an innocent mix-up, then I'm sorry." He sighed, though more to himself. "I really need to find those other pictures. It's very important."

There was an urgency in his voice. Maybe he really was trying to help that woman. "Is something wrong?"

"It's possible that someone is in danger."

Jordy stilled. *Just tell me you're her brother, or boyfriend, or husband even, so I can trust you.* "What's in those pictures?"

"I don't know."

"You don't know? I'm sorry, what was your name again?"

His eyebrows lifted, then, improbably, he smiled.

Jordy had been wrong. It didn't make him attractive. It made him downright gorgeous. "I said something funny?"

"Maybe I'm losing my mind, but I think you're telling me the truth."

"About not knowing you? I take it you're used to being a more memorable guy."

"Don't apologize. It's nice to be unremarkable."

She smiled. "Trust me. You're remarkable."

He extended his hand. "Malacai L'Baan. My friends call me Cai."

Jordy juggled the papers to one arm and shook his hand. She couldn't imagine those long, graceful fingers punishing someone's skin. Stroking it maybe. She shook his hand quickly and let it go. "Jordy." Her guard lowered slightly when he didn't push for more.

"I guess I'll go back to the ZippySnap and see what they can remember."

Jordy made an instant decision. "Maybe I can help." She didn't like the shuttered look that returned to his eyes. "Let me put this stuff away, then we can grab a drink in the hotel restaurant. Ten minutes?"

He nodded, but the smile didn't return.

CAI WATCHED JORDY walk into the restaurant fifteen minutes later. The place was relatively quiet, but she'd be hard to miss, even in a crowd. She might be short, her figure nothing to write home about, but she had a definite presence.

She certainly didn't seem like the type of wacko who could have produced those letters. She was obviously not the victim, but she'd kept something from him.

"I'm sorry, I took a bit longer than I planned."

"Not a problem. I hope you don't mind, I ordered iced tea. I'll be glad to get you something—"

She waved him silent as she settled in her chair. "Tea is fine." She was wearing a bright green tank top dress that set off her eyes and hair perfectly. He wondered if she was the type to plan out those sorts of details. He didn't think so. No makeup to speak of, apparently unconcerned about the light scattering of freckles from the sun. Her hair was cut Audrey Hepburn short, windblown and unfussy. She wore several tiny silver studs in each ear. Earthy, he thought again. Uncomplicated. And an artist, she'd said. He looked at her hands. Slender fingers, short nails, no polish, just a slender silver thumb ring she was nervously toying with.

"So, do I pass muster?" She smiled. "I tried to get the magic marker off my hands, but—" She flipped her hands over to reveal a purple streak on one palm and shrugged.

Definitely not the calculated sort. "I didn't mean to stare. Occupational hazard."

"Let me guess. Psychologist? Police sketch artist?"

The smile came naturally. "I'm a writer. I have a tendency to observe people—it's sort of a byproduct of characterization. Usually I'm not so obvious."

"And I'm guessing now that you're famous and I'm the only person on the planet who didn't recognize your name."

"Not hardly. I mean, I'm known pretty well around here, but I'm not Stephen King." His smile stretched to a grin. "Not yet anyway."

"I'm not a horror fan anyway. What do you write?"

"Fantasy."

"Ah, that explains it then. I'm more a mystery and suspense reader." She paused. "And romance. I'm a sucker for a happy ending."

"Aren't we all?"

She tilted her head. "You know, I might like your books."

She was refreshingly natural. Cai found himself wishing they'd met under different circumstances. He'd come here looking for a victim or a nutcase. He hadn't expected to find her. It had been a long time since he'd found himself attracted to someone. Too long, perhaps. Thank God Alfred wasn't here. But there was still the matter of what she hadn't told him. "If you can be of any help to me in this other mess, I'll personally sign and deliver any book of your choice."

She sobered. "First, I need you to explain something. If you dropped the film off, then why don't you know what's in the pictures?"

"I didn't take them. I was just picking them up." He noticed she was twirling her ring again. He realized something. "You lied, didn't you? About not having my pictures. Tell me what you saw, Jordy."

She sat back in her chair, not saying anything.

"If you really got them by mistake, you've involved yourself in something potentially dangerous. Just get them for me and you can be done with this whole thing."

"I didn't lie. Not technically. I don't have them."

"But you did." She nodded. "What did you do with them?"

"I gave them to the police."

"You did what? Why?" He waved his hand impatiently. "Skip that for a minute. If this was a simple mix-up, why didn't you just take them back to the photo shop?"

"I did. They looked through the other envelopes, not too well I guess. I was really concerned that the ones I returned find the right owner. As I was leaving, I saw the clerk ditch the envelope in the trash. So, I took them back."

"Why?"

"Listen, I drove all the way back down here to make sure she got them back. I couldn't just abandon her like that, could I?"

"Drove back from where? I thought you worked here? And her who?"

"The woman in the photos."

So it was real. Sweet Christ. There was a sick knot in his stomach. "Who is she?"

"I don't know. But she'd been beaten. Badly beaten."

Proof. They had proof. The threat was real.

Jordy leaned forward. "Do you know her?"

"No," he murmured.

"Well, I didn't know what else to do. So I went to the police. The officer seemed pretty outraged. I'm sure he's doing all he can."

"Why didn't you tell me this before?"

"For all I knew, you could have been the one who beat her up."

He stared at her. "What?" Then he shook his head. "Never mind. I've got to get over to the police station." He pulled his wallet out and threw some bills on the table.

"Wait, if you don't know her, how do you fit in?"

"Someone is threatening me." He headed for the door.

She caught up to him as he was unlocking his helmet from his motorcycle. "Let me come with you."

"You got your pictures back. I can take it from here."

"What about my book?"

"What?"

"You promised me a book."

She wanted a damn book?

"I'll have one sent over," he snapped and straddled his bike.

She grabbed his arm. "I'm sorry, that was stupid. It's just that I don't want to walk away. All I've done for the past two days is worry about this woman. You can't cut me out now. At least let me come to the station with you."

He frowned but he didn't refuse.

"They'll probably be suspicious too. I mean, your name *was* on that envelope. I can vouch for you, help explain. I'll follow you over in my car." She didn't wait for him to reply, but ran for her car.

Swearing, he tugged on his helmet, gunned the engine, and peeled out of the lot in a cloud of smoke and gravel.

SIX

J ORDY WAITED IN the tiny reception area while Cai made some calls from Sgt. Winston's desk. She knew the rest of the story now, though there wasn't much more to it. They still didn't know who the kidnapped woman was, or who was threatening Cai.

She doodled on a legal pad as she mulled over the whole thing. Cai was arranging to turn over the e-mails. The police were polite, but they'd made it clear he would probably face more questions. They didn't seem to think Cai was directly involved, but Jordy knew they weren't done pursuing him as a suspect either. To make it worse, the State Department would be brought into it because the e-mails were being sent from out of the country.

She angled her hand and made broad strokes across the paper. She'd just crawled out from two years of hell. What new hell had she gotten herself involved in here? The police had assured her they believed she was an innocent bystander, but she would likely be questioned by the State Department agents along with Cai. Did she regret her decision to come back? No. She had done her best to help that poor woman. She'd do it again. Her good deed had already been repaid. In returning to the Keys she'd discovered a path that might lead her to her own salvation.

"You didn't have to wait for me."

Cai's deep voice startled her from her thoughts. She looked up to find him towering over her. His expression was grim, those distinctive eyes looked weary.

"Did they tell you anything else?"

He shook his head and held the door for her.

"It all seems so hard to believe. I mean, to get so crazed over one person like that." She held up her hand. "No offense."

"None taken. It seems bizarre to me too." He seemed lost in his own thoughts. "Terrifyingly so."

"I'm sure the agents will be able to trace those e-mails back to the person responsible." She wasn't sure of any such thing, but she felt compelled to erase that helpless look in his eyes. There were many times during the past two years when something as simple as a kind word would have meant the world to her. "They'll find her. She'll be okay."

"For her sake, I hope so."

"For both your sakes."

Jordy could think of nothing else to add, but she was reluctant to let him go. She felt as if they were in this together and it didn't seem right to just go back to her own life, never to speak to him again.

"Let me give you my number at the hotel. So if you hear anything, you can—"

"The police will let you know."

He obviously didn't have the same feelings of connect-edness she did. And why would he? Feeling foolish, she stepped back. "Well, then, I guess this is good-bye. I'm glad we were able to piece together at least this much of the puzzle."

He nodded and pulled his helmet off the bike.

It wasn't until she went to get her keys that she realized she'd taken the legal pad with her. She smiled ruefully. "Now I'm stealing. And from the police." She tore the top page off and turned to go back inside. She was surprised when he grabbed her arm and pulled her back toward him.

"Wait a minute. Can I see that?"

His fingers felt hard against her skin. She liked it, liked the confidence in his touch. She slid her arm free. "This?" She lifted the pad.

He shook his head and reached for the sheet she'd torn off. "This."

She glanced down as he smoothed the crinkled paper against the shiny black surface of his helmet. She hadn't really been paying attention to her doodling. A dragon.

Her hand tightened on the legal pad. It seemed so ridiculous. But it was the first thing she'd drawn in months. It was far from great, or even good.

Maybe focusing her energy on something other than art and the damn court case had let her subconscious work through some barriers. She wanted to go off by herself somewhere and revel in this first breakthrough.

No. Being tucked away with her art all the time was what had got her into the mess with Suzanne in the first place. She liked being alone with her art and didn't think that would change. But she'd promised herself she'd find a balance between art and life.

"It's perfect," he said, still staring at it.

His words brought her back to the moment with a laugh. "I wouldn't go that far." She shrugged off his compliment when what she wanted to do was dance. "It's a habit of mine when I'm distracted."

"I thought you weren't into fantasy."

It was the first time he'd really looked at her since they'd been in the hotel restaurant. His full, focused attention was a powerful thing. And something about the way he said the word "fantasy" made her insides heat up.

She cleared her throat. "In reading, no, I'm not."

"Yet, you like dragons?"

"Adore them. Always have."

He arched a brow in silent question.

"It's hard to explain," Jordy began.

"Please. Try."

There was an urgency to his voice that she didn't understand. Malacai L'Baan was turning out to be a very compelling man. "Conjuring up dragons and wizards, griffins and other fantastical creatures is what I do for a living. Or did anyway. I'm a sculptor."

His pupils flared. Now she felt that connected feeling went both ways. It was intimidating.

She paused, trying to find the right words. "I tried to read a couple of fantasy novels when I was younger. The artwork on some of the covers is exceptional. But . . . I don't know. I guess I couldn't get lost in other people's worlds. I was too lost in my own. Does that make sense to you?" She hoped she hadn't insulted him, but one look in his eyes told her that he understood. Perhaps, too much.

"Could I pay you for this?" He lifted the drawing.

The question shocked her. She laughed. "Pay me? For that?" She looked from the sketch to him. "What do you want it for?"

He was studying the drawing once again. Oddly, she felt the attention to her sketch as intimately as if he were studying her. And perhaps he was.

He looked up. "It's my dragon."

"*Your* dragon?"

"Well, the dragon in here." He tapped his forehead. "I can create complex, highly detailed worlds with words, but I must admit that I cannot draw a straight line, or a curved one for that matter. I've been trying to get across to my editor and the art department the dragon I want on my next cover. They kept sending me sketches of these fierce, soulless dragons. I needed one with heart." He lifted his shoulders in a helpless gesture she found endearing. It so contrasted his intensity. "I wanted something *there* in his eyes, some sense of the ability to feel some ancient wisdom." He looked down at the drawing. "You've captured it here."

"It's just a crude sketch." But there was no denying the nice buzz his praise gave her. It had been a long time since her work was looked at as something other than a generalized legal summation.

"I can have my editor contact you to work out whatever contractual need you have. You'll get copyrights to it and all that." He grinned. "Alfred would love this."

"Alfred?"

"My grandfather. He collects unusual sculpture, for his garden. I'll have to tell him about your work."

"That's very nice of you, but I . . . I don't have anything for sale right now." Jordy worked hard to block out the feeling of failure. "I'll be glad to talk to whoever I need to. But as for the sketch . . ." She paused. A large part of her wanted to tell him no, wanted to hoard this first step, as a reminder that her art was always inside her somewhere. She just had to let the creature out. "It's yours, but I don't want money, okay? It's payment enough that you want it, that it found its place."

His grin faded. "You really have to, I insist. This is no small thing you've done."

"You don't understand. It's just right this way." And it was. Making the dragon a gift was sort of her way to celebrate the first step to rediscovering her talent.

"You said you used to create these things for a living. You don't any longer?"

He really didn't miss anything. "Not for a while. I'm . . . working on getting back to it."

He looked at her in that penetrating way of his, but he mercifully changed the subject. "You know, I think I've talked to more people today than I have in the last two months."

"You write about people, but you don't talk to many?"

"When did you last spend time with a dragon?"

She smiled. "Touché."

"I stay pretty secluded. Helps me stay focused."

"I understand that completely. When I work on a new sculpture, I hole myself away for weeks at a time." And it was precisely that penchant for burying her head in her fantasy world that ultimately had allowed Suzanne to screw her over.

Sgt. Winston chose that moment to push through the station doors. "Mr. L'Baan, I'm glad I caught you. I have Special Agent Proctor on the line. We could expedite things if you'd come in and talk to him."

Cai looked from Jordy to the officer.

"It's okay. I really should be getting back." Cai fascinated her, but he also overwhelmed her. It might be wiser to keep some distance.

"I really want to talk to you more. About the drawing. About a lot of things."

"The sketch is yours. I'll sign whatever release you need. I'll be here for two more weeks."

"Two weeks?" He frowned.

From their talks with the police, he knew she'd been vacationing here from Virginia, but not why. He knew she'd come back with the pictures and taken the job, but that was it. "The regular counselor will be back after that."

"You'll go back to Virginia?"

Jordy found her gaze drawn to the dragon. It symbolized so much, but so much more lay ahead. "Yes. I'll be going home." The statement rang in her head like a death knell. She really needed to work on that.

"You'd better hurry. Sergeant Winston is waiting. "I'm glad the dragon works, Cai. More than you can know."

He said nothing as she slid into her car and closed the door. She saw him disappear into the building in her rearview mirror as she pulled out of the lot. "Good-bye, Malacai L'Baan," she whispered.

IT WAS ALMOST dark by the time Cai reached the dock at Crystal Key. The whole thing was proving to be a nightmare. He was heartsick that someone out there was suffering because they happened to be a fan of his work.

But his mind was also on Jordy. She'd been invading his thoughts all afternoon, even when he'd been grilled by Special Agent Proctor. He was going to have to bring in his whole CPU for them to examine. He understood that it was to help exonerate him from being part of this in any way, but it was a major pain. He'd been able to convince Agent Proctor not to come to Crystal Key. He'd said it would be problematic for his ailing grandfather. If Alfred knew how poorly he'd portrayed him to the police, he'd have had a full-blown fit.

But it was his fervent hope that Alfred would know nothing of this. Ever.

He looked up and found Dilys standing a few feet away. "Himself is worried about ye being gone fer so long."

Dilys could handle Alfred better than Cai could himself, so if she was concerned enough to meet him out here, Alfred must really be on the warpath.

"I'm sorry," he said, never more sincere. "It couldn't be helped."

She said nothing, merely turned and began heading to the house. Then just as suddenly, she said, "If I were you, I'd tell him you were on a date. That would divert him."

Cai's mouth opened in surprise. It was rare, bordering on historic, for Dilys to comment on his social life. "How do you know I wasn't?" he said, damning himself for sounding so defensive. But he thought of Jordy and wondered how far from the truth it was. Or could have been if the circumstances had been different. "And divert him from what exactly?"

"Ye might think him senile, Master Malacai, but himself knows things are amiss. Do as I say, if ye have the heart in ye I know to be there." Without waiting for him to reply, she left Cai alone to face God knew what.

SEVEN

JORDY FINISHED HER last class of the week and headed up to her room. She'd had eight kids today, all apparently on some sort of sugar high. Perhaps finger painting hadn't been such a great idea. She smiled as she scraped a glob of red off her shoulder. Okay, so she'd had fun too, but she was beat.

She'd looked forward to a late afternoon sketching session. But right now, she was too tired to even doodle. She would have to settle for a long, numbing shower and a cold drink on the balcony.

There was a light flashing on the phone in her room when she returned. "Who called, Fred?" She took a peek in his bowl as she toed out of her sandals.

It was from Eileen Mason, Cai's editor. Jordy had already spoken to the woman twice. Eileen reminded her a little bit of Suzanne. But unlike Suzanne, Eileen didn't waste time on things like finesse or charm, which had been her former partner's stock and trade. No bullshit with Eileen. Jordy appreciated that.

Eileen was suspicious of anyone who didn't make demands and had bluntly told her it would be easier if they paid her for the sketch, if for no other reason than she would be less likely to come back and sue them later. Jordy assured her that the very last thing she'd ever do would be to sue anyone, but Eileen wasn't having it. So ten minutes into the first call, she'd relented on the payment deal.

Cai hadn't been involved in any of it.

Even though she'd pulled out of the police station five days ago thinking she'd never see him again, deep down she had hoped otherwise. She'd talked to the State Department agents, but Cai hadn't been there. A box had shown up at the desk for her mid-week, filled with a stack of books, one of which was the hardcover of Cai's newest release. The book that had started the whole mess. He'd signed them to her, but no personal message was included.

There was no reason to see him again.

She had one week left as camp counselor, then it was home to Virginia. No crazed fans, no police interrogation.

No enigmatic writer with whom she had no business getting involved.

She sat up on the edge of the bed and carefully dragged off her paint-splattered T-shirt and shorts. She picked up the sketch pad, flipping past the pages. Most of her work since the dragon had come slowly, so she tried hard not to analyze it too critically. She had begun to recapture the passion. Now that she didn't expect each drawing to be a stroke of genius, she didn't fear imperfection.

Passion. She recalled the exact moment the passion had returned. Her heart had pounded . . . but for an entirely different reason.

She wanted to flip right to it, to look at it, both with a critical eye and out of sheer curiosity to see once again what had come out of her last night. She made herself glance through her other attempts first. There was the griffin she thought had turned out fairly well. It wouldn't work in clay, but there was a spark there. There was a smaller dragon she kind of liked. She stopped pretending and flipped past the rest, stopping abruptly at the page filled with smaller, partial sketches.

This is where it had started. She'd wanted—needed—to draw him. She tilted her head and studied the series of thumbnail sketches. She'd been right. He was difficult to capture in a monochrome exercise. Charcoal hadn't done it. Nor had pen and ink. He needed color. Watercolors were too transparent. Not enough power to carry off the effect. She'd never dabbled in oils, but she thought that might be the perfect medium. He demanded color, texture, depth.

And yet she yearned to bring him to life in clay. To find those hollows and smooth planes, urge them to the surface, and clean away the excess until all that remained was the raw power of his image. The intensity of that need shocked her. And thrilled her. It was coming back.

And it had been Malacai L'Baan that had drawn it forth. Or, more specifically, her fascination with him that had.

She didn't care. She needed something to get her started, to break down the walls that two years of facing demoralizing, painful realities had built up.

She'd begun by teasing herself with the sweep of his jaw, the finely curved lips and the high formality of his forehead. She ran her forefinger over the sharply drawn lines of his cheek, then the loose strands of hair that danced around his face, just like they did in the constant tropical breeze.

The next image had come at her from nowhere. Fully realized and more completely detailed than her regular work, it had overwhelmed her. Once she started, she'd been totally immersed in it, the pen moving faster and faster.

She paused before turning the page. What if, in the light of day, it was awful? Her fingers tensed. She stared at it, the drawing that had flowed from her like a torrent. God, how long had it been since she'd felt that rush?

It was all she remembered and more.

The first image to emerge had been a gargoyle, not too

fierce, but not at all whimsical. Another matched it and behind them a deep brooding forest. A far more complex sketch began to evolve than her preliminary sculpture drawings had ever entailed. But the details came into her mind fast and furious and she faithfully released them onto the page.

The gargoyles seemed to be guarding a gate. To where she wasn't certain. The great winged horse had come next, emerging from the dark mists wafting through the gnarled trees. Astride the winged beast sat a man.

She looked again at the face that had flowed so effortlessly from her hand. Malacai L'Baan.

She remembered sitting there, stunned at what she'd created, even as she was recording it. He'd pulled at her then. He pulled at her now.

Feeling like a moonfaced teenager, Jordy flipped the book shut and tossed it on the bed.

It was just the connection of what he did for a living, she convinced herself, and her job of bringing fantastical beings to life, that had her so obsessed with him. She turned toward the bathroom, frowning. As if he needed anyone else obsessing over him at the moment.

The sudden jarring ring of the phone made her jump.

"Yes, this is Miss Decker," she replied to the elegant, British-accented query.

"This is Alfred L'Baan."

"Cai's grandfather?"

"Why, yes, yes indeed. He's spoken of me to you, then?"

He sounded delighted by the prospect, making Jordy smile. "Yes, he did. You must be calling about my sculptures. I'm very sorry, but I told Cai I have no inventory at the moment."

"Sculptures, you say? Well, now, isn't this an even more pleasant turn of events."

"You didn't know?"

"I called to speak with the woman whose imagination spawned that delightful dragon Malacai has been mooning over."

Mooning? Mooning was good. Jordy instantly corrected herself. No, no it wasn't good. Hadn't she decided that she wasn't down here to get involved? Nevertheless she couldn't seem to wipe the grin from her face.

"I'm glad that worked out for him. It was just a coincidence, really. I doodle when I'm distracted and the dragon simply evolved. He saw it and thought it would be perfect for a book cover."

"I understood that Cai met with you to look over your designs. Do you have others?"

Now it was Jordy's turn to pause. What exactly *had* Cai told Alfred? Could it be he didn't know about the kidnapping? "I'm working, but I don't have a portfolio."

"Do you sculpt delightful creatures such as the dragon?"

Jordy ignored the tiny stab of doubt that hit her when he said the word "sculpt." "My work is typically more on the whimsical side, yes."

"Malacai spoke of my garden to you, I presume. I have a strong affinity for whimsy, as you call it. No faith in what could be, in this world today. Too much black and white, not nearly enough gray. No belief in things not easily explained. Pity. What medium do you work in?"

It took a second to make the transition. "Clay mostly." Something about him, his sincerity, maybe his charming accent, relaxed her. "I've tried to work in stone, but I find it rather cold, distant. I need to feel the movement of the piece as it takes shape. Clay has life inside it. Heart." She laughed self-consciously. "That probably doesn't make any sense."

"On the contrary, young lady, it speaks volumes to me." Jordy smiled, charmed indeed.

"We must meet. For tea. Could you fit us into your

schedule, say sometime early in the upcoming week? I realize this isn't proper notice, but Malacai said your stay in Florida was to be brief."

So Cai had spoken of more than just her drawing to his grandfather?

"Sounds wonderful. I teach in the mornings on Monday, so perhaps that afternoon?"

"Delightful! We'll expect you at the docks at three."

"The docks?"

"Oh, dear, where are my manners? We reside on Crystal Key, Gulf-side of Mangrove. We use the docks at Dobs' Storage. Dobs will escort you to our slip. Malacai will collect you there if that's convenient. Or I can have him call at your hotel."

"No! I mean, that's very kind, but I'm certain I can find it. It's really no bother."

"Nonsense. The mangroves aren't the easiest to maneuver, especially for a novice. Malacai can find his way through the maze on a moonless night. You find Dobs and we'll take care of the rest. Dilys puts on a delightful tea and she'll be happy to add another teacup to the tray. We don't have many visitors out this way."

Jordy heard a trace of loneliness in his voice, and her heart softened further. And who was Dilys? Interesting name. Some British form of Phyllis maybe? Perhaps she was British as well. Odd that Cai had no accent. She wondered about that, and why his grandfather lived with him, and several other things she had no business being curious about. "Until Monday then."

Alfred rang off and Jordy finally took her shower. Maybe seeing Cai again was exactly what she needed. Perhaps seeing him in his own surroundings would deconstruct the mystery she'd spun around him.

Rejuvenated by the shower, she went to retrieve her sketch pad, but found herself picking up Cai's book instead. After all, it was this book that had indirectly brought them together.

She wandered out to the balcony, looking at the cover. The man dominating it was cloaked in a deep, black robe, so all that was visible was the bright blue of his eyes and the slash of his cheek. She curled up in the thickly padded papasan chair, laying the book open on her thighs.

Several hours later, the sun almost fully set, her Coke warm and flat, she got up and wandered inside, eyes riveted to the current page. She clicked on the lamp and crawled into bed, still turning the pages.

She'd left Florida hours before and was now deeply ensconced in Cai's world. How she could be so far from home, and yet feel she'd finally arrived there, she had no idea. She turned another page.

EIGHT

SHE WORE A sleeveless T-shirt dress of pale yellow that ended just above her knees and clung to her slight curves. Her legs were tan and bare save for her flat leather sandals. Wisps of hair blew in wild, short tendrils around her head like a fairy halo. And his reaction was like a sucker punch to the gut; hard, swift, and unexpected.

Cai hadn't been thrilled with his grandfather's sneaky liaison. With an air of wounded pride, Alfred had informed him he merely wanted to spend an hour or two in the company of a delightful young woman with similar interests.

Cai had his doubts. He never should have let him look at the dragon sketch, but it had been his cover for being gone from Crystal Key. It had seemed harmless. Now he had to see her again, when he'd worked so hard not to.

After only one meeting, she had found a way into his head and stubbornly refused to leave. For that reason, he'd gone out of his way to conclude his business with her from a distance. She was leaving shortly and there was too much going on in his life to include her on his ever-growing list of concerns.

Standing on the dock waiting for him, she was a golden

promise that his life could get real interesting, real fast, if he'd only let it. Damn, Alfred.

Cai pulled the boat up and cut the engine. He would stick to his plan. Polite within the boundaries of social acceptance, nothing more, nothing less.

She wasn't smiling. In fact, she looked every bit as wary as he did. That should have reassured him. Perversely, it did not.

He reached up to offer her assistance into the boat. Her hands weren't soft and pampered. Lean, callused, strong were the words he'd use to describe them. That jolted him like no gentle touch ever could have. He let them go as soon as she'd steadied herself.

Curling his hands deliberately around the wheel, he directed her to a seat. "All set?" The words were more curt than he'd intended, but he let them lie.

Instead of being insulted, she sighed in resignation.

"I'm sorry Alfred rooked you into this," she said sincerely. "I didn't mean to intrude on your privacy. I'm sure you have a lot on your mind."

"You have no idea," he murmured, but the roar of the engine as he swung away from the dock swallowed his words.

She said nothing until they'd cleared the mangroves and were heading smoothly across the blue waters.

"Your grandfather seems like a delightful man. Very charming."

"He can be."

The sudden touch of her hand on his arm surprised him and the boat jerked to the right before he straightened it out. He looked at her for the first time since leaving Mangrove.

"Can we talk for a minute?"

He wanted to gun the engine and race home. The term "hideaway" took on a new meaning. Instead he slowed the engine to an idle and let the boat drift. "I'm trying not to be a jerk here."

A tiny quirk of a smile teased her lips.

"Okay, so I wasn't trying that hard. It's just that things are more complicated than you realize. I don't want to upset Alfred."

"You think my visit will upset him?" Then suddenly it dawned on her. "Oh, you mean the investigation. Don't worry. I figured out that you hadn't told him about it. I think it's sweet that you want to spare him the worry. I won't say anything about how we really met."

"Thank you, I appreciate that." Maybe he was being an egotistical ass for worrying that she read more into this than a simple tea. Other than the polite thank you for his books, she'd made no attempt to contact him, either.

"He wanted to talk about my sculptures and before I knew it, we were having tea."

"Alfred can have that effect on people." On his good days. Which, Cai had to admit, he'd been having since he'd made this date. Alfred had always been reclusive, but maybe Cai had reinforced that isolation. He'd been protecting Alfred and his reputation, but maybe he'd gone too far. Did Alfred sincerely just want the company, with no hidden matchmaking agenda?

"You showed him the dragon," she said.

"I had to explain my visit to Mangrove."

"Oh, I see."

You don't see a thing, he thought. Was she disappointed? Had she liked the thought of him talking about her? Was she sitting there thinking the same things he was thinking? Could he get any more confused about all of this?

"Well, as I said, I won't blow our cover. This sounds like a bad spy novel." Then she brightened. "Oh, I wanted to thank you for the books."

"You did. I got your note the other day."

"Well, I want to thank you again. I read *Quest for the Dark Pearl,* over the weekend. I don't think I've ever been so deeply pulled into a piece of fiction. I lived it, breathed it."

Her praise disconcerted him. This wasn't like getting a note from a reader. She wasn't looking at him like he was some celebrity. She was looking at him like she saw something else there now. And maybe she did. It was unnerving.

And incredibly arousing.

He shifted in his seat. "I'm glad you enjoyed it."

She laughed self-consciously. "I guess you're used to people gushing."

He wasn't used to anything when it came from her.

She crossed her legs and he noticed she wore a toe ring. He shifted again.

"I wish I had your way with words, so I could explain how I felt when I read your book." She leaned forward, spontaneously placing her hand on his arm. His muscles twitched under her thumb.

Under her thumb. He'd have laughed out loud if his heart wasn't lodged in his throat. It was the most bizarre feeling in the world, this sense of suspense, the simultaneous dread and almost painful arousal, this certainty that everything was about to change.

"You created a world so real to me I could feel it, hear it, smell it, taste it."

He was going to implode. It took everything he had to sit still under her touch.

"Your hero really got to me. It was his flaws that drew him to me. He wasn't always heroic, but I never had a doubt he'd succeed. In fact, the more he doubted himself, the more confident I became in him. I don't think I've ever so completely identified with a fictional character." Her smile suddenly faded as she looked into his eyes. He had no idea if the ferocity of his reaction showed in his expression. Her hand tightened on him for a moment and then she pulled it away quickly as if she'd been burned.

He noticed the vein in her temple flicker, and she swallowed nervously.

He wanted to reassure her that he was harmless, however he felt anything but at the moment. He had to end this . . . possession she had of some part of him he couldn't control. He wanted to let go, to give into it and follow it where it would lead him. Lead them. She'd created the dragon after all. His dragon.

"Fairy or sorceress," he murmured. Which was she?

"I . . . I don't—" She stood and moved back. The breeze tore at her hair, sending it up in fiery spikes around her head, wrapping the thin cotton of her dress tightly against her skin.

He stood too, but moved away from her, fists tight, pulse hammering. He let the boat drift, not caring if it capsized or floated out to sea.

Jordy nervously smoothed her dress. As if that helped. Her frame was slight and yet he had this burning need to run his hands over the shape the wind had so clearly defined for him.

Insanity. He kept his gaze on the water until he could bring himself under control.

"We'd better get going," she said, her voice a bit uneven. "I don't want to keep your grandfather waiting."

Cai opened his mouth, then shut it.

He didn't speak again until the dock at Crystal Key came into view. "Thank you for helping me out with Alfred. About the investigation, I mean. It's just better if he doesn't have to be bothered with this."

"No problem."

He darted a glance her way, before maneuvering the boat up to the dock. She wasn't looking at him.

"Your home is lovely," she said, the polite visitor once again. "Is it all yours? The island I mean."

"Yes." He cut the engine and tied off the boat, but before hopping to the pier, he faced her. "Listen, I'm glad you enjoyed the book. I, uh, about back there, it's—"

She cut him off with a light smile. "No need to explain. Your job is much like mine, isolated. It's nice to know when something you've labored over is appreciated. But I'm sorry if I embarrassed you."

"You didn't embarrass me." She'd felt something of what he did back there, he knew that. But, if she was going to gloss it over with polite platitudes, he should simply let it go as well. Nothing had happened. Nothing really had changed.

He wished like hell he could believe that.

He helped her up, careful to touch her no more than he had to. "I have to work," he said shortly. "Just have Dilys come and tell me when you're ready to leave and I'll take you back."

They were almost to the edge of the yard when she stopped. "I know I'm an outsider here." There was more than politeness in her tone now. There was frost. "I know you're worried about your grandfather. You have nothing to fear from me."

Cai almost laughed out loud at that. He'd never been more afraid in all his life.

"I don't want anything from you and the only thing I want from Alfred is a nice afternoon spent discussing sculpture. I have no mercenary agenda, but I'll be baldly honest. I'm here in Florida trying to resurrect a dead career. That dragon sketch was the first thing I've drawn in months." She stopped him from speaking with a raised palm. "I'm really thrilled that it fulfilled some need of yours."

If she'd wanted to make him feel like slime, she'd succeeded. "Jordy—"

"Ah, there you are, my lady fair." Alfred's ringing welcome had Cai stepping back even before he realized he'd been stepping forward.

He made a quick apology to his grandfather for missing tea, followed by an unapologetic escape into the house.

NINE

"WELL, NOW, WASN'T that interesting," Alfred observed.

Interesting? Rude was more like it. Jordy couldn't decide what to make of Cai. Hot one second—really hot—then cold the next.

Alfred turned back to her, a smile creasing his face. His eyes were a remarkable shade of blue. She thought of the book jacket for *Dark Pearl* and felt that little shiver again.

"Welcome and good afternoon, my dear young lady. We won't waste time discussing my grandson's abominable behavior. Too fine a day for it. I thought we'd take tea on the lanai, overlooking the water. We can take a leisurely stroll through the garden afterward, if you're not tired of my company by then."

"Sounds lovely. And I'm sure I could never tire of listening to your voice." Her cheeks warmed when he winked.

"Shall we then? Dilys' teacakes are best had fresh from the oven. The things that woman can do with marmalade."

He used a cane, a gorgeous one with a beautifully carved griffin on the knob. She hoped to take a closer look at it later. He wore brilliant white duck pants and a sharply pressed blue pinstriped shirt that provided the perfect contrast to his bright eyes. His white hair gleamed as it lay softly on his shoulders. His goatee and mustache were trimmed to perfection. Elegant, yet a bit unconventional.

Jordy took the arm he offered, comfortable with him already. "Tell me about Dilys, she sounds like a wonder."

THREE HOURS LATER they finally finished tea, and she knew little more about Dilys, except that she was Alfred's rock in life. She'd come from Wales with him to care for Cai when he was quite young. His parents had been killed when their light plane crash-landed off Key West. Alfred and Dilys become instant parents to Cai.

Alfred was outspoken to say the least, sharing his opinions on everything, ranging from the marmalade tarts to the state of the union. Dilys was reserved to the point of being taciturn, though in no way subservient. The woman had an amazing ability to communicate volumes with nothing more than a slight rearrangement of her eyebrows. Jordy thought she'd have made a great dowager duchess in an old historical novel.

Alfred rose after Dilys removed the tea tray and held his arm out to Jordy. "Would you like to take that stroll, or should you be heading back? I'm sure a young woman such as yourself has better things to do than listen to an old man natter on about things of little consequence."

Her heart softened further. "You promised me a stroll. I'm holding you to it."

He nodded approvingly. "Onward and upward, then." He guided her to the wide plank steps at the back of the deck that terraced down to the ground. A path wound into a dense stand of palmettos.

Oddly enough, they hadn't talked about art at all. Cai's name had come up now and again, but other than his parents' deaths, she hadn't learned much there, either. But, she'd enjoyed every moment of her conversation with Alfred.

"I started this garden a number of years back. Some of the statuary is a reflection of my dedication to the Dark Age and the world of Arthur Pendragon, Merlin, and the others. I think you'll find some pieces most amusing."

"I don't know much of Arthurian legend, I'm afraid," Jordy said. "Although I love the romanticism of the Knights of the Round Table."

"Nothing romantic about it," Alfred snorted. "The knights were an uneducated lot mostly. More in demand for their brawn than their brains. An ungainly crew, but useful enough for their stated purpose."

She was surprised at Alfred's suddenly harsh tone. "Well, I suppose much of the past has been softened over the years, with the romantic aspect played up for its appeal."

"Wars have long been romanticized." He released her arm and waved an impatient hand in the air. "Could never understand that and told Arthur so. What is to be gained by making something, that is by its very nature destructive and violent, out to be anything different than it is? Yes, war is a glorious and, at times, necessary evil, a brash campaign of man's spirit and desire to conquer, to control, but romantic? Bah."

Told Arthur so? He'd spent so many years writing about Arthur and his life and times, she supposed it wasn't unusual for him to speak as if he'd known the man. Perhaps this was why Cai had been concerned about her visit.

Well if the man wanted to rant on about centuries-old injustices as if he'd witnessed them firsthand, it was fine by her. He did it so vividly, she felt as if she were there right alongside him. She made a mental note to look for his books.

Alfred continued to lecture as they wandered down the

path. "Arthur was a great king, but he was no hero, not in the romantic sense. That was the work of those like Monmouth, Malory, and Chrétien de Troyes, spinning yarns of what they wanted Arthur to be. They came centuries upon centuries too late, more concerned with telling a good tale, than relating the truth of history."

"But he did exist."

"Aye, that he did. But their tales, from which Arthurian legend as you know it was born, do not describe the real man. The fifth century was a dark time and little of what was recorded survived. Blaise faithfully transcribed everything, but it vanished. Nennius made a good attempt, but it was the ninth century, and already much of Arthur's role in history was lost. I don't deny them their lore, but it has forever diffused the real truth of him. The real Arthur had charm and leadership in abundance but his heart was merely that of a mortal man and, as such, susceptible to the very same things that plague all men. Lust, greed, power. He was better at managing some more than others."

She wanted to ask how he knew the truth but she was too caught up in his passionate defense to question him. "Well, there is romance in that. Some of the best heroes, the ones that are the easiest to romanticize, are the ones that are the most flawed, the most human. Maybe it was because Arthur made decisions, both wise and unwise, not simply as a king, but as a man, that made him so memorable."

Alfred stopped and turned to her, his blue eyes ablaze with an inner fire. She was a little alarmed that perhaps she'd pushed too far.

"Young lady, as fine a mind as you possess, you know naught of which you speak. Arthur was a king, no less and no more. He made great decisions and abominably poor ones. As have leaders all around the world for thousands of years. His flaws are nothing to exemplify nor worship, nor is his position as leader enough to warrant such rampant idolization. He was only as worthy as the men he commanded."

"So, are you saying that no one man should stand above another, or no one station in life should be more revered? Then is there no figure worthy of idolizing, of putting on a pedestal, of romanticizing?"

"I said no such thing!" he thundered and Jordy took a step back despite herself. "There are hundreds upon thousands of men who, during their time on this earth, have led lives that would need no inaccurate folklore, no foolish tales of great deeds passed down, to lift them to the level of hero. Arthur may have been one of them, but not in the manner he is portrayed to be." His eyes took on a faraway look. "Merlin worked his magic as best as he could, but not even one as great as he could get through to Arthur when he was being stubborn. Merlin was frustration in its purest form, I tell you. It was a difficult time and Arthur refused to see the end as we did. Had he listened, had he acted as Merlin instructed, perhaps I would be building that pedestal myself instead of spending a lifetime demystifying what never should have been. It is only by exposing the truths behind the myths and legends that we can hope to alter the tragedy that will otherwise be our destiny."

He raised a rigid, bony finger and aimed it at her. "Be warned," he said gravely, his blue eyes piercing into her so sharply she could almost feel the point of entry. "There are those who would go to lengths you cannot foresee to harm the true heroes of this world, just as there are those who would sacrifice everything to protect them. The difficulty comes in deciding who is playing which role."

He shifted his hand and cupped her chin. "Decide which role you will play, Jordalyn. Will you be protector? Or destroyer."

TEN

J ORDALYN. HER FULL name, spoken in his mellif-
luous tones, shook her badly. How had he known that?
She'd been named for her father, Jordan Decker, who'd
died when Jordy was a baby. Only her mother had ever
called her that and she had passed away long ago.

"I have done much to ensure his safety," Alfred continued. "You will play a role here. But be warned, I will be
watching." He released her chin and turned away, using his
cane heavily as he moved on down the path.

Jordy didn't know whether to run, or follow the old man
and ask him what in the hell he was talking about. Was he
simply senile, living in some imaginary world of his creation? But those eyes . . .

Alfred turned just at the bend in the path. Gone was the
fierce expression. He was once again her kindly tea companion. Poor Cai, she thought. How hard it must be for
him to love his grandfather so much and have to watch
over him as his mind deteriorated.

"Come along," he bade her, "there is much to be seen. I
want your opinion on one of my favorite pieces."

She put on a smile and moved to catch up with him.
She'd wondered about their reclusive lifestyle, but now she
understood that Cai was simply protecting his once-famous

grandfather from the prying eyes of the world. *Protector, or destroyer?* One thing was clear. Cai was a protector.

Alfred took her arm when the path ended at a set of terraced stairs curving upward. At the top, she stopped with a gasp. "Oh my." She absorbed the magical world Alfred had created in his garden. "A paradise in paradise. You did all this yourself?"

He all but preened. "Aye, that I did. It's a labor of unconditional love."

"It shows. I'm amazed you could grow all this."

"Cai and I have developed some watering systems along with soil protection units. Many of the garden plots are actually planted in movable beds that are inset into the ground. The palms, pines, and dense foliage provide protection from the winds. I have hothouses on the far side of the house. It allows me to move things about, change things. I quite enjoy it." He motioned behind her. "With the house being raised as it is, most of the rear bedrooms look out over the garden."

"You do understand romanticism."

Alfred responded with a knowing chuckle.

The garden was laid out in the old English style, entirely encased in hedgerows, with more decorative hedges shaped in curving, geometrical lines inside the large square. There were tidy flower beds, some circular, some rectangular, set in the small courtyards formed by the hedges. Yet the flowers weren't all tidy or formal. He had roses and lilies and the like, but he also had exotic island flowers, all blended together in exquisite patterns, a wild riot of color and textures.

Alfred led her down several stairs and along the inlaid path to the central courtyard.

She didn't notice the sculptures at first. They didn't stand on carefully placed pedestals as the formality of the garden would suggest. They were tucked here and there, peeking from hedgerows and underneath lush blossoms, overseeing pathways and tending to some of the flowers. "They are delightful. I love this."

"Go, explore." Alfred gave her a soft push to the elbow. "I'll sit here and enjoy your adventure."

There were gnomes, elves, and other mystical creatures she couldn't identify. Jordy followed the sound of a small, trickling stream to find a burbling water fountain in the center of a pond filled with water lilies. And floating on them were tiny marble fairies. She knelt down and marveled over the intricate detail carved into each one.

"They are each different, to my exact specifications."

Alfred stood at the entrance to this particular quadrant, looking at her like a father would a child of whom he was particularly fond. She wanted to bask in the warmth of his smile.

She'd enjoyed her solitude, her focus on her work, but in that moment she realized what she'd forfeited. The wealth of emotion, the rich reward, that came from truly connecting with another human being. She wouldn't make that sacrifice again. She couldn't, now that she'd felt this sense of belonging. She thought of Cai and the tense moments they'd shared on the boat. Belonging . . . longing . . .

"This is a wonderland, Alfred. I hope you're as proud of this as any other achievement you've made." She turned a slow circle, surveying what she could see in this area, and found several more sculptures she'd missed. "It's magical. I feel as if I've been transported to some other realm, where things aren't what they seem, but exactly what you want them to be. That sounds silly." She grinned at him. "But maybe you of all people would understand."

"Your heart is a pure one, Jordalyn."

Like a sharp pin, that name burst the bubble.

"Come now, don't let the magic go." He stepped closer

to her and she saw, behind the caring grandfatherly gaze, a
deeper fire there, pulling at her.

She stepped back without really understanding why. She
didn't feel at risk. Or did she? But it was a risk that tantalized, challenged. Just as his grandson had tantalized and
challenged her earlier. "How do you know my full name?"

His smile didn't falter, neither did the intensity—or
warmth—of his gaze. "After we spoke on the phone, I was
interested in your work, so I looked into it. You should use
your full name, it is quite lovely you know."

"Thank you." She signed her work Jordy, always had.
Her business had all been done in that name. But she
wasn't going to quibble with him. He'd obviously dug it
up somehow. Information was much easier to come by in
these days of high technology.

She turned her attention back to the statuary. "You have
some wonderful pieces here. I'd love to know about the
artists."

"Most of them came from the same woman. She resides
near my home in Wales."

Surprised, she asked, "Do you still have a home there?"

"I haven't been back in a very long time," was all he
said. "I commission pieces from Mara through the mail and
over the phone. A delightful woman."

"Well, she does wonderful work. Very inspiring."

"She'd be flattered. I'll pass along your comments. Come
this way and see the piece I wanted you to look at."

"I don't know how you keep this up without any help."

"Digging my hands into the earth helps me maintain
balance. There is nothing like sifting dirt between one's
fingers to keep in mind the eternity of life and one's minus-
cule part in it."

She sighed. The man did have a way with words. "I've
never had much of a green thumb, but just being out here
makes me want to grow something."

"Well then, grow something you shall. You must see the hothouses. I have the perfect new hybrid to start you on."

Her heart kicked in at the mere suggestion. She wanted to stay, get more involved. Badly. Maybe too badly. The sense of belonging only increased and she hated to remind him, and herself, that she was merely a guest here. Had she been so starved of people?

Once she returned to Virginia, she'd make a vow to become involved. Perhaps a senior citizen home would be a place to start. The plan only assuaged a little of the pain of her following words. "Oh, Alfred, that is really sweet of you, but I couldn't." His face fell so swiftly, she felt terrible. "It's not that I don't want to, it's just that you've been so kind and—"

He squeezed her hand. "No, I understand, dear one. I've already taken up too much of your precious time."

"It's not that at all. Actually, I could spend hours here. Days. It makes me want to learn all about gardening."

"Then I see no reason why we can't schedule some more time together. You'll come again, and wear something suitable for working the earth."

Jordy felt as if she were awakening from a long sleep. And she hadn't missed the stirrings of imagination she felt just standing here. She could create here. She knew it, felt it. But she couldn't intrude further on Cai's hospitality. Could she?

She had less than a week left before she had to return home. She would never have this chance again. She could even find her own transportation over to the private Key, so he wouldn't feel put out.

She smiled at Alfred, responding before she realized she'd made the decision. "Would Wednesday be too soon?"

Alfred beamed. "Wednesday would be fine. Same time?" He rubbed his hands together like a child in anticipation.

"Would you mind if I brought my sketch pad?"

"Certainly not. I was hoping to discuss that with you anyway. I would like to commission something for the garden. Perhaps we can work on that Wednesday."

Jordy smiled, even as her heart clutched at the thought of trying to work for anyone but herself. She'd have to explain things to Alfred. He'd understand she couldn't commit to anything quite yet. But at least she'd found a place to start. "I would love to." On impulse she stepped forward and kissed his cheek. "Thank you, Alfred. This means more to me than you can know."

Cai suddenly appeared on the path in front of them. "I'm sorry to intrude, but I need to take Jordy home. Now."

ELEVEN

ALFRED DIDN'T SO much as blink at the sudden intrusion. "There you are, Malacai. I was just about to show Jordalyn the dragon in the corner."

"I'm sorry, Grandfather. There's a storm coming. I'd like to take Jordy back to Mangrove now."

"I saw nothing on the news about a storm."

"It's just been announced."

It hadn't escaped Jordy's attention that Cai hadn't once looked at her. She didn't know what was up, but she suspected this wasn't just about a storm. Had he overheard their plans to meet again?

"I don't see where fifteen minutes will make that much difference."

Jordy stepped in, not wanting such a wonderful afternoon to end on a sour note. "I'm sorry," she said to Alfred, never more sincere. "But it's probably wise for me to head back now anyway. I didn't realize how late it was." She squeezed his hand and leaned closer to him. "Until Wednesday," she said quietly. "I'll bring gloves."

He squeezed back. "No gloves, my dear. One must feel the earth to understand it's ways."

She nodded. "Okay, then. I'm looking forward to it."

The sudden pressure of Cai's hand on her lower back was

like a hot brand. She tensed, but smiled at Alfred. His gaze deepened for an interminable moment, once again leaving her to wonder just what went on behind those magnificent blue eyes of his.

He placed a courtly kiss on the back of her hand, then bowed his head slightly. "Until then." Without looking at his grandson, he turned and spoke as he walked away. "I want to check on a few things at the hothouse. Tell Dilys I'll be in after an hour or so."

"The storm—" Cai broke off.

Alfred had already moved off and didn't respond. Cai had been clearly rebuked and dismissed. Jordy made only a token attempt to hide her amused smile.

With a scowl, he took her elbow and began to move her down the path, but she tugged it away and held her ground.

Cai frowned. "We really must head back."

"You really must not lead me around like a pony," she replied. "I don't know where you learned your manners, but it wasn't from your very gentlemanly grandfather."

"I apologize. We still need to hurry," he said.

"Listen, if you're worried about my seeing Alfred again—"

"Again?"

So, he hadn't been eavesdropping. "Yes, again. On Wednesday. He's going to teach me to grow things and we're going to discuss my work." Because he irritated her, she added, "He wants to commission a piece." She moved closer. "Were you really so worried about my visit with him that you had to cut it short?"

"It doesn't have anything to do—"

"Because I think I understand your concerns about Alfred and I can put your fears to rest. I would never harm him, or embarrass him."

"What do you mean?"

"I understand, about his . . . you know, his spells, or whatever you call them. I understand that his mind slips a little now and then. You know, with all the study he's done on the man's life, it's not all that surprising that his senility would—"

"He's not senile," he said a bit too forcefully. "He's an eccentric in every definition of the word. Always has been."

"And he's a delightful one." Seeing Cai's skeptical look she added, "I know what it's like. I do. My mother passed away when I was in college. She had cancer, which I know is totally different, but it was debilitating. I was in denial far longer than she was. I'm not sure who helped who more." She placed her hand on his arm, more reassured than alarmed at that sudden connection they seemed to make. "I won't hurt him, Cai. I enjoy him and I think he enjoys my company as well."

He shifted away from her touch.

She straightened her shoulders. "I won't let anything slip about the investigation. I can keep him occupied while you deal with everything else."

Cai looked down into her too-green eyes and wondered why her perfectly sensible arguments scared the daylights out of him.

It was obvious that Alfred was charmed by her. But too much was going on . . . and little was getting done about it. All he had to show for a full afternoon was a blank computer screen and a headache from trying not to think about her. He should have been thrilled with the chance to work uninterrupted. Instead he'd spent the greater portion of the time staring at the copy of her dragon sketch. Her laughter had found its way to his open window again and again during tea. When they'd finally, mercifully, finished and left for the garden, had he gotten to work? No. He'd stared out the window after them like a moonstruck calf.

And now she wanted to spend another day here? He

didn't think he'd survive it. Hell, this one wasn't even over yet.

"We can talk about it on the boat. Come on."

"Okay, okay." She moved past him, tucking her elbow against her side as she passed him. "I know you don't want me here. I understand."

"You don't understand anything," he muttered.

"It's not like I'm going to be hanging around here all the time, you know," she went on. "I'm going back home this Sunday."

He knew that. There was an undeniable sinking feeling in his chest. Yeah. He knew that. Another good reason to nip this in the bud.

"I'll find my own way here and back."

"I'll come and get you." The offer was made gruffly and totally against his better judgment.

"Thank you. I think." At his raised eyebrow, she said, "This sudden rush isn't just about a storm, or Alfred, is it?"

Cai had to get away from her. Something as simple as her hand on his arm had made him painfully aroused. He was beginning to wonder if Alfred was right about his sex life, or lack of one. Maybe he should get out more.

"Jordy, please." But it was clear she wasn't budging. "I have to get over to Mangrove. On business. Now."

Understanding dawned in her eyes. "This has something to do with the investigation, doesn't it?"

He paused a heartbeat too long.

"Is it another e-mail?"

"I don't want to involve you any further."

She bristled. "I am involved. I'm going to find out what's going on anyway. The local police are keeping me filled in. Are they waiting for you to bring it to them? Couldn't you just forward it?"

Cai shook his head. "They don't want anything sent out

from here. No electronic trail connecting me with the police."

"Do they honestly think she can track that kind of thing? And don't you think she'll figure you went to the police anyway, once you got those photos?"

"We don't know what she thinks, or what she's capable of. They aren't taking any chances."

"What does this one say? Does she make any other demands? Have the agents decided how you should respond to her e-mails?"

"I thought they were keeping in contact with you."

Jordy flushed, but held her ground. "It's not like I'm on their speed dial, okay? Why are you so worried about my involvement anyway?"

"The bigger this thing gets, the harder it will be to keep Alfred from finding out."

"I know you want to protect him, but you might have to tell him at some point. He's not a child."

"You've spent all of one afternoon with him and you think you're qualified to tell me how to take care of him?"

She sighed. "All I'm saying is that you should be prepared to tell him if it becomes necessary."

Cai blew out a long breath and raked his hand through his hair.

Jordy's expression softened. "Cai—"

"I know how much Alfred enjoyed having you here today."

"I enjoyed it, too."

There was something special in those eyes of hers. He wanted to know her, to know what she was thinking when her eyes went all soft like that. "He doesn't get much company and under normal circumstances, I'd welcome anyone who could bring him happiness."

"But?"

"But if you're involved in this other stuff, you'll want to

talk about it, like we are right now, and I can't be worrying about what Alfred might overhear. He saw the first e-mail and that triggered a 'spell,' as you call it, that lasted a great deal longer than your little chat in the garden. They drain him enormously and cause him pain. It would just be easier if—"

"If I went away?"

He swore under his breath. "I'm not handling this right."

"Perhaps if you dealt with people more often, you'd be better at it."

"Your people skills being so highly evolved and all?"

That hit a mark, but she came right back. "My people skills seemed fine to your grandfather. Could you try and see past your own problems long enough to think that instead of being a burden to you, I might be able to help? I want to spend time with Alfred. It's not like I'm going to be here forever. We're talking one week. It means more to me than you can possibly understand. And if there is anything I can do to make your life simpler while I'm here, then I'm all for helping you out. The whole world does not have to rest on your shoulders."

He shouldn't smile. He shouldn't. But he did.

She put her hands on her hips. "I'm glad I'm so amusing to you. Do you think you're the only one with problems? I could give you a rundown of my last twenty-four months that would make you think otherwise. But it is precisely because of those last twenty-four months that I need this so badly." She stepped closer to him. "I can take care of myself around Alfred for a visit or two. Then you don't have to deal with me anymore. I know you don't want me here, okay?"

Cai's heart pounded. She was magnificent. "You have no idea what I want."

"You've made it plain enough. You don't look at me

unless you have to, you go out of your way to keep from touching me."

Cai moved right up to her, but kept his hands by his side. "And why do you think that is, Jordy?"

Her eyes grew large, but she didn't back away. He watched her throat work and dug his fingertips into his thighs.

"It's not only Alfred I worry about, or the investigation. It's myself I'm protecting here."

"From what?"

"From getting involved in something I have no business even starting." He touched her cheek with his fingers and traced the soft line of her jaw. They both shuddered. "See what touching you does to me?" He took her hand and placed it on his chest. "Feel what looking at you does to me."

She looked at their hands, pressed together over his heart, then up into his eyes. Hers had gone dark with need.

"So don't tell me about what I want." He tugged her against him. "This is what I want, Jordy." She gasped at the contact. He stopped just shy of touching his lips to hers. "Tell me what you want. Tell me so I can take that mouth of yours the way I've been dying to since the first time you spoke to me." He brushed his lips lightly across hers, then moved his mouth to her ear as she shuddered against him. "Tell me."

TWELVE

J ORDY COULD BARELY breathe. "You . . ." She
cleared her throat. "You said you didn't want this to happen. That you shouldn't do this."

"What I should want, and what I do want are so far
apart I'm having a hard time reconciling them."

"Then maybe it's up to me to stop this."

"Can you?"

It was the challenge that lent her the strength to move
away from him. "Both of us are fighting against this. Isn't
that reason enough to stop?"

Cai held her gaze for an interminable moment. If he
touched her again, she wouldn't be able to say no. But he
didn't. Jordy's heart was still pounding and the needy ache
was a knot inside her. "Maybe we should get over to Mangrove so you can deliver that note."

He said nothing, but led the way down the path that ran
alongside the house, toward the dock. She walked behind
him.

The tense silence began to gnaw at her. "I didn't get the
chance to thank Dilys for the wonderful tea. Could you
please tell her for me?"

"Yeah."

She frowned at the terse reply, but pushed on. "Your

house is beautiful." It was that and more. An unusual sprawling wood structure, with rooms added on here and there, all connected by closed-in walkways. And the whole thing was on stilts, a nod to the tempestuous weather in the Keys. Fittingly, it was as unique as its residents. "It's a very impressive structure."

"Thanks."

Jordy stared at his back as they crossed the yard and headed down to the docks. "It's sort of like a Robinson Family treehouse kind of thing. I'm surprised at all the windows, though. Don't you worry about hurricanes?"

"Some."

She stopped. It took him several seconds to realize she wasn't still behind him. He turned and braced his hands on his hips. "Now what?"

"So, we either drag each other to the ground and have hot, torrid sex, or we speak in monosyllabic sentences? Are those the only options here?"

His expression grew dark, formidable. Then he stalked back up the path, his gaze pinning her down like a helpless butterfly. Only she wasn't helpless. She chose not to move. Because, she realized, she didn't want to.

He closed in on her and didn't stop. His hips bumped against hers as he took her head in his hands, levering her mouth up to his as he pressed her back against the pathway railing. He didn't ask, he just took.

His mouth was warm, his tongue hot and she was well acquainted with both inside the first two seconds. He demanded she respond, not willing to let her get away with him doing all the taking. She would take as well, or the kiss would end.

She took.

He welcomed her seeking tongue, and held it hostage, torturing her, pleasuring her. His hands slid down to her shoulders, then down to her elbows, where he urged her

arms up, urged her to touch him, hold him. It was an
invitation she couldn't resist.

He felt as glorious as he tasted. She ran her hands up
over his back, then slid them to his neck and dug her
fingers into all that beautiful hair. He was as decadent as
Alfred's lush gardens and far more drenching to her senses.

He pulled his mouth from hers, making her whimper,
only to trail kisses along her jaw to the soft spot beneath
her ear. His hips pressed more intimately against hers and a
small moan slipped from her lips.

"That's our option, Jordy. Do you understand now?"

Her fingers were shaky when she uncurled them from
the nape of his neck. She smoothed them against her
thighs, acutely aware of how closely aligned hers were with
his. They would fit so perfectly, too perfectly. She somehow
found the will to slip out from the narrow space he'd
backed her into. "I . . . yeah." She turned to look out
over the water. "Understood."

She felt his breath, his heat. "What's it going to be,
Jordy? All? Or nothing?"

"Nothing." She choked on the word.

He stepped back. "Fine."

"Fine." Screw fine, she wanted to say, come back here
and do that to me again. But she didn't. She'd done the
right thing. For both of them. She waited another moment,
until she heard his footsteps retreat down the path, before
turning and following him.

BACK AT MANGROVE, Cai watched her climb into her
car and drive off, then headed to his bike. Thankfully Dobs
wasn't about. He wasn't up for any small talk at the moment. What in the hell had gotten into him back there?
Jordy Decker had worked her way under his skin and then
some, but when push came to shove—and they'd done a

little of both there on the pathway—she'd done the right thing and ended it before it went any further. Damn good thing it had been up to her, he thought darkly. Or they'd be butt naked and going at it even now. Christ, what a mess.

Almost a mess, he corrected himself. They were both adults and had made their decision. No harm, no foul. And better yet, Alfred knew nothing about their little interlude. Thank God. Now *that* would have been disastrous. The boat ride over had been painfully strained, but they'd manage it. They'd manage it again. After all, it was one lousy week, how hard could that be?

He swore under his breath as he slid onto his bike. If he revved it a bit too high and laid down just a little rubber exiting the parking lot, well, so what? Damn, but that woman made even his teeth ache.

It wasn't until he pulled into the police parking lot that his mind finally shifted to what it should have been focused on all along. He unfolded the printout of the e-mail as he walked inside the station. Sgt. Winston looked up and immediately signaled Cai to his desk.

Winston smoothed the paper out on top of the open file in which he'd been writing. He read over it silently, but Cai already knew the words by heart.

No response, my Heart's Keeper? Surely you understood my request was not merely a query to be considered, but a demand that must be fulfilled. You are the only one. You cannot escape your destiny.

Are the stakes not high enough? Have I insulted you with only one life in peril? Please know that you have my humblest apologies. I will take care of this oversight with due haste. So many devoted to you, finding another will not take long. I will send along proof of my next claim.

I pray you begin your journey quickly. For endless patience is not something I possess. But I will possess the Dark Pearl. And I will possess you.

"She doesn't seem to realize that I've contacted the police," Cai said to the sergeant.

"I've seen more than a few whackjobs in my career." Winston smiled up at Cai. "I worked up in Jersey for twenty years before heading down to the sun and fun of Florida. I thought I'd left this behind." He shook his head. "She really believes all this stuff."

Cai could only nod. "This stuff" of legends and quests was what he did for a living. He knew it was fiction, and that he wasn't responsible for the mental capacities of his readers, but to think that because of a story he told, someone would suffer . . .

"She'll do it, won't she?" He didn't really need to ask. He knew the answer.

Winston nodded, then sipped his coffee. "They pinpointed the last e-mail as originating in Wales. They haven't been able to track the other two yet. But it doesn't look like she's here. They'll trace this one, too. Anyhow, as of now, we're officially out of it. State Department will be handling it. You need to hand this over to them right away." He fished around on his desk and came up with a card. "This is the number to call."

"I have their cards from the other day."

"This is a new one. Apparently the suits here earlier just do prelim work. You've been officially assigned to a separate task force now. Some sort of adjunct agency or something to the State Department dealing specifically with electronic crimes. This is the guy." He tapped the card. "You can use my phone."

Cai looked at the card again. Special Investigative Agent John Kuhn. Special Taskforce. U.S. Department of State.

Cai sighed, and picked up the phone. How were they going to stop her? There *was* no freaking pearl. But maybe it didn't matter. An idea hit him as the line rang in his ear. Maybe any pearl would do the job.

The call was picked up and Cai asked to speak to Mr. Kuhn. He had the plan all worked out by the time the agent finally came on the line.

FORTY MINUTES LATER, the moon hidden behind the clouds and rain starting to lash down, Cai stormed out of the police station swearing a blue streak. The last thing he needed was to find Jordy climbing out of her car.

She started to say hello, but he cut her off. "What are you doing here?" he demanded. "Checking up on me? I thought we agreed to—"

She snapped open an umbrella. "We agreed to steer clear of each other, that's it. I figured you'd be gone by now." She moved to go around him, but he put his arm out and stopped her.

"There's no point going in there."

"I can go wherever I damn well please. I may not be involved with you but, like it or not, I am involved with this case and I plan to keep track of their progress."

"Jordy—"

"This isn't about you, Cai. It's about the woman in those pictures. I'm worried about her. Is that so hard for you to understand?" Her anger seemed to blow over as quickly as it had come up. She sighed. "I see her face, Cai. I see it all the time. When I'm awake, when I sleep. I need to know she'll be okay. Or . . . or that she won't."

Cai wanted—needed—to be mad, and he was mad, just not at her. He blew out a long breath, then let his hand drop. "Yeah, okay."

"Thank you." She pushed past him.

He was soaked, but he still had to get his bike to Dobs and maneuver the boat back to Crystal before the storm really set in. He should leave now, let her find out on her own who had the case and steer as clear of her as he could. He was discovering that there were a lot of things he should be doing where she was concerned, just as he was learning he wasn't too good at doing any of them.

"The locals don't have the case anymore."

That stopped her. "What? Why?"

"They tracked the last e-mail and it originated in Wales. It's officially a State Department case now."

"I thought they were already in on it." She stepped closer and leaned her umbrella over him to share her shelter.

Way too cozy. "They were, in a preliminary way. Now they've officially assigned it to some new agency task force. There's a new investigator."

Jordy tilted her head. "I take it you two didn't hit it off too well."

"You could say that."

"Is this about the last e-mail?"

"Partly."

"Can you just make an exception to our no-talking rule and tell me what happened?"

That was just it. Talking to her was easy, very easy. Too easy. "I had an idea on how to catch her, but Special Investigative Agent John Kuhn didn't see it that way."

She nodded, but he saw the little smile.

"I'm so glad this amuses you," he said, parroting her earlier words.

"It's not that—"

"Since you seem so worried about the victims, I'd think you'd be a little more concerned."

"Victims? There's more than one?"

Shit.

THIRTEEN

H<small>E WASN'T SURE</small> why, but ten minutes later he was sitting in a donut shop with Jordy, drying out, sipping hot coffee, eating sweet buns, and talking about the case.

"Let me see the note."

"I was asked not to show it to anyone."

She put her cup down, wiped the powder from her lips, and stuck her hand out. "I'm not just anyone. Give it up."

Cai gripped his coffee cup tighter. They were talking about torture and kidnapping and all he could think about was licking that powder from her fingertips. He pulled the note from his pocket. "I faxed it to Kuhn from the station. They're tracking it."

"Did they find out a last name? Any name?"

Cai shook his head. "No. No fixed address either. Every one of them was bogus."

"How about the phone numbers? I mean, if they tracked down the call from when she signed on to send the mail, that had to give them something."

Cai had hoped for the same thing. "Nothing. She may be nuts, but she's not stupid."

She read the printout quietly. "She'll do it. What are we going to do?"

"We? We can't do anything."

"But you said you had a plan. What was it?"

"I thought we should respond by my finding the Dark Pearl and contacting her for a meeting."

She leaned forward. "But there is no Dark Pearl."

"She doesn't believe that. It's all fiction, so why not just create a 'real' Dark Pearl?"

"Kuhn says no?"

Cai shook his head. "No civilian input."

"So what's his big plan?"

"He didn't say, other than to inform me they were handling it. He didn't even listen to my idea. Officious type. A real asshole. Pardon me."

She shrugged it off. "I've met my share."

"I just want this nightmare over." It was already interfering with his work. Eileen was treating him like one of her more neurotic writers, which he hated. She said he needed a distraction. He watched Jordy read the note again, watched her eyes, the way they tilted down in the corners when she frowned.

"What sort of assholes do you meet?" The question just popped out.

She looked up, startled. "What?"

"You said you'd met your fair share of assholes and I just asked where. Sculpting seems as reclusive as writing."

She looked wary. "Haven't we covered this ground?"

"No, we covered sexual attraction and decided it was best if we didn't go there. I'm being a good boy and sitting over here keeping my hands to myself. But I want to know you better. You're getting involved with my grandfather and I'm just looking out for him."

Jordy laughed. "Oh, I see. How noble of you."

Cai leaned back, relaxing a little for the first time all day. Maybe Eileen was right about needing a distraction, though he'd be the last to tell her so. And Jordy was proving to be that and yet so much more. "Exactly what I thought."

She stared him down as she took another lengthy sip of coffee, but finally answered. "I used to own a business, or co-own it anyway."

"Selling your work?"

She nodded. "I started in college. My roommate was majoring in business and marketing. She was the brains behind the selling part of it. I could never have gone out and pushed my work on people. She saw the potential, though, and she went after it. We opened a small shop in Warburg right after graduation. I concentrated on my work and she had a product she could sell. We were friends. The best of friends. It was a perfect partnership."

"So what happened?"

"Suzanne was pushing for us to grow bigger, to branch out, but I knew with that kind of pressure, I'd never be able to maintain my creativity. I was perfectly happy with the way things were going. We weren't rich, but we made out well enough."

"What did she do? Sell out?"

"No. Suzanne had a lot invested in our business and she knew the clientele. We sold pieces to many prominent families and Suzanne enjoyed the spotlight moving in those circles afforded. She loved the wining and dining, going to gallery openings and the like, always drumming up new clients."

"But you didn't."

Jordy shook her head. "I was relieved she liked all that stuff because it was great for business, but no, I was very happy staying behind the scenes." She twisted her thumb ring. "I'm not exactly the socialite type."

Cai thought she'd knock any crowd on their collective butts, but all he said was, "So, what did she do?"

"She started to work behind the scenes to expand our

asset base without telling me. She did some investing without my knowledge, forging my signature, and when that
started to go well, she did more."

"She forged your name? Didn't you know what was happening?"

Jordy kept her chin up. "I really didn't pay attention to
the books. Suzanne hired the bookkeeper and our accoun-
tant. I know it sounds stupid now, but I trusted her completely. I just wanted to sculpt, so I let her take care of
business. Later on, when things started to go bad, I saw the
signs, but I ignored them."

"I take it the investments went south?"

"Pretty much. But she kept going, she was in too deep
then and had to find her way out. So she started siphoning
off what profit she could and investing it personally, leaving our creditors hanging. I didn't want to believe that she
would run out and leave me to hang. But that's exactly
what she planned to do." Jordy stared into her cup.

"Listen, I didn't mean to drag you through a bad time."

"No, it's okay. I mean, the whole thing was very not
okay. I've never talked about it, though. Maybe it's not so
bad to get it out."

"You had no one to talk to? No one on your side?"

She smiled a little. "You're not the only recluse on the
planet. But there wasn't anyone I trusted at that point. Just
me and Fred, and he doesn't really count."

"Fred?" Cai was totally unprepared for the sudden jab of
jealousy that shot through him.

"My goldfish. He's the short, fat, silent type."

"A goldfish?" He was ridiculously relieved.

"He goes with me everywhere. Great listener, but not
too good at dispensing advice. Still, he's all I've got." She
laughed. "Well now, that sounds pathetic, doesn't it?"

"I've never had a pet, not even a fish."

"Really? Okay, that's even more pathetic. But you do

have your grandfather, and Dilys. That's wonderful. I'd
love to still have a family. It would have made the trial
almost bearable."

"Trial?"

"It was long, ugly, and complicated. I was forced to sue
Suzanne and she counter-sued and in the course of that, we
both came under indictment for criminal charges."

"You, too?"

She nodded. "When it all hit the fan, she tried to twist
it all around and blame me. She was pretty damn convincing. She'd made up phony records. I had nothing to combat
them with."

"Some best friend."

"What was amazing to me, and really humbling, was
that she actually convinced a good number of our clients
that she was the wronged party. I wasn't just behind the
scenes, I didn't exist. I was like the hired help or something. The whole thing lasted over two years. In the end,
my business and my career were history. I lost everything I
owned, including my house. But fight it I did. And I won.
Two weeks ago today. Funny, but I didn't feel victorious."

"Just two weeks ago? Jordy, I—"

"But you know what hit me the hardest? It was realiz-
ing that I'd let someone else run my entire life. Actually, I
let her have my life. I thought I could sit alone in my
studio and create. I believed that this life she'd built
around me was actually part mine. But it wasn't. The only
thing that was mine was my craft. I had no real life. It was
all hers. The clients, the parties, the support, the friends,
all of it. I had nothing. And you know whose fault that is?
Mine. If you don't participate in life, you don't really have
one. I'm thirty-one years old and it took losing everything
to make me understand that." She laughed without humor.
"Now *that's* pathetic."

"No, it's not. You're lucky."

"Excuse me?"

"Not everyone gets the chance to figure that out."

"So says the man who lives on an island?"

Cai smiled wryly. "Yes, well, maybe that's why I have this point of view. Some days I wonder how I ended up like I did, so removed from the world. Most days I like it, other times I wonder if we did the right thing." He thought of Arthur and Dilys and the difficult road that lay ahead for all of them as aging took its inevitable toll.

"That's just it," Jordy said. "I liked my solitude. Still do. But I can't just rely on the rest of the world to take care of everything else except what interests me. And if I do, then I damn well can't complain if I get shafted. You have to pay attention to what's important, whatever that is. I'm just starting to figure it all out."

"It sounds like you're doing just that. You have learned a great deal about life."

"Oh, I learned. I learned not to trust people. I learned the legal system isn't about who's right and who's wrong but who has the most well-paid shark in the courtroom."

"You trusted your lawyers. You did win."

"It had nothing to do with trust. I swam with the sharks. It was bloody and damned expensive. All to prove I didn't do anything wrong in the first place. Except trust the wrong person." She drained her coffee, crumpled her napkin up, and shoved it inside the paper cup. "Maybe this wasn't such a good idea after all. We came here to talk about the case, not about me."

"Tell me one more thing."

The wary look returned. "Depends."

"You'd just walked away from the two-year battle from hell. You come down here to wash the blood off and I guess try and figure out where to start over again. Why on earth did you get involved with this case?"

She fiddled with her cup. "Because I was concerned

about her. Because I know how it feels to not have anyone to turn to." She finally looked at him. "And because I didn't want to go home yet and I thought helping someone else might give me a clue as to how to help myself."

"You were going to give up sculpting?"

"For a long time I didn't think I had a choice. I thought it was lost to me."

"Until the dragon."

She suddenly stood. "Yeah, well, maybe that was a fluke."

He caught her by the arm. "Wait a minute."

"It's really late and it looks like the storm finally let up. I should go."

Cai stood, but didn't let go. "Tell me about the dragon."

She looked so vulnerable that he almost let her go. But he didn't. She said she needed to talk. Well, this time there was someone interested in listening.

"Why did you give it to me?"

"I told you already. It was a gift. To us both. For you it was the perfect solution. To me it was. . . . It was hope." She pulled her arm free. "Satisfied?"

"No, I'm not. I wasn't trying to hurt you. I'm honored you wanted me to have it. I'm glad you took the contract. Gift or not, you deserved payment. And now Alfred wants to commission a piece. You should be happy."

"Yes, everyone is happy." She started to move away.

"I'd be terrified if I thought I couldn't write, so I think I have some idea how hard this is for you."

She faced him fully. "With all due respect, no, you don't. I came here to sort out my life, and I stayed to help a complete stranger get hers back. I was given a chance to teach some kids about art and, in the process, I'm beginning to relearn a bit about my own. I met your grandfather, walked through his amazing garden, and for the first time since the courtroom battle, I wanted to work. I wanted to feel the clay under my hands." She paused, then said, "I've never taken my talent for granted. I thanked God every time I came up with a new creation. But to just lose it, to lose your faith in yourself . . . There is this sense of being abandoned. By your own self. It's the cruelest trick. Unless you've been through the hell of losing your gift, you can't possibly know what it means to me to think I might get it back."

Cai listened to her passionate defense and thought about the blank monitor screen he'd been staring at for a week. "Oh, yes, I do," he said quietly.

"Then you know it's twice as terrifying wondering if it's back to stay."

He reached out to touch her, but she immediately stepped back. That hurt, but he didn't blame her. He'd gotten his distraction, but he hadn't intended this. Which was exactly why he should just stay on his damn island and not get involved with people.

She was at the door when he spoke. "I'll pick you up to see Alfred whenever you want. Just call."

She turned. She looked tired. Very tired. "I get done with the kids early on Wednesday, by noon at the latest. Any time after that would be fine." She paused a second, then added, "Thank you, Cai. I appreciate it." Then she walked away.

He sat back down and stared out the window. The parking lot was unlit, so he couldn't see her climb in her car and leave, but he saw her just the same. He saw how she looked at him when he made her smile. He saw the smile shift to a frown when she was upset. He saw the vulnerability she hid behind bravado. He saw the concern and warmth that filled her eyes when she talked of Alfred. He saw those same eyes go dark with desire when he pulled her into his arms. He saw her spit fire at him when he set her off.

He saw her all right. With every breath he took, he saw her. He balled up his napkin and shot it hard into the trash, then stalked out into the night.

FOURTEEN

JORDY MADE HERSELF comfortable on the stone bench and flipped open her sketch book. She smiled when she spied the dirt under her fingernails. Alfred had been right, it was better to sink bare hands into the soil. There was life there. Just as there was in clay.

She'd left Alfred behind in his hothouses and headed to the gardens. She chose a fountain pen with a fine nib, checked the ink cartridge, then focused on the small figures she'd chosen to draw. She'd decided to begin by sketching whatever caught her attention. Her pen moved swiftly and the small pond lily fairies came instantly to life on the paper.

She had no idea how long she'd been at it when Dilys suddenly appeared.

"Sorry to startle you," Dilys said perfunctorily.

"No, no problem." She noticed the older woman carried a silver platter laid for tea.

"I thought you might like to break for some tea."

Jordy set aside the pad and pen and stood, reaching for the tray. "Thank you. You didn't need to go to all this trouble, though."

Dilys regarded her silently. The look on her face made it

clear that she felt it would be an act akin to blasphemy to skip tea.

"I'll bring this back to the house when I'm done," Jordy said.

"No need. I'll be back in one hour." She turned and left as silently as she'd arrived.

Jordy sat there, bemused by the interesting woman, until another thought entered her mind. Perhaps Dilys' sudden generosity had more to do with protecting Cai's privacy by keeping her away from the house than with her overriding concern that tea time be observed.

Jordy had called and spoken to Alfred earlier that day, letting him know when she'd be at Dobs' dock, once again offering to hire someone to make the short boat ride. He'd heard none of that and she had braced herself for the trip over with Cai. She hadn't spoken to or seen him since she left the donut shop two days ago. To her surprised relief and perverse disappointment, Dilys had been the one waiting in the boat when she arrived. The trip had been quick, silent, and efficient. Dilys' hallmark traits.

She looked at the variety of delights Dilys had prepared. Knowing that Dilys wouldn't stand for anything but an empty tray when she returned, Jordy poured herself a cup of tea, then selected a warm scone.

She sighed in deep appreciation at the first bite, then picked up her sketch pad to look over her afternoon's work. She smiled at the first drawing. The pond lily fairies were too delightful to enhance with any of her own ideas, so she'd recorded them faithfully. She really wanted a chance to meet the wonderful artist. Why had she never sought out other artists before? Art was, by its very nature, a reclusive occupation. But certainly she could have made it a point to make contact with another artist whose work she admired, and there had been more than a few over the years. She'd simply never presumed to. She'd had Suzanne and with such a flamboyant friend, more would have been exhausting.

Jordy realized now how wrong she'd been. She decided right then and there to ask Alfred for a way to contact Mara. Seeking out new friendships was a step in the right direction with her new life, she thought. So long as she didn't give that friend control of her life.

Thoughts of burgeoning friendships had her thinking of Alfred, and even Dilys. She wouldn't call the latter a friend, but she was certainly on her way to building a new circle of acquaintances. Eccentric ones, to be certain, but then, she was an artist, so wasn't that appropriate? She chuckled as she picked up another biscuit.

"Dilys doing something funny to the scones again?"

Startled, Jordy almost spilled tea on her lap.

"I'm sorry," Cai said. "I'll beat the bushes with a stick next time I approach."

She expected him to be smiling, but when she looked up she found him staring at her, in that unnerving, I-can-see-your-soul way that he had.

He walked over to the stone bench. "Can I join you?"

"There's only one cup. Besides, I think you're ruining Dilys' master plan by being out here."

Cai took a seat on the other side of the tray. "Master plan?"

Jordy willed her heart to slow down. But he looked incredibly fine in black jeans and T-shirt, his dark hair blowing in the light breeze. She tried not to stare at his mouth or to remember the kiss they'd shared. She wasn't too successful at either. She turned her attention to her tea cup.

"I think she agrees we shouldn't spend time alone together," Jordy said. "Isn't that why she came and got me at Dobs' today?"

"She had to come in to pick up Alfred's monthly prescription refills and I had an emergency call from my editor, so it just seemed easier." He picked up a marmalade tart and sunk his teeth into it, groaning in pleasure.

Jordy had to stifle one of her own. His teeth were strong and white and looked way too sensual sinking into that tart. She had no problem transferring the visual to a more intimate type of nibbling.

"I'm not trying to avoid you," he said, while popping a small sugar cookie into his mouth.

Jordy wanted to remove the sprinkles of sugar that dusted his lips. With her tongue.

"Don't ever tell her I said so, but Dilys is a food goddess."

She smiled at that, but it quickly faded. She was hot, achy, itchy, and needy, and it was all his fault dammit. "Maybe it's better that way. Avoiding each other, I mean."

"Maybe. Probably."

That stung, even though she'd said it first.

"There you are. And Malacai as well, how perfect." Alfred moved slowly into the small courtyard.

For two people who'd just agreed that they shouldn't be alone together, Jordy noticed neither one of them appeared thrilled at Alfred's sudden intrusion.

And Alfred might be up there in years, but he wasn't so old as to miss the tension in the air. "I've interrupted something. My apologies."

"No, it's fine," Jordy quickly said. "We were just enjoying Dilys' fabulous tea pastries. Please join us before Cai demolishes the rest."

Jordy could feel the apprehension all but rolling off Cai.

"I think I will pass on the tarts, thank you." Alfred said. "So, how did you fare today, Jordalyn?"

"I . . . well . . . fine." She glanced at the sketch pad, and felt a thrum of excitement. She'd done some good work today. She smiled at Alfred. "Very fine, I think."

Alfred tapped his cane. "Splendid, indeed."

"I think I might even have an idea for you. It's very preliminary," she hurried to add. "But it's a start." She'd explained her background to him earlier and he'd been as understanding as she'd expected. But he'd also refused to listen to any concerns and was convinced she would create a fine piece for him. She wished she had a bit more of his confidence. Still, it meant a great deal to her that she had anything to show him. One look at the smile in his eyes and she knew he understood that, too.

Alfred waved his cane like a wizard might a staff. "Very good indeed and I'm certain you've crafted a gem. I'm anxious to discuss every detail, but first we must discuss my plans."

"Plans?" Cai spoke for the first time.

Alfred didn't look at Cai but continued to address Jordy. "I have a small outbuilding adjacent to the gardens. I had originally intended to use it as a potting shed, but after the hothouses were constructed, I found little need for it. I fear it requires some maintenance, the salty air here isn't conducive to keeping paint on things, but it should fix up quite nicely with a little attention."

"Fix up? What have you cooked up now?"

Alfred turned to his grandson and smiled kindly, as a patient parent would to a recalcitrant child.

"Rest assured, I have not cooked anything. I leave that fathomless function to Dilys, with all of her inimitable talents." He turned his attention back to Jordy. "I plan to consign you to sculpt several pieces."

His vote of confidence both reassured and terrified her. She forced a confident smile. "That is wonderful to hear, truly." Her smile slipped a bit as honesty forced her to add, "But Alfred, I can't guarantee—"

"Ah, my dear, those are two words I don't want to hear

passing from those lips again. You can and you will. Has this garden inspired your creativity?"

"Yes, but—"

"Am I right in thinking that you would enjoy continuing to work in this environment?"

"Well, yes, but I have to go—"

"She can't stay."

"Says who?" Jordy asked. It irritated her that he was making decisions for her. Even if it was the same one she'd been about to make. "I finish working with the kids this Friday." To Alfred, she added, "After that, my plans are open."

"After that your plan was to return to Virginia and start your business again," Cai said pointedly.

"You said you understood why I was here. You don't understand at all."

"I understand perfectly. You don't want to go home and face what lies there. I don't blame you. But hiding out here isn't going to solve anything."

"Who said anything about hiding out?"

Cai turned to Alfred. "You want to make the potting shed into a studio and move her in here. Am I correct?"

Alfred beamed. "Always were a sharp boy. Precisely my idea. Golden, isn't it?"

She stared back and forth at both of them. "Whoa, wait a minute. Let's all just back up a few steps." She addressed Cai first. "I do have to return to Virginia. At some point." She raised a finger when he started to speak. "I'm not running, or hiding, by admitting that working here would be a tremendous boost for me. If you couldn't write any longer but found there was a place where you thought you could, would you let anything stop you?"

Cai stared at her, but said nothing.

"You are making a wise decision, my dear," Alfred said.

She turned to him and her expression gentled. "Alfred,

it is very kind of you to make such a generous offer, but I can't accept."

He looked so crestfallen she felt like she'd kicked a puppy.

"He's a genius at looking wounded," Cai said. "Don't let it sway you. Trust me."

She shot Cai a quelling look, then took Alfred's hand. "Cai is right, I do have to get back home, but I'd like to extend my stay on Mangrove just a little longer and I'd be greatly appreciative if I could come and sit in your marvelous gardens. Whenever it's convenient." She turned to include Cai. "I really have no intention of intruding."

Cai muttered something under his breath that she didn't catch, but Alfred apparently did. "I did not raise you to be impertinent to guests. Crystal Key is as much my home as it is yours. I'm certain Jordalyn and I can work out a suitable arrangement that won't require your presence."

Cai started to speak, but those crystal blue eyes stopped him. "Make wise choices, Malacai. Don't mistake fear for weakness. The consequences could be dire."

An odd, eerie silence descended over the garden at this proclamation. She was uncomfortably reminded of the feeling she'd had that first day in the garden when Alfred had gone a little batty on her. But just as he had then, he seemed very much aware of exactly what he was saying.

In the next instant, the look vanished, replaced once again by the warm, grandfatherly gaze she'd grown attached to.

"I would think, however," Alfred went on, as if the moment hadn't occurred, "that you'd be somewhat more grateful to the woman who, with the stroke of her pen, saved your publisher's abysmal marketing campaign." With a dismissive nod that made it clear the subject was closed, he smiled at Jordy. "Now, come dear, and we shall look over those drawings. I really would like you to see the potting shed. Cai here will be glad to remove the tea tray."

Jordy didn't have to look at Cai to know he was steaming. She could feel the heat. She also knew Alfred had every intention of trying to talk her into staying.

And if she stayed, despite their best intentions, she'd end up all tangled with Cai. She knew it, and she was certain Cai knew it.

Which was why she had to nip Alfred's grand scheme in the bud. She would find a way to work here, for at least a few more visits. Too much was riding on this. Surely she and Cai could steer clear of each other that long.

"I'll be taking you back to Mangrove later," Cai said.

She let Alfred walk ahead before turning back to him. The silver tray, gleaming in a beam of sunlight, was balanced easily on one wide palm. He should have seemed ridiculously out of place, all rugged and dangerous looking in his black clothes, holding a tray filled with delicate china, surrounded by hothouse flowers and whimsical fairy creatures.

And yet, he looked perfect.

She recalled the sorcerer in his latest book, the one who had held her as spellbound as the author himself. She wondered if he had any idea how strongly she was beginning to identify him with that troubled hero. Did he see that in himself? Or was it an unconscious manifestation?

She shivered. There was another woman out there who identified Cai with his sorcerer. And Jordy had the cold realization that if that woman were to see the way he looked right now, she would feel vindicated for all her beliefs.

"I'll . . . I'll meet you on the docks in an hour." Without another glance, she clutched her sketch pad to her chest and raced to catch up with Alfred.

FIFTEEN

CAI STOOD ON the rear deck and watched Alfred give directions to the three-man crew he'd hired to renovate the potting shed. He tried not to think about the blank monitor sitting on his desk, the cursor blinking at him like an irritating accusation. He couldn't sleep. He was too tired to think. And when he couldn't think, he couldn't create.

He fell into bed at night exhausted, only to have nightmares of that woman being beaten, and when he focused closely on her face, he saw only Jordy staring back at him. Alfred was also there, snapping in and out of his Arthurian mode, casting prophecies with that bony finger. Threading through it all, the madwoman responsible for the whole thing appeared. Faceless, nameless, in a dark shroud, telling him he could end all this agony if he would only bring her the pearl.

He'd wake up sweating and crawl out of bed to the haven that was his computer. He craved the alternate world of his own creation, seeking the solace and escape it had always provided him. But he found, like Jordy's sculpting, his own art had abandoned him in his time of need. A cruel trick indeed.

Alfred had been more even-keeled since he'd met Jordy.

His new goal of having her work on Crystal Key kept him mostly focused. Still, Cai worried. Alfred was becoming attached to Jordy. It was perfectly understandable, Cai thought with aching frustration, but she *would* eventually leave.

His eyes narrowed when he saw Alfred wave his cane and begin to expound to the startled crew. He moved to intervene, then spied Dilys running to the rescue. He puffed out a sigh of relief. He didn't think he could handle another confrontation. He'd tangled with Alfred over this every day, since he'd escorted Jordy back to Mangrove four days ago.

She'd promised that she would only stay long enough to finalize the preliminary plans for the pieces Alfred wanted to commission. He had no doubt she'd keep her word. But, he knew his grandfather. He was a very persuasive man. He'd seen the looks the two of them had shared when she'd come back yesterday morning. He knew their special bond was deepening every moment they spent together.

The phone rang and jolted him out of his thoughts. He seriously considering letting the machine pick up. He answered on the third ring.

"Hello, Eileen."

After a smoky exhale, she jumped right in. "What does it say about a man's social life when he automatically assumes the only person who would call on a Saturday is his editor?"

"The same thing it says about editors working weekends."

Eileen's hoarse laugh filled his ear. "I've gone over your revisions on Book Two and everything looks fine. It's on schedule. But I need to give Lawrence a date on the partial for Book Three. He's got it tentatively scheduled, but he wants to see some of it before meeting with the new team from marketing. He's really happy with the new cover concept for the second one, by the way. Maybe we can get Jordy to think about contributing to your next cover as well."

Jordy, Jordy, Jordy. How had she so quickly found her way into every aspect of his life? Irritated, but knowing this was a safer topic than the proposal he hadn't made a page of progress on in the past week and a half, he said, "She's a sculptor, not an illustrator."

"I don't care if she's a librarian who doodles in book margins. She's hot and Lawrence likes her work. I can have the art department talk to her directly."

"Don't do that."

The pause was slight, but told him he'd blown it. "Oh? Trouble in paradise? I thought she was getting all chummy with Alfred. Isn't that a good thing? She's keeping him out of your hair, so you can concentrate on your work."

"It's more than that," he muttered.

There was a sharp inhale, followed by a long, contemplative exhale. Eileen could say more with a simple drag on a cigarette than others could in an entire speech.

"I see."

Having Eileen on his case about work was one thing, having her involved in his private life at this point was another. "Listen, I have to get back outside with Alfred. I'll call you back soon with a date." She was still exhaling when he hung up. It rang again almost immediately. "C'mon, give me a break." He snatched up the phone. "Listen, Eileen, I need some—"

"Mr. L'Baan? Special Agent Kuhn here."

Cai swore silently. He'd rather deal with Eileen. Hell, he'd rather deal with Alfred. "What can I do for you?"

"We've done additional traces on that last e-mail. She used a service provider out of London, but the call originated in the same area of Wales as the others."

Well, duh, Cai thought uncharitably.

"The trail ended there. Another alias and phony address."

None of this was surprising. It had been the same with the others. "Thank you for letting me know, Kuhn."

"You're welcome, and it's Special Agent Kuhn."

Cai had to resist the urge to hang up on the pompous jerk. "I still think we should discuss my idea about contacting her. What have we got to lose?"

"Mr. L'Baan, we have special training in these matters and I believe we have this under control, but I appreciate your concern."

"Well, I hope the woman who's suffering God knows what kind of torture right now as we swap ridiculous formalities shares your confidence, *Special Investigative Agent* Kuhn."

"This is no time to lose your cool, Mr. L'Baan" he said tightly. "Rest assured everything is being done to locate the woman."

"Not everything. We could still—"

"If you receive anything else you will inform us immediately. Still nothing regarding proof of the second threatened kidnapping?"

Cai controlled his temper. "Nothing."

"We'll take that as a good sign. I'll be in touch. When you hear something, contact me immediately."

"Yes, sir." Cai disconnected, replacing the phone carefully. It was that or rip it out of the wall.

Dilys chose that moment to enter his office. "Himself is needing your attention," she said shortly. "He's in his gardens. I'm bringing out tea." She left without waiting for a reply.

She knew Cai would do his duty by his grandfather. He wished he could go away somewhere, worry only about himself for just a little while. The guilt hit him immediately. He rose to go find Alfred.

On the walk there, he stared out at the gardens and thought about what Jordy had said about finding a haven where she could finally work, and the lengths to which she'd go in order to be there. For her, it was here, on Crystal Key. This had always been his haven too, but it wasn't right now. He had to admit, if such a place were to pop up this instant, he'd move heaven and earth to go there. So he did understand.

As he neared the steps leading up to the garden, he heard Alfred expounding on Merlin's merits as a great magician. It mattered not that his audience was made of stone. Cai found Alfred, cane lifted high like a staff, orating with clear, elegant prose to a group of marble fairies.

Cai's love for the old man ached in his chest and burned behind his eyes. He owed him everything. Everything.

Alfred wasn't a burden, he was a gift.

To remind himself of that fact, Cai quietly took a seat on the nearest bench, to listen, and to learn.

"IF THINGS WERE different," Jordy tapped fish food into the bowl, "I'd move to Crystal Key in a heartbeat."

Fred swished around, catching the falling flakes in an awkward sideways grab.

"I know. I'm supposed to be in Warburg right now, getting on with my life." She'd called her landlady earlier that day and asked her to water her plants for another week. She smiled, thinking of her. Mrs. Isaak was a sharp-tongued woman who didn't hesitate to share her opinions on anything, frequently and without provocation. For whatever reason, probably because it went against public opinion, she'd taken a shine to Jordy. She gave her a good deal on the rent and, in return, Jordy patiently listened to her daily rants without interruption. Mrs. Isaak had offered to bag up her mail and send it to her. Of course, she'd added in her raspy voice, the postage would be added to next month's rent. Jordy had thanked her for her consideration.

The Mangrove Hotel manager, grateful for her help with the camp, had given her a break on the room for a week, but it still put a serious dent in what she laughingly called her budget.

There was still a lot of work to be done on the preliminary sketches for Alfred's dragon. She smiled as the warm thrill raced over her again. He'd approved of what she'd done so far and his sincere enthusiasm had her actually believing she could pull this off.

Alfred had been certain, so much so that he'd offered to pay her a small advance up front. She'd refused, but, in typical Alfred fashion, he didn't give her much chance to argue. And, truth be told, the money was a godsend. The check from the publisher wouldn't be coming right away.

She tried to view it as motivation and not be intimidated by the deadline she now had. And Alfred wanted more when she finished this. She kept that promise locked away in her heart, but there was no denying that the small seed of hope had been planted.

In the meantime, she focused on details. She'd have to find someone to fire her pieces until she had a place for the kiln she had in storage. Next she'd convert her tiny living room into a makeshift workshop. She tried not to think of Mrs. Isaak's reaction to the dropcloths and wrapped bundles of clay, not to mention the tools that would likely litter the tables, sinks, and every other available surface in the place.

It was all coming back to her. She could do this. With Alfred's encouragement, she'd find her way. This time, she wasn't alone. The feeling of security he gave her should have been alarming, relying as she was on someone else.

But it was different this time. It was teamwork of the best kind. And it was real.

The sketches were only a start. There was still the clay to face: sinking her fingers into it, smoothing her fingertips along the cool, damp surface, finding the curves, discovering the angles, letting the creature out.

Jordy stood at the balcony door and thought of the potting shed, that perfect little cottage set on the edge of wonderland. A wonderland created by a delightfully eccentric old man and watched over by an equally enigmatic younger one. It caught at her heart and made her pulse race. But her destiny didn't lie down that path.

She turned away and picked up her sketch pad.

She had work to do.

THOUSANDS OF MILES away, on the windswept moors that ran along a Welsh river, a scream went unheard as another victim was taken.

SIXTEEN

"ALFRED, YOU REALLY shouldn't have done all this." Jordy gaped at the amazing transformation he'd wrought to the potting shed in only three days.

He'd had the roof freshly shingled. The graying stone walls, previously covered in island vegetation, had been scraped clean and repainted a pale shell pink. The splintered, rotting window frames had all been replaced, and the glass panes were shining. He'd even started a small garden plot alongside the small stoop. The stone walkway, once thick with weeds and uneven stones, had been cleared and reset. As a finishing touch, a woven doormat had been laid on the stoop.

"Nonsense," he said, beaming with pride. "It had to be done."

She turned to him, trying to keep the shine of excitement from her eyes. She'd made a promise to herself. She had plans. "It's wonderful, but I told you, I can't come to work here. I'm going home in a week." She talked over Alfred's response, rushing the words so she could pretend this wasn't killing her. "I've been working on your dragon and I think I have the concept finalized. I don't want to do much detailing, since I prefer to let that emerge as I create. I've worked out a schedule and even a tentative delivery date. It will be better for me if I have a deadline to work toward. We'll have to decide on shipping and such, but seeing as you get most of your pieces shipped from Wales, I'm sure we can come to a suitable arrangement to get the dragon here from Virginia."

Alfred listened patiently, then spoke as if he hadn't heard a word. "You should be able to move your things in by week's end. I'm having the interior worked on, putting in a small bathroom and running a stronger electrical line. I wanted you to look at this today before they start so you can give me your input on the lighting." He moved to the door. It too had been refinished. "Naturally, you'll stay in the house, but Dilys can show you your room when we're done here. Perhaps later, after tea."

Jordy saw that he was leaning more heavily on his cane than usual. She wanted to believe he was just playing on her sympathy. But as she watched him work the knob on the door with difficulty, she frowned. She rarely thought of Alfred as being frail, but today it was hard to ignore the obvious signs. "Here," she said, stepping forward and gently moving his hand aside. The knob turned easily. She didn't say anything, but casually took his arm as they stepped over the raised entry board.

That he allowed her to take some of his weight as they crossed to the middle of the room alarmed her further. Once he had his cane carefully positioned on the uneven flooring, he let go. As he described his plans, she studied him. He seemed a bit pale, but he had on a wide-brimmed straw hat today, so it was hard to say for certain in the dim natural lighting.

"We'll put a narrow table alongside that wall, and cupboards over there for your supplies. You'll have to give me the specifics of your needs in regards to worktables and the like. The bathroom will be in that corner there, with a utility sink on the opposing wall of the bathroom sink."

He turned to her with a twinkling eyes. "What think you, my dear?"

Only because she'd spent a great deal of time when he wasn't aware, studying him, assessing his features, for later study with ink and paper, did she see the slight pinched lines at the corners of his eyes.

But worse than that, far worse . . . she saw hope.

Feeling more torn than she could ever remember, she went on instinct. She walked up to him and kissed his cheek, then laid her hand over his and looked him straight in the eye.

"It's beautiful, Alfred. It's like something from a fairy tale, and I'd be lying if I said I didn't want to work here."

"But?" His expression was one of infinite wisdom . . . and regret.

"I have to go home," she said gently. "I have to start rebuilding my life. You've given me an immense gift by bringing me here even for such a short time."

"Build on your dream here." He covered her hand with his. "You get very few chances to realize a dream in this life, Jordalyn. Don't be hasty in throwing this one away."

"Alfred—"

"I didn't make this offer lightly. Don't regard it only with logic. Logic can cloud the heart. Instinct is a powerful guide most never learn to follow." Alfred's gaze shifted past her shoulder. "Come now, Malacai, let us not add skulking to the list your lamentable character traits of late."

Jordy turned in time to see Cai fill the small doorway.

He looked to Alfred. "Would you excuse us for a moment?"

To Jordy, Alfred said, "Instinct, my dear. It guides the heart, which in turn can teach the mind."

Jordy nodded, then turned and stepped past Cai. They

walked to the garden. "Was that really necessary? I told you I'd handle it."

"I know Alfred," was all he said.

Since Alfred had been doing a pretty fine job of destroying her defenses, she had to bite down on her retort. "Why did you want to see me?"

She hadn't seen Cai at all on her last two trips to Crystal Key. He looked tired. Instead of the frustration and sexual tension that always seemed to simmer just beneath the surface whenever they were together, she saw weariness. He looked almost . . . haunted.

"Are you okay?" She stepped closer. "You look terrible."

His dry smile was fleeting. He was clearly torn about something and she had a pretty good idea as to what it was.

"You're right, you know," she said. "Alfred does make a very convincing argument, but I've made some plans of my own. They don't include staying here. You can take that off your list of things to worry about."

"That's just it. I don't want you to turn him down."

She gaped. "What? What are you saying?"

"I'm saying I changed my mind. I want you to take Alfred's offer." He held up his hand to forestall her response. "Hear me out. I've given this a lot of thought. I know we agreed to go our separate ways, and that it was best for both of us not to get involved."

"And now you're saying . . . what exactly?"

"I want you to stay, for Alfred."

"I thought it was precisely because of Alfred that you didn't want me around."

"You told me to look past my own problems, to do what was best for him. Maybe I wanted you gone because it would be easier for me, but maybe what's easier isn't what's best." He stepped closer. "You do want to stay, don't you? I know you care about him."

"I do care for him, a great deal." She was suddenly

concerned. "Is there something wrong with him? Is he ill?" She remembered the pinched lines around his eyes, the slowness in his step. "Is that why?"

"He has been more easily fatigued lately, but it's not only that. Maybe I was being selfish in trying to prevent him from having a meaningful relationship because I thought it would hurt him too badly in the end." Cai moved even closer and looked down into her eyes. "He's grown very fond of you. When you're here with him, he . . . I don't know, he seems more like his old self."

"I don't want to hurt him either, but just because I'm going home doesn't mean I don't plan on keeping in touch."

"My thought exactly. It wouldn't have to end completely when you leave. And I know you want to work here. Maybe I was being selfish there, too. I do understand about needing to be where you can work. You could finish the pieces Alfred wants and maybe begin others you could ship back to Virginia as a portfolio, or whatever you call it. Something to start on."

It was too much, to be handed a dream twice.

Instinct, my dear. It guides the heart, which in turn can teach the mind. She swallowed hard. "Just how long are we talking about?"

Cai's relieved grin elicited a dangerous jump in her pulse rate. He might have come to terms with being around her, but she was quite certain she hadn't.

"How long do you want?"

"I . . . I don't know about this," she hedged. "Maybe this isn't such a good idea. We agreed to stay out of each other's hair. How can we do that if I'm living here?"

Cai closed the rest of the distance between them. "I've given that some thought, too."

She put her hands up and backed away. "You said we were doing this for Alfred."

He covered her hands with his and pulled them up to his shoulders. "We are. And with everything we have going on, it would be logical for us not to confuse things further with this." He let his mouth drop to hers and took her in a blood-stirring kiss. She was breathless when he lifted his head. "But maybe I'm letting logic cloud my instincts there, too."

Jordy's head was spinning. It was too much, too fast. "But what about Alfred? What will he think about us . . . getting involved?"

The hands that had begun to slide down her back stilled. "I think he'd understand."

"And when I leave? What then? I do plan to keep in touch, but I don't want to hurt him by giving him false hopes about . . ." She had to swallow before she could say it. "About us. About . . . this."

"This," he repeated. "I've tried getting over *this,* I tried ignoring *this.* It's not working. How about you?"

She could only shake her head.

"Then maybe we look beyond our problems on this, too. Go through it, see where it leads. You told me to let Alfred be an adult. Maybe you were right. So we'll tell him up front, so he doesn't get any grand ideas."

She smiled wryly. "And here you said you knew the man. Do you honestly believe he won't think whatever he damn well pleases?"

"We could be worrying about nothing. For all we know, we could be sick of each other inside a week."

"Yeah, right." Jordy snorted, then felt her face go red. "It could happen," she muttered.

He tipped her chin. "Yeah," he said, then took her mouth again.

They lifted their heads, only to find Alfred standing just beyond the opening in the hedgerow. Gone was his fatigue. His eyes were bright and his step more lively than it had been in days. "I misjudged you, Malacai." He shifted his gaze to hers. "Instincts aren't such a terror, are they, my dear?"

Before either could speak, Dilys stepped through the hedge opening at the opposite end of the small garden. She motioned to Cai, who walked over to where she stood.

"What is it?" he asked.

"There is a delivery, at the dock. The gentleman will take only your signature."

SEVENTEEN

CAI FELT HIS stomach drop. "I'll be right there," he said. He turned to Jordy. "Why don't you and Alfred finish discussing your plans for the cottage, then come up to the house. Dilys will show you to your room. We can make the rest of the arrangements at tea."

Jordy frowned. "What's wrong?"

He held her gaze, silently telegraphing her to let this drop while Alfred stood so near. "I have to go take care of something. I'll see you at the house later."

"Wait, I want to go with you."

"Jordy—" But he could see from the stubborn set of her jaw that she wasn't going to be left behind.

She turned to Alfred and Dilys. "I need to talk to Cai. Why don't I meet you back at the house? We can finish discussing this there. Is that okay?"

Cai swore silently as Alfred's eyebrows lifted in curiosity. He looked from Cai to Jordy, then smiled benevolently. "You've spent more than enough time humoring this old man," he said, eyes twinkling. "Dilys and I will be in the house whenever you two finish . . . talking."

For once, Cai was actually relieved to see the matchmaking glint in Alfred's eyes. He'd set him straight later. Or try to. What he was going to say to convince him after the kiss he'd witnessed, he had no idea. Hell, he wasn't even sure how *he* felt about this new turn in their relationship.

But it was better to deal with Alfred's scheming than with his curiosity. Cai had a very bad feeling about the package that awaited him.

"Thank you, Alfred," Jordy said, her cheeks a little pink. "We won't be long."

Cai nodded to Alfred and Dilys, then waved to Jordy in front of him down the path.

"What's going on?" she asked, as soon as they were out of earshot.

"Package at the dock needs my signature."

Jordy paused and put her hand on his arm. "Do you think it's from her?"

Even with his mind in total turmoil, her touch drew his attention like a brand. He had a good idea he'd need all his wits about him right now, so he slid his arm from her touch. He'd much rather go back to exploring the kiss they'd just shared than deal with what lay ahead. "Yeah, that's exactly what I think. Come on."

The boat that awaited them at the dock wasn't from any of the usual delivery services that operated out of the Keys. The deliveryman had on a black tank top and khaki shorts. He was of average build, in good shape, and appeared fairly young, in his early twenties. His dark sunglasses and plain black cap hid his features effectively. There was no sign anywhere of what company he worked for.

Cai slowed as he neared the end of the dock.

"You Malacai L'Baan?" the young man called out.

Cai nodded and kept Jordy angled behind him as the young man lifted a wooden crate onto the dock. It was about a foot and a half tall and half as wide.

He lifted a clipboard. "I need you to sign for this." When Cai made no move to come any closer, he beamed a smile, showing a row of perfect white teeth. "Boss lady gets a bit antsy about deliveries. You know how it is. I don't come back with a signature, I get docked my percentage of the delivery fee."

"Boss *lady*?" Jordy whispered.

"Stay here," Cai ordered, then walked closer to the crate. "What company are you delivering for?" he asked the young man.

The young man waited a beat too long in answering. "Union Parcel."

"Never heard of them." Cai stepped closer. "What's in the package? Who sent it? I'm not expecting anything."

"I don't know about contents." He tried the smile again, but it wasn't as confident as his earlier one. "I just deliver 'em. It doesn't say here who sent it, just an address."

Cai was close enough now to read the address label plastered on the side of the crate. There was a customs stamp on the side. He looked more closely at it. United Kingdom. The pit in his stomach grew deeper.

He looked back to the young man, who shifted from one foot to the other under Cai's silent scrutiny.

"If you don't mind, I'm sort of on a tight schedule here." He lifted the clipboard again.

There were no other packages in the boat. Cai glanced at the clipboard. There was a manifest on the top, with Union Parcel in bold black print. Maybe the kid was legit, but he still had a bad feeling about this whole setup. He reached for the clipboard. "Your boss works you pretty hard, does she? I wasn't aware delivery service was such a big business in the Keys."

The young man just shrugged, eyeing the clipboard as if willing Cai to sign it and hand it back to him.

Cai flipped up the sheet of paper. It was the only one on the clipboard.

Jordy moved beside him. "For someone in a hurry, deliveries are kind of light today."

Cai glared at her, but she wasn't looking at him.

"I, um, I only do, you know, one at a time." He laughed, but didn't pull it off too well. "Things are spread out down here. I have to turn each sheet in."

Cai scrawled his name on the line. "What did you say your name was?"

"Uh, Cliff."

"And your boss, what is her name?" Jordy asked.

His gaze darted between the two of them and he swallowed visibly. "Why do you ask? I mean, you're not going to complain about anything, are you?"

Cai studied the young man. He'd watched enough people over the years to understand body language. He's bet his next advance that this kid wasn't simply worried about keeping his job. He seemed too nervous, as if his fear went a bit deeper than employment. Was the kid working for Margaron? It made sense for her to have someone down here. It explained how the film was delivered to the ZippySnap. He looked down at the manifest and recognized the neat, block lettering that had also been used on the photo envelope.

He smiled at the young man, hoping it didn't look as feral as it felt. "No complaints. But I send a lot of packages out and I'm always on the lookout for new delivery services. Competition is a good thing, right?"

The kid bobbed his head and reached for the clipboard. "Yeah, sure."

"Why don't I just jot down your number." Cai looked back down at the manifest. There was an address, a post office box on one of the larger Keys, but that was it. Cai looked up. "Funny, there's no number on here. Awfully hard to do business when you can't take calls."

The man suddenly lunged up on the edge of his boat and snatched the clipboard right out of Cai's hand. He stumbled back into the boat and scrambled for the controls.

"Hold on there!" Cai shouted, but the kid was already gunning the engine.

The boat ripped away from the dock, whipping the rope he'd loosely tied up with off the piling.

"Cai, look out!"

Cai swung around just as Jordy grabbed him by the shoulders and pushed him to the dock. The rope whistled by, just over their heads.

"Dammit to hell!" Jordy climbed off Cai and they both scrambled to stand up. Cai ran for his jet boat.

"Where are you going?"

"He works for Margaron, I'd bet my next advance on it."

"You'll never find him in the maze of mangroves."

Cai jumped onto the boat. "I know these mangroves better than anyone. I'll find him. Stay here with the crate. Don't let Alfred or Dilys near it. And don't open it!" he yelled over the roar of the engine.

Jordy looked at the crate and back to the house. She hated being left behind, and eyed the other boat, but there was no way she could maneuver at any speed through the maze of waterways that snaked through the mangroves. It was better if she stayed and guarded the crate. Dammit. "Be careful!" she shouted, already worried for his safety.

CAI SWUNG AWAY from the dock and spent the next thirty minutes looking for the delivery boat, but with no luck. He scooted over to Dobs' dock to see if he'd seen anything. But Dobs was out fishing. And there were no water marks from the tires of a trailer or truck at the launching pad.

Cai smacked the steering wheel. "Damn, damn, damn." Reluctantly, he gave up and returned.

Jordy was there, waiting for him.

"I lost him. No sign where he went."

"Damn." She gave him a hand up to the dock. "Listen, I've been thinking. You said there was an address on the manifest. Do you remember it?"

"It was a post office box on Key West. But I can't take the time to head down there right now. I have to get a look in this crate before Dilys and Alfred come snooping around."

"They haven't been out here." Jordy leveled a look at him. "And you're not opening this alone. If we're going to see where this relationship leads, then you best be warned that the investigation is part of the rest of it. Don't lock me out."

"I wasn't locking you out. I trusted that package to your care. I thought it was more important than tagging along with me on a wild-goose chase."

Her defiant posture softened and her chin lowered. "You're right. It's just that I let other people make my decisions when I should have made my own. I'm still trying to find my way here. It isn't as easy as I'd hoped it would be."

"Nothing worth having comes easy."

She moved closer and looked up into his eyes. His muscles tightened when she said, "No, it doesn't."

They both shifted their attention to the crate. Despite the searing heat of the sun directly overhead, Jordy shivered and rubbed her arms. "How can a harmless box of wood seem so ominous?" She stepped closer to it. "This is her proof, isn't it?"

He nodded. "It doesn't look like photographs this time, either."

When she shuddered again, Cai ran his hand over her bare arm.

She laid her hand over his. "I like it when you touch me.

I like the warmth and strength." She held his gaze again. "Only this time, I want to share it. Not hide behind it."

He didn't miss her meaning. He nodded. "Let's take this inside and find out what she sent us."

JORDY LOCKED THE door behind them as Cai set the crate on his desk. They both stared at it in silence for several long moments.

"It's from the UK," she said unnecessarily, wanting to break the silence. "I don't see a return address on it anywhere." She tore her gaze away from it and looked at Cai. "I know it's from her. Should we call the task force guy? What was his name?"

Cai's jaw tightened. "Kuhn."

"Well?"

Cai stepped closer to the crate and began prying off the wooden slats with the screwdriver he'd picked up on the way into the house. "I'll decide after I see what's inside. She knows where I live, obviously. And just as obviously, she has other people working for her. For all we know that kid, or someone else like him, could be watching the Key, reporting back to her."

"Then you think she knows about the police? About Kuhn?"

Cai shook his head. "I don't know. I don't think anyone followed me, or observed me when I went into the station, but I wasn't really looking for that. There isn't much traffic on Mangrove, so I think I would have noticed."

"She hasn't said anything about it, or warned you. Maybe you're right. Maybe we're getting too paranoid here."

Cai leveled a look at her. "She is torturing at least one innocent woman, possibly two. She knows where I live and is targeting me. That's not paranoia, that's fact. I'd rather not give her the benefit of the doubt and assume the worst, okay?"

Jordy nodded, her icy fingertips pressing into her palms as he took the final panel off.

Inside was an oak box, polished to a high sheen, obviously expensively made. There was a gold clasp on the front, and dangling from it was a tag.

Cai went to reach for it, but Jordy stopped him. "Maybe we shouldn't touch it. There might be fingerprints or something."

Cai scowled, but picked up the card by holding the edges between two fingertips so none of the surface was touched. "It's sealed." He picked up a letter opener and slid it carefully inside, slicing the tape that held the card shut.

A tiny gold key was taped to one side. On the other side was a handwritten note in elegantly stylized script.

> *Here is your proof, Malacai. Another soul to rescue. Torture is such an elemental way to gain attention, but wonderfully effective. Your path is now clear. Your quest has begun. Do not deny the destiny that is ours, for the result will not be to your liking, or to that of the innocents in my care. Bring me the Dark Pearl, and bring it swiftly. The clock of life is ticking away . . .*

It was signed Margaron.

He let the card dangle once again as Jordy sucked in a breath. "She has to be stopped, Cai. This is sick. Truly sick."

He nodded, then studied the clasp.

"Maybe we should contact Kuhn."

"Screw Kuhn. So far he's done nothing to solve this case but follow a cold paper trail. He will demand we turn it over and then we'll never know what's going on. I'm opening it. Once I see for myself what she's sent, then I'll decide what to do next."

"You're probably right."

He studied the clasp. "There's no keyhole."

Jordy picked up a pen and flicked the clasp open. "It isn't locked." She looked at Cai. "Maybe what's inside the box is."

Cai laid the box on its side, careful to touch only the edges. He blew out a deep breath, then glanced up at Jordy. "You want me to look first?"

She smiled, though the fear was still plain in her eyes. "Yes. But I'm not going to let you."

Cai admired her courage, but wished she'd let him handle this.

"Share the burden," she said quietly.

"Yeah," he said, just as quietly. He slid the letter opener into the open seam beneath the clasp. "Here goes." He had no idea what he expected, but it wasn't what he found.

"It's a wizard." Jordy was obviously just as surprised.

It was a foot-tall statue of a wizard, made of some sort of heavy-looking gray stone, with an intricately carved face, long, flowing beard, and voluminous robes. He held a tall staff in one hand, the head of which was carved to look like an uncut precious gemstone, all jagged, spear-like crystals.

"The craftsmanship is stunning." Jordy stepped closer. "It's probably pretty old. That particular type of marble is rare and hasn't been commercially available in ages. You see it used in some work from several centuries ago." She looked at Cai. "Usually in museums."

"You think it's stolen?"

"I hadn't thought about that. Just that whoever had this kept it for a very long time." She studied it more closely. "It hasn't been handled much. The detail is impeccable. Perhaps the stone is old, but the carving newer. I can't be certain."

Cai picked up the card by the edges again and looked at the key. "I wonder what this is for, then?"

"Look!" She pointed. "Here. And here."

Cai had to lean in close to see them. Two tiny hinges were tucked into the rippling folds of the wizard's robes. "It opens."

"Yes, but where is the lock?"

They both leaned in close. Cai found it. "There." He pointed to the carved pendant that hung from the wizard's neck. It was shaped like the sliver of a waning moon. The keyhole was there.

Cai stared at it, cold dread sitting heavy in his stomach. Just what in the hell had she tucked inside this thing?

He slit the tape holding the key to the card, then picked it up. His heartbeat was a thundering sound in his ears. His stomach felt like he was on a tiny boat in the middle of a severe storm. How in the hell were they going to find her and make this nightmare end?

Somehow he knew, as he slid the key in the lock, that in the end, it would be up to him. And only him.

He turned the tiny key and opened the statue.

Eighteen

JORDY LEANED OVER him as Cai lifted a clear glass frame, about four inches square, from the statue. There was something pressed between the two sheets of glass. It looked like a ragged piece of fabric.

"What is it?" Jordy whispered.

He turned it over. Jordy stifled a scream at the same time Cai swore. It wasn't fabric. It was a piece of human flesh. It had been tattooed with some sort of symbol.

"Dear God, Cai. I can't believe she'd . . ." She had to turn away as bile rose in her throat.

Cai placed his hand on the back of her neck. "Why don't you go on outside and get some air."

She lifted her head, but could not bring herself to look at what he held again. "I'll stay here." She took a deep breath, then several more. "So, this is the proof?"

"Looks that way." Cai laid the frame back inside the open statue. His face was a little pale as well.

"We have to give this to Kuhn," Jordy said.

Cai's jaw flexed. "For all the good it will do." He pushed off the desk and walked to the window. "What in the hell is happening, Jordy? Things have gone crazy, too crazy. Kuhn isn't doing shit and I can't sit here while—" He raised his hand in the direction of his desk, then let it drop.

"The symbol." She latched onto the one thing she could to keep her stomach from heaving. "Did you recognize it? Is it from one of your books?"

"No, it's not. I don't recognize it, but it looks Celtic."

"Maybe Alfred could—"

Cai spun around and pinned her with a dark glare. "Absolutely not. He is to know nothing of this."

Jordy didn't argue with him, because she understood his need to protect Alfred. To a point. "Maybe we could do some digging ourselves."

He relaxed slightly. "Yeah. I want to do some checking on that Union Parcel."

There was a sudden knock on the door. "Malacai, I believe you've captured our fair Jordalyn and don't plan to share her. Dilys has tea on."

Cai shot Jordy a look, then took a deep breath. "We were just talking about her staying here."

"Splendid. Glad you've both come to your senses."

"I've agreed to no such thing," she said in a heated whisper.

Cai stood and directed Jordy to the door. "I don't want him in here," he said under his breath. "Please go have tea while I contact Kuhn, okay? We'll work it out later."

She was out the door before she could respond. Cai leaned out behind her. "You'll have to forgive me, Alfred, but I have some work that must get done right away. I'll join you both later."

"I suppose I can't be cross with you if you've convinced Jordalyn to accept our hospitality," Alfred said.

Jordy slipped her arm through Alfred's. "I didn't realize how hungry I was. Tea sounds like just the thing."

If she spoke a little too brightly, Alfred didn't notice. The very idea of tea made her stomach churn, but she accepted Cai's need to keep this latest twist of events private. The least she could do was help him out.

"Well, then, let us not waste another moment. We have much to discuss."

Jordy sent a narrow look to the closed door at her back. "Yes, it appears we do."

IT WAS NOON the following day when Jordy carefully placed the Tupperware bowl on a small maple table near the big picture window in her new room. "We're in Wonderland, Fred."

The view was almost too beautiful. To her left she could see a portion of the gardens, below the lushly bordered walkway that led to the front of the house and the dock. Straight ahead was a dense row of mangroves, and beyond that the sparkling blue water, which spanned out toward Mangrove Key.

She walked back to the bed and flipped open her suitcase. She'd spent last night tossing and turning over her decision to come here. Alfred had made it no secret that he was delighted. But she hadn't seen Cai again since she'd abruptly left his office yesterday. When tea was finished, Dilys informed them he'd taken one of the boats over to Mangrove. Jordy managed to slip away long enough to search his office. The wooden box and statue were nowhere to be found. She could only hope he'd gone to Mangrove to deliver the statue.

They needed to find some trace of evidence that would provide a lead to the identity of the abused woman, although she wasn't optimistic. Margaron seemed far too crafty to make such an easy mistake.

Crafty. She shuddered. Twisted, was more like it. She'd had nightmares about the woman in the pictures, which had only been compounded by this new evidence. In contrast, her worries about moving temporarily to Crystal Key had seemed trivial.

But she couldn't leave now. She had to see this through. Both the investigation, and this new turn in her relationship with Cai.

She wished she'd had the chance to see Cai one more time before leaving the island. That kiss in the garden seemed like a million years ago. She shuddered in remembered pleasure. The way he'd felt beneath her hands, all hard, sinewy muscle. And when he'd pulled her against him . . . She swallowed hard and wet her suddenly dry lips.

She'd hoped to spend time alone with Cai on the trip back to Mangrove, but Dilys had been the one to take her back last night. She'd arranged for Dobs to ferry her and her belongings over to Crystal Key this morning.

Jordy had liked Dobs the first time she'd met him. If for no other reason than he was the only human being with balls big enough to hassle Dilys. Jordy hadn't thought the woman could turn so many shades of red. She also hadn't missed the twinkle in the old man's eyes. Dilys had harrumphed all the way back to the docks. Despite the day's events, Jordy had enjoyed their interplay.

Investigation or not, there was no denying the fact that she was growing attached to this eccentric family. And now that she was here, it was impossible to regret her decision. Her call to Mrs. Isaak this morning had cemented it. Her landlady was going to arrange to sublet the apartment to an elderly friend of hers who was in town helping out a niece with a new baby. Mrs. Isaak said she figured six weeks would be what she'd want.

Six weeks.

Her mail was being forwarded. She had her car at Dobs', enough clothes, and Fred. Everything seemed perfect. Except there had still been no sign of Cai.

There was a heavy knock on the door. She jumped up, smoothing her hair off her face. "Come in."

She tried not to look crestfallen when Dilys bumped into the room carrying her ubiquitous silver tray.

"I didn't think ye'd enjoy lunchin' alone downstairs. So I brought this up for ye."

"Thank you." Jordy moved to take the heavy tray, but Dilys was already setting it down. "Where is everyone?"

"Himself is napping. Master Malacai is in his office. I don't expect we'll see them until supper."

He was here. And he hadn't said so much as hello. She smiled through her disappointment. "This looks wonderful. You didn't have to go to the trouble, I could have fixed myself something."

Dilys' implacable expression turned fierce. "I'll tend to the meals. You've only to ask."

"I meant no insult." Dilys' expression relaxed a tad. "Can I bring the tray down for you?"

Dilys nodded tersely. "Yer to go to the cottage when you've a mind to and make a list of the supplies you'll be needin'. Bring it to me when you're finished."

"I've already explained to Alfred that I'm purchasing my own supplies. He's done so much already. You all have."

"Either you make the list or himself will be doin' the orderin'. I figured you'd rather be the one."

Jordy knew it was time to put her foot down. She'd already had an argument with Alfred over paying rent on the cottage and something toward her room and board. He'd turned a deaf ear. She doubted Dilys would be any easier of a sell.

"I'm having my own tools sent down. I've already placed an order for the rest of the supplies I'll need. The clay is ordered as well." Which was only a little fib. She had the lists made and the numbers to call, but she hadn't placed the order yet. "I will need help when it comes in, getting it over here. I can talk to Dobs about that, I'm sure he won't mind."

The mention of Dobs had the calculated effect on Dilys that Jordy expected. Dilys puffed up like a blowfish. "We'll no' be needin' that scoundrel's help. When word comes, you see me."

The door clicked shut and Jordy sat back down on the bed. Her mouth twitched. It was an eccentric family she'd inherited all right. But, for now, they were hers. They wanted her and, for better or worse, she wanted them back.

CAI PICKED UP the copy he'd made of the glass-framed flesh before turning it over to Kuhn. He had offered to help determine the meaning of the tattoo, but after Kuhn had ascertained it hadn't come from one of his books, he'd coolly dismissed Cai's offer. Officious son of a bitch.

Cai hadn't told him about the Union Parcel deliveryman. If Kuhn thought someone was spying on them, he'd have men all over Crystal Key. Cai wouldn't risk that. Not yet. Besides, he wanted Kuhn in Miami.

And he couldn't shake the eerie feeling that he was the one who'd eventually have to deal with Margaron.

He'd run the jet boat all through the mangroves last night and again at daybreak this morning. No sign of the boat, or the delivery kid. Hopefully, he was nothing more than an errand boy.

Cai clicked to another website on his computer. He'd been searching all morning for information on the Celtic sign and had come up with precisely nothing. Nothing even close. He'd sketched the tattoo as best he could then scanned and e-mailed it to one of the university researchers he occasionally used. Eric was a genius at finding the most arcane information. And he didn't ask questions. Cai had checked his mail every fifteen minutes, but so far nothing.

He stood and stretched, then picked up the copy once again. The whole thing was so grisly. He stared at the ragged edges of the piece of flesh. This hadn't been done gently.

There was a light knock on the door, then it cracked open. Jordy's face appeared. "I'm sorry to butt in to your work time. I need to talk to you."

"Come on in."

She entered the room, his domain. All day he'd found his mind straying to her, to how natural it seemed to have her involved in his life. It was perhaps the worst time to be starting something like this. That indecision had kept him from calling her last night, or greeting her at the docks this morning. But now that she was here, he knew he wasn't going to walk away from it.

"Are you all settled in?"

"Mostly, yes." She sat, then stood again, pacing the length of the narrow room. She stopped in the center of the wall-length window. "You have the same view as I do, only a bit lower to the ground. I didn't notice yesterday."

"You came to discuss the view?"

She turned. "No. I came to thank you."

"You're welcome. For what?"

She lifted her hands. "Everything."

"You should thank Alfred. This was his brainchild."

"You've changed your mind then." She swore under her breath. "You should have said something. I changed my mind about a thousand times last night. I knew you were worried about Alfred finding out about the statue and used me as the distraction. When I didn't hear from you, I wondered, but I came anyway. You know, a phone call would have saved me—"

"Did you decide to come here because of me?"

"No," she said after a moment. "No, I came here because of me. Despite everything else, I need this. And Alfred seems to need me."

"I agree. And so you're here. What has this got to do

with me?" It was selfish, he knew, but he wanted to hear her say she needed him, too.

She sat. "If you've changed your mind about . . . us, I'd rather know right now."

Cai crossed the room and tugged her to a stand. "I thought I made it clear in the garden exactly what I wanted."

"I thought so, too. So why are you avoiding me? If I'm being self-absorbed here, tell me. I know you have a lot on your mind. Did you deliver the statue?"

"Yes. Kuhn wasn't thrilled with our interference."

"Okay, maybe your absence had nothing to do with me."

"I won't lie to you, Jordy. The statue complicated things. I wondered if maybe this wasn't the best time to explore whatever it is we seem to feel when we're around each other." Her magnificent green eyes dimmed. "Maybe there never is a good time for something like this."

"Like this?"

"Yeah. You remember. This." He dipped his head, half expecting her to pull away. It was nothing less than he deserved for yanking her emotions around like he had been. But his own emotions had been none too steady either. He captured her mouth with his, and all the confusion and frustration he'd been tangling with these last forty-eight hours seemed to come down to one tiny decision.

Continue this or regret it for the rest of his life.

She opened her mouth under his. He felt her hands touch his shoulders, tentatively at first, then more surely when he pressed deeply into her mouth. He spread his legs and she moved between them and up against him so naturally that his knees threatened to buckle. "Jordy—"

"Shh," she said against his lips. "No more interruptions. I want to kiss you until I'm finished."

But there seemed to be no end to the kiss. The need only

grew the longer he tasted her. His hands started at her shoulders, then traced lightly down her back. He wanted more. He wanted to turn and lay her across his desk. Rip the shirt from her body, see her, touch her, taste her. Take her.

And she was here now, under his roof, within his reach. Twenty-four hours a day. Day in, day out. He'd experienced passion. But he'd never, not once, known what it was to be so close to losing total control. To want to lose control.

Her hands were all over him. In his hair, on his chest, running down his thighs. How in the hell was he supposed to hold back when she was doing to him what he so very badly wanted to do to her?

He wrenched his head up, sucking in air. She pulled back too, a somewhat dazed look on her own face.

But they left their hands on each other.

"Wow," Jordy said, breathless.

"Exactly," he said. They continued to stare at each other, and then Cai chuckled.

She smiled, then laughed. "What's so funny?"

"I make my living with words. And *wow* is the only one I can think of right now."

"Wow's not so bad. I can live with wow."

Cai wanted nothing more than to keep her in his arms, laugh with her, kiss her again. How easy it would be to love her, he thought. He knew he was on dangerous ground when the panic that usually accompanied such a thought didn't come.

"I can live with it," he said. "Trouble is, can we work with it, too?" He slid his hands to her hips and tugged her up against him. "You feel how badly I want you? I have an idea it's going to be like that all the time."

"All the time," she echoed. Her eyes darkened and he wanted to drown himself there.

"You're here to work. I can't ignore mine either."

"No," she said, shaking her head. "Can't ignore work."
But she was staring at him with naked hunger. It was so
pure, so honest, it made him want to get on his knees and
beg her to take him, take him now.

"Ah, hell, how long can wow last anyway?" he murmured. He pulled her mouth to his and lost himself all
over again.

NINETEEN

AI SLID HIS lips to her ear, pulling the lobe in, groaning when she moaned against his throat. Her shirt was a thin knit thing, turquoise blue, with a dozen tiny buttons down the front. He started to undo them, letting his fingers slip between and caress her skin. She wasn't wearing a bra and by the time he finally slid the last button free, he was crazy with the need to taste her.

But first he had to look. "It's beautiful you are, my Jordalyn," he said, his Welsh accent a fine imitation.

Her fingers, already deep in his hair, clutched tightly at his head. "Please, Cai. Look later."

A short laugh burst out, but he didn't need any urging. She was small, but perfect, and filled his mouth so sweetly he could have died in that moment and been a happy man.

She held him fiercely to her, bending her own head so she could kiss his hair. "Let me, let me." She pushed at him until he was forced to release her. She nudged his head up and captured his mouth again while her fingers busied themselves with his shirt.

At the first touch of her cool hand on the warm skin of his chest, he thought he'd come. It was that exquisite. "Don't ever stop touching me." He was begging. He didn't care.

"I want to sculpt you," she said, her lips pressed against his heart. She smoothed her cheek along his chest, leaving a trail of soft hot kisses. "I don't think I could capture what I feel, what I taste, this . . ." She trailed off when he took her mouth again.

He moved his hand to the waistband of her shorts and she fought to get to his at the same time.

"You're driving me insane." His voice was a hoarse rasp against her throat. He pushed her shorts down over her hips.

"I know." She yanked at his zipper. "I know."

"Jordy, we need—" A deep groan abruptly stopped his words when her hand wrapped around him.

"We need this."

Her single-minded focus made him smile even as his body jerked at her touch. "Yeah. A lot of this."

He slid back on his desk, heedless of papers and books being pushed all over. She kicked her shorts free and he pulled her easily onto his lap.

He looked into her eyes, wanting to see everything she felt, everything she was. "This is insanity," he whispered.

She nodded, and pushed herself down on him.

He saw her eyes widen, her mouth open, her head fall back. Then she began to move and his world went dark. His mouth was on her, her hands were all over him. And they moved, the rhythm grinding, demanding, fulfilling. It was a kaleidoscope of touching, tasting, and just plain feeling.

Her head jerked forward just as she tightened on him. Their eyes met.

"Come to me." With one hand, he pulled her mouth to his, coaxing her over the edge by pushing his tongue into her mouth with the same rhythm she rode him.

She leaned into the kiss, pushing him deeper inside. He swallowed her scream when she came. He took every sweet pulsation, held her tightly as she rocked, then closed his eyes, pulled her hips down, and let himself explode.

He opened his eyes at the same moment she did.

"Wow," they gasped in unison.

Jordy stared down into his eyes. "I can't believe we just did . . . what we just did."

She went to move off of him, but he wrapped a tight arm around her back, holding her to him. "Good can't believe? Or bad can't believe?"

"You can ask that with a straight face?"

"Well, I can honestly say this isn't a regular part of my daily routine."

"I make a habit of jumping men in their offices all the time," she said dryly. The reality was she'd just done exactly that. "God."

He leaned up and caught a kiss from her before she could cover her face with her hand. "It's a little late to be embarrassed now." He sat up, holding her on his lap.

"Cai, anyone could have walked right in. It's one thing for Alfred to catch us necking, but this . . . Jesus, I didn't even stop to think about that. I didn't stop to think about anything. I'm not, this isn't—"

He stopped her with a hard, fast kiss. "I'm not either. I've never gotten carried away. Not like this. Not ever. And I didn't stop to think either. About a couple of things." He cupped her face. "For that, I'm sorry. I'm healthy, no ugly surprises there, but I've always taken responsibility for protection, always, but with you . . ."

She touched his face. "And I'm healthy, too. We're—I'm protected. I've been taking the pill forever, it takes care of some other problems."

He blew out a breath. "Thank God."

Jordy agreed with him. So why was there this little pang down deep inside her? With everything else that had been going on, the status of her biological clock was way down on her list of things to worry about. Now, suddenly, it moved up a few notches.

"What are you thinking about?"

She smiled at him. "I'm thinking, 'How am I going to get off his lap and get dressed without being mortified by what I just did?'"

He smiled in return. "Like this." He slid her off his lap, then reached down and snagged their clothes. He handed hers to her. "We'll do it at the same time and be mortified together."

It shouldn't have been so easy . . . so natural. But it was. He brushed her hands aside and buttoned up her shirt, then held her gaze for a long moment.

"I don't want you to think that, because we . . . because of this . . . that I automatically expect this to happen again."

Insulted, she said, "You don't?"

"I'm not saying this right. I meant there's no pressure on you to have to do anything, with me, whenever."

"Oh. No pressure." She felt an ease with him that surprised her. She trailed her hand along his shoulder and up the back of his neck. He shuddered and his eyes went dark. She smiled. "No pressure at all."

"Exactly," he managed, swallowing hard when she moved against him. "No pressure."

A sudden rapping at the door made them leap apart like guilty school children.

"I'm looking for our Jordalyn. Are you keeping her prisoner in there, young Malacai?"

Cai groaned.

Jordy stood straighter and moved over to the window as Cai opened the door. She was sure she had "hot sex" written all over her face.

Alfred was leaning heavily on his cane. Embarrassment forgotten, she immediately went to his side. She hooked her arm through Alfred's, gently taking some of his weight. She let him guide her to the set of chairs, and gracefully accepted the first one, knowing he wouldn't sit until she did.

"I've been out to the cottage, Alfred. It's amazing." Maybe if she chattered enough, he wouldn't detect the remnants of sexual tension that were still screaming around the room. "You must have had a crew of fairies and gnomes working all night to get that much done since yesterday."

"Nonsense, my dear." His vivid blue eyes twinkled. "Gnomes don't work at night."

Jordy laughed and began to relax.

Cai stepped in. "Why don't we go down and check out the progress. Jordy said she still needed a few things."

She shot him a dark look.

"Then you got Dilys' message," Alfred said approvingly.

"I explained to Dilys that I was taking care of getting my supplies. I've already accepted too much of your hospitality, and no matter how much you protest, I am paying you some form of rent or room and board."

Alfred waved his cane, then stamped it authoritatively on the floor. "Nonsense. If you must, think of me as your benefactor. It is my choice to play the philanthropist. Who are you to tell me I can't spend my well-earned money to nurture the art of a young, talented woman?"

Jordy sighed and looked at Cai. "How do I get around this?"

Cai smiled. "You know, I think I'm going to like having you here." He shifted so his grin encompassed them both. "Two against one might even the odds a little."

Alfred sniffed and stood. "If you think to intimidate me, he who has withstood the whims of kings, you are sadly misinformed, young whelp."

"Well, this whelp has held his own fairly well for all his thirty-four years," Cai answered.

Alfred grunted, then turned a beatific smile on her and held out his arm. "Shall we, my dear?"

Jordy slid her arm through his. Cai moved to step in behind them, then his gaze fell on his desk. Jordy saw a flash of something almost . . . visceral in his eyes and followed his gaze to his desk. It was a mess and she felt the embarrassment climb again, but it wasn't the signs of their frantic lovemaking that had put that look on his face.

It had to be the statue. Or more specifically, what had been inside. He'd probably been doing research on the symbol all morning. She felt a moment of shame, for the pleasure she and Cai just shared, while those women suffered.

"I forgot," he said, distractedly. "There is something I've got to attend to. I'll meet you at the cottage in a little while. Or at supper."

"Let me stay and help you," she said, but he shook his head and sent a quick glance to Alfred. She understood what he meant, even if she didn't like being shut out.

"Fine," Alfred said as he moved into the hall. "Oh, and you might want to turn your shirt right side out before you see Dilys. You know how particular the woman is about clothing."

Cai was dumbstruck and Jordy didn't know whether to laugh or start digging a hole to crawl into.

Alfred winked at her. "Come, my dear. I have some other ideas I want to share with you." She didn't dare look at Cai as she followed Alfred from the room.

CAI WINCED WHEN he looked down and saw the seams of his polo shirt staring back at him. Well, the jig was up now for sure. Cai knew he was going to have a hard time explaining to Alfred that his relationship with Jordy wasn't permanent.

Permanent. He'd never used that word in conjunction with a woman before, and why did it sound so good when he thought about Jordy?

All in all, he'd rather deal with Alfred than what lay on his desk. His desk. Visions of what he'd been doing on it minutes ago had him shaking his head. "Yeah, Mr. Smooth. That's you, L'Baan." On his desk. Christ, what had he been thinking? Well, he knew what he'd been thinking with. But even if the venue hadn't been perfect, if he could turn back time to when she walked in that door, he couldn't say he'd change one thing. In fact, if he had his way, he'd steal her away from Alfred, shove away everything else, and tuck her in his bed for the next two days. Or three. Maybe a week would do it. She was here for six of them.

He purposely turned to the paper lying on his desk. The harsh reality of what was happening a world away struck him hard. There had to be a way to end this nightmare.

TWENTY

❧❧❧

CAI FOUND HER in the cottage. It had only been a couple hours since they'd eaten breakfast together, but it seemed like an eternity. He'd made love to her for the first time yesterday afternoon. That, too, seemed an eternity ago.

She and Alfred had stayed up late, enthusiastically reviewing details for the final cottage renovations. He had spent the evening in his office, waiting for replies on his e-mail queries and trying to get some writing done.

It had been an impossible task. When he looked at the screen he saw only her face. She was staying. There was no need to rush things. He'd told himself that a hundred times. Yet his hunger for her was already an outrageous thing.

Her sunny smiles and pensive frowns had made an indelible imprint on his mind. She had a smart mouth, so at odds with the shadows of vulnerability that flitted behind those green eyes of hers. She entranced him.

What would it be like if she were within his reach, all of the time? That thought had kept him aroused and completely crazy the entire night.

They'd slept apart. Or maybe she'd slept. He'd lain

awake all night, talking himself out of going to her, wishing like hell she'd come to him.

It was the last night he intended to spend that way.

He stood in the open doorway unnoticed. She was measuring the corner walls, stopping to scribble down numbers, measuring the floor, then scribbling again.

He could already see her here, sitting on a stool in front of the rear window, the sun shining on her hair, and the gardens laid out behind her. This was only her second day living under his roof, and already he couldn't remember a time when she didn't.

He wanted to watch her create, to know that part of her. That she'd found her spark here, in the place he called home, filled him with a sensation he couldn't describe.

"If you're done staring at me, you can come hold the end of this," she said without raising her eyes.

Cai took the end of the tape measure and held it to the spot on the wall she pointed to. "What are you measuring for?"

"Shelves. I need a place to dry my pieces before firing them."

"I can picture you working here, in front of the window."

She looked up at him. "I was thinking of setting up in the center of the room. I like space. I need to move around my work in progress. Three dimensions taken into consideration at all times. It comes alive for me faster that way."

"Yes," he said almost absently, totally taken with simply watching the excited sparkle leap about in her eyes. "Did I remember to tell you how stunningly beautiful you are?"

Her smile was cocky. "Why, I don't believe you did."

He dropped the tape and pulled her to her feet. "You are stunningly beautiful." She came so easily into his arms, as if they had been sculpted together that way.

"Cai, we really shouldn't—"

"Waste time." He dipped his head. "I totally agree." She only resisted his kiss for a nanosecond, and then she opened her mouth under his.

"We're never going to be able to work if we can't keep our hands off each other."

"Work?"

"We're going to have to set some guidelines."

"Like off-limits time? I'm banned from the cottage for certain hours?" He was grinning, but she wasn't.

"That's just it. I don't work under set hours. I might leave a piece alone all day, then work all night. Or I might work for a few hours, then let it sit for days until I decide where I want to go with it. I do preliminary work on other pieces then, or the post-firing work. Glazing or bronzing, applying patina." She rolled her eyes. "Which is why I ended up in court, because my business had fallen apart around me and I was too busy in my own little world to notice." She moved out of his arms. "I want it to be different this time. I will learn to manage my own business, but I'm not exactly sure how to do the rest of the 'getting a life' thing. I work when I work, and when I work, I'm totally involved. I don't think I can change that part."

She was serious, worried, but he heard the spark of excitement beneath her words. She couldn't wait to get back to it, to let it consume her. He, of all people, understood that.

"Just answer me this. With all the demands of your craft, do you think there is sufficient downtime that you could devote to me?"

"Yes."

The unhesitating answer made his pulse thrum.

"But I can't promise—"

He pressed a finger to her lips. "I'll make the promise. I promise to let you work, but I also promise to make you play. I get lost in my work, too. Maybe we'll both tend to

surface more often knowing there is something else . . .
some*one* else, demanding our attention."

"You could have a point there." She smiled. "What
about Alfred? Has he said anything else to you since
we . . . you know."

"No. Did he say anything else to you last night?"

She shook her head. "I know he knows exactly what is
going on, though."

"He approves. I'd have heard about it by now if he
didn't."

"It's just that I know how determined he can be about
things and I don't want him mistaking our relationship for
something . . ." She trailed off on a light shrug.

"Permanent?" There was that word again.

"Yeah," she said quietly. "Permanent."

"I don't think it matters what we say. He'll push us
together anyway. He likes you and he thinks my sex life is
terribly neglected."

Her eyebrows lifted. "Oh? And is it?"

He pulled her close with a growl. "I can't seem to remember."

Her eyes went dark again and he had to work at not
backing her up to the nearest wall.

"He'll push," he said, "but I don't want you to feel
pushed, okay? I don't want to hurt him, either, by letting
him think this is something it isn't."

She shrugged out of his arms. "I'll be leaving eventually,
he knows that."

Cai knew that, too. Too well. He found a smile, even
though what he felt was dread. "He won't let a little thing
like that stop him."

She didn't smile back. Instead she walked to the rear
window and looked out over the gardens.

He moved behind her, but didn't touch her. "I've never
had a woman live here before." When she didn't say any-

thing, he continued. "Partly because I've never felt strongly enough about anyone to take that step, but mostly because I've never met anyone who understood Alfred. He deserves to live out his days in peace, with a family that understands and accepts his eccentricities." She turned then and he traced his fingers down the side of her face. "You understand him. You have a connection with him that even I don't fully comprehend. It's not about me. It doesn't exist because of me. Whatever happens with us . . . or doesn't, you and Alfred will still have that special relationship."

She covered his hand with her own. "I lived in a small town most of my life, except for college, which was just another small town, really. But even though I was surrounded by people, I was as much a recluse as you and Alfred are. It suited me, too, even if my reasons were a bit different." She rested her hand on his chest. "This is as much a new path for me as it is for you. And maybe it's what we need. My life is in Warburg, and for me to build my business, I'm going to have to learn not to be so reclusive, to deal with people, broaden my horizons, take risks. Your life is here on Crystal Key, where you can work and care for Alfred and Dilys. But they won't be here forever, and if you don't want to be alone, you're going to have to learn to broaden your horizons, too." She reached up and kissed him. "So let's view this as a learning experience for all of us."

"A learning experience, huh?" he said, shoving aside thoughts he shouldn't even entertain. She smiled and his own came naturally. "Well, I'll leave you to your measuring while I get some work done myself. Then maybe we can convene for a class later on. Seduction 101?"

"I believe you aced that one earlier."

"I thought I'd go for my master's." Her mouth dropped open and he took full advantage of the opportunity to kiss her. He left her standing by the window, staring dazedly after him.

His mind was still on her and his disconcerting feelings about their future, so he didn't see Alfred turn the corner around the hedgerow until he almost ran into him.

It took only a second for Cai to realize that Alfred was not well. He was flushed and his pupils were the size of pinheads.

He shook a bony finger at Cai and demanded, "What have you done?"

Cai was momentarily stunned by the outrage in his grandfather's voice. He'd honestly thought Alfred applauded the personal turn his relationship with Jordy had taken. Still, this was the man who'd raised him, and thoughts of what he and Jordy had done yesterday on his desk had him flushing despite himself. "I—I can explain."

"Than I shall hear it, and hear it now." Alfred was almost shaking with anger.

Cai's guilt instantly ceded to his immediate concern for Alfred's well-being. "Grandfather, calm down. It's not so bad, is it?"

"Calm down? Calm down?"

Cai tried to take his arm and lead him to the closest bench, but he'd have none of it. "We're consenting adults, Alfred. I thought you understood what was going on and approved. You like Jordy. I won't do anything to harm your relationship with her." He put a gentling hand on his shoulder. "I want her here as much as you do."

"What nonsense are you raving on about?" His gaze had been pinned on some point past Cai's shoulder and only now did he seem to snap out of it and look directly at him. "I'm not talking about your carnal relationship with Jordalyn. Of that I approve heartily and can only say, don't screw it up."

Nonplussed, Cai stepped back. "Then what—"

The rage came back to his crystalline eyes. "This."

For the first time Cai noticed the paper Alfred held. His heart dropped to the pit of his stomach. It was the copy of the symbol.

Alfred suddenly clutched at his chest and stumbled back a step.

"God, no." Cai rushed to him and carefully helped him to the stone bench. He yelled for Dilys, but it was Jordy who came running.

She skidded to a halt when she saw them. "Oh no! What happened?"

"I need you to run to the house and get Dilys to call Alfred's doctor immediately."

"Is he having a heart attack? Shouldn't we get him over to the Keys? Where is the closest hospital?"

Though his breathing was labored, Alfred said, "My heart is strong and will endure this, too, Jordalyn." He took another breath. "I don't need a doctor, I need to speak with my grandson."

Cai turned to him. "You need the doctor, just to make sure." He checked his pulse, which, though a bit rapid, was strong and regular. "Then I promise we'll talk as long as you want." He looked up. "Run and have Dilys call."

Alfred didn't object this time. He leaned his weight forward on his cane, and seemed to stabilize with the help of Cai's arm around his shoulders.

"You should have told me," Alfred stated.

"I didn't want to worry you. You've been excited about having Jordy here and I wanted you to concentrate on that."

Alfred pierced Cai with an electrified look. "The symbol. Do you know what it means?"

"No. No, I don't. I have some queries out now, but I haven't received any responses yet."

"They will not be of help to you."

His grandfather's arrogance was usually well earned, but, out of habit, Cai said, "You don't even know who I asked."

"It matters not, Malacai. I knew when I read that note on your computer that the time had come. I foolishly thought I had you protected. That she'd be unable to do anything if you ignored her. I should have known that she'd not abandon the campaign once she'd begun it."

Cai didn't know what to say. "I never answered her," he got out.

Alfred wasn't listening. "One thousand years spent as the stronger one, the worthier one, and in one quarter century I've allowed my pride and ego to overcome me. I've risked everything." He leaned closer. "She's taken someone, hasn't she?"

Cai couldn't lie to him, but he didn't have to tell him there was more than one victim. "Yes, she has."

Alfred had gone off on delusional rants more times than Cai could recall. But he'd never sounded like this. Fear was like a fist in his throat. "I think we should get you into the house. Let Dr. Fashel look you over and make sure nothing is seriously wrong. Then we can talk."

"Ah, but there is no time to waste. Had you told me, I could have done something." He seemed to wilt within himself and Cai's alarm grew. "Or perhaps not. My magic is not what it once was."

Cai swallowed hard and silently willed his grandfather not to drift further off into one of his fantasies.

"Let's get up to the house, okay?" He started to rise, helping Alfred to his feet, but his grandfather clutched at his sleeve and with surprising strength, pulled him to the bench again.

"She has made her mark now," he said. "She won't stop until she has the Dark Pearl. And, I fear, she wants you as well." Then he collapsed into Cai's arms.

TWENTY-ONE

***

J ORDY PACED OUTSIDE Alfred's bedroom door.
Dilys had come and gone several times since the doctor's
arrival several hours earlier, but she'd said nothing. Her
demeanor had been even more formidable than usual, making Jordy feel every bit the outsider she was. Still, she
wouldn't leave until she heard the doctor's prognosis.

She couldn't erase the image of Cai carrying Alfred into
the house. He'd looked impossibly frail and thin against
Cai's broad chest.

She turned abruptly at the sound of the door opening.
Cai was shaking the doctor's hand as they left the room.

"It wasn't a heart attack, Cai, but I still wish we could
get him to consent to come in for some testing."

"I can try, but other than drag him bodily, I don't think
I'll have much success."

"I understand. The most important thing is to not upset
him, and I don't want him doing anything strenuous for a
day or two. If he's doing okay, then moderate activity after
that. But make sure someone is right there with him, at
least for the first week or so."

"I will. Thank you, Frank, for coming out here so
quickly."

"I'll come back out at the end of the week. Keep him calm, Cai, and call me immediately if he has any trouble."

Cai nodded and looked at Jordy. "I'll be back after I take Dr. Fashel to the dock. Alfred's asleep, so why don't we meet in the living room."

The doctor held out his hand to her. He was older, short, trim, with only wisps of hair on his head. He had a warm smile and serious eyes. "I'm Frank," he said with a quiet smile that matched his demeanor. "You must be Jordalyn."

"Yes, I am. I'm just . . . I was worried about Alfred."

"He asked after you."

Cai nodded in agreement. "He wanted to make sure you weren't upset. I told him you'd come in after he'd had some rest."

She had been in the room initially, but while Alfred's room wasn't small, it was cluttered with furniture and stacks of books and folders and such. Once Dr. Fashel had arrived, she'd thought it best to give them as much room as possible. And she hadn't wanted to intrude.

"Is he okay?" she asked.

"I think he'll be fine, once he gets some rest. But it might not hurt if you go in and sit with him a bit. Just don't disturb him."

"I won't. Do you mind?" she asked Cai.

"No, of course not. I know he'll be happy to see you when he wakes up."

She wanted to ask more questions, but now wasn't the time. Cai looked weary and worried and she wondered if there was more going on than they were willing to tell her. She quietly entered the room, and closed the door behind her.

She didn't notice the interesting clutter this time. All she could see was a fragile old man in the big, feather-stuffed bed. His white hair flowed around his head on the dark pillowcase, making him look like an otherworldly angel. She smiled at that and wondered what Alfred would think.

She wanted to pick up his hand and warm it in her own. But not wanting to disturb him, she opted to carefully move a brocade chair to his bedside and sit as close as she could.

He'd never seemed a robust man to her, but there had always been an energy about him. Now he looked brittle, and she didn't feel his energy. It frightened her. She couldn't imagine what this was doing to Cai.

The door opened silently and Dilys entered, a smaller china tray in her hand. "I thought you'd like some tea." She set the tray down on the small table next to her chair. "There is a pitcher of shaved ice there too, and a glass, for himself, if he should waken thirsty."

Jordy watched Dilys arrange the pitcher and glass just so on Alfred's nightstand and thought it must be as hard, if not harder, on Alfred's longtime companion. "How did you come to be with Alfred, Dilys?" she asked softly.

She surprised Jordy by answering. "My family has worked closely with his for many, many years. It is an alignment that has been beneficial to us both."

Jordy remembered Alfred had told her that Dilys' name was Welsh for loyal. "I see," she said, though the explanation created more questions than it answered.

"I thought you might be wantin' this." From the deep pocket of her apron, she pulled out one of Jordy's sketchbooks and her ink pen.

Surprised, but touched, Jordy took them from her. "Thank you, Dilys. Yes, I would like them very much."

Dilys paused at the door, her hand on the knob. After a silent moment, she said, "Yer good for him. And for Master Malacai."

Stunned by such an admission from someone like Dilys,

it took her a moment or two to answer. "They are both good for me, too. I'd never do anything intentionally to hurt either one of them. I hope you know that."

Dilys looked at Alfred and there was no mistaking the fierce loyalty in her gaze. When she shifted her gaze back to Jordy, she felt the intensity of it like a wave crashing down on her. "Ye have a purpose in being here, Miss Jordalyn. Be there for them when the need comes, or they will suffer for your lack of courage." She was gone before Jordy could respond.

Not that she had the slightest idea what she'd have said.

"She's right, Jordalyn."

The croaky whisper brought her attention back to Alfred. She grasped his raised hand and held it between her own. "How are you?" Her eyes widened when he tried to sit up. She stood and leaned over him. "No, please lie back. You're not to exert yourself. Please."

"Dilys speaks the truth. 'Tis not for myself I worry, but Malacai. He is to be tested, and I fear you are a part of this." His attention seemed to drift. "I should have seen that you would serve a greater purpose than rightfully filling the void in Cai's life. I was too relieved that you'd finally come. Too charmed by your presence and talent to question it further." A rattling sigh left his chest and she bent over him.

She didn't know what to say, but she knew it wasn't wise to let Alfred go on. "You need to rest." She reached for the pitcher. "Would you like some ice chips?" She didn't wait for his answer, but slipped a few of them into the glass. Supporting his back, she tilted the glass to his lips and let the slivers of ice wet them.

He didn't speak until he was resting comfortably. "You must promise you'll stand by Malacai when the time comes."

Her heart dropped. "Don't talk like that. Get some rest. You've been overdoing it lately."

"Haven't done near enough," he muttered. "I should have felt her evil, but I'd let myself become enchanted. What do you know of her treachery?"

Dear God, he'd found out about the kidnapping. Is that what had caused him to collapse? How much did Dr. Fashel know? She and Cai hadn't had a moment alone to talk. "Maybe we should talk about this later, once you've rested."

He tried to rise again, eyes flashing. "I've rested too long as it is."

Alarmed, she rose and soothed him back to the pillows. She knew from the look in his eyes that there would be no avoiding the subject. She sat back down, his hand gripping hers. "What do you know?"

"I know she's taken someone, marked them. I've seen the symbol. Do you know of it?"

There was no point lying to him now. "Yes, I do."

He relaxed slightly. "At least he's not keeping it from you. The boy tries too hard to protect those close to him. I fear I am to blame, encouraging him to remain in this reclusive enclave as I have all these years, but I did it to protect him."

Jordy wondered if he knew that Cai stayed here, at least in part, to protect his eccentric grandfather. But what did Alfred think Cai needed protecting from? She tried to lead him to a safer topic. "This is a beautiful place. What child wouldn't love growing up in paradise?"

A distant look came into his eyes. "It was the home of Malcolm, my only son. He was a writer as well, of textbooks. He and his wife, Laura, an American he met while at university, moved to Florida after they wed. She had only her mother, who lived in Key West and was ailing. They loved it here and I can say it suited them both. I didn't worry about them here. Laura's mother passed on shortly before the accident." He focused on Jordy again. "They were returning from a brief trip to the Caribbean, their plane went down. Malacai had been left behind with friends. He had only myself and Dilys left to protect him, then."

"You both left Wales to raise him here?" She knew part of this story from their first meeting. But she humored him to keep him talking. "That must have been difficult."

"It was for the best. He was far removed from the dangers I knew one day would surface." His expression grew troubled. "And now they have."

Jordy struggled to keep him focused. "Have you been back to Wales recently? Has Cai ever been there? Do you miss it?"

"Wales will live on in my heart and mind clearly enough for me to ever feel the loss too keenly. I am content here and would not trade the years I've had with my grandson."

"You've never been back? In all that time?"

"No. It was for the best."

She didn't want to push, he'd quieted down now.

"Life has not slighted the L'Baan men, my dear one." His eyes began to drift shut. Relieved, she went to settle back in the chair. He spoke before she could sit. "Her evil will not conquer us, Jordalyn. I have not lasted this long to let her succeed now." His eyes closed and he fell fast asleep.

Alfred veered swiftly and all too believably between reality and fantasy. It was growing more difficult to take his statements as nothing more than baseless ramblings.

He recognized the symbol. He knew something about it, of that she was almost certain. She sat for another fifteen minutes, until she was certain he was sleeping comfortably. A minute later, she was knocking on the door to Cai's office.

•   •   •

CAI PULLED HIS attention reluctantly from the monitor. He still had no luck in finding the symbol's meaning. Frustrated and worried about Alfred's renewed involvement in this mess, he barked, "Come in."

Jordy poked her head in. "I need to talk to you."

Cai went to stand. "Is Alfred—?"

She waved him down. "He's fine, sleeping like a baby." She stepped inside and closed the door. He saw her glance at his desk and despite everything that was tearing at him, he felt that insistent tug.

Apparently she wasn't thinking about that. She stood across from him, arms folded. "Alfred knows something about the symbol."

Cai blew out a long sigh. "I know. He found it on my desk. It's what caused his collapse."

She shook her head. "No, no. I mean, he knows something about its origins."

Cai stood. "You didn't badger him about it did you?"

Hurt stung her eyes, but her jaw firmed. "No, I didn't badger him. In fact, I steered him as gently as possible away from the topic since it was obviously alarming him."

"Alarming him?"

She lifted her hand. "He's okay. I eventually diverted him into talking about your father and Wales and he finally drifted back to sleep."

"My father? Wales?"

"He didn't say much really, he was explaining how you came to live here." She folded her arms again. "Apparently all the L'Baan men have a strong protective streak. He says he decided to raise you here to protect you. It's also why he's never returned to Wales. He says he's protecting you from her evil."

Cai didn't like the feeling of dread that invaded his body.

"I know he does this sort of thing often, going off on these tangents, but this time . . ." Her anger dissolved into concern. She sank into the chair. "Cai, it seemed more . . . real. I know it's crazy, but do you ever question what he says? Think there might be more to it?"

"Not since I was about twelve." He saw she was very serious, so he rose and walked around the desk. "What else did he say?"

"He kept referring to 'her', saying that she was evil. He made it clear he knew about the kidnapping, so naturally I assume he's talking about Margaron. But he talks of her as if he's known her for a long time." She rubbed her arms and looked up at him. "I know it sounds crazy, Cai, but do you think it's possible he might actually know the woman who's doing all this?"

TWENTY-TWO

C AI SHOOK HIS head. "That seems too far-
fetched."

"Have you heard anything back from the research guy?"

Cai blew out a sigh of disgust. "Eric's stumped." He
lifted his hand to stop her. "I know where you're headed
with this and the answer is no. You saw what just looking
at the thing did to him. I'll figure this out on my own."

This time she wasn't hurt. She was angry. "On your
own? This involves *us* whether you want it to or not. *She*
involved us." Jordy went to him, slid an arm around his
waist, and stroked his cheek with her fingertips. She looked
directly into his eyes. "I'm here. I'm involved. Get used to
it, Cai."

A man could get lost in those eyes, he thought.

"Answer me this," she said. "Is this relationship just
about great sex?"

"Of course not."

"Then we share the good with the bad, and even the
ugly sometimes. Otherwise, this is all just a vacation fling
or something."

"We don't know what this is."

"Well, I know what it isn't. I'm not just dallying here
for the fun of it. I don't know what will happen between

us, but I'm not interested in some whirlwind romance where the real world doesn't intrude."

He held her gaze for a long, silent moment. "I don't want that either." Suddenly he realized just how much a reality she'd become to him. To all of them. She was becoming a true member of this family, important to each one of them. Which brought his thoughts back to Alfred. "Let me help you, Cai. Have you heard anything from Kuhn?"

"Not a word. I've put in several calls, but we're being ignored."

"What about Union Parcel?"

"I haven't had much chance to look into it yet, but there is no listing for it in the yellow pages."

"We need to check that post office box." She quietly added, "And we need to ask Alfred about the meaning of the symbol."

"No way. I'm not dragging him any deeper into this. He can't take it."

"I don't think you can stop him now. And if he knows something that can help find this madwoman, then don't we have an obligation to let him help us?"

"Not if it means more episodes like today. Or worse."

She moved back to the window. "If he recognized the symbol, then it must be Welsh or Celtic." She faced him. "From his years of writing, Alfred probably has tons of research materials, right? Would he have books on Wales, myth, legend, things like that?"

"Bookcases full. But his office is his private domain. Dilys is the only other person who goes in there."

"Maybe he wouldn't mind if we just looked at some of his books."

"I have always respected his privacy in regards to his office."

"Would you rather ask him for permission?"

Cai sighed. "No. Dilys is over in Mangrove filling some of Alfred's prescriptions and picking up a few things. If we're going to do this, we'd better do it now."

JORDY CAREFULLY SLID a slim volume out from the crammed shelf. Cai was working on the higher shelves, while she was seated on the floor. She opened the cracked leather cover and flipped through the glossy pages. "More legends, mostly pertaining to Arthur. Nothing on symbols."

"There is no way we can get through all this," he said, sliding another volume back in place.

They'd been in the office for over a half hour and hadn't found anything helpful.

"Most of the older volumes have no title on the spine. We'd have to look at every one of them."

They'd realized that if Alfred had a filing system for his books, it was beyond their comprehension. Most likely he shoved them wherever they'd fit. Judging by the dust, most of them hadn't been touched in years. Dilys might have access here, but it was obvious Alfred drew the line at letting her keep this room in her typical spotless fashion.

Jordy took the hand Cai offered her and got up from the floor. Brushing at her shorts, she said, "Maybe he'll just tell us. I don't think he's done talking about it anyway."

"I don't want him worked up again."

She surveyed the office, wondering if they'd missed anything obvious in their zeal to look at his books. It was an amazing workspace, as eccentric and delightful as the man who'd created it. Aside from the shelves lining two of the walls, there was a massive hardwood desk and antique leather chair, several filing cabinets, a brocaded, high-backed chair with matching ottoman, and a floor lamp with a fringed shade placed next to it. An old-fashioned rotary phone and an antiquated black typewriter sat on his desk, amongst piles of books, folders, and other clutter.

The walls were covered with framed awards, newspaper clippings, reviews, and whatnot. But what made the room distinctly Alfred's were the smaller versions of the whimsical creatures found in his garden. They were cast in a variety of materials. Made of brass, pewter, glass, clay, ceramic, wood, and stone, they dotted every available surface in the small, crowded room.

"Why doesn't Alfred allow you in here?"

"He's never said. As a child I never intruded here and he never invited me in. I respected his privacy. I understand the need to have a place to think and write without worrying about distractions or untimely intrusions."

"He comes into your office. That's how he found the copy in the first place."

"True. But I don't mind the interruptions. If I'm on a roll with an idea or scene, I tell him so and he leaves." He shrugged. "Each of us has our own way." He took her hand. "We'd better go. Dilys should be back any time now."

She was reluctant to leave, not knowing if she'd ever get to come back in again. She looked around one last time, more to imprint the details of the room on her mind than anything else. Perhaps that's why she noticed the book.

It was ancient looking and huge, stuffed between two of the filing cabinets. There was no title on the spine, but the sheer size of it intrigued her too much not to check it out.

"Wait a minute." She knelt down and worked the book free without harming the ancient, cracked leather binding. She sat it on her lap—it covered the space from her thighs to her knees—and carefully opened it. She gasped. *"Incantations, Spells and Other Magicks,"* she read aloud.

"We really should leave."

He was right. She hadn't missed the sound of the boat

engine. She closed it gently, and tucked it against her chest as she stood up. "Do you think he'd miss this for a few hours? I can return it later after everyone is asleep."

Cai clearly didn't like the idea, but nodded. "I don't think he'll be back in here for a day or two anyway. Come on." He closed the door quickly behind them and followed her to her room, which was closer than his office. They were less likely to cross paths with Dilys this way.

He stood in front of her as she sat on the bed and opened the book across her lap. "This isn't exactly the way I pictured coming to your bed for the first time."

Jordy looked up at him and smiled. His smile didn't reach his eyes. There was worry there. And a little fear. She patted the bed beside her.

He sat and pulled half of the big book onto his lap.

She turned past the first few pages. "I don't see any publication date or anything like that. It looks almost hand drawn." She looked at Cai, suddenly uneasy. "Maybe we should have left this alone. It looks like an heirloom. I'm almost afraid it will disintegrate in my hands."

But Cai wasn't paying attention, his gaze was riveted on the page. She looked down and gasped.

The page was filled with hand-drawn symbols. Words in some other language were written beneath each one. Cai traced a finger lightly over the many columns, coming to one figure that stood out among the others.

She saw it the same time he did.

It was the symbol that had been marked on the flesh, and directly beneath it, the words: *Mae olion ar y cnawd y sawl sy'n uffuddhau.*

TWENTY-THREE

IT WAS AFTER midnight when Cai quietly closed the
door to Alfred's bedroom and moved down the hallway.
His grandfather wasn't doing as well as he'd hoped. He'd
expected him to be bristling mad at being kept in bed.
He'd also been prepared to deal with the subject that had
sent him to bed in the first place. None of that had happened. Dilys had been there when he'd come in, feeding
Alfred soup like one would a child.

Seeing Alfred like this scared Cai. Pale, weak, and too
tired to do much more than sip down the broth, the day's
activities had obviously taken far more out of him than Cai
had realized. A day or two of rest, like Dr. Fashel had said,
and he should be good as new.

He clung to that hope as he went to Alfred's office.

His thoughts turned reluctantly to the symbol and the
words beneath it. Growing up around Alfred had taught
him a smattering of the Welsh language, but not enough to
do translations.

Jordy was standing at the door when he got there.

"I'm not surprised to find you here," he said.

"You didn't really think I'd gone off to bed, did you?"

"It's where you should be." But he didn't push it. Truth

was, he was glad to see her. He didn't really want to be alone. "Come on."

They searched the shelves and found several Welsh language reference books. It took a long time to find the meanings of the words. He pieced it together as best he could. "Marked is the flesh of those who will obey."

Jordy shivered. "Alfred's right. She is evil."

Cai didn't want to think about Alfred and what he knew right now. He saw the fatigue lining her face and his concern shifted immediately to her. "Why don't you turn in for the night?"

She stilled, then said, "What about you?"

He felt the instantaneous tension between them. He wanted nothing more than to crawl into bed with her and forget everything else except the sweet taste of her skin. "It's been a difficult day. We both need sleep." He reached out and ran a finger along her cheek. "If we spend the night together, neither of us will get any rest."

Her eyes darkened. "True."

He leaned in before he could stop himself and kissed her. It started softly, a goodnight kiss, then quickly got out of hand.

She pulled away first. "I'm not feeling restful here."

Cai gently touched the smudges under her eyes. "But you need to. I've got some work to finish up." He chanced a kiss on her forehead. "I'll see you in the morning."

"Anything I can help you with?"

"No, it's regular work stuff."

"Okay." She looked disappointed.

He wasn't exactly overjoyed about sending her away either. "Tomorrow morning I want to run over to Key West and check out that post office box. You want to go with me?" He hadn't heard or seen anything more of the deliveryman, but he couldn't shake the feeling that he should keep those he cared for close to him.

She immediately brightened. "Yes, I would."

He smiled, telling himself the contentment was due to the knowledge that he could keep a close eye on her. Truth was, he wanted to spend all his time with her and it had little to do with keeping her safe.

"We'll see how Alfred is doing in the morning. If he's calm, Dilys can keep watch over him for an hour or so."

She reached up and kissed him. "Goodnight, Cai." She retreated quickly.

Cai sank into his chair. Somehow, in a very short span of time, Jordy had come to mean a great deal to him. And to Alfred as well. She was making a place here, in his home, in his life. In all their lives.

Alfred was more than fond of her, she'd become very important to him. Cai understood that feeling perfectly. It should surprise him, but somehow it didn't. Already he couldn't imagine waking up and not finding her here.

In a more perfect world, he'd be crawling into bed with her tonight, sinking himself into the oblivion only she could deliver.

But it wasn't a perfect world. Far from it.

The dreams haunted him nightly. Dreams of a dank, dark place, far from here. A place where evil flourished. He heard screams echoing through the night and saw all sorts of unspeakable horrors. It was the curse of his vivid imagination that it only worked to torment him, never to help him. His book sat unfinished, his current chapter barely touched.

He swore under his breath as the other pressures he faced crowded in on him. He punched up his internet account and signed on. He had to send Eileen an e-mail asking for more time, something he wasn't looking forward to.

His mind went to the investigation and its lack of progress. He spent a moment or two entertaining the idea of

going ahead with his plan on his own. But even if he
contacted her on his own and agreed to meet her, made up
some fake Dark Pearl . . . Margaron was in Wales. He
couldn't race off halfway around the world. Not with Alfred in such bad shape.

The incoming e-mail filtered onto the screen and Cai
froze. There was another e-mail. From Margaron.

His fingers trembled as he shifted the cursor . . . and
pressed the icon to open it.

> *Who is she, Malacai? You are promised to me and*
> *none other. I will not tolerate even a pretender to your*
> *affection. You dare to dally when all your energies are to*
> *be focused on your quest? Do not make the mistake of*
> *underestimating the power that I wield. Or the lengths to*
> *which I will go to secure what is mine.*
>
> *Dally no longer, Keeper of My Heart. Or the pre-*
> *tender will pay the price for your arrogance.*

Cai sank slowly back in his chair, icy fingers of fear
clawing at him. She knew about Jordy. He remembered the
haunted screams of those women in his nightmares. He
squeezed his eyes shut to block them out, but they
wouldn't go away. And in their place, he saw Jordy and
heard her screams, which were much too real. No. No way
in hell was anything going to happen to her!

The ferocity of his reaction was not lost on him. And it
went beyond the horror he'd felt on behalf of the women
already put in that position. That she might walk out of his
life in six weeks was something he could shove aside, deal
with later. That someone could mean to remove her permanently from his life or anyone else's shook him badly.

He swore long and loud. "How in God's name could she
know—" The deliveryman. Jordy had been on the dock.
He'd obviously reported back to Margaron. Cai slammed

his fist against the desk, scattering papers. He jumped to his feet and stalked to the window. Lights flickered in the distance on Mangrove Key.

"Are you out there watching me now, you bastard?" he murmured under his breath. Cai wanted to take the boat out, search for the sneaky son of a bitch, and beat answers out of him. But even though he knew the mangroves well, the middle of the night was no time to go on the hunt.

Fine. As soon as the sun rose, he'd be on the water. He'd still take Jordy with him and keep her close. Alfred would be safe here with Dilys. After they checked the mangroves, they could head over to Key West.

Armed with a plan, he should have felt better. Instead he felt vulnerable. Too damn vulnerable. Damn, damn, damn. He was only one man. How was he going to protect them all?

He turned abruptly and left his office. He needed to sleep, be sharp for the morning, but adrenaline was a live thing inside him now. It took every bit of self-control to keep from going directly to Jordy. He wanted her within arm's reach, so he didn't have to live in fear of losing her. But she needed her sleep and wouldn't thank him for disturbing her. He almost smiled thinking of exactly what she'd say about him needing to protect her.

He paced the hallway outside her room. He told himself that she was fine, safely tucked in a bed under his own roof. He thought about sending her home, back to Warburg, but he knew she wouldn't go.

And, he had to admit that he wanted her here. Close. He only hoped to God he could keep her safe. If anything happened to her . . .

He ended up on the dock. The moon ducked in and out of the clouds. The air was breezy but warm. He barely noticed. He paced the planks. There had to be something more he could do. Logic said he should contact Kuhn.

Instinct told him it would be a mistake. Kuhn would invade Crystal Key. Cai wouldn't have that. Maybe he should move them all off the Key, temporarily. But Alfred was in no shape to deal with something like that right now.

He paced to the end of the dock and stared out at the water, but no other solutions were forthcoming. Worry consumed him, the sense of helplessness was enough to make a man insane. Then the air shifted, and he felt her. She'd made no sound. But when he turned, Jordy was there, at the end of the walkway leading to the house.

Soft, thin cotton clung to her lean curves, the flicker of moonlight silhouetting them as she lifted her arms to him. "You're not resting either. Come inside, Cai."

It was a different sort of insanity, what she did to him. But this insanity he could do something about.

They didn't make it to the house. He pulled her against him and took her waiting mouth. She opened for him, took him in, reached for more. The frustration and helplessness that had come so close to consuming him took on a different course, that of devouring her, claiming her, exerting some control in a world that he no longer commanded.

He filled his hands with her, touching, tasting, reveling in her scent until he thought he would drown, could drown, and finally find peace. Or oblivion.

She writhed against him as his demands intensified. He slid a hand up her thigh, pushing her nightshirt up, sliding fingers over her bare hip and around back . . . and down. She crumpled against him in a deep moan of pleasure as he found her, wet and wanting him.

He wanted, too. Now. Here. Deep and fast, hard and forever. He pushed her back against the dock railing and shoved at his pants even as he lifted her up so he could take her.

She gripped his shoulders and flung her head back as he pushed inside her on a deep, shuddering groan. "Yes, Cai.

Now! Yes." He did as she demanded. She dug her heels into him and climaxed instantly, ripping him over the edge with her.

He held her close as they both shivered and shuddered around each other. He buried his face in her neck, knowing he should be feeling some shred of remorse for taking her like a wild animal, with no thought to modesty; his or hers.

Then she kissed his neck and nipped his earlobe and chuckled against the damp heat of his chest. "We're dangerous, Malacai L'Baan," she said. "Totally and completely irresponsible."

"Totally and completely." He carefully shifted her to her feet and helped her straighten her clothing, then took care of his own.

"Wow," was all he could say.

TWENTY-FOUR

F OR THE NEXT four days, Cai spent as much time with Jordy as possible. It still wasn't enough. He'd held her through each night, making love to her until they both lay spent in each other's arms. He resented the sun for rising, knowing he'd have to share her with the rest of the world then. They had made certain they were down at breakfast while Dilys was still busy preparing it in the kitchen. Not that she wasn't aware of what was going on, but because he knew Jordy was a little uncomfortable with the situation. They couldn't keep their eyes off of one another as they ate, stifling laughter as Dilys eyed them knowingly the entire time she served them.

Still, the real world managed to rudely intrude. The post office box number had proven nonexistent, as had Union Parcel. Cai hadn't said anything to Jordy about the last e-mail, nor had he forwarded it to Kuhn. He had heard nothing from the agent and Cai no longer trusted him to handle this. Not that he was any more certain he could handle it himself. But he did his best to maintain a vigil over those he cared about while trying to figure out what to do next.

Nothing else had happened in the intervening days. Cai made regular morning and evening runs through the mangroves and despite the reason behind them, had come to look forward to the quiet time spent on the water with Jordy. They'd talked about the dragon she was going to start for Alfred. She was excited, but she'd been unable to hide her fear that when it came right down to it, she wouldn't be able to find the creature in the clay.

Her supplies had come in and she'd begun preliminary work on the formative structure she'd build the piece on. He'd wanted to stick close, watch her work, not simply for safety, but because he wanted to be a part of that reawakening. But he better than anyone understood she needed the time alone, to find her way back in. Cai had given her that space, had used the time to try and find his way back into his own neglected work. He had actually managed to write a few pages. He wasn't all that happy with them, but it was a start. He might have accomplished more if he weren't so worried about Alfred. He wasn't recovering as fast as they'd hoped. Dr. Fashel had been out again, and could find nothing wrong with him, but agreed it was best for him to set his own pace.

Not for the first time, Cai was faced with his grandfather's advancing age, but this time it really hit home. They'd all expected Alfred to be up and about long before now, brandishing his cane and sermonizing.

At best Dilys managed to get him into a chair by the window for an hour or two, where he could look out over his garden. He'd said nothing else about Margaron or the symbol. Cai had been relieved at first, but now he'd begun to wish that something would shake his grandfather out of the stupor into which he seemed to have willingly fallen.

Cai refused to believe that his grandfather might never return to his old self. He hoped now that Jordy had begun work on his sculpture that it would spark some interest and life back into him. Again he was faced with how important her place in their lives had become and again, he'd worked to ignore the growing clutch in his heart at the knowledge that she'd eventually leave them. It would tear a hole in their lives he wasn't sure could ever be filled.

Cai fought the need to go to Jordy at the cottage for the hundredth time today. Today was the big day, when she actually began working the clay. He wanted to be there to support her, but she hadn't asked. So he'd stayed in the house.

He forced his attention back to his computer screen, then impulsively clicked on the icon to retrieve his e-mail. No note from Margaron, thank God, but nothing from Kuhn either. Dammit!

These past four days had taken a toll on him and on Jordy. She felt as helpless as he did in this mess. Cai felt a tiny stab of guilt for not warning her of Margaron's most recent threat, but as long as she was here on Crystal Key, under his care, she was safe. She had enough to worry about right now. Today was a huge step for her. He refused to put more pressure on her.

But he couldn't escape the feeling that time was dwindling. Margaron wasn't simply going to sit and wait for him to figure out the next step in this macabre dance she'd begun.

But, dammit, what could he do? Leaving Alfred now was absolutely out of the question.

Then again, maybe he didn't have to go anywhere.

Cai sat up straighter in his chair as the idea formed more fully. He could set up a meeting with Margaron and simply have the police, or whoever, show up in his stead. Surely someone could pose as him and nail her. He kicked himself for not thinking of this sooner. Kuhn would be mad as all hell, but fuck Kuhn. Cai was done with waiting around while Kuhn strutted about with his Special Investigative Agent finger up his ass.

Cai pulled up the last e-mail, the one threatening Jordy, and hit *Reply*.

> *I have taken on your quest. I now possess what you so avidly seek. I have only to present it to you so that we may join forces. The world will be ours. You must tell me where you wish to meet and I will be there. Yours faithfully, Malacai L'Baan.*

He punched *Send*. His wait for a response was brief. The mail came back as undeliverable. No account in that name.

"Shit." If he *had* been insane enough to take on this task of hers when she first contacted him, how in the hell did she expect him to find her once he'd done it?

He shoved away from his desk and stormed out of his office. He hadn't realized his intended destination until he was standing in front of the cottage door. He raised his hand to knock, then pulled it away. He needed her, needed to touch her, hold her, reassure himself he was doing the right thing by keeping her here by his side, but he couldn't intrude. Not today.

He reluctantly turned away, but stopped as his gaze passed the small front window. She was working chunks of clay around the armature she'd erected. Her back was to him at the moment, though she moved around the work-table as she continued the task. It was a much larger piece than he'd realized, almost two feet tall. He couldn't imagine how she looked at that mass of clay and envisioned the dragon she planned to create.

Just then she looked up and saw him standing there. She grinned and motioned for him to come in.

It was a simple thing, the instant welcome, and yet it meant everything to him. Whatever guilt he felt for intruding was overwhelmed by his need to be with her.

He stepped inside and she met him at the door. "I really

didn't mean to interrupt your work." He smiled when she raised an eyebrow. "Okay, so, I did. But I was trying to leave. Honest."

She grinned. "It's okay. I'm just beginning."

She had clay rubbed into her jeans. Her hands and arms were smeared with it, a dried, powdery smudge streaked her forehead and chin. Her eyes were shining.

"You're incredibly gorgeous," he said.

She laughed. "You can come around all the time if you say things like that." She reached up and kissed him lightly on the lips, then backed away when he would have pulled her tight for more. Much more.

"I'll get you all messy."

"Maybe we'll both get a little messy." Her eyes went dark, the way they did when she wanted him. He hardened immediately. "Jordy."

She backed further away. "You have to behave in here. You promised."

"I was in a weakened state when I said that."

"So am I, all the time. That's why I haven't asked you to come out here."

He felt better than he had in hours. "How is it going?"

There was no faltering in her beaming expression. She swept her arm out. "Pretty damn good, actually. What do you think so far?"

He dragged his gaze away from her. "Well . . . It's . . ."

"A lump of clay, I know. But I'll tell you a secret."

He moved closer. "I want to know all of your secrets."

She grinned slyly, but wisely stayed just out of his reach. "There's a dragon in there," she whispered. "But not for long." Her eyes danced gaily. "I'm going to set him free."

He shifted at the persistent pressure she aroused so effortlessly, wishing she'd free him as well. He forcefully turned his attention to the clay. "I'm glad you can see him in there. I don't know how you do it."

"I don't know how you create those stories in your head and transcribe them into words either. It's magic, I guess."

"Magic, yes," he agreed, though he wasn't thinking about his writing. "It's bigger than I'd expected."

"Me, too." She shrugged at his confused look. "I hope Alfred doesn't mind. But when I started building the armature, he just sort of grew on me. This is just how big he is."

"Sometimes my characters lead me instead of the other way around. I guess it's sort of the same thing." He wandered around the rest of the room. It smelled of freshly painted walls and of sawdust from the recent addition of shelves.

"I'm still waiting on a few more things. Dilys said she'd make a run over to Mangrove tomorrow."

There was a workbench running the entire length of one wall, with drawers underneath. He pulled one open and there were trays of neatly stowed tools. He removed one, a small curved blade and tested the edge.

"Careful," she warned, but it was too late.

He sucked the small bead of blood from his fingertip. "Remind me to be more careful around you. I didn't know you were armed."

"Maybe we'll get you to behave in here yet."

He raised his hands. "I'm behaving, I'm behaving."

She grinned as she tucked the tool back in the drawer. "I saw Alfred this morning. I told him I was beginning the piece today. He was happy about it."

"He was sleeping when I went in. So, he seemed better to you?"

Worry entered her eyes. "Not as good as I'd hoped. I thought he'd be more energized, but he seems just as drained as yesterday, and the day before. He was asleep when I left. I know Dr. Fashel said this wasn't entirely abnormal for a man his age, but I can't help but worry."

"I know. I wonder if we shouldn't try and get him over to Mangrove and run some tests or something, just in case Fashel is missing something."

"I thought you'd already asked Fashel about that and he said he didn't think it was necessary?"

"Well, maybe it's time to ask him again." He paced the room to the window overlooking the gardens. "You said he was excited about the sculpture. It was all he talked about before . . . before he got ill."

She came up behind him and wove her arms around his waist, resting her cheek against his back. "He asked some questions about it, said he approved, but there was no spark in his eyes like usual." She hugged him. "I can only imagine how hard this is on you. I'm so sorry, Cai."

He was silent for a moment, staring out the window. "What about your grandparents? Did you know them?"

"No. They died when I was young. My dad, too. I was only a baby."

"You lost your mom young, too. I can't imagine not having anyone."

Jordy squeezed more tightly. "I'm glad for all the time we did have, though. It was her dream that I graduate and do something with my art."

He covered her hands with his. "And you did."

"Yes. I did."

He tugged her around in front of him. "And you will again."

She lifted her chin and looked him in the eye. "Yes. I will."

He respected her courage and determination. Yet at the same time, there was a pang deep inside his chest. Her success meant her eventual return to Virginia.

"I cherish the time I've had with Alfred," he said. "But even now it seems like it's running out too soon."

"He is proud of you, too, you know. You two have created quite a legacy."

"I don't know about that, but I do know he is proud of my work. I've never taken that support lightly." He found a smile. "And now he's spread that support to you."

"I know. It's somewhat intimidating, having someone like him as a patron, or whatever you'd call it." She stepped away from him and looked out the window. "I so want to prove to him his faith and investment in me is a worthy one."

"You've earned his respect. Just enjoy finding your muse again and that will be enough."

"I'm doing my best." She turned to face him. "And I am excited. But I'll feel even better when he's up and around again. I guess I sort of figured he'd be out here, popping in and checking up on me. At first I was worried how I'd handle that. I don't usually like anyone to see my work until it's done. Now I'd give anything to see him walking up the pathway to the door."

For once, the tension in the room wasn't sexual and Cai felt bad for coming out here with his worries. "Maybe I should go check on him and let you get back to work."

"Okay." But concern was still present in her eyes. "I'll come up and sit with him later this afternoon, tell him about my progress." She waited until he was at the door, then asked, "Any word on the investigation?"

"No." Cai stood on the threshold and debated telling her that he'd tried to contact Margaron. The e-mail hadn't worked, so there was no reason to upset her. He realized he wanted to anyway, that he wanted to share all the details of his life with her, important or not.

She rubbed her arms, as if suddenly cold. "I wish there

was something else we could do. This can't go on indefinitely."

"I'm beginning to wonder," he muttered.

"Has Alfred said anything about it at all?"

"No, and I'd like to keep it that way."

"Well, I was just thinking that— No, never mind. It's
foolish."

"Say it. What?"

"He was so worked up over the symbol that he collapsed. He obviously knew what it meant since he figured
out about the kidnapping."

"He saw Margaron's first e-mail, before she threatened
to do that. He just put it together. And we already know
what the symbol means."

"I know, but I can't help but feel there's more to it than
that. Remember I told you he acted like he knew her, had
known her for a long time."

This wasn't the first time she'd brought up the subject,
but Cai had always managed to distract her from it. He
didn't want to think about Alfred's possible connection to
all this, he couldn't. It would mean believing there was
more to Alfred's ranting than that of a man whose mind
was slipping. It was too difficult to consider. He simply
couldn't go there.

"What are you suggesting?" he asked warily.

"I think that maybe his listlessness is more distraction
than fatigue. Maybe he's not so much frail as consumed
with thoughts of something else."

"If that were the case, he'd be busting to get up and do
something about it. It's not like him to just lie down and
let something roll over him."

"Did you tell him you had the police working on it?"

"No."

"Maybe you should talk to him about it now." She
talked over his refusal. "Something is still bothering him

about this, Cai. The more I think about it, the more I'm sure I'm right."

"There is no way I'm going to upset him."

"But—"

"No. I'm not going to risk it. And don't you talk to him about it either. If he wanted to talk about it, he's had ample opportunity."

"He knows more about this. I'm sure of it, Cai."

"I don't see how that's possible. Just because he recognized the symbol doesn't mean anything. You're reading too much into his fanciful stories."

She looked mutinous.

"Promise me, Jordy. He's my grandfather and my responsibility."

"I think you're making a mistake."

"Then that's my cross to bear. It won't be the first one and it likely won't be the last."

"Fine. I understand I'm the intruder here. But I care about him, too. And maybe because I am an outsider I can see things in a clearer perspective than you can."

"You're not talking to him about this. That's my final word on this."

"Final words have a way of coming back to haunt you. If he doesn't start to come around soon, at least promise me you'll give this another thought."

She was wrong. Alfred needed rest, not more talk about the symbol and the kidnapping.

"Promise me, Cai."

Nothing was likely to make him change his mind, so he spoke the words she wanted to hear. "I promise."

And he'd make a promise to himself, too, that he'd find some other way to end this thing, without involving Alfred.

TWENTY-FIVE

JORDY WRAPPED THE clay in plastic and gathered her tools for cleaning. When had it grown dark? She'd missed dinner by now, but she'd already instructed Dilys not to interrupt her in the cottage if she missed a meal. She smiled, remembering the woman's obvious disapproval. Her stomach rumbled just then, making her chuckle. "Guess I'll have to bow and scrape for leftovers now."

She entered the back of the house but heard nothing. She'd seen the light on in Alfred's room, but he hadn't been at the window. Hoping that meant Cai was visiting him, she went to the kitchen. Dilys was commanding the stove like a captain would a ship.

"Coming in finally, are you?" she said without looking up from the giant pot she was stirring.

The steamy smells emanating from it made her mouth water. Her stomach chose that moment to chime in. Dilys' jaw tightened as she continued to stir. Jordy had made a private pact with Fred that morning that she wasn't going to let the woman cow her any longer. Another rung on her self-improvement ladder. It was a big step.

She moved a foot inside the door. "I tend to lose track of time when I'm working. I really don't want to upset your schedule though. I don't mind fixing myself a—"

"I've a plate for you warmin' in the oven. I've done it often enough for Master Malacai." Dilys pointed the wooden spoon at her. "Don't be complainin' if the meat is a bit dry now. It was meant to be enjoyed fresh off the roast."

Properly chastised, she took another bold step into Dilys' domain. "I'm sure it will be wonderful. I appreciate you going to the trouble."

"Have yourself a seat in the dining room and I'll be in. Or would you prefer a tray in your room?"

"No. Downstairs is fine. Actually," she took another step into the room, "I'd enjoy eating right in here, if that wouldn't bother you too much."

Dilys stiffened, something Jordy thought impossible, seeing how rigid she was on a normal basis. "It's just that, well, I love the smells and warmth of a kitchen. I used to sit and talk to my mother while she cooked. It was the favorite part of my day. This room reminds me of that."

In truth, this kitchen was nothing like the tiny, cozy one she'd grown up in. This kitchen was massive, white-tiled, white-walled, with gleaming white and chrome appliances and miles of pristine white counter space. Cold, austere, just like the woman who ran it.

She purposely didn't look at Dilys, and went instead to the table that fronted a bay window. She could see across the dark water to the lights twinkling on Mangrove. "Lovely view."

The stirring had stopped. Jordy sat down. And waited.

After an interminable silence, her silverware and a crystal glass of iced tea were placed just so on the table in front of her. The plate of steaming food was delivered moments later.

She took a bite. "The roast is delicious." The buttered roll melted in her mouth. The mashed potatoes were perfect. "You're incredible, Dilys."

The silence was deafening. Maybe she'd pushed too far.

But now that she was here, in the inner sanctum of the woman who knew Alfred best, she took advantage of the opportunity she'd created.

"I'm worried about Alfred." There was a pause in the stirring, then it resumed. She swallowed a sigh, but persevered. Rome hadn't been built in a day. "His spirit is so vital, I really thought he'd be doing better by now." Still nothing. She took a measured sip of tea, then turned and faced Dilys.

Her silver hair was pinned neatly behind her head, not a strand out of place. Her cheeks were a bit flushed from the rising steam, her apron flecked with broth and other bits. If it weren't for the narrowed black eyes, she'd look the quintessential grandmother. Jordy thought more in terms of the dragon she was presently unveiling out in the cottage. Only unfriendlier.

She stood and carried her plate to the sink, earning a sniff from Dilys. Apparently she'd crossed another invisible boundary. She didn't care. If Cai wouldn't, or couldn't, see that Alfred needed a strong nudge, then it was up to her. She'd promised she wouldn't do it herself, but she hadn't promised she wouldn't find a proxy.

She went directly to the opposite side of the counter that ran along the back of the stove and stood straight in front of Dilys. "Has he said anything to you about what upset him that day in the garden?"

Silence.

"Dilys, this is important. I need your help."

"What you need is to leave it be. Himself will find his way. He always does."

"But he's never been so listless like this, has he?" She pressed her palms on the counter. "It's not like him, Dilys, is it? To just give up?"

Dilys slapped the spoon on the counter. "Ye'll leave him be. Himself will find his way."

"Find his way where? You told me I'd be needed, that it would be my courage that would help him. Well, I'm here. And I'm not going away until someone listens to me. Something is wrong, terribly wrong. I can feel it."

Dilys' eyes narrowed and she felt a cold chill race up her spine. "What is it you can feel, young miss? What is it you think you know of Alfred and his woes? Ye've been in this home naught but a week and yer tellin' me what to do about a man I've assisted for more years than you can possibly ken. Ye'll be tested, ye will, but not this way."

Jordy was rattled by her ferocity, but she'd seen something flicker in Dilys' dark eyes besides anger. Fear. She was afraid, but of what?

"He warned me, just as you did," she said. "He's afraid for Cai. He thinks evil is coming for him. Well, evil has already come and we don't know how to fight it. I think Alfred can help us, but Cai is afraid to ask him, fearing he'll grow worse." She leaned over the counter. "It took all of our strength to keep Alfred in bed that first day, to calm him down. Now, it's as if he's forgotten the whole thing. Only I don't think he has. Something is going on. Can you please help me?"

Dilys held her gaze for what felt like an eternity, before she finally spoke. "There is an evil that has plagued Alfred for many years. By remaining here, with Master Malacai, he has achieved a balance of sorts and protected him from what would harm him." She looked away, picked up the spoon, then put it down again. After a deep breath, she turned to Jordy once again. "He fears he no longer has the strength to protect, that she knows this and has found her way in."

"She who? Margaron?"

"Is that the name she's usin'? Always the clever one."

Jordy wished she felt happier about being right. This was all beginning to freak her out. Alfred spouting about

King Arthur was one thing. Dilys talking about all this like it was fact was almost too much. "There is a task force already on this case," she said. "If you know anything that might—"

"The police are involved?"

"There is a special task force from the State Department working on it. I don't know who their counterparts are in Wales. But they aren't making any headway."

"They'll not catch her like," Dilys murmured under her breath. But before Jordy could question her, she flipped off the burner and headed out of the room.

Jordy followed her, but when she disappeared inside Alfred's room, the door was shut tight and she heard the lock tumble. She put her ear to the door, but heard nothing.

She leaned against the wall. She'd done the right thing by telling Dilys.

Dilys and Alfred knew something more than they were saying. Could they really know this woman? Had she been a threat before? A crazed fan of Alfred's perhaps? It made sense. Maybe Alfred had come to Florida to escape her.

She was on the right track, she knew it. If she could just get a name from them, something they could send to Kuhn, this whole horrific episode would be over. God, could it have been this simple all along?

Voices were raised behind the door. Jordy spun around and tilted her head, straining to hear.

"You must! I've done what I can from here."

"I willna leave. And neither will you."

The latter had been Dilys.

"We're fine, right here," she went on. "And safe."

The voices subsided to unintelligible murmurs.

"Damn." Jordy paced again. What was it Alfred wanted Dilys to do? She was gratified that Dilys had roused his anger. Any emotion was better than the hollow man he'd been the last couple of days.

Safe. Dilys wanted them to stay here. Which meant Alfred wanted them to go somewhere. Wales? Back to whomever was threatening them? If they knew who it was, why on earth wouldn't they just say so and let the police handle it? Dilys was right. They were all safer here. Let the law enforcement people do their jobs.

She had to go in there and talk some reason to them both. Her hand was raised to knock on the door when her arm was pulled back and she was spun around.

Cai towered over her, his gray eyes cold as ice and just as hard. "You gave me a promise."

"I kept it." The voices on the other side of the door raised again and she winced. "Sort of."

He pulled her not so gently away from the door. "What in the hell have you done?"

TWENTY-SIX

❧❧

JORDY YANKED HER arm from his grasp. "I knew there was something more to all this. And I was right."

Cai didn't want to hear her excuses, he wanted to go in and make sure his grandfather wasn't having a stroke. He heard Dily's voice beyond the door, then things quieted down to a murmur once again. "So help me, if this makes him worse, I will never forgive you."

"Did you hear what I said? I was right. They know something, both of them."

"Move." He reached for the door.

She grabbed his arm and held on. "They know who the kidnapper is, dammit. Will you listen to me?" She was keeping her voice to a low, furious whisper, but her short nails dug into his skin. "We have to make them tell us."

Cai let go of the doorknob. "What are you saying?"

Jordy pulled him a few feet down the hall. "I talked to Dilys tonight. I asked her if Alfred had said anything to her about this. It was too strange that he just clammed up like he did, when before we could barely restrain him."

"You promised."

"I promised I wouldn't talk to Alfred. But if anyone knows what's happening inside his head, it's Dilys. I didn't know she'd go straight to Alfred and upset him." She stood taller. "But I'd do it again. They know this woman, Cai. Maybe she was a threat to Alfred in the past. Dilys all but said so. I think they know her from their days in Wales and she just now caught up with them."

"You must have misunderstood."

"I didn't misunderstand. And now Dilys is in there talking to him. He was demanding she do something, I don't know what, but she refused and told him it was best for everyone to stay here. That we'd all be safe here."

"Maybe she's gone batty right along with him," Cai muttered. His head throbbed.

"Dilys is rock solid. And she's worried, Cai. I saw it in her eyes. She's afraid. Something is wrong here, far more so than we even imagined." She let him go. "Go in there and talk to them. Get them to tell you what Margaron's real name is. Call Kuhn and give it to him. It could be as simple as that. And this nightmare will be over."

"Jordy—" Was the whole world going insane around him? Just then the door opened and Dilys stepped out.

She didn't seem surprised to find them both there. She pulled the door shut behind her and stood guard. "He'll want to rest now. Give him until morning."

"Jordy thinks you know something about all this. Do you know who the woman is?"

"Yes. I believe I might."

Even though he'd been warned, the straightforward answer hit him like a harsh blow. Had he been so blind in wanting to keep Alfred from harm that he'd put them all in danger? He straightened his shoulders. "I want to go in and check on Grandfather, then I want us all to go to the living room and discuss this."

Dilys put her hand on the knob. "Ye'll not be going in there tonight, Master Malacai."

"Is there something you're not telling me?"

This time her gaze held firm. "He needs to rest."

Other than bodily removing her from the door, there was little he could do but heed her indomitable will. He would come check on him later, after they were done talking. "Fine." He waved his arm. "After you."

DILYS MOVED THROUGH the living room toward the kitchen. "I'll get us some tea."

"It's late. Let's get on with this."

Dilys' eyes narrowed. "You've never had need to take that tone of voice with me before, Master Malacai. You willna be startin' tonight. You may not need fortification, but I do." She left the room.

Cai spun on his heel, swearing. He caught the barest hint of a satisfied look on Jordy's face. It was all the goading he needed. "We have two women being tortured, my grandfather so ill he can't leave his bed, and Dilys treating me like a snot-nosed child. Which part amuses you?"

"I'm not remotely amused. Perhaps if you realized that we're all adults and somewhat capable of taking care of ourselves, you wouldn't find yourself treated like a snot-nosed child."

"I'm just trying to protect my family."

"Maybe there's a line between protecting and controlling. You're making decisions they might be capable of making themselves." She crossed the room and softened her tone. "You were trying to protect him, when maybe the best thing you could have done was to include him."

"When he went off after seeing that first e-mail, I didn't even understand half of what he said. It took him two days to calm down, then he never brought it up again. I was happy to leave him out of it."

"Maybe it's not about whether he could have helped. He's a member of this family. If something is happening to you, then he'd want to know about it, even if he couldn't do anything to help." Cai turned away, but she moved in front of him again, stopping his pacing. "Ask yourself this: if the tables were turned and he was the one in trouble, wouldn't you expect him to confide in you even if there was nothing you could do about it?"

"Of course, but that's different. I'm not in frail health. I'm the one taking care of him."

"For far more years it was the other way around. He's still the man who raised you. Maybe he's earned the right to expect confidence from you, no matter how old or feeble he might be."

Dilys chose that moment to enter the room.

Cai took a deep breath when the older woman ignored him as she set about pouring tea. At any other time he would have smiled at the fact that she was stubbornly preparing three cups. "I was just trying to protect him, Dilys. Maybe that was wrong. Maybe I should have included him."

"Perhaps ye'd be better off delivering this speech to himself."

"Oh, I plan to. I didn't want either of you to have the extra worry. I know Alfred hasn't been doing well—"

"Himself has done fine enough for many years and he'll continue on for more. T'would be of more help for himself to be treated as such, rather than as if he were on his last legs. A man should be able to depend on his family to turn to him in a time of need no matter what."

Cai didn't think he'd ever felt so abashed. "You're right." He sat on the couch, feeling unbearably weary. "So, what do we do now?"

Jordy placed her hand over his. "We find Margaron and end this thing." They both looked to Dilys for her input, but were forced to wait for her response until she finished serving the tea.

Then, Dilys began. "Many years ago, when your grandfather's first book on Arthur came out, there was a popular female critic who took great delight in savaging his work. He ignored her insults at first, but after she tore apart the second and third book, he fought back. He wrote letters to her editor, and at one point even took out ads to rebuke her. He was that angry with her, and he also knew that the public loved such an open battle between critic and author, so he gave them a good one. His book sales skyrocketed as a result of their publicly heated quarrels."

Cai placed his cup untouched on the coffee table and stood. "Dilys I know this story. Alfred has told the tale of Isolde Morgan many times. They feuded for more than two decades. What does this have to do with the kidnappings?"

"You don't understand. She is evil."

Cai swallowed a sigh of disappointment. Another fantasy. "Dilys, are you saying that you believe Isolde Morgan kidnapped these two women as some sort of ongoing vendetta against Alfred?"

"It's exactly what I'm sayin'."

"But that's—"

"Crazy," she finished for him. "You may think so. She certainly is. Crazy like a fox. She is a wily one she is, waiting all these years to make her move. Waiting for the sign." She sat her cup down and gave Cai a look so sharp it made him sit straighter. "You gave it to her, you know. You gave her the sign."

"All I did was write a book."

"Where did you come up with the idea for your Dark Pearl?" Dilys prodded, still holding his gaze.

"It's fiction." Cai faltered then, thinking back, remembering. "Alfred told me stories of the Dark Pearl as a child. I don't even really remember them, just the magical Pearl. I used it, but only that element. The entire story surrounding it is completely mine. The characters are pure fantasy. I don't see how—"

"Of course you do not see!" Dilys stood, rattling the china as she bumped the table. "Isolde isn't coming for you because of your fantastical tales. It is the Pearl itself that called her here. You made her aware you knew of its existence. It was all the sign she needed." She moved past him at a surprising speed.

He caught up with her at the door. "Wait a minute. If what you say is true, then why on earth would she do something so horrific? She is still in the public eye."

"She retired at the same time your grandfather did."

"But she's just as much an icon as he is. Why would someone of her stature risk everything to do something like this? It makes no sense. So they had a long-running feud. It was a war of words, not one of flesh and blood. Certainly it was no cause to kidnap and torture innocent women. And a decade later for Christ sake!"

Dilys turned in the doorway. "Believe what you will, Master Malacai. Himself has done all he could to protect you, has sacrificed more than you'll ever know to keep you safe. Maybe he was injudicious in telling you tales as a boy, tales he perhaps thought you'd forget. Perhaps we'd both become too complacent. I told him to get you to change the Dark Pearl book." The ferocity drained from her tone and her face. She seemed to slump in on herself. Suddenly, she looked every bit as old and frail as Alfred. "But the sign has been given. She will not stop now until she has it." She was talking to herself now. "And then it will all be for naught. Centuries of work, of sacrifice, gone."

Cai took her arm as gently as he could without letting her pass. "If this is really true, we can stop her, Dilys. There are law enforcement agencies already working on this case. She won't get away with it."

Dilys laughed. It was an eerie, hollow sound that sent a cold chill sliding down his spine. "They will not be able to stop her. Her power is too strong. Evil's always is." With that she broke loose and left.

Cai debated going after her, but it wouldn't do any good. It was late and he needed to regroup.

"Cai, do you think she was telling the truth? I mean, it's pretty unbelievable."

He slumped down on the couch. "You're the one who thought they knew the truth."

Jordy shrugged off the barb. "But Isolde Morgan?"

"It's all unbelievable, Jordy. The kidnappings, the tattooed flesh, all of it. She sounded just like Alfred," he said quietly. "Talking of centuries of time, of magical pearls, evil powers. Maybe they're both loons. Maybe we are, too, for even wanting to believe them."

"She seemed very certain." Jordy shook her head. "You're right, though. If Isolde is really this insane, then why wait ten years to do something like this? And what does she hope to gain by torturing your readers? Why you and not Alfred? It's all too weird."

"She wants this mythological Dark Pearl. And because I wrote about one, she thinks I'm the only one that can give it to her."

Jordy rubbed her arms. "What were the stories Alfred told you about it? Can you remember any of them?"

Cai shook his head. "No. I'm not even sure why I remembered the Pearl at all. I was developing my next trilogy idea and I knew I wanted it to be a quest series. I didn't want the object to be anything ordinary. I wanted something magical, something mystical. For some reason the Dark Pearl came to mind and it was perfect. But that's all. The rest is purely made up."

"If you can't remember the stories, then how can you be sure? Maybe there are some elements in there that came from your subconscious."

"Even if they did, how could I have known it would

trigger something like this? Alfred talked about Isolde, but not about anything like this. She was an acid-tongued bitch who liked to pick on his work and he enjoyed battling right back. They both prospered from the public battles, so none of the rest of this makes any sense. I was a kid when they were fighting. It had pretty much burned out by the time I was a teenager and ended altogether when Alfred stopped publishing. I had just begun my career and we never really talked about her after that."

"Did Alfred read your book before it was published? Did he say anything about the Pearl? Dilys said she tried to get him to make you change that."

"I know." He shook his head. "He read it, but he never said anything. If they really believe all this, then maybe he left it alone precisely because it was a tale of pure fantasy." He dipped his chin and massaged his temples. "Magic pearls, evil powers, it's all nuts."

"Are you going to tell Kuhn?"

"I don't know. If I do, he'll want to talk to Alfred. I know I promised to involve him, to give him the chance, but to subject him to one of Kuhn's interrogations . . . I don't know."

"Maybe you could talk to Alfred instead. Record the conversation or something. The tape would be proof enough."

"It's possible." He blew out a deep breath. "We can figure out what to do in the morning."

Jordy walked over to him and he tugged her down onto his lap. "None of this is your fault, Cai." She pressed a kiss along his jaw. "It's a chain of events no one could have predicted or prevented. I don't know what the truth is any more than you do, but I do know that you'll feel better once you've had a talk with your grandfather."

"Will you come with me?"

He'd surprised her with that one. "Are you sure?"

"He likes having you here. Maybe it will make it easier. On all of us." He tilted her chin and kissed her deeply. It was damnably easy to get lost in her, even now, when his world was falling apart. Maybe especially now. "I won't be able to sleep tonight."

"Neither will I."

"Then why don't we not sleep together."

TWENTY-SEVEN

JORDY FOLLOWED CAI into Alfred's room the following morning. She should be thinking only of the conversation they were about to have, but she couldn't get her mind off last night. Cai's lovemaking had been slow and thorough, devastating any defenses she had left. Lovemaking. That's exactly what it had been. She felt different.

She felt loved.

There had been no declarations or words of commitment. Not that she'd expected any. But, in the truthful light of morning, when she'd awoken first to lightly stroke her hands over his chest and face . . . could she deny she'd wanted to hear them?

"Is that you, Jordalyn?"

Alfred's voice, thready and rough, pulled her from her reverie.

"Yes, yes it's me." She moved past Cai and went to his side. Taking up his hand, she was dismayed to find it cool, his skin papery and dry. "How are you this morning?"

He didn't answer. Instead he shifted his attention to Cai. "Malacai, I'm glad you've both come. The time has come to talk."

"Yes, Grandfather, we must." Cai perched on the edge of the mattress while Jordy took the chair next to the bed. "I should have come to you sooner. I didn't want to upset you. But I should have told you what was going on."

"We all make mistakes," Alfred answered. "Those made in the name of love are the easiest to forgive." He shifted on his pillows. "I, too, have made mistakes. While mine are also of the heart, I fear they are far more dire in the consequences they have created."

"Dilys says you think the kidnapper is Isolde Morgan," Cai said bluntly. "Do you honestly believe she'd go to these great lengths for a feud that ended more than ten years ago? What could she hope to gain from it? Where does the Dark Pearl fit in to all this? It doesn't make sense."

Alfred's blue eyes were as sharp as his voice was weak. "Oh, the feud reaches much farther back than you can know. That Isolde is responsible for this, I am certain. But then, so am I to blame." He looked away and his shoulders seemed to sink into the thick bedding.

"Nonsense," Jordy responded. "There is no way anyone could have predicted that Cai's book would have triggered this kind of insanity."

Alfred thumped the bed with surprising vigor. "I knew! Or should have known. I was well aware that the Dark Pearl was the focus of Malacai's latest work and yet I said nothing. The book was fantasy and this was his finest story yet. I was smug in my assurance that I'd kept the secret safe for so long that I could stave off any threat it might provoke. How wrong I was, and now we all will pay."

"Alfred, we have people working on this," Cai said. "The State Department is on it, both here and in Wales. Once we supply them with her name, if she really did kidnap those women, then it will only be a matter of time until the truth comes out."

"They will never find her or anything resembling the truth. She is far too skilled for that. No, this is a battle that only I can take on."

Cai went still. "You can't get involved, not directly." He gentled his tone. "With all due respect, you can barely leave your bed."

Alfred started to speak, then stopped. He held their gazes, then took a deep breath and released it slowly. "Perhaps you are right, Malacai. My power has weakened. I have spent these past days doing my best, but I no longer have the strength to hold her off."

He looked so defeated it broke Jordy's heart. "Alfred, we can wait for the task force to—"

"No more waiting! I have perhaps ruined what chance I had by wasting these last days. No, I fear I must tell you everything. Joining our forces is the only way to stop her. I had hoped that this would never be necessary, certainly not until you'd had a child of your own. Then the truth would have presented itself."

Cai looked at Jordy. She knew what he was thinking. If Alfred went off on another one of his rants, getting useful information about Isolde to pass on to Kuhn would be difficult, if not downright impossible. And could they trust any information he gave them anyway when he was like this?

"Alfred, I don't understand what the Dark Pearl has to do with your feud. Why does she want it, assuming it really exists? Is it so valuable? Enough to warrant kidnapping and torture to own it?"

"Oh, it exists. It's value as a gemstone would be astronomical on the current market. It is immense and flawless. But that is not why she wishes to possess it." Alfred patted the bed. "Come, Jordalyn. Sit beside me so that I might hold both of your hands as I tell you a story."

Jordy met Cai's eyes once again. He nodded and she sat on the opposite edge of the bed. Alfred took her hand, Cai held his other one.

"I know you have thought me eccentric, even senile,

with all my talk of Arthur and Merlin." He waved away their discomfort. "Whether or not you believed me hasn't been an issue, so I have not forced it. Until now. Now it is vital. What I'm about to tell you will challenge your beliefs in what is truth and what can be."

Both Jordy and Cai sat silently.

"Malacai, you were born into a family whose history predates time as you measure it. You know little of your actual heritage because I determined it was better that way. You were not born of the gift. Your father was. In time, he would have told you of his duties, if for no other reason than to protect you." His eyes shifted away for a moment. "I disagreed with that decision, and it is only now that I realize he was right. I, too, should have confided in you."

"Confide what? About Isolde?"

A spark of fire returned to Alfred's eyes. "Isolde is only part of this. I misjudged her as well as my own abilities. I thought that once she knew you weren't the one, she would leave us be. And for ten years, she has. The story will take some time in the telling and I will brook no more interruptions." He slipped his fingers around Cai's and squeezed. "You will need to open both your mind and your heart. Trust in what you know, not only in what you can see."

There was nothing to do but follow Alfred's lead. "For a weak old man, you have an amazing ability to control those around you," Cai said.

Alfred smiled for the first time in days. "A skill you would be wise to learn, young lad."

"I tried, didn't work too well." Cai smiled, but couldn't swallow the worry that grew ever deeper. Alfred was teetering on the edge of complete irrationality. He wasn't sure he'd recover this time.

Cai looked up to find Jordy gazing at him. She had a way of looking into him that was more intimate than a touch. Her heart ached for Alfred, too. But there was something else there, a spark. She was falling under Alfred's spell and urging Cai to follow. He sighed inwardly. She didn't know Alfred like he did.

"I suppose I will begin where it started," Alfred went on. "The L'Baan's have existed for tens of centuries. It was known immediately upon my birth that I would be the next Keeper. I was apprised of my future role and prepared for it, but my other skills had to be developed first. I was taken to court as a young boy by my father for training. A Keeper must learn the full extent of his powers if he is to fulfill his duty. It is a long, arduous task, but I was fortunate. For he apprenticed me to Merlin."

Cai sat up straight. He wanted to indulge his grandfather, but this was too much. He couldn't just sit here and watch the last of his grandfather's mind desert him. "Merlin, Grandfather?" he said gently. "That was over a thousand years ago."

"I asked for only your silence," he said pointedly. "I will take nothing less."

Cai frowned, but nodded.

"Merlin was a difficult taskmaster, but I learned my calling well. I spent a great deal of time in Camelot, even traveling with Arthur on occasion. Later on, I would accompany other knights. Perceval on his hunt for the Grail." Alfred shook his head. "A time that was. Fraught with arguments. Many a time I thought to leave him to it, but we managed well enough in the end. If he knew that Galahad would go on to reap most of the glory . . ." He sighed, a smile curving his lips. "Ah yes, those years were some of the best of my long life. But that is the way of youth, the memories retaining more luminescence than perhaps the actual time warranted."

He gestured for his water and Jordy quickly positioned the glass and straw in front of his mouth. He sipped, his mind seemingly miles—or centuries—away. "I was entrusted with a great deal of responsibility as I moved through various courts and kings over time. But none so powerful as that given to me as birthright. That of Keeper of the Dark Pearl. It would take all of my training to maintain that balance of power. My father knew of that power, as had his father before him. L'Baan's had been Keepers since before time was recorded. The position was exalted and feared, the Pearl greatly desired, its possession savagely sought. They did not understand that its power was only worthy in that it balanced an equal evil. Wielding it for the sake of greed would bring such devastation mere mortals could not comprehend.

"So, the Keeper before my father, my great-grandfather, secreted the Pearl away. Tales of its powers were passed down amongst the masses but, as generations passed, those tales eventually were seen as myth. After time even the myths were no longer repeated. By the time I became Keeper, knowledge of the Dark Pearl had disappeared from recorded history altogether. I was known to courts and kings as a great magician. But only the Keeper knows of the Pearl and her history, has her secrets, knows where she is hidden. The Keeper and one other."

"Isolde." Jordy whispered the word.

Alfred merely nodded. "Isolde is the descendant, yes. She and I came to power at about the same time. She was apprenticed as well, to a magician as powerful as Merlin though his magick was dark, evil, as was the one before him. His realm, and hers by association, never crossed into Camelot. Not then. But I knew from my father of her existence. She learned well, grew far more powerful than even my father had predicted. We met for the first time on the eve of the second millennium." He fell silent, his expression troubled.

At any other time, Cai would have been enraptured. Alfred spun nothing less than gold. But this was no story.

Not to Alfred. How long had Cai deluded himself that his grandfather's flights of fancy were harmless? If Cai had been less doting and more vigilant, perhaps he could have found help for him earlier on. But even as he thought it, he discarded it. Alfred's eccentricities were intrinsic to the man he was. To take that from him would have been like stealing his soul.

Who was he to judge if this fantasy world was where his grandfather chose to go when his time on earth was drawing to a close? If it gave Alfred peace, then Cai would find peace there as well.

"I could have finished it that night," Alfred went on. "But I was arrogant. She taunted me with her designs to take the Pearl from me, to shift the balance of power to evil. I all but dared her to try." He snorted in disgust. "She was an apt pupil and I had to spend enormous amounts of time and energy to maintain my edge over her. Energy better spent elsewhere.

"Our battle continued for centuries more and with all my time spent staving her off, my continuing studies in the realm of magick, and time spent in service to kings and their crusades, I remained alone. This was not my father's dying wish. I knew I must find my mate and produce an heir to my position. Were I to die without benefit of an heir to my powers, she would win. I could not let that happen. Yet I had to marry wisely. Not every union would produce a Keeper. I was fortunate. Meet her I did, and our union made us more powerful still. Isolde was furious and went into seclusion for the duration of our time together.

"Your grandmother died in giving birth to your father. It was both the greatest and most tragic day of my life. But I knew as soon as his eyes opened and he looked upon me that we had succeeded. She had not given her life in vain." Alfred suddenly gripped his hand. "Her life pulsed in your father, and his pulses in you."

Cai could only stare into his grandfather's fierce blue eyes and hold on.

"And yet I have no special powers," Cai said quietly.

"Your father did not love as wisely as I. He was not a focused pupil. I fear I doted on him too much and with not as firm a hand as I should have. But he was all I had. Isolde had not shown herself in over a century and I naively thought I had all the time in the world to show him the way. I let him wander and as a result he fell in love with your mother." Alfred smiled warmly. "She was a lovely creature, full of life and energy. I could not fault him for wanting the union. I didn't encourage it, but neither did I worry overmuch. I knew his time would transcend hers and that he could go on to produce his heir with the right mate."

"Instead he had me."

Alfred nodded. "Indeed he did. And a fine lad he sired in you. We knew immediately you would not carry the gift, but that didn't lessen his love or devotion to you. I worried that time was wasting. Isolde had surfaced once again, gloating a bit over my mistakes with your father. He had come to live here in Florida and had no interest in his lessons with me. Yet, I still believed we had time and let him have his youthful fling." His eyes grew glassy. "Had I been more strict, he would never have fallen prey to that faulty plane machinery. His magic should have been strong by then." He lifted his hand and stroked Cai's arm.

Once again he seemed to fade out. Cai looked over at Jordy, but her gaze was focused rapturously on Alfred's. Tears made her eyes look like bright, glistening emeralds. She was completely transported. Cai found his own smile, even as his heart ached. Alfred's own life might be waning, but his true power hadn't abated one bit.

Alfred cleared his throat. "I gladly took on your care, knowing that the seed for salvation lies within you. I kept

you here, away from Isolde's prying eyes, raising you myself, encouraging our cloistered lifestyle. When the time
came, I would guide you to your mate, see that you produced the heir to the Pearl."

Cai surprised them both by grinning.

"You find this humorous, young sire?" Alfred demanded.

"It's just that some of the women you've tried to hook
me up with don't, uh, exactly seem to meet the criteria of
this perfect mate I'm supposed to find."

Cai expected to be blasted for his insubordination, but
instead Alfred's cheeks colored slightly and he shifted a bit,
picking at the sheets. "Well, I wasn't getting any younger.
Your complete inability to maintain an ongoing relationship with any woman, much less the perfect mate, was
more than a little alarming. I knew I would not have centuries with you as I did your father." He harrumphed. "I
did what I had to do."

Cai didn't know whether to laugh or cry. He could have
done both, and perhaps that was Alfred's lasting legacy.
The idea that this incredible man would leave him forever
hit him hard and swift. He leaned over and kissed Alfred
on the cheek. "I love you," he said. "I wish I had the words
to explain all the reasons why."

Alfred's eyes misted and he didn't seem to know what to
say. He cleared his throat and gestured for more water,
which Jordy provided. "I love you like my own son," he
said finally. "I only kept you here to protect you. Perhaps if
I'd told you sooner, encouraged you to live more openly, I'd
be training my replacement by now."

He took their hands and joined them over him. "Fate
works in strange ways, however. I knew as soon as I saw her
dragon that she was the one, Malacai." To Jordy he said,
"You will do well by him, I know this to be true. Your soul
is pure. My heart will be with you always, Jordalyn." He

refused to let them respond. Gripping their hands more tightly and with some urgency, he said, "I have not been completely foolhardy with my birthright. Knowing time was waning, I have spent these last years putting to paper everything I have learned in my long time on earth. The volumes are hidden. I fear they are not complete, but there is enough. Dilys has the only key. I may not be here to do my duty by him, so you will need them to train the child you will create. He will be the Keeper, I feel it."

· TWENTY-EIGHT

CAI CLOSED THE door to his office. Jordy walked
to the window. They had both remained silent since leaving Alfred minutes ago.

Alfred's final proclamation had barely left his mouth
when his eyes drifted shut. He'd fallen asleep with their
hands still joined in his tight grip. Cai had known a moment of soul-deep panic, uncertain if his grandfather had
fallen asleep for the night, or all eternity. But his chest rose
and fell evenly. They'd stayed with him until he'd relaxed
into deep sleep.

"What do we do now?" Jordy asked.

"I honestly have no idea." Cai was exhausted both mentally and physically. He couldn't think rationally, then
again, nothing about the last hour had been rational. He
was no longer certain where reality ended and fantasy began.

"Do you think there's a chance Alfred is right?"

He turned and took her hands in his, holding them still.
"Even if he is, I can't see him convincing anyone else of it."

Jordy looked deep into his eyes. "Did he convince you?"

He spent a long time staring back at her before answering. "I don't know."

"He makes me want to believe," she said softly.

Cai could drown in her eyes. Alfred said she had magic. Maybe there was a little of the believer in him after all. He surely felt spellbound.

"Maybe we should ask Dilys for the key," she said. "To Alfred's papers."

He had to let her go, stop touching her, if he was going to think straight. He walked around his desk and sat.

She sat, too. "We have nothing to lose by looking at them. And you never know, maybe there will be some kind of documentation of his claims against Isolde."

"Claims that they battled over a powerful magic pearl a thousand years ago?"

Jordy slapped her knees and stood. "Fine. Just fine. You sit here and wallow in your self-pity and pain then. I'll go talk to Dilys."

"No."

She lifted a brow. "No? Alfred made it clear that he expected both of us to have access to those papers. I suppose it will be up to Dilys to decide."

He swore when she walked from the room. But he didn't go after her. Self-pity? He wanted to reject that, but he couldn't. He was human, his emotions were raw, his defenses drained, and yes, he resented Alfred's slow descent into madness. Pain? Well, yes, dammit, he was in pain. So much so he ached with it. His grandfather was fighting a losing battle and Cai could do nothing but watch.

He wished he could believe Alfred's story. How wonderful it would be if life were that simple. But life wasn't like that. He tilted his head back. No, his life wasn't like that.

THE KITCHEN WAS empty, so Jordy went to Alfred's room first. She listened at the door, but heard no voices. She peeked inside, but Alfred was alone and still sleeping. She tried his office next, but it was also empty.

She went through the rest of the house, even going so far
as to knock on the door to Dilys' private quarters. If she
was there, she wasn't answering.

It was the middle of the day. Where else would she be?
She doubted Dilys was out wandering the gardens alone.
Jordy walked out to the docks, but there were no boats
missing. Hell, for all she knew, she might have been chasing her in circles. It was a big place.

She headed back to the house, but instead of going inside, she veered toward the path to the cottage. With Alfred asleep, Dilys missing in action, and Cai closeted away
with his thoughts, there was little she could do anyway.

Maybe working on the dragon would help her sort out
her thoughts.

"Hi, Fred." She went over to the bowl and picked up his
fish flakes. She'd moved Fred out here earlier, since this was
where she figured she'd be spending most of her time. She
sprinkled a few flakes in the water, then froze. Her mouth
dropped open. Fred was swimming upright. She bent down
and looked through the side of the glass, then stood and
looked into the water again. There was no mistaking it.
Fred looked . . . normal. She walked around the bowl,
unable to believe what she was seeing. His crooked tail still
bent at a slightly funny angle, but it was no longer twisted.

"How did you manage this?" she asked in wonder.

" 'Twasn't difficult if ye know the words."

Jordy spun around, hand to her chest. Dilys stood inside
the door. She looked different, too. Not in any specific way.
Her hair was still sleeked back into a tight chignon, her
clothes spotless and ruthlessly crisp.

But there was something . . .

"*You* fixed him?"

Dilys walked toward her and the fishbowl. "Aye, not
that the wee thing was complainin'." She smiled tenderly

at Fred. "Though I'm certain he willna mind seein' the world right side up for a change."

That was it, Jordy thought, stunned. Her tone had softened, her eclectic dialect emphasized by the change. The cold austerity was gone from her. Dilys radiated . . . warmth.

She turned to Jordy. "I did it because I felt ye needed a sign."

"A sign?"

"I feel yer faith is strong, perhaps more so than Master Malacai's. But then that one takes too much on his shoulders, he does. You hear with your heart as well as your head. I thought it might not hurt to nudge you along a bit."

She didn't wait for an answer, but moved over to the plastic sheet that covered her dragon. Without asking permission, she uncovered it. A smile split her normally tightly drawn features. It transformed her, so much so Jordy swallowed a gasp of surprise.

"Ye have the magic in ye, aye, and that's the honest truth. Himself saw it in ye right off, he did. I wasna so certain, until I had myself a peek at your drawings."

"You went through my sketch books?"

A tinge of the old Dilys surfaced as her shoulders straightened a bit. "I didn't paw through your things, if that's what you mean." She gentled a bit then. "When I brought you yer sketch pad as you watched over himself when he took to his bed. I took the liberty of looking through it. I suppose I was lookin' for a sign, too."

"Did you find it?" The question was out before she could stop it.

"I believe so." She looked again at the beginnings of the sculpture. "This here is further proof. You know where the slumbering creatures lay."

"I'm a sculptor. Finding the creatures, as you say, is

what I do. I don't know that there's anything particularly magical about it. This one is barely begun."

Dilys' smile remained intact as she covered the dragon back up. "Ye've been through a lot in your young life, Mistress Jordalyn. Enough to thwart a trusting nature such as yours. And yet, you still want to believe. That is why I've come."

Jordy looked at Fred, then back at her. "How did you fix Fred's tail?"

"Are you asking because you are ready to know?"

She wasn't sure of any such thing. Dilys was right about one thing though. What had happened with Suzanne had made her less likely to trust anyone but herself. And yet the L'Baan men had gained her trust in precious little time.

"They are deserving of it," Dilys said, as if reading her thoughts.

The idea that she might be doing just that spooked Jordy into backing up a step. This whole thing was making her more than a little edgy. "I was looking for you. Before I came out here."

She nodded, her knowing smile doing nothing to calm Jordy's jumping nerves.

"Do you have the key?"

"Aye."

Jordy rubbed her suddenly sweaty palms along the sides of her shorts. Now what?

"What is it ye seek there?"

"Proof. About Isolde."

Dilys laughed, startling her with the rich, deep sound. "The most important possessions one owns are the least tangible. Faith, hope, trust." She walked to Jordy and laid her hand over her own. Her palm was warm, her fingers were strong, and Jordy felt oddly reassured in her presence.

"What you need is in here." She tapped Jordy's chest,

right over her heart. "Ye only need this"—she tapped her forehead—"to guide it." She turned to leave.

"Wait! What are you saying we should do?"

Dilys turned. "I believe you've been shown the path."

Jordy thought back over what Alfred had said. "You mean about finding Isolde?"

"I mean about finding the Dark Pearl. Ye must retrieve it, bring it home to him. He'll need the strength only the Pearl can give him if he is to defeat Isolde this final time."

"The Dark Pearl?"

Dilys' smile was not unkind, but there was a trace of worry in her eyes now. "Faith, hope, trust. Those are the only tools you'll need." Her hand was on the doorknob. "That and a passport."

"But—"

She was gone.

She couldn't be serious. Jordy turned back and stared helplessly at Fred. He was swimming in circles.

Right side up.

I thought you needed a sign.

"SHE WANTS US to what?"

Jordy sat down across from Cai. "She wants us to go to Wales and retrieve the Dark Pearl for Alfred."

Cai started to speak, then stopped and sat heavily in his chair. It was all too much. His family was falling apart around him. Someone had to be the voice of reason.

"What should we do?" she asked.

"You should sculpt, I should write, and Dilys should continue to take care of Alfred."

"Oh, fine. And when we take our heads out of the sand, and acknowledge this won't go away on its own, then what?"

"Then I get him help, that's what!" Cai spun his chair

around and lunged out of it. "What the hell do you want me to do, Jordy, huh? My grandfather has slipped permanently into la-la land and Dilys is on the track right behind him. You can't expect us to go hopscotching halfway around the world on some wild fantasy chase after a magic pearl." And yet he feared that was the only path left to them. Maybe some part of him had known it all along.

Cai stopped pacing. "No matter what else happens at this point, Alfred's not going to rest until he feels it has been taken care of his way."

"So, what do you suggest?" she asked.

"I don't have any answers. I just keep getting more confused."

"Me, too." She went to him, tugged at his crossed arms until he let her in. "I want to help him, too. Do what's best. I wish it were easier to figure out what that means."

Cai held her cheek to his shoulder and rested his head on hers. They stood that way, drawing comfort from one another, for several silent moments. Maybe this was all family could do in a case like this, stay close and draw comfort from one another.

The fact that she considered herself family at this point was not lost on her, nor was the warm way it made her feel. These weren't the best of family times, but a real family didn't only rally in the good times. She wanted to be a real part of this family. Maybe she was finding that new path after all.

"There's something else I have to tell you," she said into the comfort of his shoulder. "Dilys did something else today." She felt him stiffen. "She called it a sign."

Cai leaned back. "What are you talking about?"

She looked him in the eye. "She fixed Fred."

Clearly surprised, Cai took a moment to respond. "Fixed Fred? As in . . . like, neutered? I didn't know you could fix a fish. And what in the hell for?"

Jordy laughed. It felt good after a day of heavy emotions. "No, no, not that way. She fixed his tail. He's swimming right side up, or was when I left him."

"How on earth did she do that?"

"I asked her and she said 'it's easy if you know the right words.' I think she meant . . . you know . . . a spell."

Cai groaned. "Not this again."

Jordy stepped back. "Well, there's no denying that whatever she did, Fred is swimming upright for the first time ever. His tail is still a bit crooked, but come on, this isn't a normal type achievement here."

"And she said this was a sign?"

Jordy nodded. "To help me follow my instincts and believe what Alfred says. Then she asked me to go to Wales and retrieve the Pearl."

"I suppose this is so she and Alfred can say some kind of incantation over it and make the evil Isolde go away? Did she give you a treasure map with a big X on it, too? I can't do this anymore today, Jordy. I'm tapped out on playing Fantasy Island. I'm glad Fred is fixed, but I'm not buying into the rest of it."

"Precisely what she predicted." Jordy shivered.

"And your job is to do what," Cai went on sarcastically, "seduce me into going to Wales with you?"

"I know you're upset, but that was low and totally uncalled for."

He sighed. "I'm sorry. You're right. Which is why maybe we should just leave it be for right now. Okay? Just get back to the status quo for a bit, let things sort themselves out."

"Toddle off to the cottage and play with my clay, is that it?" She stalked to the door. "Men." And slammed it shut behind her.

TWENTY-NINE

CAI RAN DOWN the path to the cottage. His heart was pounding, and panic began to swell inside him. "Slow down," he schooled himself. "I'm sure they're both there."

They had to be.

He hadn't seen Jordy since she'd stormed out of his office the previous afternoon. She'd missed dinner. Dilys had told him she was working late. She'd still been out there when he went to bed. He'd woken up alone. She hadn't been on the dock at daybreak for their morning cruise, either. So he'd gone on his own.

He hated having her angry with him. He'd barely made it around the Key when he'd turned back, intent on apologizing. He'd taken a shortcut he hadn't used in years. It was only because he was in a hurry that he'd even remembered it. The mangroves were overgrown and a real bitch to maneuver in.

It was there he'd spied the boat.

Little bastard had been out there the whole time. And Cai had been doing just what Jordy accused him of, burying his head in the sand, wishing the whole thing would go away.

Then, to top off the morning, he'd arrived back at Crystal Key to find a boat gone. He'd told himself it was no big deal, probably just Dilys running an errand. But the whole house had been empty. Once he'd got over the shock of not finding Alfred in bed, he'd convinced himself that he would most likely be with Jordy in the cottage. Dear God, let that be the case.

He rapped on the door.

His heart stopped, then started again when Jordy cracked the door open and peered out. Her hair was literally standing on end in ragged spikes. Her face was smudged with dusty dried clay. She wore baggy khaki shorts that rode low on her hips and a loose, midriff-baring tank top. There were circles under her eyes. She was the most beautiful sight in the world to him.

"Thank God you're okay."

There might be dark smudges under her eyes, but they exuded that inner fire she had when she'd been focused on a task. She didn't look too happy at being distracted from it. "What? Why wouldn't I be?"

All he could think about was pulling her tightly into his arms and begging her forgiveness for putting her in danger's way. He didn't want to alarm her, but he'd have to tell her about the boat.

"I was just worried. You weren't on the docks this morning." He touched her then, had to, just a trace of a finger down her clay-smudged cheek. "I'm sorry, Jordy. More sorry than I can possibly say."

The abstract look faded from her eyes. "I'm sorry, too, Cai. I know this is difficult for you. I just get impatient."

"I think we should talk to Alfred about all this again. Can I come in? He's here, isn't he?"

"Alfred? Here? He's not in his room?"

The panic resurrected itself. "No. I was hoping he was out here with you."

She shook her head, as if to clear it, then stepped back from the doorway, opening it wider for him to come in.

As disturbed as he was about Alfred's whereabouts, Cai couldn't help but be immediately drawn to the piece of sculpture that sat at the center stage in the small room. It could have commanded that spot in an auditorium.

He walked past her and stared at it. "It's . . ." Suddenly words failed him. He walked all around it in awe. After a long while, he looked at her. The fatigue showed clearly now, along with obvious discomfort. "He's magnificent. You're . . ." His gaze was drawn to the dragon. "You're incredible."

"He's not done," was all she said. She pushed by him and flipped the plastic over the beast.

As a writer, Cai understood the vulnerability that came with the feeling of someone looking over his shoulder while he was working. But it didn't stop the hurt he felt at being so cleanly shut out. Not that he deserved her trust right now. "I'm sorry," he said. "About everything. I wouldn't have intruded. But we have to talk. It's important. We've got to find Alfred, first."

Jordy's irritation fled as concern filled her face. "You say he's not in the house anywhere? What about Dilys? Could they be off somewhere together? Did you check his office?"

"I checked everywhere. Dilys isn't home. One of the boats is gone, so I figure she's in Mangrove."

"Could he have gone with her?"

Dread doubled up like a fist in his stomach. What if Alfred had collapsed again? Or worse. "Oh God." He turned and took off at a run.

Jordy was hot on his heels. "Wait, I'm barefoot, I can't keep up."

"I've got to call Dr. Fashel." He never should have taken the jet boat out alone. He should have been here.

Jordy caught up with him in the kitchen.

"No note." There'd been none in his office either. "Run to my room and check for a note while I call Frank."

Clearly alarmed, she did as he asked without questioning him. She came running back as he hung up the phone. "Nothing."

"Damn!" Cai dug his fingers into his hair. "Fashel's secretary says he's been gone all morning and there was no call from Dilys." He called information and then dialed the number for the closest hospital. He argued with the admissions nurse, then, frowning, he hung up. "He hasn't been admitted and there's no record of him in emergency." He swore viciously under his breath. "I should have been here, dammit!"

"You couldn't possibly have known—"

"I found the delivery boat this morning, Jordy. The son of a bitch has been out there watching us the whole time."

Jordy sank into the nearest chair. "You don't actually think that he . . . that someone came right on the island and—" She broke off and covered her mouth with her hand.

"I don't know what to think. The boat was tied up in the mangroves, but empty. I'm not sure where he was." He slammed a fist on the counter. "Damn it to hell, how could I have been so arrogant to think I could handle this."

Jordy went to him and held his face in her hands. "Stop it, this isn't going to help them."

He looked down into her eyes, feeling like a failure. "I left him alone, Jordy. And you. Dear God, she could have tried to do what she threatened to do. When I couldn't find you—" He buried his face in her hair.

Jordy tensed. "What do you mean, threatened to do?" She pulled from his grasp and looked up at him. "What didn't you tell me, Cai?"

The time for protecting her was over. Little good it had done him anyway. "I should have told you, I know that now, Jordy. I was stupidly trying to protect you, to protect Alfred, oh hell." He rounded away from her and stalked to the window. "Margaron sent an e-mail almost a week ago. Apparently our deliveryman passed on word of your existence to her. She wasn't happy." He slammed his palm against the wall. "And I've been parading you under his nose all week. I should have sent you home to Virginia, but no. I thought you'd be better off with me. Goddamn it, how much more of an ass could I have been!"

"Stop it!" Jordy yelled. "Stop. It's done. I'm here, I'm okay."

He turned on her, strode across the room, and took hold of her arms. "I was selfish. I wanted you with me, for myself, for Alfred, for your art, for all the wrong reasons. I should have sent you home, Jordy."

She looked him dead in the eye. "I wouldn't have gone, Cai. But you're right, you should have told me."

"Do you have any idea how much I care about you?" he asked bleakly. "It makes my heart hurt, makes my head stupid." She smiled a little at that and he relaxed a fraction. He kissed her then, and his world tilted a bit closer to center. "I want to do the right thing, Jordy," he murmured against her mouth. "By you, by me, by all of us."

"Then let me help you instead of trying to take this on all alone. When will you realize that I'm not a burden to be shouldered, but a woman who can share the burdens with you?"

"Maybe now." He held her tight.

She reached up and kissed him again. "I'm not going anywhere, Malacai L'Baan. I'm in this for the long haul. Get used to it."

"Maybe that's just it, it's very easy to get used to you being here. Always."

She faltered a bit at that and he felt the pinch of pain around his heart. Now was not the time to pressure her for future plans.

"You said a boat was gone," she said. "Something tells me our deliveryman isn't involved in this little caper of theirs. I can't see him ordering Dilys to do anything she doesn't want to do. And if Alfred had become sick again, she'd have come to the cottage and told me, or left a note." She took his hand. "Come on, there has to be a note somewhere around here. Dilys wouldn't have just left without a note, no matter what the circumstances." Her eyes widened and she turned back to Cai. "Oh, God! You don't think . . . They wouldn't do it themselves, would they?"

"Do what?"

"Go to Wales. To get the Pearl. They wouldn't up and go there on their own, would they?" She put her hand to her forehead, understanding dawning in her eyes. "That's what Alfred wanted Dilys to do! When I heard them arguing. He wanted her to help him retrieve the Dark Pearl."

Cai didn't want to believe it, but even before he left the kitchen to search Alfred's room, he had a sick feeling that was exactly what had happened.

He stared into Alfred's closet. Clothes were missing, as were two of his suitcases. "Shit!"

Jordy picked up the phone on the nightstand.

"Who are you calling?"

"Dobs."

Cai started to question her, then nodded in approval. "Good thinking." He had to calm down, try to stop worrying so much, it was clouding his judgment.

She hung up moments later. "The boat is there, but he was out fishing this morning. It was in the slip when he got back. He doesn't know anything."

Cai grabbed the phone and punched in information, then called the airport in Miami. Minutes later he slammed the phone down. "Only one flight to London this evening that wasn't already booked up. They wouldn't tell me if Dilys or Alfred is on the list of passengers." He grabbed her hand. "Come on, we have to go check. There's time to get there before they board."

The phone rang and they both jumped. Cai picked it up. It was Kuhn.

"We want to come down there and talk to you," he said without preamble. "This afternoon. Your grandfather, too."

Cai's gut tightened. "I'm sorry, but that won't be possible. Listen—"

"You don't have a choice in this matter, L'Baan. We've traced the meaning of the tattoo. It dates back to the Dark Ages. Your grandfather is an expert in that area, isn't he?"

The suspicious tone sent the hairs on the back of Cai's neck standing on end. Kuhn suspected Alfred now? This he did not need. Not now. Thinking quickly, he said, "There has been a new development. I was just about to call you."

"Oh?" The suspicious tone increased, making Cai want to throttle him. "And what new development would that be?"

Cai reined in his temper and spoke as clearly as he could. There was no time to waste. "We're being watched. I found a boat in the mangroves just off the Key less than an hour ago. It's the same boat that the deliveryman used to bring me the crate containing the statue."

"Deliveryman? You mean someone actually brought it out to the island?" Kuhn's temper exploded. "Why in the hell didn't you give us this information before?"

Cai's own temper seethed. "Because I didn't think it was important at the time." *And because you're an incompetent asshole.* "The man worked for a company called Union Parcel. Got a pen? Here's the serial number that was on the boat." Cai looked at the palm of his hand, the only thing he'd had to scribble the number on earlier this morning. He read it off, rapid-fire, not really caring if Kuhn got it or not. "If you find anything out, call me. I'll talk to my grandfather about setting up a meeting." He hung up while Kuhn was still shouting orders in his ear.

"He really is an ass," Jordy said.

Cai blew out a frustrated breath. "I couldn't agree with you more."

"What did he want?"

"He wants to talk to Alfred. I think he thinks we have a more direct role in this than that of innocent bystanders."

"But that's ridiculous!"

"Yeah, well, that's Kuhn for you. He doesn't have anything else to go on, so when he found out the symbol on the flesh was from the Dark Ages, he immediately linked it to Alfred." He grabbed her hand once again. "Come on, I don't want us to be here when he or his men arrive. I gave him the deliveryman and boat info to buy us some time, but he'll be hot to talk to us for sure now."

"You didn't tell him about Isolde."

He stopped and turned back to her. "I'm not going to, not until we find Alfred and find out what's going on. Kuhn couldn't find the truth if it was engraved on an invitation and handed to him. Let him chase down our spy. I want that bastard out of the way, anyway. I don't want him following us to Miami. And who knows, maybe we'll finally get lucky and he'll tell Kuhn himself who his boss lady is. My main concern right now is Alfred."

"Do I have time to run upstairs and change clothes?"

He kissed her hard on the mouth. "Just hurry."

"We'll find him, Cai. It will turn out okay."

"I hope to hell you're right."

She smiled, though there was honest fear in her eyes. "Aren't I always?"

He tried to smile too, but all he managed was another fast kiss. "Hurry, meet me on the docks."

He was halfway down the path when she shouted from her bedroom window. "Cai! It's a note, from Dilys."

She held up her hand. "And the key."

THIRTY

J ORDY'S FINGERS TREMBLED as she read the note again.

> *Jordalyn.*
> *I was wrong to assign you a task that was mine to fulfill. I tried to convince himself to stay behind with those who love him, but he has his own obligations in this matter and his will would not be thwarted. Master Malacai will worry, but ask that he understand why we must make this pilgrimage. It is his grandfather's rightful deed and he does it out of honor and love and for his family. The Dark Pearl must be protected. We will send word when all has been resolved. We will not fail, for all will then be lost.*

She looked up when Cai entered the room. "Read this."

She watched his face as he read it. Anger, betrayal, fear, confusion.

"You said she gave you a key?" he asked.

She nodded and showed him an elegant silver antique key. "It was in a velvet pouch next to the note."

"Why should I have expected anything less?" He sighed, then frowned.

"What?"

"It just occurred to me that they could have chartered something private to fly them over. It would be just like Alfred."

"Do they have private planes for overseas flights?"

"If they did, Alfred would find one."

"Then they could already be gone." She cupped his cheek when she saw he'd already come to that conclusion.

"Then we follow them," he said. "You get to go to Wales after all."

Her eyes widened at that, although she already figured that might be where this was headed. "We don't know where they went."

"Then we find whatever this key unlocks and take it with us. There has to be a clue somewhere in his notes."

Jordy was surprised he'd mentioned the notes. He hadn't believed in them before. But much had changed with Alfred's sudden disappearance. "What about where Alfred lived in Wales? You must know——"

"No, I don't. Not specifically. North Wales is all I know. Somewhere in Anglesey, I think."

It should have surprised her that Cai couldn't tell her where his grandfather was from but knowing Alfred and everything else he'd kept from Cai, it wasn't so odd. "Well, it's a start."

He searched Alfred's room but found nothing that the key would fit. "Let's check Dilys' room."

Jordy followed him to the door, then stopped short. "If they're not in Miami and we have to go on to Wales . . . I don't have my passport." Her heart sank.

"Damn." He turned to her. "Maybe you should go back to Warburg, let me go on over there if I have to." His tone was sincere, but his eyes were filled with regret.

"Cai——"

He moved closer and pulled her into his arms. "Margaron knows about you. You might not be safe. I have no idea what's going on over there or where this all might lead." He stroked her hair, then her lips. "It might be for the best."

She shook her head. "Dilys said I had to have courage, that I couldn't let you down, that I was part of this, too. I believe that, I feel that. In ways I can't even explain. I don't want to run home to Warburg and hide." She held his gaze. "I want to be with you, I want to help you."

"Truthfully, I don't want you out of my sight. But with no passport . . ."

She swore under her breath and was surprised when he smiled. "I can't imagine what you find so funny at a time like this."

"You." He held her tightly. "Me. We're both too stubborn for our own good." He looked down into her eyes. "Promise me you won't leave my side the entire time."

Her heart sped up, but hope died quickly. "How?"

"I've got an idea. You search Dilys' room. I've got some phone calls to make." He kissed her hard and deep and left her standing there, dazed and reeling.

JORDY SLID INTO her leather seat on the Concorde and carefully stowed her canvas bag under the seat in front of her. "Be a good fish, Fred," she whispered, careful that his ventilated Tupperware bowl was securely tucked in. Another great thing about having fish for pets, they were easy to smuggle. A little Ziploc baggie of water in a coat pocket, through the security check, then a quick transfer back to his covered bowl, and *voila*! Cai had had a fit halfway to Richmond yesterday when he'd finally realized what was in the bag. He wasn't much happier about it now.

"Do you realize what kind of international laws you're probably breaking?" he whispered in her ear.

"Like I said yesterday, I'm not leaving him behind. Besides, he loves to fly. He did really well when Suzanne and I took him to Mexico. I couldn't leave him with anyone. The one time I had someone watch him, they almost flushed him because they thought he was dead."

"He doesn't swim upside down anymore," Cai grumbled, but he let it go.

Jordy hated the tension she saw in his face. She was really worried about him. Despite the complicated plans he'd made to retrieve her passport, she knew he'd hoped that they'd intercept Alfred and Dilys in the airport in Miami. They'd tried everything to find out if they'd booked a flight, but it would take the FBI to get information on the passenger manifests.

The flight to Richmond had been tense. She had barely made it to her bank in Warburg in time. It had felt so strange being back home again, but Cai had been so upset and they were in such a hurry, she'd hardly had time to figure out how she felt about it. It certainly wasn't the homecoming she'd planned.

She was worried about Alfred, too. How was he holding up through all this? Thank God he had Dilys with him. It was the only thing that eased either of their minds.

She thought about the binders tucked in the bag beneath Fred. She'd found them in an old trunk in Dilys' closet. Stuffed full of Alfred's notes, they were thick and somewhat heavy. She'd been able to bring only a handful.

Jordy buckled her belt, her shoulder rubbing against Cai's. His face was turned to the window. Strain drew his features into tight lines. Neither of them had slept well the night before, too worried to do much more than hold on to each other in the dark. She slid her hand to his thigh and wove her fingers through his. Without looking at her, his fingers tightened almost painfully on hers.

As the plane lifted from the runway, her eyes blurred and she tried not to wonder how this was all going to end.

WITH THE JUMP in time, it was dark when they landed at Heathrow. They'd slept fitfully on the flight and both were ragged around the edges.

"Come on, we have one more flight to catch."

She transferred Fred back to his water-filled plastic baggie and they trudged through Customs. An hour later, they were on a private plane to Manchester.

It was the early hours of the morning when Cai finally checked them into a modest hotel. Even though, U.S. time, it was evening, she felt every bit as tired as if she'd stayed up half the night.

"Any news?" she asked, once they were settled in their room. She put Fred on the nightstand.

Cai hung up the phone. "No messages from Alfred or Dilys. Several calls from Kuhn." They both grimaced. "Naturally, he left no word on the boat or deliveryman."

"Figures. What about Eric? Did he call in?"

Cai had contacted his researcher before they took off from New York and asked him to check into Isolde's address in Wales.

Cai nodded. "Isolde has homes in London and Paris, but she also has family property in north Wales that apparently dates back quite a ways. I asked Eric to look into Alfred's past here, too."

"He didn't think that was odd? You asking about your own grandfather?"

"I ask him to look up all sorts of weird stuff. His head is always in a book, he doesn't ask why, he just loves the hunt. That's why I use him." Cai paused, then nodded to the canvas sack on the foot of the bed. "Did you find anything useful in his books?"

Jordy was surprised. Even though it had been his idea to bring them along, Cai hadn't once asked her what was in the books. She knew he was still having a hard time believing anything Alfred had said. She wasn't sure how much she believed herself. "A few place names, but I have no idea how they might relate to Isolde, if at all. We'll need a map to locate them." She sat on the edge of the bed and waited for him to ask what else the books entailed, but he didn't. "We have to talk about this at some point, Cai. The information he's recorded goes way beyond some fantasy he's created in his head. The notes are very detailed."

Cai's face, lined with exhaustion and worry, tightened further. "Does it say where he hid the damn Pearl?"

She shouldn't have brought it up. "No, it doesn't. He's written this as if that knowledge is already known. He does relay the history. The place names he mentions are the ones I copied down. It might be a start."

He nodded wearily. "Fine."

She stood and moved into his arms. She kissed him and kept on kissing him until the tension ebbed and he was returning her kisses with equal ardor. "Come to bed, Malacai," she whispered against his mouth. "We'll find a more productive outlet for all this frustration. And then we'll sleep."

She didn't get any argument from him.

THIRTY-ONE

FRED'S BOWL WEDGED perfectly between the seat of the little Ford they rented the following morning. It felt weird sitting in the left seat with no steering wheel in front of her. The landscape west of Chester was captivating. So this was the land Alfred had been raised in. Even in the dead of winter, it was stunning. She wondered how he could have stayed away from this for so long. Chilly blue skies, a constant wind, snow dotting the peaks of the Clwydian Range, and fields so bright the color defied description. Stone farmhouses and sheep dotted the fields, their black faces making her wish she were sharing this with Alfred.

It was late afternoon when they closed in on their destination. "Get off here and cut across to Ty'n-y-Groes. It's only a couple of miles to Llanbedr-y-Cennin. However the hell you say that."

Fifteen minutes later, Cai pulled up in front of the small bed-and-breakfast he'd made arrangements with back in Manchester.

"Just bring the one bag in for now. And stow that damn fish." Cai hefted his gym bag and climbed the stone steps to the porch of the small farmhouse.

Jordy made a face at his back, but did as asked. She

knew his stress was at max load. However, as soon as they closed the door on their room, she turned to him. "I know you're worried, Cai. I am, too, but you could be a bit nicer to me. I am just trying to help."

He waited a long moment, then finally said, "I know. I'm sorry."

"Now," Jordy began, "you said Isolde's family land is close to here. We can check it out before dinner." She bent a little and went to him. "We're here, Cai, we're doing something to help."

"But it's just . . . something doesn't feel right."

"What do you mean?"

He swore under his breath and leaned back in the doorway. "I expected the place to be somewhere more, I don't know, populated. We're out in the middle of nowhere."

"You said the property has been in her family a long time. So it's not that surprising that it doesn't fit in with her jet set glamour reputation, is it? Maybe this fits perfectly. I mean, an isolated place like this would be perfect to hide . . . you know . . ." She shuddered, unable to put it into words. When he didn't respond, she said, "It's more than just the location, isn't it?" She saw it in his eyes.

"Ever since we drove through Ty'n-y-Groes, I've had this, I don't know, this . . ."

"Say it."

"This weird feeling. I can't explain it, Jordy."

She took his arm and pulled him to the door to the hallway. "Come on."

"Where?"

"We're going right now. We're going to check the place out, see what we're dealing with. We can ask our hostess, Mrs. Evans, if she's heard of two older Americans staying nearby."

"Alfred is Welsh. And Dilys is . . . well, I haven't a clue, but at least part Welsh anyway."

"Okay, okay, but any visitors at this time of year have to be a bit unusual. It won't hurt to ask."

Cai nodded, and they went downstairs.

Mrs. Evans was very nice, but not very helpful. She was attending some local women's club meeting that night in Conwy and said she'd ask around. Jordy didn't want to admit that she wasn't much more hopeful than Cai.

They were at the door when Mrs. Evans said, "You say you're heading to the old Morgan property?"

Something in her tone had them both nodding warily.

"Was rumored to be a llys on that site in ancient times, but they never dug there as it's still owned by the family."

"Llys?"

"An ancient palace of sorts. A noble house." She shrugged. "They're just starting to dig for them, made a great discovery in Rhosyr. Great sand blow buried most of them well back as I understand it. The Morgan place survived better, being up in the mountains and all. A shame they won't let them excavate it."

"How long ago was it buried?" Jordy asked.

"Oh my, well, we're talking back in the late thirteenth century or thereabouts at least. I'm not good on dates."

She tried not to show her disappointment. "Is there a house there now?" Jordy asked. "A family residence?"

"No, no. Just the ruins as I understand it. Never been up there myself."

Cai swore under his breath, as Jordy thanked her for her help.

"I don't know what connection you have to the Morgans," Mrs. Evans went on, "but I suppose you know the current holder is none other than Isolde Morgan herself. Not that she's come around these parts."

"Yes, we heard that."

She smiled. "Lovely, then. Perhaps you know of its curse as well?"

"Curse?" they said simultaneously.

"Yes." She laughed. "We Welsh can be a superstitious lot. The story has been passed down for years, supposedly started way back in the Dark Ages. It is said that anyone other than a Morgan descendant who has tried to make a home on that land has either gone mad or disappeared." In the uncomfortable silence that immediately followed, Mrs. Evans waved her hand and chattered on. "Of course, no one has lived there for hundreds of years."

"Of course," Jordy said weakly. Mrs. Evans continued to smile brightly, only now it was beginning to creep Jordy out. Suddenly magic pearls and ancient curses weren't sounding quite so unreal.

USING THE MAP Mrs. Evans had kindly drawn for them, Cai turned on the dirt track that wound up into the mountains and slowed to a crawl. Heavy rains and snow runoff had left the narrow lane deeply rutted. With the coming dusk, it felt more than a little ominous. He thought about Mrs. Evans' tale, told in her irritatingly chirpy little voice. Cursed. Just what he needed. Along with a magic Pearl and a grandfather claiming to be a . . . a sorcerer or . . . something.

"I don't know what to look for," Jordy said.

"I have a feeling we'll know it when we see it."

They bumped up another hillock, then went around a sharp turn. Cai brought the car to a jarring stop.

"Damn," Jordy whispered.

"Yeah." Cai said. "Damn."

Mrs. Evans hadn't been kidding about there being a ruin. All that was left were the outlines of a few walls and the remains of a stone fence that rambled all across the hills.

Cai jammed the car in reverse. "This was a waste of time."

"Wait. Why don't we get out and look around. There's enough daylight left."

"Look around for what? Do you think Isolde is hiding under a rock? Or maybe she can turn herself into a toad."

She rolled her eyes at him. "I'm just saying we should look around. This is the only property we have a record of her owning in Wales."

"The place *is* cursed then," Cai said. "Because you're nuts if you think we're going to find anything out here."

"Fine. Nutty me will go by myself."

"Jordy—"

She ignored him and climbed out of the car, then began picking her way up the rocky hillside.

Cai watched her trip and almost fall before he slammed out of the car. "Jordy, come on. It's too dark too see anything anyway." He was walking up the hill after her.

"Cai, come here!" Jordy knelt in front of the stones that once had formed part of the doorway or entrance. "Look!"

He made his way there and stood over her. "What is it?" The heavy sense of foreboding hanging over him had only grown worse the closer he got to the ruins. "Back out of there, Jordy."

She looked back over her shoulder at him. "What? Look, there are symbols carved in this stone."

He leaned forward and grabbed her shoulders just as she went to run her fingers over the badly worn symbols. The air seemed to shimmer around them for a second. Cai blinked, thinking his vision had blurred, knowing it hadn't. "Come on. Now!" He didn't wait for her to argue, but grabbed her hand and all but dragged her downhill to the car.

"Get in." He opened the door and shoved her inside, then climbed in his side.

"What in the hell has come over you?"

Cai didn't answer, he was too busy trying to back down the godforsaken mountain onto the main road.

"Cai, I think those symbols are like the one she sent to you. We need that book of Alfred's. Dammit."

Once he was on the main road back to Mrs. Evans' he thought he'd feel better. Safer. But his foot pressed even heavier on the gas pedal.

"When you put your hand near that symbol, did you . . . you know, feel anything? Anything unusual?" He'd meant to keep it to himself, but found he couldn't.

Jordy shifted in her seat. "Unusual how?"

He hesitated, then spoke. "Something's not right about that place. I can't explain it any better than that."

"Maybe it was just Mrs. Evans' talk about the curse. She was even creeping me out there toward the end."

"Yeah, maybe." He sure as hell wanted to believe that.

"You know, now that I think about it, something did strike me a little weird. The symbols were definitely not new, they were well worn, but you'd think, with all that wind and rain and being exposed to all the harsh elements, that they wouldn't still be readable at all hundreds of years later. And being in the entrance, wouldn't they have been even more worn down by the inhabitants treading over them every day?" She sat back and stared out the window. "I'm surprised they're still there."

Cai had thought the very same thing. But the possible explanations for that, and for that odd sensation he'd had, were in the realm of things he badly wanted to leave unexplored. "I'll get a call out to Crystal Key and see if they've called in. Maybe Mrs. Evans will have found out something at her meeting."

He felt her eyes on him. She wasn't going to let this slide. But she said nothing. Instead she slid the map book from the visor and dug a pencil out of her purse. She turned on the overhead light and made a quick sketch on the inside cover.

"What are you doing?" he asked.

"I'm making a sketch of the symbols while I can still remember most of them."

It didn't make any sense, but he didn't like the idea of even a sketched representation of those symbols riding around in the car with them. But short of ripping the map book from her hands and tossing it out the window, there wasn't much he could do. He'd already alarmed her with his behavior back there. Hell, he'd alarmed himself.

She flicked off the light as they pulled up to the small white stone house. In the sudden silence after he cut the engine, she said, "We're going to have to talk about this you know."

"Jordy—"

"You said we were in this together. Don't shut me out now. What happened to you back there?"

He hesitated, then said, "You're a lot more willing to jump headfirst into all this magic mumbo jumbo."

"Does that mean you're beginning to believe in some of what Alfred said?"

He turned to her then. His eyes were adjusted to the dark now. She was beautiful in the patchy moonlight. Shadows shifted suddenly across her face, casting her features in a wash of deathly white. He felt a sudden chill, as if something portentous was about to happen. He had this insane urge to grab her and hold on as tight as he could, as if some unseen forces were about to rip her away from him.

"Let's get inside." He didn't explain—couldn't—he just knew they shouldn't be out here, in the car. Out in the open. "We'll talk inside."

Mrs. Evans was still out. Cai added a chunk of coal to the stove she'd left burning, wondering if there was a heat pervasive enough to ward off the cold that seemed to have taken up residence inside his very bones.

He sat on the small couch and Jordy sat beside him. He kept his gaze on the fire as he spoke. "When you went to touch that stone it was as if the air almost, I don't know, shifted or something. I felt this dark sense of dread, like something bad, something irrevocably bad, would happen if you touched those symbols." He finally looked at her. "I had to get you out of there."

She rubbed her arms and he pulled her into his lap, giving in to the need to hold her close. To keep her safe. "I'm worried, Jordy. About Alfred, about Dilys. About you. About all of this." She tried to look up at him, but he didn't want her to see what was in his eyes. His fear was deeper than worry, more pervasive than concern. He was scared. He was feeling things that made no sense. And yet, the feelings were undeniably there.

He stroked her short hair, weaving his fingers through the wisps that framed her face. The power of his feelings for her washed over him once again. If anything happened to her . . .

He tilted her mouth up to his then and took it, pouring in everything he felt, but could not say.

When he lifted his head, he found her staring deeply into his eyes. "Cai, what can I do to help you?"

"Stay here. Right here."

"I'm not going anywhere."

They sat like that, for a long time, until the coal had almost burned down to nothing.

"You know," he said into the shadows. "For someone who makes his living with words, I can't seem to find the right ones to tell you how I feel about you."

Obviously surprised, she leaned back and looked up at him.

He smiled a little and pulled her head back to his chest.
"And it's even harder when you look at me like that."

"Like what?"

He heard the smile in her voice, and relaxed slightly.
"Like you see all the way down inside me."

She rubbed her cheek against his chest. "Well, isn't that
interesting. I've felt the same way about you. I chalked it
up to all that people analyzing thing you do for your writing."

"This has nothing to do with that."

"Yeah. I didn't buy it either."

He pressed his lips against her hair. "Jordy, when this is
all over, whatever happens, I—"

Just then, the front door banged open and Mrs. Evans
bustled in, her arm full of bags. Cai and Jordy moved off
the couch and relieved her of some of the heavy ones.

"So, did you enjoy your trip to the ruins? I see you made
it back in one piece," she said, bubbly as ever. "No word
on your friends, I'm sorry to say. But I thought you might
find it an odd coincidence that Isolde Morgan made the
evening news. Apparently she collapsed in some restaurant
near her apartment in Paris and has been taken to the
hospital there for observation." She lowered her voice. "The
same one where they took Princess Di. I hope they do
better by Ms. Morgan, if you know what I mean." She
tsked. "Such a tragedy that." She shifted her parcels and
smiled brightly again. "Well, I'll ring when dinner is
ready." She bustled out, leaving Jordy and Cai dumb-
founded.

THIRTY-TWO

I DON'T SEE any of them listed in here." Jordy tossed the map book on the nightstand. Dinner was over and Mrs. Evans was out for the evening, leaving Cai and Jordy alone.

Cai stood and paced to the window and back. "Isolde is in a Paris hospital." They'd seen the reports themselves now. "The places in Alfred's notes appear to be nonexistent." He shrugged helplessly. "I'm not certain he ever really had a clue about what was going on, with the kidnappings, the whole thing."

She walked over to him and tugged him around. "You don't want to believe in this. No rational person would."

"But?"

"But you felt something on that mountain this afternoon."

"Nerves. Exhaustion. Jordy, there are a million explanations for what I thought I felt."

"And Dilys? She believes him."

"What are you saying? That you believe he's lived as some Keeper of a magic pearl for over a thousand years?" He stepped back. "Do you honestly believe that?"

"Rationally? No. In here?" She tapped her forehead. "No. But here?" She laid her hand on her heart. "Here, I'm not so sure what I believe. Your grandfather is a powerful storyteller, Cai. He makes me want to believe." She looked past him, outside, into the dark. "And here, in this country, a place so old, so filled with history that I almost can't comprehend it. Anything seems possible here."

"I just want to find my grandfather and Dilys and take them safely home."

"What about those two women? Do you not believe in them, either?"

Cai stalked to the other end of the room. "I don't know what the hell to believe anymore. For all I know, Alfred is wandering around Miami in some hallucinatory fog and I'm half a world away chasing shadows and demons that only exist in his disintegrating mind."

"Then what do you want to do?"

"I said I don't know, dammit!" He swung back around, then stopped abruptly. He lifted his hands, then let them fall helplessly to his side. "I'm supposed to take care of him, Jordy," he said bleakly. "And I don't know how to do that anymore." His breath caught. "I'm afraid I'm not going to find him until it's too late."

She stopped fighting and went into his arms then. And held on. She just held on.

JORDY AND CAI thanked Mrs. Evans for breakfast the following morning. They'd barely touched it, but had forced down enough so as not to insult their hostess.

They had argued on the next step to take, but hadn't come to any conclusions. "I just wish we'd been able to find out more about Alfred's past here," she said.

They'd received a message from Eric about where Alfred had lived in Anglesey, but the house had been razed long ago for a row of shops.

"I can't believe we can't find anything more about his

younger years. What about his parents? Where did they
live? You'd think there would be a paper trail."

"We checked into all that. Nothing."

"Maybe we should go to Paris," Jordy said as they
climbed the steps back to their room.

"Excuse me?"

She sat on the bed. "Just because the e-mails came from
here, doesn't mean she was here. If she hired some guy to
watch us in the Keys, who's to say she didn't hire someone
to send the e-mails? But we know where she is now. Maybe
that's where she's holding the women. And if she collapsed,
then they might be trapped somewhere. And nobody
would know about their existence."

He crossed his arms. "I'm no longer so certain Isolde
Morgan has anything to do with this. I think it's a fantasy
Alfred concocted in his mind, maybe from their past history together or something, and has somehow managed to
convince Dilys of the whole thing. She's not exactly in the
spring of her youth either."

Jordy crossed her arms. "Okay. Then explain what you
felt yesterday at those ruins?"

"I told you before. It could be explained a million different ways, Jordy."

"I want to go back and check out that symbol again. I
didn't get it all down. It could be an important clue."

"Absolutely not."

She cocked an eyebrow. "If you don't think she's connected, what difference does it make? What's the worst
that could happen?"

I could lose you. The words just came into his head, but
once there, they wouldn't be dismissed.

"I know how hard all this is on you, but if we really are
relying on each other, we're going to have to learn to trust
each other. It's important to me to check those ruins out

again. That's all I want. After that we'll do whatever you think we should do next."

Cai felt the tension knot up in his neck, but he nodded. "I do rely on you, Jordy. More than you realize. And I do trust you. It's just hard, when what's in the balance is so critical, to let anyone else be part of the decision making process."

"You've been making all the decisions on your own for a long time."

"Not entirely. Alfred has been there." A ghost of a smile curved his lips. "And Dilys' commands have saved me from making numerous decisions."

"I relied on Suzanne far too heavily for too many years. Once the trial started, I found out quickly it's not much fun being the only one in charge. The key, I guess, is balance. I think you had that with Alfred. I'd like for us to find that, too."

"So would I." He took her face in his hands and kissed her deeply. "I want you to stay close to me, though. And don't touch the symbols." She gave him a look and he could only shrug. "So, I don't want to take any chances. Promise me, Jordy."

"I promise. And thank you, Cai."

He wasn't so sure she should be thanking him. He had a very bad feeling about this.

CAI TURNED SLOWLY onto the rutted track. This was just a quick stop, he told himself as he stopped the car when the ruins came into sight once again. That unexplicable dread filled him once again, both frustrating and angering him. This was all nonsense! And he wished like hell he could believe that. He wasn't suffering from jet lag now.

Jordy ran a finger along the crease beside his tightly

clamped lips. "Are you sure you want to walk up there with me?"

He wanted to back down the hill and get as far away from this place as he could. "Come on, let's get this over with."

They climbed the hill and stopped several feet away from the entrance.

Jordy saw it first.

"There's something stuck in the wall remains, next to the entrance. See it?" She was already walking closer before Cai caught sight of the fluttering piece of white.

He reached out and pulled her back. "Wait here."

She opened her mouth to argue, but shut it again and nodded. "Be careful."

His lips quirked. "That would be the last thing you have to worry about. Fox Mulder I am not."

Jordy smiled, but it wasn't too reassuring. A shiver raced over his skin as he walked closer. There was no wavering shift of the air this time, just the steady chill breeze. The sky was metal gray, lending to the ominous feeling.

"It's a piece of paper," he called out. But it was no errant piece of trash. The paper wasn't snagged in the rocks. It had been purposely pinned down.

Cai walked to the wall. He could read the neat black writing from where he stood.

> *She is a beautiful one, Malacai, but the Dark Pearl she is not. I warned you to leave her behind once before. Do not test me any further. Do not return here again with empty hands or you will not enjoy the consequences. Neither will she.*

Jordy watched as Cai turned back to her, face as pale as the piece of paper he'd been studying. "What?" She stumbled up the slope.

Her movement seemed to galvanize him into action. He took her elbow. "We have to get out of here. Right now."

"What's wrong? Tell me. What was on the paper?"

"A note." He pinned her with a dark look. "From Margaron." He said nothing, but went back to the car.

They were backing down the rutted path when she asked him what the note said.

"She said not to return empty-handed again."

"How did she know? She's in a hospital in Paris."

Cai stopped at the bottom of the track. "Obviously Margaron is not Isolde. I don't know who in the hell we're dealing with."

Jordy sat back, rubbing her arms, trying to take it all in. "How does she—whoever she is—know we're here?"

"I have no idea. But she has to be connected to Isolde somehow. This is her property."

"You think they are working together or something?"

"Your guess is as good as mine at this point."

"She knows we're here. So she's close by." The realization made her shudder.

"Which is exactly why I have to get you the hell out of here."

He put the car into gear and didn't speak until after they were back in their room.

Jordy sat on the bed. "You know, if Alfred sees on the news that Isolde is in a hospital in Paris, do you think he might go there?"

Cai paced. "He might. It's been three days. I don't know where he is, what kind of shape he's in, what his plan is." He raked his fingers through his hair.

Jordy rubbed her chin. "She wants the Pearl."

Cai looked at her. "I don't think I want to hear this."

She took his hand and wove her fingers through his. "I think you should give her what she wants, Cai. Lure her out and end this part of it. We even have the perfect way to

communicate. You can leave her a note at the ruins. Tell
her where to meet you. We'll call the police here. Someone
will know who we should contact on a case like this."

Cai knew she was making sense. Far more rational sense
than he was making. But the sense of danger was palpable.
He had been warned not to go back there empty-handed
and he was just spooked enough to not dare it. Not with
Jordy here. And there was no way he was leaving her unat-
tended while he went alone.

"She must have some way of spying on the ruins, and
that's how she found out we were here," Jordy said. "But
how did she know you didn't have the Pearl? I mean, how
big is this thing supposed to be? We need to know that if
you're going to pull this off."

Cai wasn't at all sure he liked this plan. He blew out a
deep breath and looked at her. "Does Alfred describe it at
all in his notes?"

"No. The notes aren't really directly about the Dark
Pearl anyway. They're . . . I don't know, lessons. Of a
sort."

"What kind of lessons?" he asked warily.

"Well, I guess you'd call them magic lessons. You know,
casting spells and such. I couldn't comprehend much of it,
but he was amazingly thorough on various subjects."

Cai felt his heart squeeze. Alfred had ranted and railed
often during their lifetime together and many of his flights
of fancy had revolved around his "contemporary" Merlin.
But to make reams of notes on the subject? Was he so far
gone he could sustain that sort of detailed fantasy? If not,
what was the alternate explanation?

Just then Mrs. Evans called up the stairs. "I'll go see
what she wants," Jordy said. She kissed him and held his
gaze. "Don't worry about the rest of this now, okay? One
thing at a time."

She disappeared down the stairs, leaving Cai alone with

thoughts he'd rather not be having. He found his gaze shifting to the Tupperware bowl. The goldfish swam crookedly, but upright.

Cai thought back to what Jordy had told him the day before Alfred and Dilys had disappeared. Dilys had fixed Fred as a sign to Jordy that she and Alfred were legit.

Cai watched the fish for several moments, then reached for the canvas bag. He slid one binder out and opened it to the first page. It was handwritten in elegant script. Something struck him as familiar, but he couldn't place it. Of course, he'd seen Alfred's handwriting many times, albeit not quite such a formal rendering of it.

He stilled as the connection hit him hard and all of a sudden. He knew where he'd seen this script before. He was surprised that Jordy, with her eye for detail, hadn't seen it, too. The handwriting was the same as that in the book of incantations in which they'd found the symbol. A book that was far more ancient than Alfred's eighty-some years.

He didn't have time to think any more on it as Jordy burst into the room. "Cai, come quickly. Dilys is here. Alfred's in trouble."

THIRTY-THREE

DILYS DROVE TOO quickly on the tight, windy roads. Cai held on to the door handles of the little Citroën while Jordy braced herself in the cramped back. Dilys had told them that Alfred had collapsed and they must come at once. When they asked her how she'd known where they were, she'd said only, "It wasn't much of a challenge."

Cai figured she'd gotten the message he'd left on the voice mail back on Crystal Key, explaining where they were in case she or Alfred had checked in.

"If you knew we were here, why didn't you come for us sooner?" he asked.

"It wasn't time. We weren't done yet."

Struggling with his patience, he said, "Where are we headed? Where have you been staying?"

"I must concentrate on my driving."

Given the way the car careened around each bend, Cai wisely fell silent.

They headed south, past Tal Y Bont and Dolgarrog, where Dilys turned onto a narrow paved track. The road, such as it was, turned and twisted, until they could no longer see the valley below them.

Dilys took a tight corner, almost putting the car on two wheels, then came to a bone-jarring stop.

Once Cai could pry his hands from the dash and door, he looked ahead and his jaw dropped. A massive, two-story stone house stood just in front of them. It was obviously ancient, and yet amazingly well preserved. At one end was a large, round tower that jutted higher than the rest.

"Come now. We must hurry." Dilys was out of the car and picking her way up the rock-strewn path before they could answer.

The ground was icy and the wind had a steady bite. Cai held on to Jordy's hand as they made their way behind Dilys to the front door.

They stepped inside, closing the heavy wooden door behind them to block out the cold and the wind. It took Cai several moments for his eyes to adjust to the deep gloom. They were in a large foyer illuminated by gaslit wall sconces. He felt Jordy shiver beside him.

Two rooms opened off the foyer. There was a wide staircase in front of them, and a hallway to the side of it that disappeared into shadows. It was too dim to make out the wall-hangings.

"Where is he?" Cai demanded.

"This way, Master Malacai." There were two lanterns on a small, ornate wooden table in the foyer. Dilys quickly lit one and handed it to Cai, then lit a second one for herself. "Watch the stairs, they're not uniform."

Cai noticed the stairs were stone, as had been the foyer floor. It was mostly covered by thick rugs, but the stairs were bare. He didn't have time to study anything else as he followed Dilys' quickly retreating figure.

Please let him be all right, Cai silently prayed. He had never been so relieved to see anyone as he had been to see Dilys standing in Mrs. Evans' parlor. But his relief had been cut short by the even greater fear that Alfred might not survive long enough for Cai to reach his side. Dilys had said little, other than that the situation was grave.

They quickly moved down the hallway. Sconces along the walls provided small pools of yellow light. Doors lined each side, all of them shut. The place was drafty and chilly. Jordy was beside him, her hand still tucked firmly in his. He held on tightly, perhaps too tightly, but he couldn't seem to do otherwise.

The hallway went on, seemingly forever. Cai wondered why, if his grandfather was so ill, he had been put in such a distant room. He didn't have time to ask.

The hallway came to an abrupt end at a set of double doors. Dilys set her lantern down on one of the small tables that framed the doorway and turned the doorknobs. They both opened soundlessly, swinging wide into the room.

"Do you want me to stay here?" Jordy whispered.

"No. Alfred will want to see you." He looked down into her eyes for the first time since entering the house. "I need you, too."

She squeezed his hand. "I'm right here, then."

They stepped into the room.

Cai didn't know what he'd expected, but it wasn't this. He stopped dead in his tracks, awed by the sight before him. They were in the tower. The room was huge, with steps leading down to the floor area. Round in shape, it was filled with tables, which were in turn filled with glass bowls and tubes and all sorts of odd instruments. Bookcases lined the steep walls, with a circular metal stairway on the opposite side, leading to a catwalk that circled the shelves at the level of the entrance they stood in. The ceilings disappeared into the shadows from which wires extended downward with varying shapes affixed to them. They shifted this way and that, like some huge mobile. It looked like some medieval chamber.

Like something from Merlin's time.

"Come, come, we're wasting time we do not have."

Dilys bustled them down the stairs and through the

cluttered area, giving Cai no time to dwell on that unsettling comparison.

"Wait here." Dilys stopped in front of narrow door on the opposite side of the chamber. "I'll only be a second." She disappeared inside.

"This is incredible," Jordy said in hushed tones. She tugged on his hand. "What do you make of all this?"

"I just want to see him," was all he said, all he dared to say.

Jordy turned back and looked over the room, craning her neck to look up into the darkness above.

Cai was just about to open the door himself, when it swung open and Dilys motioned them inside. "He's only aware every so often. But if you'd sit with him, hold his hand, let him know of your presence, that will do." She put a hand on Cai's arm as he made to go past her. "Be patient, Master Malacai, and when he does speak to ye, heed his words. I fear these will be his last."

His heart burned in his chest as his worst fears were put into words. He stepped around her and stopped short once again, surprised by what he saw. The room was mostly in shadows, he had no feeling for how large or small a place it was, since it was lit only by a small lamp that sat on the table next to Alfred's bed. Alfred's enormous bed. It was a monstrosity of wood, with heavy beams at each corner, all deeply carved. There were heaps of bedclothes and a number of pillows tucked against the equally massive, carved headboard.

Amidst all this, Alfred's frail form was barely noticeable.

Cai went immediately to his side, Jordy right behind him. He took his grandfather's hand in his.

"Grandfather, it's Malacai. I'm here. Jordalyn is here as well."

Jordy reached around him and placed her hand on Alfred's arm. "I'm right here, Alfred."

Cai waited expectantly, but Alfred's eyes didn't so much as flutter. He anxiously looked at his chest and was relieved to notice its shallow rising and falling. He was weak, far weaker than he'd been at any time back home. The ache was so deep, so all consuming, it made his breath catch and his eyes burn.

"Alfred," he said, his voice breaking. "Grandfather."

Jordy's grip tightened to where Cai thought his fingers would break. He welcomed the pain.

He stepped up and sat on the edge of the mattress. He stroked his grandfather's flowing white hair, stroked his arm, held his hand. He thought of all this man had done for him, all they had shared, and knew he'd been incredibly fortunate to have spent even part of his life with him. He didn't regret any of it, and sitting here now, he didn't wish any of it different.

"I love you, Grandfather."

At that, he felt the slightest of pressure from Alfred's fingertips. Then his eyes fluttered once, then a second time, before slowly opening. "Malacai." His voice was brittle and Cai leaned closer to hear him more clearly.

"Yes. I've come, so has Jordalyn. We're both here."

"Dilys said she'd bring you," he said haltingly. "Never failed me yet, that woman."

Cai wanted to ask him what he'd been doing, what this place was, and a million other things, but mostly he wanted Alfred to keep holding his hand.

"We came right away," Cai said. "She drives like a madwoman."

Alfred's lips twitched and a light wheeze rattled his chest in what might have been a chuckle.

Alarmed, Cai stroked the back of his hand. "Have you seen a doctor over here?"

He slowly shook his head. "It is my time."

"Grandfather—"

"I have kept going a long time, Malacai, knowing I'd failed to train my replacement. This has haunted me. It will haunt me even as I move onward to the next realm."

"We have your notes, now," Jordy said.

Alfred shifted his head slightly, and his lips twitched again when he found her. "Ah, Jordalyn. My light. You give me hope. Promise me you won't fail Malacai."

"I promise." Her own voice caught.

Alfred shifted his attention back to Cai. His eyelids fluttered shut, and Cai quickly checked his chest. It still rose, and he swallowed hard once again.

"I have retrieved the Dark Pearl." Alfred's voice was thready, his eyes remained shut. "It is here."

Cai stilled. "Here?"

"I am too weak to finish." His fingertips brushed against Cai's hand. "You must finish it. I am sorry for that too."

"No more apologies, Grandfather. I would do anything for you. And it still won't compare to all you've done for me."

"I've left you unprepared," he said, a trace of heat entering his weak voice.

"Shhh," Cai soothed. "We'll handle it. Whatever it is, we'll handle it."

"Dilys will do what she can, but in the end it will be up to you."

"Okay." Cai kept stroking Alfred's hand.

Alfred's eyes opened. The blue that had been weak and watery was once again fierce. It took Cai's breath away. "I thought it was Isolde. I was wrong."

Cai stilled completely. "She's in a hospital, in Paris."

"I am aware of her collapse." A smile that could only be described as pure satisfaction curved his lips. It made Cai's blood chill.

Alfred's grip suddenly tightened, surprisingly so. "She kept her existence from me. I should have suspected. She was growing weak, as was I. She would no more leave this earth without an heir than I would. I should have known!"

"Alfred, calm down. It's okay."

This only served to rile him. "It's not okay. It's anything but okay." He wheezed then, wracking his thin body with a series of coughs.

"Grandfather, please. You need to tell me what I must do." Cai knew Alfred wouldn't rest until he'd got whatever was bothering him off his chest.

"Isolde had a daughter. She died well before your father. I should have known when I read that first note she sent. I thought she was merely being clever." His breathing was rapid and shallow, but he continued. "She was clever all right. She has a granddaughter, secreted away all these years. Her daughter named her after the Pearl."

THIRTY-FOUR

JORDY GASPED. "MARGARON."

Cai nodded. "Welsh for pearl."

"I wasted the last of my power on finishing Isolde." Alfred shifted restlessly. "But she was not the source of this threat."

Jordy moved closer and stroked his hair. She looked at Cai and was shaken by how hollow his eyes were. She wanted to hold him, stroke him, tell him it would all be okay. But she knew it wouldn't be. She'd felt it when she'd stepped into the room. Alfred embodied this place, this incredible place. And yet she felt his spirit waning.

"Margaron is the force pushing this toward an ugly end. It is not time. The next Keeper has not come yet. I understood that. Isolde understood that. But the impatience of youth . . ." He let the words trail off and once again his eyes closed.

"We'll find her, Alfred," Cai said. "We'll end this."

He said nothing. After a few moments, it was obvious he'd fallen back asleep.

"Cai, maybe we'd best let him rest for a bit."

"I'm not leaving his side."

"I think we need to talk to Dilys. Find out what's going on."

"That can wait until . . . until later."

Jordy didn't agree, but she nodded. She leaned down and kissed his forehead, then his cheek, then his mouth. "I'm so sorry, Cai. I'm glad you're with him."

His eyes were glassy. "I know it's time, but I'm not ready."

"I don't think we ever can be. But he is. Can you feel that?"

Cai looked at his grandfather, then gave a quick nod. "I just don't want him dying thinking he failed. Whatever else, I don't want him leaving thinking that."

"Then we'll make sure he knows we'll finish what he started."

Cai looked up at her then, and she saw the fear in his eyes. "I want to." He broke off and shook his head. "It's all so damn confusing. What is this place, Jordy?" he whispered. "What is really going on here?"

"We'll find out. We'll finish it." She kissed him again. "I'm going to go find Dilys and see if I can't get some answers. I won't be gone long."

"Stay close. I'm not sure how much longer . . ." He shrugged and swallowed hard.

She moved closer then and hugged him with everything she had. "Oh, Cai."

He pressed his face against her chest and wrapped one arm around her waist. He held on tight and she felt his broad shoulders heave. She kissed him and stroked his hair and let him hold on.

When he let her go, he kept his face averted, looking at his grandfather. His hand still covered Alfred's. "I'll be here," he said roughly.

"I won't be long." With an aching heart, she stepped out into the cavernous room and was once again struck by the enormity of it all.

Dilys was sitting at one of the tables, perched on a high stool, pouring over a large book.

"I need to talk with ye," she said, without looking up.

"Alfred said he has the Pearl."

She looked up then. Her dark eyes narrowed. "What else did he tell ye?"

"That Margaron is the one responsible for the kidnappings. That she's Isolde's granddaughter."

Dilys nodded tightly. "That she is, the witch."

"Is that what she is, Dilys? Really, I mean." Standing here, in this room, it seemed like a perfectly plausible question.

"She is far more than that. She is everything Isolde ever was and more, I fear." Dilys marked her place in the oversized book and slid from the stool. "She should have waited, but she knows she is strong."

"Margaron?"

Dilys nodded sharply. "When Master Malacai wrote of the Dark Pearl, she took it as a sign. Mad that one is, far more dangerous than her grandmother ever was."

"You know about Isolde's collapse."

"Oh, aye. Satisfyin', that was. A fittin' way for Alfred to end things." Her expression darkened. "Had that been the end." She slapped the table, making Jordy jump. "How we missed her spawning I have no idea. Devil's spawn, from all accounts."

Jordy thought of the tattooed piece of flesh and found herself agreeing. "She's here, Dilys. She left Cai a note in the ruins on Isolde's property. She knows he's here."

"I know she's close. We feel her evil."

"If you know where, then you have to tell me. We can call in the police and end this. I know you think they can't help, but they can. They have more force than we do. We have to free those poor women, Dilys."

"I understand yer feelings for the misfortunates. But

they are the least of the worries we will have if Margaron gets her hands on the Dark Pearl."

"We don't need to let that happen. We can use it as a lure. Once she's out in the open, the police will catch her, take her into custody."

Dilys smiled in a maternal way as she had what now seemed like eons ago back in the cottage. "If it were only that simple, dear Jordalyn."

"It can be."

"No. Yer heart is there, Jordalyn. You are on the brink of understanding that this extends beyond the realm of the rational, are ye not?"

She wanted to say no. She wanted to say that this horrific crime was a police matter, nothing more, nothing less.

"If Alfred could, he would end this himself. It is his place. But he cannot."

"Cai doesn't want Alfred to die feeling he's failed."

"Neither do I. But I am afraid that Malacai can only finish this if he believes." She walked over to Jordy. "He must believe, in his heart, or he will fail."

"He wants to. I want to. But it's not that easy. You can't just say to yourself 'believe this' and, bingo, that's it."

"Look around you, Jordalyn. What do ye think this place is?"

"I—I don't know. Show me the Dark Pearl," Jordy said suddenly.

Dilys shook her head. "I cannot." She lifted a hand at her protest. "It is no' because I doubt yer intentions with it. It is simpler than that. Ye will no' see it if ye dinna believe in it."

"Show it to me. If I see it, then that will be proof enough that I truly believe, will it not?"

"The time will come. Go back to Master Malacai. He will be needing you shortly."

"We won't fail him, Dilys," Jordy said, holding her direct gaze. "Whatever it takes, we will do it."

Dilys nodded. "I believe ye mean it. If willingness were only enough."

"If Alfred is going to— If this is the end, don't you think you should be in there as well?"

"I am doing what I must, what he has asked of me. We have made our peace." She nodded. "Go on."

Jordy went back inside the bedroom. Cai still sat on the bed, Alfred appeared to still be sleeping. Cai reached for her hand as soon as she stepped close enough.

"Is he okay? Has he said anything else?"

"He's sleeping."

She slid her arm around Cai's shoulder. "Dilys thinks the time is soon," she said quietly.

Cai only nodded.

"I asked to see the Pearl."

Cai said nothing, his attention remaining on Alfred.

"She wouldn't show it to me. She said it can only be seen by those who believe." When Cai still said nothing, she said, "I asked if they knew Margaron was here. Dilys knows where she is, Cai." She felt him stiffen. "I told her she had to tell us, but she won't."

"The police cannot be of help to you in this." Alfred's weak voice got their abrupt attention.

"Grandfather," Cai said. He stroked his forehead. "Just rest."

"There is no time to prepare you, Malacai. You have not the power, but you must wield the Dark Pearl for me." His hand fluttered against Cai's. "I will be there, in spirit, guiding you. You must listen." His eyes opened. "You must believe. You must!"

"I will."

"Do not placate a dying man, Malacai."

Abashed, Cai opened his mouth, then closed it again.

"Dilys will show you, will teach you the words. But without belief, the Pearl will not exist for you. Trust in it, Malacai." His grip tightened. "Trust in me."

"I do trust you."

"You love me. It is why you did not tell me of Margaron's evil."

"I do love you, more than anything."

"Then let that love expand, Malacai. Let it expand into a place where rational ideals are no longer the only truths. Where anything is possible."

"I want to."

"It is the legacy I leave you, it is all I am, all I have lived for, beyond you. Do not fail me, Malacai. For you are the hope of the future." His voice broke and Jordy felt Cai's breath come in heavy gulps.

He leaned down and kissed his cheek. "Please know that you have done everything right by me. You have been everything to me. I love you."

"I have done what I have done. I hope it will be enough. It is now up to you." He looked past Cai to Jordy. "And to you."

She came closer and sat on the bed, stroking her hand over his forehead and hair. "I'm here, Alfred. I'm here."

"I love you both. Do not forget, you are the future. Conquer Margaron, then fulfill that future promise."

Tears on their cheeks, they could both only nod.

"I will always be with you. Believe that, and you will hear me when you need to." Alfred smiled then, his gaze fixed on some spot beyond them. His gaze remained fixed there, his smile beatific, even as his chest stopped rising and falling.

Jordy's heart shattered as she watched Cai's face crumple. He laid his head on Alfred's chest and wept.

THIRTY-FIVE

⋘✕⋙

ALFRED WAS BURIED three days later in a small cemetery in Anglesey, near what once was his home. Cai had thought to bring him back to Florida, to bury him with his son, but Dilys had intervened, saying it was important that his remains be buried where he was born. She'd insisted that he not be interred near the stone house, for she didn't want the property in the public spotlight.

She had gone to a nearby town and contacted a coroner who had come and silently taken care of moving Alfred to Anglesey. Cai and Jordy hadn't questioned her choice, figuring as long as she trusted the man, they should as well.

Dilys had apparently chosen wisely, because no word of the other residence had appeared in any of the news stories. And there had been many. All had said he died in Anglesey, near where he'd been born.

The funeral had been private, but the media had picked up on it almost immediately. While he wasn't keen on the intrusion, Cai was glad to see Alfred get his due respect from his peers. Most of the news stories were reverential, glowing tributes to his remarkable career.

Most of them. More disturbing was the fact that Isolde had passed away the same day as Alfred. Several less respectable media sources had enjoyed making much of the irony of two life-long foes passing on the same day. No mention was made of any family attending Isolde's funeral. Cai tried to ignore that as much as possible.

He and Jordy were packing the things they'd bought for the funeral in preparation for returning to the stone house.

Alfred was gone.

Cai was still coming to terms with the void. It had been easier when there had been plans to make and paperwork to file. Now Cai had to face what came next.

"I'm worried the media will follow us," Jordy said.

"I've been thinking about that, too."

Another ugly result of the publicity surrounding Alfred's death was Kuhn finding out. He had tracked Cai down at their hotel and after delivering a perfunctory platitude on his grandfather's passing, began a blistering lecture on not alerting him to their plans. Cai had delivered one right back, putting the question to Kuhn as to why his task force hadn't been able to follow up on the lead the deliveryman no doubt been able to provide. In clipped tones, Cai was informed that the young man hadn't survived to be taken into custody and questioned. Apparently, he'd opened fire on the agents during the chase and had been gunned down in the battle. Kuhn then informed him that he was coming to Wales and demanded Cai make himself available for questioning.

Cai had told Kuhn exactly what he could do with his questioning, following that with a detailed description of what he thought of his skills as a Special Investigative Agent, then very satisfactorily hung up on him in midtirade. For that reason alone he was glad to be going back to the stone house. There were no phone lines there.

He wasn't certain he was ready for the rest of it.

"I'm hoping the media won't be interested now that the funeral is over," he said. "Maybe we should return to Mrs. Evans' first, get our stuff." They'd called her the day following Alfred's death and filled her in. With a grimace, Cai recalled how she'd twittered on about how delighted she'd been to find she'd been housing a celebrity but how sorry she was for his grandfather's passing. She kindly told them she wouldn't be charging them for their room and they could retrieve their belongings whenever they wanted. Cai imagined she'd be dining out for years on this story, so he accepted her hospitality with a polite thank you.

"I'll go tell Dilys we're almost ready," Jordy said.

Cai caught her hand before she could leave and pulled her to him. "I know I've been swallowed up in the arrangements for the funeral and I haven't said much, but I want you to know how much it has meant to me that you stood by me through all this."

She looked surprised. "Of course I would."

"There's no of course about it. I've been difficult and hard on you. Not everyone would have stayed."

She grinned. "I'm not everyone."

There was no truer statement than that. He tugged her close. "I'm not sure how I would have dealt with all this if you hadn't been here."

"You would have handled it, Cai."

"Maybe." He grew serious. "If you want to go back to Crystal Key, or even home to Virginia, I'll understand."

"Is that what you want?" She looked insulted. And hurt.

He felt only relief. "No. I don't want to let you out of my sight." Ever.

She tensed at that. "Are you still worried about me? Because you have enough—"

"I've been numb for the past three days. I do worry about you. Until this whole mess is taken care of, I don't think that will stop. But that's not the only reason." He wanted to tell her how he felt, that he was falling in love with her. Had already fallen.

"Well, I'm not going anywhere, you can stop worrying."

"Good." He held her more tightly. "Good." It had been an emotional week for them both. Now wasn't the time for declarations of love. She was here and she was safe. For now, that would have to be enough.

"Unless you want Dilys to claim the driver's seat," she said, "we'd better get downstairs."

"Thank you for that, too." At her questioning look, he said, "Making me smile. It feels good."

She reached up and kissed him. "Yes, it does. Alfred would approve."

DILYS DIDN'T WASTE any time once they returned to the stone house. She settled them in a room not far from Alfred's massive chamber and instructed them to come downstairs at five for supper. After that, they'd begin.

Neither of them had asked begin what.

After a supper of wine, cheese, bread, and soup, the latter prepared on a black iron coal stove in a kitchen only slightly less massive but far darker than the one back on Crystal Key, they ascended the stairs and walked the long hall back to the set of double doors.

"We must begin right away. These past days were spent revering the dead, as must be, but if we are to truly honor himself, we must now work ever harder to attain our goal." Dilys went around the room and lit the sconces. The yellow haloes illuminated the room, but didn't reach beyond the catwalk above their heads. "Sit there," she instructed, motioning to two stools near a table, cluttered with books.

They sat.

Dilys explained again about the role of the Keeper. Cai did his best to open his mind and try to embrace what she was saying as the truth. Even sitting in this remarkable room, it was difficult to grasp. A quick look at Jordy proved she wasn't having as much difficulty.

"Tomorrow morning, we will go over the steps you must take if you are to overcome Margaron. The time is drawing close I'm afraid. The confrontation is unavoidable."

"Do you think she knows we are here, in this house?" Jordy asked.

Dilys nodded. "Of that, I am certain."

Cai's skin prickled at her admission. Despite his loathing of law enforcement at the moment, he was tempted to find some way to contact the special agents on the case here in Britain. If Margaron was close, then how hard could it be to trap her? He schooled himself to be patient. All he had to do was go along with Dilys, follow her directions. At some point, it meant dealing directly with Margaron. That was all he needed.

Dilys pinned him with a dark look that had him straightening in his seat. "Do nothing foolish, Master Malacai. You would not dishonor your grandfather."

"No. Of course not."

She stared at him a moment longer, then waved her hand. "Off to bed with ye, then. Breakfast is at eight. We will work the rest of the day."

Relieved, Cai slid from his stool and walked with Jordy to the door. He was looking forward to curling up in the massive bed in their room. He desperately needed to lose himself in her.

"Ye'll need yer strength, Malacai, so make certain you sleep as well."

She couldn't have possibly read his thoughts, but his face colored nonetheless. "Yes, ma'am."

JORDY WOKE FIRST. Cai was sprawled facedown next to her, gloriously naked with his hair tousled on the pillow. She stroked a gentle hand down his back and reveled once again in the night they'd just shared. He'd been so needy and yet he'd done most of the giving. She loved him.

The revelation rocked her and yet she shouldn't have been surprised.

With slightly trembling fingers, she continued to trace the path of his spine. So much had happened to the two of them in such a relatively short time, perhaps she was confusing empathy—and incredible sex—for love.

But she didn't think so.

Love.

In love. She grinned, wanting to hug the feeling to herself, revel in it for a while without examining it.

Cai didn't stir. He was exhausted. He'd held it together incredibly well over the past few trying days, dealing with everything, and then the press as well. She'd been very proud of him, but she worried, too. Despite what he'd said in Anglesey, he'd closed a part of himself off from her. It was understandable with everything going on, but she'd still worried that he'd continue to pull away. Last night that had changed. He'd been more open with her than ever before.

In love. Was there a chance he felt it, too?

She couldn't sit still, but she couldn't disturb him either. He needed the rest.

She slipped from the bed, shivering even though the floor was covered with a thick rug and a fire still burned low in the grate. She dressed quickly and went downstairs, thinking she might help Dilys prepare breakfast.

There was no sign of her in the kitchen. Jordy thought she'd surprise them both and begin breakfast herself, but she had no idea how to use the stove. It couldn't be too complicated if she could just light the coal. But there were no matches about.

She wandered back to the grand foyer and peeked in the two rooms that were connected to it. Both had high ceilings, though nothing like Alfred's chamber. One was lined with bookshelves, but they were empty, as was the room, save for the rug on the floor and the heavy drapes on the tall window.

The other room had a large, bare fireplace and a grouping of furniture in the middle of the room, all underneath white sheets. It struck her then that the place wasn't dusty. If this was where Alfred had spent his time before coming to Crystal Key, than it had been closed up for twenty-some years. Jordy went to the window and pulled the draperies back. She gasped at the sight before her.

The sun was coming up over the mountain peaks. It was dazzling red, making a gorgeous backdrop to the pristine white snow that lay beneath it. She grabbed her coat from the rack in the hallway and slipped outside. It was freezing and she thought about going back in, but the sunrise was too beautiful to be viewed behind the thick, wavery panes of glass.

She wandered up a small footpath to the left of the house. The house was close to the peak and if she got to the top, the view would be spectacular.

The wind bit at her cheeks and ears and she flipped the collar of her coat up, then stuck her hands in her pockets. It was worth it. This sunrise was like a new beginning.

She thought of Alfred and the pain was still there. She missed him terribly, ached that he'd never see her dragon, that they'd never again walk in his gardens.

But when she looked at this sunrise, she wondered how many he'd seen, perhaps from this very spot, and she felt close to him again, as if he were right there next to her.

"I knew you'd come."

Jordy whirled around so fast she almost lost her footing. A woman in a dark cloak stood not ten yards away.

"Who are you? Where did you come from?" Had she

been so caught up in her thoughts she hadn't heard her approach?

"You know who I am." She stepped closer. "You shouldn't have left his side, you know." Her eyes glowed an unnatural shade of bottomless black. Her mouth curved in an evil smile.

Evil. A sick ball of fear formed deep in Jordy's gut. "Margaron."

THIRTY-SIX

CAI SAT BOLT upright in bed. Disoriented, coming out of a deep sleep, it took him a second to process what had awakened him.

He was alone.

"Jordy?"

No answer. The space next to him was cold. A look at the clock told him the sun had barely risen. She was probably downstairs talking to Dilys. Or, knowing Jordy, snooping in Alfred's chamber for the Pearl. That latter thought should have made him smile.

But it didn't. He'd smile again when he found out where she was.

He was pulling on his pants when there was a banging on his door.

"Master Malacai, come quick."

Dilys sounded frantic. Even more so than when she'd come to fetch them back to Alfred's side.

He flung the door open. Dilys' white face only jacked up his fear. "What is it? Where's Jordy?"

She clutched his arm. "Why did ye let her leave yer side? Oh, Master Malacai, she's got her, too. Dear merciful God."

His heart plunged to his toes. "Who has her?" he choked out. But he knew. It was what had woken him up.

"Margaron." Dilys was in a panic. "The poor sweet one. She's strong, but she won't stand up to it, Malacai. Margaron will have it in for her. She's a threat, she is. I should have cautioned you."

Cai took hold of her shoulders. "Stop it! Listen to me. Where is she, Dilys? Where is Margaron? No more games. You tell me and tell me now!"

"Ye canno' get to her. No' without the Pearl."

Cai shook her even harder, losing his control by the moment. She couldn't do to Jordy what she'd done to— No. He shut that down completely. It would destroy whatever chance he had to save her. "No more talk of Pearls and magic, Dilys. This is life and death. Jordy's. Do you hear me? If anything happens to her—Goddammit, tell me where Margaron is."

Cai's fury seemed to snap Dilys out of her panic. She wrested her arms from his grasp, her expression now every bit as fierce as his own. "She's in the ruins. Ye've been there. Did ye see her? She saw you. Ye tell me how to get to where she is, if not with magic?"

Cai pushed past Dilys and ran down the hallway. If Margaron were anywhere on the godforsaken mountain he would find her.

Dilys shouted, "If ye go off now, she will surely be lost. Margaron wants the Dark Pearl. It is yer bargaining power for getting Jordalyn back."

Feeling the cold sweat trickle down his neck, he turned back to her. "Where is it? Get it and let's go. You can give me instructions on the way."

"It's no' that simple."

"It is now," Cai stated. "I'll be in the car."

Dilys stood in the hallway.

Cai took the stairs to the foyer, grabbed the keys off the

table, and went to the door. It didn't open. He yanked, checked the lock, swore, pulled again, then stormed to the rear of the house through the kitchen. No door. By the time he reached the foyer, his fury was complete.

"Dilys!" The roar echoed up the stairs.

She stood calmly at the top of them. "Ye canno' leave without the Pearl. And ye canno' take what ye canno' see."

She descended the stairs with a small ornate trunk. About a foot long, half as tall and wide.

Cai was shaking. "Dilys, we can't waste time." His voice began to break and he used all his will to marshal it back under his control. "I can't let her suffer."

"Then you would be wise to listen to me."

There was anger in Dilys' voice.

"I'll do anything, just let's get on with it," Cai begged.

"You told your grandfather you wouldn't fail him. You canno' fail him in bringing down Margaron, and you canno' fail him in rescuing Jordalyn. For it is with her the future of the Keeper lies. Do you understand?"

Cai nodded, panic rising again within him.

"It's no' in your eyes. Ye'll say anything, make any promise, but they are hollow unless ye believe."

She was right, he was willing to do anything, say anything, to make it okay. But he couldn't force himself to believe in something just because he was told to. Even when Jordy's life was at stake.

He took a shaky breath and forced his clenched hands to uncurl. "I want to believe, Dilys. I want to do whatever I must to end this. I don't know what else I can do."

"Follow me." She turned to go back up the stairs.

"Dilys, we can't stay here."

She turned. "You wish to believe. Until you do, it matters not where we are, for Margaron will be unattainable. As will Jordalyn."

Rationality told him to batter down the front door if he

had to, to shatter the windowpanes, to escape this sudden asylum, and drive as fast as he could to the ruins. And yet, even if he could break free, would he be searching the ruins in vain? He had been there, and beyond that tumble of rocks, there was nowhere to hide. It was the hardest decision he'd ever had to make.

His thoughts battered, a cold chill crept into in his heart, and he turned to the stairs. He slowly took the first step.

Above him, Dilys smiled and nodded.

JORDY WOKE UP to darkness. It was cold. Damp. She rolled over slowly and instinctively swallowed the moan that came to her lips. She was stiff and sore. Probably from lying on the cold stone. For how long, she didn't know.

It was too dark to get her bearings, so she lay perfectly still and willed her eyes to adjust to her surroundings. But it was simply too dark.

She focused on recalling what had brought her here and an array of thoughts tumbled through her mind. One image stood out. Margaron.

She shivered and it had little to do with the chill in the air. She very slowly moved to a sitting position. She wasn't bound or shackled in any way. She seemed to be on the floor, since there didn't appear to be any end to what she sat upon. She reached out around her, but felt no walls either. She sat still, collecting her wits before making another move.

Margaron. Jordy remembered wondering how a smile that evil, and eyes that cold, could be a part of face so indescribably beautiful. Her features were perfection. Flawless lips, exquisite cheekbones, a high proud forehead, all framed with dark, thick hair that fell well past her shoulders. Stunning. Angelic. Had it not been for those eyes. And that smile.

She had walked toward her and Jordy remembered not being able to move. Margaron had reached out and touched her face. She recalled shuddering in revulsion, then Margaron's fingers had slid to her neck. She'd said something Jordy hadn't been able to understand, in Welsh perhaps? Then her world had gone dark.

It was still dark. Only she was awake now. And she had no idea where she was.

As her head cleared, she thought immediately of Cai. Oh God, he was probably panic-stricken. She would never forgive herself for putting him through the torture of this, and so soon after dealing with Alfred's death. She had to find some way out of here.

Wherever here was.

It was then she heard the moaning.

Even in her muddled state, she thought she knew what—or who—it was. One of Margaron's victims.

It was only then it fully struck her.

She was now one of those victims.

She ran her hands over her arms and legs, her face. But her aches and pains seemed to be muscle stiffness only. She recalled once again the empty light in Margaron's eyes and doubted she would suffer only this.

Tamping down the rising panic and blocking the images of those pictures, the tattooed piece of flesh—having only marginal success in either—she rolled to her knees and carefully, slowly, stood.

As long as she kept thinking, planning, doing something toward getting out of here, the terror wouldn't consume her.

The moan came again.

It sounded close by. She edged one foot forward and put out her hands. The dark was so damn disorienting she almost lost her balance. She closed her eyes and pretended she was in a well-lit room, walking across an uneven floor and trying not to bump into furniture. She clung to that vision and moved forward slowly. The room still seemed to sway beneath her feet, but she held her balance.

Her fingers and toes hit the bars at the same time.

She stilled. With great determination, she slowed her breathing with long deep breaths. Then she reached out her other hand and felt for what she knew was there. Prison bars.

She felt along them, hand to hand, bar to bar. The space between each bar was fairly wide, but not wide enough for her to squeeze through. Again, she felt the room spin and she was forced to stop. She rested her head against one bar and held on to the next. Her foot slid forward between them . . . and dropped down. Gasping, she pulled it back in, then knelt and reached her hand out, and down.

Nothing but air. She crawled along the bars, trying once again not to panic, and realized two things: there was no flooring beyond the bars, and her prison was round.

"If you lie still, the spinning will stop."

The roughly whispered words stilled her movements. Once she could hear beyond her own pounding heart, she chanced a response. "What spinning?"

A different voice answered. "Why, your bird cage, my finest canary."

And then it sounded as if a giant match had been struck, and the chamber glowed with the bright yellow light of fire.

She squinted against the sudden brightness, then slowly opened her eyes. She wished she hadn't.

What she could see now was too surreal to believe.

She was indeed in a cage, suspended by a heavy linked chain from the ceiling somewhere far above. The bars were heavy black iron. Suspended nearby were three others. Two of them inhabited. One form was curled into a small ball on the floor, unmoving. The other was kneeling, clothes torn and filthy, looking out of swollen, hollow eyes at Jordy.

It was the woman from the photos.

Shaking uncontrollably now, Jordy forced herself to look down. Margaron stood at the doorway. Two enormous torches were now lit on either side. The chamber was immense, very much like Alfred's. But there the similarity ended. Where Alfred's had looked like the chamber of some medieval chemist, this looked far more like the chamber of a medieval sadist.

And Jordy knew that was exactly what it was.

"You will not escape your pretty cage, my sweet."

Jordy didn't know where she found the courage, but she stood straight and looked down on Margaron. "Go to hell."

Margaron's smile faded. She didn't so much as blink, but there was a heavy jolt, then the sound of screeching metal.

Jordy was forced to grab the bars to say upright as her cage began to descend to the floor of the chamber.

"Time to clip your wings, my bold little bird."

THIRTY-SEVEN

DILYS SHOVED BOOKS aside and sat the trunk on a chest-high table. "Sit."

Cai didn't waste precious time arguing.

Dilys nodded. "Open the trunk."

Cai reached over and shifted the trunk around so the lock faced him. Even for a small trunk, he was surprised by its lightness. "It feels empty."

Dilys said only, "Open it."

There was a lock on the front hasp. Only, when he looked at it more closely, he realized it wasn't an ordinary lock. There was no keyhole, no combination dial. In fact, it looked more like an amulet of some kind.

"How am I supposed to open this?"

"Precisely."

"I don't have time for games, Dilys."

"This is no game, Master Malacai. Most problems in life can be resolved if one knows the right words to say."

"Abracadabra?"

Dilys' lips were tight with disapproval. "There is also something to be said for the sincerity with which the words are spoken. Empty vows are never a solution."

"Teach me what to say."

Dilys opened the book next to her. It looked almost

exactly like the incantations book they'd found the symbol in at home. He remembered what he'd thought about the handwriting in Alfred's notes. He turned the book around and looked at the words. The pages were yellowed, the edges ragged. The script looked handwritten in rusty brown ink. The words were in Welsh, or something like it. The handwriting was familiar.

"Did Alfred write this?"

For the first time that day, warmth entered Dilys' dark eyes. "Indeed, this is his work." She motioned to the shelves that ringed the room. "As are most of these."

Cai knew his expression was disbelieving. There were hundreds, possibly thousands, of books lining those shelves.

"His achievements in Arthurian lore were a small hobby, but one in which he took great pride," she went on. "These are his true life's work. These and the volumes of notes he left behind for you. For your son."

Cai couldn't think that far into the future right now, it was too much. So he simply nodded and said, "Teach me the words to the combination. I don't know how to pronounce these. You know Alfred gave up trying to teach me Welsh."

"That would have been helpful, but this is an ancient form that was influential in creating the language."

Impatience clawed at him. "Teach me to say them."

Dilys went over the words once, then several more times. Eventually she had him say them, one at a time, after her. He couldn't get the inflection and the guttural sounds right. He finally slapped the table. "Is this really necessary?"

Dilys slapped the table even harder. "Do ye think I'd put ye through this, let Mistress Jordalyn sit in that spawn's lair for one second if this weren't the only way?" She spun the trunk around to him. "Wrap your hand around the lock and speak the words. It matters more that they are from your heart, than that the inflection is just right."

Cai wrapped his hand around the amulet and read the words that he had now memorized. Nothing happened.

"Ye're reciting them as a schoolboy would his letters. Speak them and believe. Speak them as if your life depended on opening that box."

His life did depend on it. His mind went to Jordy, to wherever she was at this moment. He spoke the words again.

The amulet grew warm in his hand. He could see its glow seep out between his clenched fingers. It slid free of the hasp, then went dark and cold. He quickly opened the trunk. There was nothing inside but a thick bed of deep blue velvet.

He looked up at Dilys. "Where is it?"

"It's right there."

He blew out a harsh breath and swore. "Fine. Then get it and let's be going."

"Yer strong, loving heart was enough to open the box, but it is only yer mind that will let you wield the Pearl."

"It's enough that it's in here."

Dilys slid the trunk from his grasp, having correctly assumed he was about to take off with it. "One thing a true Keeper learns is that life is long, and patience is not only a virtue, but an intrinsic element of that life. You are not a Keeper. You do not have the luxury of hundreds, perhaps thousands, of years to learn the folly of impulse." She stood and somehow seemed to tower over him. "Sit down and heed my words and those of your grandfather. Do not again defy me, Master Malacai, or you will lose everything you hold dear. Everything."

The rage of impotence was there inside him, but he had

to manage his emotions. She was indeed his only hope. He couldn't afford to lose her.

"If I could wield the Dark Pearl, I would have done so. I have no Keeper's blood in me," she said. "It is not enough to open the trunk. Margaron believes. And she could wield the dark Pearl to the destruction of us all. Were you to carry this to her, how easily she would take from you what you cannot see. And once in her possession, all is lost. Jordalyn's life would only be the beginning of the suffering. She would consume you as well. And then there would be no future Keeper. Your grandfather, and the L'Baan's before him, would have spent their centuries on this earth for nothing because of the impatience of one arrogant mortal man." She stalked off into the shadows of the far side of the chamber.

Cai looked into the box. He thought about all his grandfather's ravings. It was impossible to grasp it, to wrap his mind around it. Somewhat like being asked to understand all the mysteries of the universe without any proof other than the stars twinkling above. He created fantasy, but believing it to be real was something else all together. He stared as hard as he could into the depths of the dark velvet, willing the Pearl to appear.

Nothing.

He stared harder. He thought of Jordy, let his heart go out, let the pain in, felt the fear, the terror, felt his throat burn and his heart break. Nothing.

He slammed both fists on the table, but he did not take his eyes off the interior of the box.

What do you want of me? he begged silently. His throat was raw from constriction against the tears of frustration that wanted to flow. He held them in check, allowing nothing to blur his single-minded determination to will the Pearl to appear. *I'll do whatever you want. Just end this torture, prove to me you exist. I'm here, I'm willing, what more can I do? Appear dammit!*

You must believe in it, Malacai.

He jerked his head up, but Alfred wasn't standing there. He'd heard the words as clearly as if Alfred were right there next to him. Anguish ripped through him. He was so exhausted now that his mind was playing cruel games on him as well.

He should leave, find the police. Get helicopters, search dogs, whatever they had at their disposal, and crawl all over that mountain until they found her hiding place.

He looked up, but Dilys was nowhere to be seen. He looked at the trunk, picked it up. He could leave, take this to the ruins. Have the police with him as well. Surely they could take her down.

Do not fail me, Malacai.

He pressed his hands to his head. Surely he was losing his mind. He was crazy from grief, from fear for Jordy.

And yet he knew he was not.

He looked into the trunk. It was still empty.

"Dilys." He spoke without taking his eyes off the blue velvet.

"Yes?" She spoke from just behind him.

"What do I have to do when I have the Pearl?"

"You cannot wield what you cannot see."

"Just tell me what to do, dammit!"

She said nothing for a moment, then, "You say nothing. You hold it in your hand and lift it out toward the force of evil. The energy within you, the belief in what is right, will transfer into the Pearl. The Pearl will project that, magnified beyond any mortal power."

"You said only a Keeper could wield it. I am not one."

"No, you are not. But you have the Keeper's blood in your veins. That and your will should be enough."

"If it stays here. If we do nothing, then what?"

"Then it will be only a matter of time before she comes to you. She knows you possess it now. You are not a Keeper, you cannot protect it. She will simply take it."

"Then why hasn't she? Why take Jordy?"

"Because she wants more than the Pearl. She wants you."

"Why? I am nothing."

"You may not be the Keeper, but only you can create him. Perhaps she wishes to be the one to carry that child. And the way to get you is through Jordalyn. Margaron, if she is like her grandmother, enjoys confrontation. She enjoys a grand display. And that is what she has set up here. She will wait for you. She knows you will come."

In his heart, whatever else he believed or did not, he knew this was Margaron's plan. He had only to think over her letters and know the truth of it. And still, the trunk was empty.

"I can't see it, Dilys."

"Ye didn't question the lock growing warm in yer hands, nor the glow it emitted. Nor did you question how it came off. Why?"

"It did what it was supposed to do. I didn't have time to question why."

"Ye heard him, earlier, did ye no'?"

He looked at her sharply. "Yes."

"How did ye know wha' I meant just now? That ye heard himself inside yer head. How did I know that?"

"You know every other damn thing. I just know you did."

Rather than get mad, she nodded in satisfaction. "That is how ye must think of the Pearl. You must 'just know' it will work, that it will be there when you call upon it, without questioning it."

Cai looked back to the trunk. "Maybe we have to take the trunk to her. Trust that it will be there when I need it."

He looked to her. "I don't know what else to do. I'm willing, Dilys. I will do anything I have to in order to free her, and the others, you know that. I can't sit here any longer."

She studied him, then nodded. "Perhaps you're right. Ye remember the words to open it?"

He nodded.

"Then it's time we go."

THIRTY-EIGHT

JORDY SQUEEZED THE bars and willed her legs to stop shaking and her heart to stop pounding as the cage touched the stone floor. She called on some deep reservoir of strength and did whatever she had to, to maintain eye contact with Margaron.

The beautiful young woman arched a perfectly sculpted brow and Jordy knew she'd surprised her. She moved on the advantage. She'd had all she ever wanted of being a pawn in someone else's game.

"You didn't have to take them," she said.

Margaron didn't pretend not to know what she meant. "Oh, yes, I did. I had to present Malacai with a challenge equal to his abilities."

"He's not a Keeper." Another surprise. Good. "He has no powers. He can't use the Dark Pearl. He doesn't even know where it is."

Margaron's expression hardened. "I see I have underestimated him. And his choice in mates."

Jordy forced a laugh. "I am nothing to him. We're just having a fling."

"You traveled halfway around the world with him. For a fling, as you call it?"

Jordy shrugged, even as she held on to the bars for continued support. She'd sat in that courtroom and watched
Suzanne work the jury as well as their friends and clients.
Maybe she'd picked up a pointer or two. "He has money. I
flew on the Concorde. I get to see the British Isles. Not a
bad fling if you ask me."

Margaron eyed her, but remained silent.

She had her thinking now. Jordy pressed on, careful not
to overplay her hand. "He had no idea about Alfred's past.
We didn't find out until it was too late. And even then, he
believed it was just a senile fantasy."

This provoked a livid scowl and Jordy braced herself.

Margaron remained where she stood. "He will not stand
by while you suffer. He will use that pathetic excuse for an
assistant Alfred had tagging along with him all those years.
She will help him, teach him."

Jordy lifted one shoulder. "Dilys? He thinks she's as
batty as Alfred. You know, he wasn't thrilled about what
you'd done with those other women. But he never thought
of this as a real quest. He called the police, he wanted them
to handle it."

"Yet, he is here," she raged. "He came to me!"

"He came to find his grandfather. We found him, we
buried him. We were preparing to go back home. Dilys
just wanted to take some of Alfred's things with her. Then
we were off to the airport."

"Liar!" The screech echoed off the chamber walls, elicit-
ing moans from above her head.

She'd gone too far. Margaron came closer. Her expression was murderous. Jordy tried hard not to cower.

"He will come for you, this I know. I've watched you
both. I've seen the way he looks at you. You have be-
witched him." She moved closer still, a sudden smile curving her lips. "But this will not last. Once he is with me,

you will be forgotten. He will realize that I am the one, the only one, with whom he can create the ultimate Keeper of the Pearl. The child will be mine. Then the power of the Pearl will be mine, too." An unholy light flickered in the depths of her black eyes. It made Jordy's flesh crawl.

Margaron reached out a long, elegant finger and touched first her cheek, then her chin.

"You play at being strong, my little canary. But you cannot mask the terror in your eyes." She looked down and the evil smile turned into a frown so ugly it marred even her perfect features. "Do you carry his bastard within you?"

Jordy stepped back then, but stopped short of protectively covering her stomach.

"He will not be the Keeper. If you planned to trap him that way, you will not. No mere mortal can produce the child I could." She ran her hand along the metal bar and a gate door that Jordy could have sworn was not there moments ago, swung open. "Come here."

"I am not pregnant."

"I will be the judge of that." She motioned to a table several feet away. There were heavy leather straps at the foot and the head of the bed. "Lie down."

Jordy began to shake in earnest then and no amount of will would stop it. Dear merciful God, what in the hell did she think she was going to do? "No, thanks."

Margaron looked amused.

Bluffing time was over. Jordy did the only thing left to do. She ran.

CAI DROVE TO the ruins, questioning Dilys the entire way. It had proven useless as she refused to tell him anything more. He stopped the car and got out, carrying the small trunk with him. Nothing had changed. It still felt empty. He hadn't known what he expected, but he felt a stab of disappointment and fear. Had he done something wrong?

"This way." Dilys picked her way up the rocky slope toward the remains.

"There is no one here."

"Do not trust only what your eyes can see. Your grandfather tried to explain that to you."

Cai swore under his breath, but moved up the slope after her. She stopped in front of the entrance.

Then Cai recalled the shimmering air, the strange feeling he'd had once before. "The symbols. What do they mean?"

"I cannot follow you in," was all she said.

"Why not?" In truth, he didn't want to put her in jeopardy, but she seemed to be the only one who knew what in the hell was going on. "I need you to guide me. I don't know what to do."

"Your heart will guide you. Remember, trust what is, act on it. Do not waste time seeking explanations where there are none." Dilys stepped closer and laid her hand on his chest. It was the first time he could ever recall her touching him. It stopped him from saying anything further. "You will succeed, but only if you have faith in yourself. And you must have faith in her as well. She is not weak."

"Margaron?"

"Jordalyn. You are a team. You are the future. You are not here to simply rescue her, or the others, although you must succeed in that endeavor as well. You are here to secure the future for us all." She reached up and kissed his cheek. "I have faith in you, Malacai. As does your grandfather. If you need him, he will be there for you. All you have to do is listen."

Cai could only nod. He was terrified. Terrified of failing Dilys, Alfred, the two women who were innocent victims in all this, and most of all he was of terrified of failing Jordy.

"Do not forget the words."

"I won't."

"Do not expose the Dark Pearl until the time is right. Wield it wisely. Never let it leave your possession. You will prevail."

"What do I do now?" Cai asked.

Dilys stepped back and motioned to the entrance. "Cross the portal."

Cai looked to it, then back to her. A blank look had come over her face and she slowly began reciting words.

Cai wasn't sure if he was supposed to wait for her to finish. She continued and he turned uncertainly toward the portal.

He stepped closer, placed his foot on the threshold. The air began to shimmer around him. He looked back at Dilys, who was still chanting. Her image was wavering and it was hard to see her. He faced forward and stepped fully inside. Everything went black.

Cai stood perfectly still. He was fully conscious, fully aware, but it was dark, completely dark. He looked behind him and he could still see Dilys standing just beyond the doorway. Oddly, the light from outside didn't filter in at all.

In. He was inside. The doorway was a real one, with walls on either side and a roof overhead. He reached out and felt the door itself. He looked to Dilys again, but if she could see him, she gave no indication. He swung the door shut. Instantly there was a glow of light. Yellow haloes similar to the ones in Alfred's stone house. He turned back to the room and noticed the sconces lining the walls. The room he was in was big and empty, more than a foyer, but seemingly unused. A hallway stretched before him, also lined with small dots of light.

He had no idea what sort of optical illusion could create the appearance of ruins where there was obviously still a building standing, but he did not question it. That was his mantra now. Don't question what is, just act.

Jordy was in here. There was no time to waste. He strode toward the hallway with the trunk tucked tightly under his arm. Should he practice opening it again, at least once, to make sure he could?

He continued down the hallway, keeping an eye open for any sign of Jordy. He noticed that there were no doorways off the hall and it ended abruptly at a wide door. He listened closely, then opened it. He entered a stairwell, with a short flight up and a longer one heading down. He could hear nothing. It was dark, but the glow from the hall showed a lantern on a hook. He used a wall sconce to light it, then held it up to see better.

Instinct told him if anyone were being held here, they were likely down below. He swallowed hard, and headed down. It was cold and dank, with a moldy smell in the air. He thought of the two women trapped in this place for weeks now and shuddered. And now Jordy was here as well. He moved faster, despite his continued doubts about taking on a madwoman with nothing more than an empty ancient trunk. Whatever it took, he was not leaving here without Jordy and the other two women.

The short hall ended at another door. It was massive and made of beamed wood with heavy hinges bolted across it. This was it. He felt it.

Do what you must to insure the future.

Alfred. Cai's hand stilled on the heavy iron handle.

Use the Dark Pearl wisely, but use it you must. There is evil beyond the door. Don't let it distract you from your ultimate goal.

It was as if his grandfather were standing just behind

him, talking into his ear. If he turned fast enough, he wondered if he'd see him.

Don't question it, just act, Cai repeated silently to himself.

He turned the handle and pushed the door open.

Nothing could have prepared him for what he saw.

THIRTY-NINE

H E'D WALKED INTO a living nightmare. He was
in a chamber, much like Alfred's, and yet nothing like
Alfred's. Alfred wouldn't have four cages, three suspended
from the ceiling, two with tortured victims trapped inside.

And Alfred wouldn't have tables filled with torturous
implements that would have made the Marquis de Sade
drool.

But most of all, Alfred would never have Jordy, clothes
torn apart, tied to a wooden slab, wrists and ankles
strapped helplessly apart.

A woman stood over her with her arm raised. She had
long black hair and wore a form-fitting dress of midnight
blue velvet that flowed to her ankles. It was the glint of
light bouncing off the silver blade she held that finally
snapped him out of his crippling horror.

"No!"

The woman's head snapped up. The intensity in her
dark eyes was demonic. But it was the smile that slowly
curved her lush lips that gave him his first real jolt of
sickening fear.

"I knew you'd come."

"Margaron." Cai didn't know which to focus on, her

. . . or the blade. He purposely didn't focus on Jordy, he couldn't, or he'd lose what little control he had left.

"Yes, my love. You're just in time."

Cai wanted to leap across the room and rip her throat out. The force of the hatred he felt stunned him. He couldn't let her see that. She was a delusional psychopath. An armed delusional psychopath. *Don't let the evil distract you.* He had to make each move very carefully.

"Just in time for what?" He forced the words out.

"Why, sterilizing her, of course."

He gagged on the acid that rose in his throat. It took an act of superhuman proportions for him to calmly say, "Why on earth would you do that?"

"She wants to carry your child. She insists she does not, but I have watched her. She has beguiled you. She wants what you could create inside her. The next Keeper." She stepped to the head of the table, away from Jordy's bared abdomen. "She tried to run." Her smile grew smug. "She has no idea of our power, does she?"

Cai clutched at the trunk to hide his trembling fingers. He was too far away to get to her before she could turn and plunge that knife into—

"She is not carrying my child," he ground out.

"When I am done, she never will." Margaron laughed, then. The perfectly pitched, musical sound made his skin crawl. "You know that I am the only one, Malacai. I forgive you this transgression, although I must say your appalling lack in taste somewhat disturbs me." She dangled the knife over Jordy's gagged mouth, then traced the tip down her throat and along one half-exposed breast. "How a man with your hungers can feast at such an abysmal offering of flesh and be remotely satisfied . . ." She lifted an elegant shoulder.

Cai's attention was riveted to the edge of the blade caressing Jordy's pale skin. Skin he had run his fingers and lips over, skin so soft and perfect it made him ache just to think about it. If she so much as pricked that skin, she would suffer the same and worse.

He dragged his attention away, willing his gaze to fix only on Margaron. One look into Jordy's eyes and he would lose it. If he was going to help her, save her, if he was ever going to hold her in his arms again, taste her, touch her, then he couldn't let himself think about her, about how much she meant to him.

Like a character he'd create in a novel, he would have to write himself a role to play. Only this time, pulling it off would be a matter of life or death.

He looked up at Margaron, who was studying him intently. He had a good idea of what she'd just seen on his face, so he purposely made himself smile. A grin as wide and wicked as he could create. With Jordy bound up not ten yards away, it was the hardest thing he'd ever done.

But if it was the dark sorcerer Margaron wanted, than that was exactly what he would give her.

He shut Jordy out, put himself in the story, and wrote his dialogue as he spoke it. "She was a distraction. I was bored. She was available." He shrugged. "You weren't."

Fury sparked her eyes and he wondered if he'd calculated wrong. She moved away from the table, toward him, and he had to stifle a sigh of relief.

"You knew where to find me," she said.

"I don't take commands well."

She stopped just in front of him. Her remarkable beauty struck him hard. How could someone so exquisite be so depraved?

"And yet you obeyed. You are here." She looked at the trunk, lips glistening as she moistened them. "And you've brought me the Dark Pearl."

"I am here because I am ready to claim my rightful place." He said a silent apology to Jordy and stepped closer to her. He looked directly into her mad black eyes and said, "I am ready to claim you."

He saw the spark of desire then, of surprise, and knew he'd chosen the right role.

"If you are truly my mate," he continued, "then you will do as *I* command, not the other way around."

She was clearly interested, but she raised a brow. "You are not the Keeper."

"I carry the seed."

Her eyes glowed.

"And I carry the Pearl. You are nothing to me and I am everything to you. You want what I have, and you will obey me," Cai said.

A tiny flicker of indecision marred her perfect countenance. She masked it quickly, but it was a chink in her armor he intended to exploit.

"You underestimate my power," she stated. "I can destroy you."

"Ah, but destroy me and it will end all your plans for the future."

"Open the trunk, I want to see it."

"I thought I made it clear. I don't respond to commands." He made another calculated move and turned his back on her. He strode across the room until he stood next to another table, situated directly beneath two of the cages. A third one rested on the stone floor a few yards away. Had she kept Jordy in there? He had to smooth the rage from his expression before turning back to face her. "Such archaic methods. And so unnecessary."

"I thought you would appreciate the challenge. You write of noble quests. I knew you'd find it amusing to think of yourself as the white knight."

Cai slapped the table hard, pleased to see her eyes widen in a moment of confusion. "I do not find it amusing to see innocents punished to satisfy your schoolgirl fantasies. Grow up, Margaron."

He held her gaze and watched her swallow hard. Fury dueled with desire and he wondered which would win. He didn't give her the time to decide.

"I will not tolerate your little games," he went on. "I came here expecting to find the woman who claims to be my equal and I find this . . . this . . . sophomoric display." He strode toward her. "Release them. You and I have business to get on with."

She regrouped faster than he'd expected. "Be warned. I don't take commands either, Malacai."

He snatched the blade from her hand before she could realize his intent. He dipped the tip of the blade into her plunging neckline. She gasped, but she stood still. He saw the heat of desire leap in her eyes. She would enjoy the pain he so badly wished to inflict on her. Sickened, he plunged the knife point down into the wooden table, inches from Jordy's thigh. He gripped her chin and pulled her face up to his. "Listen well. I came here to take you, to claim you. And I plan to enjoy this lush bounty you so willingly wish to give me. I will make you scream, Margaron." He dropped his hand and strode to the door. "But I will not do it with an audience." He turned to her. "When I take you, you will see only me."

It was the biggest gamble he'd ever taken. He walked out the door. He was ten paces down the hall when she called out.

"Yes, Malacai."

She'd hissed the words, but it was enough. He turned back. "Do it."

She leveled a finger at him. "Just know this. I will make you scream as well."

He was glad she turned her back to him then, because his revulsion for this game almost consumed him. His muscles cramped from the effort it took not to shake. He prayed silently as she unbuckled Jordy's arms and legs. She wasn't completely compliant, as she quickly rebound Jordy's wrists behind her and she kept the gag in her mouth. She dragged her roughly from the table and shoved her toward the door, doing nothing to cover her or adjust her torn clothing.

Come on, just walk out of here. Cai repeated the phrase over and over, but Jordy turned and looked up at the cages, waiting while they were lowered. It was all he could do not to drag her out of there to freedom and Dilys' waiting car, but he held his own.

The first cage was opened and Margaron roughly dragged the beaten woman from the cage. Her face was so disfigured, that Cai could no longer discern if she was the woman in the photo or not. That question was answered when the other cage was opened and Margaron kicked her toe at the human lump that was curled up inside. The lump moaned, but did not try to get up. Cai gagged when he saw the dried, bloody clothing stuck to her back. The tattooed flesh.

"I have not come this long way to be kept waiting," he said. "Untie her so she can carry that . . . thing out." His throat burned with the effort to stay in character.

The beaten woman crept to the other cage and tried to help the woman to her feet. She moaned and swayed to her knees, but it was clear she wouldn't make it on her own.

Cai strode back into the room. He was this close to victory, and he wasn't willing to relinquish his hold on the trunk in order to help carry the woman. He hadn't come this far to make a foolish gamble. He studiously avoided looking at Jordy and walked over to Margaron. "A little overexuberant, wouldn't you say?"

Margaron looked up at him, the mad gleam dancing

once again in her eyes. "With your creativity, I thought you'd find it clever."

"Clever, yes. Now it's merely inconvenient. Let's get on with this, shall we?" He nodded to Jordy. "Release her hands. Between the two of them, they should be able to get her out of here."

Margaron clearly wasn't happy with being ordered about. "I could rid us of their existence far more quickly."

Cai stilled for a split second. "We have far more interesting ways to spend our energies, don't you think?"

He swallowed another shaky sigh as she untied Jordy and shoved her toward the cage. Jordy and the other woman quickly hoisted the moaning woman between them and stumbled slowly to the door.

Jordy was still gagged but Cai felt her eyes on him. He purposely didn't look at her. If she had any ideas about trying to do anything other than getting the three of them the hell out of there, he was not going to encourage it.

At the door, Jordy made noises behind her gag and stopped. She motioned to the other woman, nodding, trying to make her understand while they struggled to hold the dead weight of the now unconscious woman between them.

Through a mouth so swollen it was hard to understand her words, the beaten woman said, "Where do we go?"

With a smug smile, Margaron looked at Cai and responded for him. "Down the hall, up the stairs, and out the main hall to the doorway. There will be an older woman waiting out there with a car. I care not what you do from there."

Cai said nothing and tried not to think about how she knew of Dilys' existence. With all her spying, she could have some vast system of surveillance cameras all over the place. He'd put nothing past her at this point.

"And I wouldn't advise that you rush to find help. Anyone returning to this place will find nothing but a pile of rocks." Margaron stepped closer to Cai and ran a possessive hand down his chest and cupped his groin. With a pointed look at Jordy, she said, "Besides, there is no longer anyone here requiring rescue."

FORTY

CAI WATCHED JORDY go, praying she and Dilys would leave and get those women to safety.

His job was not done yet, however.

Cai had no idea how he was going to end the threat she posed. He could just walk out, but that wouldn't stop her from starting this nightmare all over again. He'd have to restrain her somehow, then go get the authorities. If he could enter this place once, he could do it again.

Strapping her to that same slab and leaving her here indefinitely would give him great pleasure.

"Come with me," Margaron instructed. "It's finally our time."

He gripped her wrist and removed her hand, pulling it up between them. He was needlessly harsh with his grip, but he knew she would respond to pain with pleasure. "I don't wish to waste any more time."

"We can find our comfort upstairs."

He yanked her arm up behind her back, pressing her full breast tight against his chest. "I didn't think comfort was high on your list of needs."

Her eyes lit with approval. "You understand me better than I had anticipated."

"I will never understand you," he said. It was the easiest

line he'd scripted so far. "But then, complexity intrigues me. You understood I enjoyed a challenge. You just misjudged the sort." He nodded to the table Jordy had so recently departed. "Perhaps we can unveil some of those complexities right here." He pressed her back, biting his nails cruelly into her skin as he leaned into her body with his. "Or have I misjudged you as well?"

"No, you have not." If he'd thought her eyes demonic before, they were downright satanic now. "Put down the trunk. We will have time to revel in the powers of the Dark Pearl later." Her skin was flushed, her lips wet. "After you have bred me."

Her eyes were exclusively on him and Cai debated the wisdom of putting aside the very item she'd gone to so much trouble to get. She also wanted him. Or, more precisely, what she thought he could give her. Question was, which did she want more?

If he could just get her on the table . . .

"I want to see it, on your skin." He motioned to the thick slab of wood. "Lie back for me."

She arched her brow and raised a finger. "I said, put it down." She flicked her finger down and a sudden surge all but yanked the trunk from his hand.

Had his fingers not been locked around it from all the time spent gripping it so hard, he would have dropped it. As it was, he caught it to his stomach and held it with both hands. How had she done that?

Don't question it, just act.

He wasn't sure if he was hearing his words or Alfred's. Both voices echoed in his head.

He drilled her with a look. "I said, spread yourself for me."

She closed her eyes and murmured several words under her breath. The trunk slid from his hands to the floor.

She opened her eyes and laughed. "You not only don't

understand me, you underestimate me. I thought you were a believer."

He went for the trunk just as she flicked her finger upward. The trunk leapt to her outstretched hand. He went for it, but she held him back with a mere raised hand. As if a barrier had been erected between them, he could not move closer to her.

She narrowed her eyes. "Now, you spread yourself for me."

Things were happening too fast for Cai. Her sleight of hand trickery had cost him dearly, but he wasn't in this to lose. "It's empty," he said.

She laughed even more gaily. "To most people. But then, we both know you're not most people." She gripped the amulet and began to murmur the words. The amulet glowed, but she dropped it with a scream. The acrid smell of burning flesh filled the air. "What have you done to it? What spell have you put on it?"

"I am a mortal, remember? I cannot cast spells." But it was clear there was something more than stage magic going on here. *Don't ask for explanations where there are none.*

"Alfred. I knew he would reach me from beyond the grave." She flung the trunk at him and stalked across the room. She took a large blue glass bottle from a table and slid the stopper out. She poured something foul smelling on a piece of cotton batting and pressed it to her palm.

"The bastard thought he could change fate by reaching his claws out to my grandmother." Her laugh this time was cruel and cutting. "He stupidly thought she was capable of this. The old man, so lost in his mortal world of acclaim, smug in his safe little bubble he created to house the seed of his son. I could have told him my grandmother had weakened long ago." She peeled the cotton off and rinsed her palm with another solution, sucking in a breath, savoring the sting, before looking at him again. A slow smile curved her lips. "I surpassed Isolde long ago. She was no longer any use to me. Clinging, demanding, irritating. Alfred did us all a favor by bringing her sorry existence to an end."

"Alfred wouldn't kill anyone."

"That is where you're wrong. For the right reason, Alfred is capable of quite a few things I daresay would shock you. Have you not read any of his past works?" She chuckled. "You have sorely deprived yourself of quite an education." She walked back to him. "Pity you will not be able to avail yourself of them later. Right about now, that whole place should be a smoldering pile of stone rubble."

Any other time, Cai would have laughed incredulously at such a bald statement. Now he gripped her hair at the nape and yanked her head back. "What have you done?"

His actions only increased her delight. "Hedged my bets."

"Liar." She might be well-versed in any number of parlor tricks, but she wasn't capable of long-distance arson. Unless . . . "When did you take Jordy? From where?"

"Your door." She wrinkled her nose. "Fresh from your bed, from the smell of her."

Cai wanted nothing more than to yank her head back even harder, snap something. Disgusted, with her and with what she was capable of making him feel, he dropped his hand and walked several feet away.

"So, who is going to take whom?"

"You burn my grandfather's possessions and expect me to bed you? To plant my seed inside"—he gave her a derisive once-over—"this?"

Her hair seemed to lift away from her scalp, her face contorted in rage. "How dare you revile me."

"Quite easily."

"You'll pay for that." She raised her hand, but he raised his first.

"I'd be careful where you point that thing. I won't be of much use to you if you aren't careful. Though I confess I'm not all that enthusiastic about the chore any longer."

"Chore?" She fairly screeched the word. "No man can resist the pleasures I alone can offer."

"We'll see about that."

"Yes, we will."

He gestured to the table, prodding her. Goading her, as had been his intent all along.

"Not here. We will go upstairs."

He closed the distance between them and walked her backward until the table met her back. "We go nowhere. I will take you here, against the wall, if that is how it is to be. But I want this done and over. Now."

Her breath came rapidly. "So be it." She ran her finger-tips over the neckline of her dress and it dropped to the floor in a whispery heap. She was perfection. She turned his stomach. She placed a hand on his chest. "But answer me this. Can you open the trunk? Have you done it?"

He nodded.

"Prove it. Then I will show you the bliss that will be our future." She ran her hand down the length of his torso. She smiled up at him and curled her fingers around him. He felt nothing but revulsion. So, it came as a rather horrifying shock when her fingers vibrated lightly and he stirred beneath her touch.

Fear stirred within him, too. Just what in the hell had he let himself in for? That she had done . . . whatever the hell she'd just done, terrified him like no threat of torture could have.

"Open the trunk."

He was out of his league. He no longer knew what in the hell she truly was, but he knew that he didn't have what it took to beat her at her own game.

Open the trunk. Use the one weapon you have. Aim it at her heart.

Maybe he'd known from the beginning it would all come down to this.

It would all be decided on his ability to trust, to have faith. In Alfred. In Jordy. In what he could not understand.

In himself.

He moved back from her and shifted the trunk to face him. He wrapped his hand around the amulet. Now he purposely blocked Margaron from his mind. He thought of Jordy, of the many ways she challenged him. He thought of Alfred, and the many ways he challenged him still.

He didn't have to understand. He only had to believe.

He said the words, quietly, under his breath. The amulet glowed, the light seeped once again from between his clenched fingers. The amulet released.

He closed his eyes for a moment as he rested his hand on the lid. *It will be there. As it would have been for my father, as it has been for Alfred, and all the L'Baan men before him.*

The trunk grew heavier. He opened his eyes, and lifted the lid.

Nestled in the deep folds of blue velvet rested a black pearl. Immense in size, stunning in it's perfection and lustrous sheen. Cai was awed. Not by it's beauty, which was doubtlessly unsurpassed.

It existed. The Dark Pearl existed.

He didn't question it. He acted.

He lifted the Pearl and let the weight of it roll into his palm. It fit perfectly. As he somehow knew it would, should.

Margaron's sharp inhalation drew him back to his purpose. He looked at her. Her naked beauty would humble most men. He was not most men.

He lifted his hand and aimed the Pearl at her heart.

FORTY-ONE

J ORDY RESTED HER hand on the chamber door. Her head thrummed with pain where Margaron had struck her when she'd tried to run. She hadn't even seen what hit her. Her wrists and ankles stung and her body ached. Just thinking about that blade over her belly made her want to throw up. She had no idea what help she could be. But she could not leave Cai behind.

Dilys was gone. She'd taken the other two women to the closest medical facility. She'd begged Dilys to call the authorities. She'd agreed, but said, "By the time they arrive, what will be done, will have been done."

She had no idea what help they'd be anyway. As soon as she'd stepped through the entrance toward where Dilys stood, she was once again in the ruins.

She hadn't wasted time wondering about that, but demanded that Dilys get her back inside to help Cai. She'd been surprised that Dilys hadn't argued with her. She'd given Jordy her jacket to cover up in, and said nothing else, as if she'd known all along.

She'd stood behind her and instructed Jordy to simply walk through the entrance, then she'd begun chanting words softly, under her breath. The air had shimmered, and Jordy had stepped back into the gaslit hall.

Now she stood at the chamber door. She could hear no voices through it, so she carefully, slowly opened it.

Her hand flew to her mouth. He'd done it!

Cai held the Dark Pearl.

And a very naked Margaron beckoned to them both.

It was hard to draw her gaze away from the young woman. She seemed to radiate such exquisite perfection, that it was difficult not to simply stand there and reflect upon it. But the Dark Pearl surpassed even her beauty and drew Jordy into the room as if in a thrall.

"Let me hold it," Margaron commanded. "We will both hold it as you enter me. To ensure the passing of the right seed." She stepped forward.

Frowning, Cai continued to aim the Pearl at her.

"Come to me, Malacai. The time we have waited for is here. Now." She strode forward, hand outstretched.

Still frowning, Cai looked from the Dark Pearl to Margaron, seemingly transfixed. He shook his arm, his expression fierce, and yet nothing happened.

When Margaron was less than a step away, Jordy spoke.

"It's not your time, Margaron," Jordy said loudly. "Your time will never come."

Cai jerked his gaze to her. "Get out of here, Jordy. This isn't about you."

Margaron hadn't flinched in surprise, nor had she taken her eyes off the prize.

"This *is* about me." Jordy ran to him, stumbling on shaky legs. "This is about us."

Margaron made a grab for the Pearl, but Jordy leaped between them, knocking Cai's arm aside. He held on to the Pearl, but Margaron managed to grab Jordy's arms and throw her to the floor. She hit it far harder than seemed possible. Her head rang and pain sang up her arms as she broke the fall with her hands. Scraped and bruised, she didn't stay down, but rolled to her feet.

"You can do this, Cai," she said.

He didn't answer, and he didn't move. His expression was pure concentration and he held the Pearl as if his life depended on it. It very well might, she thought, gauging the dark look in Margaron's eyes.

"You won't win, Margaron. Not Cai, not the Pearl."

Margaron didn't take her eyes off the Pearl, but swung her arm wide and pointed at Jordy, who knew enough to duck.

Jordy came up behind Cai, using him as a shield, knowing Margaron wouldn't risk hurting him.

"Do it," she whispered to him.

"I can't," he said.

"Maybe not alone." She slipped beneath his arm. "But we can." Just as Margaron came at them, she reached out and placed her hand over the Pearl.

"NO!" Margaron's scream echoed through the chamber.

"Yes!" Cai's and Jordy's voices rang out in unison. Hands joined on the Pearl, they lifted it, but looked at each other. "Yes."

Margaron leaped at them, but as they repeated the vow, her body jerked hard and continued to spasm as she fell to the floor. She screamed in agony. "This will not be the end, Malacai," she growled. She managed to lift her head, her smile was pure evil joy, even as her body continued to writhe in unimaginable pain. "It won't end with me."

Her threat was blood chilling and Jordy began to falter. Cai locked his gaze on hers, willing her to go on. To finish this once and for all. The Pearl grew hot in their hands, but they held on. Both their arms shook with the strain.

The room fell suddenly silent.

And just as suddenly, they were standing amongst the ruins once again, as if the chamber never existed. Cold wind whistled through the winter air. Margaron lay, still and naked, at their feet.

They both shuddered not only from the cold, but also from the shock of what had just transpired. The Pearl cooled and Jordy finally released it. Cai's arm dropped to his side. He placed the Pearl in the trunk, then pulled her into his arms and held on as tightly as he had held on to the Pearl.

"Is she . . . dead?"

Cai went to bend down, but Jordy pulled him back. "It might be a trick of some kind."

"I have to know." He knelt and placed his fingers along the side of her neck. He looked up at Jordy and nodded. He pulled at the dress that was pooled beneath her legs and tossed the edges over her, covering most of her torso and head.

Jordy's heart clutched. "Dear God, what have we done?"

Cai stood and shook her arms. "You know we did the only thing we could. She wouldn't have let you walk out of here twice. Remember what she did to those women."

"But how did she die? What exactly just happened?"

Cai shook his head. "I don't know. I'm not sure we'll ever know. But I know it was right."

Jordy turned her face toward his chest. "Dilys took the two women to the closest medical facility. I don't imagine that's anywhere close to here, but she promised to call the authorities and send them out here." Jordy buried her head against him. "Thank God you're okay."

He lifted her chin. "Are you okay? Did she— Did she do anything to you, Jordy?"

She shook her head, tears clinging to her lashes. "No. I'm okay. I'm okay."

Cai walked several yards away and put the trunk on a rock, then pulled her tightly to him with both arms.

"The Pearl—"

"Has done it's job. I thought I was going to lose it completely when you came back, Jordy."

"I had to, Cai. I promised Alfred I wouldn't fail you. I couldn't leave you to do this alone."

Just then two cars rounded the bend and came to an abrupt stop. Three men emerged, guns drawn.

Cai pulled Jordy behind him and raised his arms. "Don't shoot, we're unarmed."

The men pulled back, but kept their weapons out. "Are you L'Baan?"

Cai nodded.

The men lowered their guns. One stepped forward. "I'm Special Officer Davies. We're with a task force, adjunct to CID. We're working with an Agent Kuhn over in the States." He knelt and checked out Margaron, giving a quick shake of his head to the other two officers. "Is this the kidnapper?"

Cai nodded.

"What happened?"

"She took Jordy this morning, while she was out walking. I . . . I was able to follow her here."

"You're saying she had the victims here?"

He nodded. Jordy shivered under his arm. "Listen, it's cold and she's had a rough time. I'd like to have her checked out."

"We'll take care of all that, but we'd appreciate a few more answers." He tipped his head to Jordy. "With your understanding, ma'am."

Jordy nodded shakily. "She said she was Isolde Morgan's granddaughter. That's why she came here. It's family property. She had the other two women with her. Have you talked to them?"

Cai caught her gaze and squeezed her. Neither of them was going to tell tales of shimmering air and medieval torture chambers, but they couldn't control what the other two women said.

"We have men with them right now. I only know what I

got over phone, but one of them is in pretty bad shape. Hasn't regained consciousness."

Jordy shuddered at the news. Cai was right. It would only have got worse.

"The other seems pretty confused," Davies went on. "She hasn't been able to give a clear account."

The officer checking out Margaron spoke. "No gunshots, no apparent blunt force trauma."

"How did she die?" Davies asked. "And can you explain how she came to end up like this?" He was obviously referring to her state of undress.

Jordy spoke up. "Dilys had come with Cai. She took the other two women down to the medical facility when Cai got her to release us. He traded himself for us. She was delusional and thought Cai was a character from one of his books. When Cai told her they could never be together, that he and I were lovers, she stripped off her clothes, trying to seduce him. Then, she had some sort of seizure and collapsed. You got here minutes after it happened."

Davies looked to the other officer, who nodded. "She's still warm. No rigor."

Just then another car pulled up. Dilys climbed out and ran toward them as quickly as the rocky ground would allow. She hugged a surprised Cai first, then Jordy. "So, it's done." She'd spoken so only they could hear her.

"How are the other women?" Jordy asked her.

"They're being seen to," she said. "It doesn't look good for the one, but the other will do okay. She won't remember much."

Cai shot Dilys a hard look, but all he said was, "Have you been to the house? Margaron said she'd burned it."

"The house is fine." Her smile was smug. "It's well protected, even in Alfred's absence."

Davies stepped in and motioned Cai and Jordy away

from the body. Dilys moved a few feet, but remained closer to the other officers, watching their activity.

"We'll need to question you more thoroughly once we've had you checked out," Davies said, escorting them to the car. "She said she was related to Isolde Morgan?" When they nodded, he shook his head. "She had a connection to your grandfather, didn't she?"

Cai nodded. "She was a critic that reviewed his work."

"Odd that they both died on the same day." He tipped his hat to Cai. "My condolences."

"Thank you. This whole thing took a toll on my grandfather. Perhaps it did on Ms. Morgan as well."

"True. If this one really was her granddaughter, then I imagine the strain of dealing with one such as her might have been enough to put her over." He opened the car door. "Here we go."

As Davies walked to the other side of the car to talk to the other officer who had come with Dilys, Jordy tugged on Cai's coat sleeve. "What about the trunk?"

Cai jerked his head around. The trunk was no longer on the rock where he'd placed it. "Get in. I'll be right back."

"No. I'm not leaving your side."

Davies looked up as they moved away from the car.

"I'm just getting Dilys. Is it okay for her to come in with us?"

He nodded. "We'll have questions for her as well."

Dilys stepped toward them keeping herself between them and Margaron's body. "Alfred is resting peacefully now," she said. "It's proud ye should be of what ye've done."

Jordy's heart skipped a beat and her eyes stung again. She felt Cai tense beside her. "Where is the trunk?"

She smiled at him. "Why do ye ask me?"

Cai held her gaze. "Because I just know it, okay?"

"As well ye should by now." Her smile faded. "Still

there are questions within ye." She sighed. "I suppose for some, that is the way of it." Surprisingly, she patted his arm. "The Dark Pearl is where it should be. We'll speak of it again when the time is right."

"That's precisely what I'm afraid of."

Dilys merely tsked. "Your time will come, Master Malacai." She took their elbows and gently urged them toward the car. She cast one last look at Margaron's body, a satisfied smile briefly crossing her face. "Come now, we must answer the good gentlemen's questions and leave these men to their duty. It will all work out as it should."

FORTY-TWO

CAI THOUGHT HE had never seen anything as beautiful as Crystal Key. He chugged the boat slowly toward the dock, wanting to savor every tiny detail.

"It feels like we left a lifetime ago," Jordy said.

The clutch in his heart wasn't new. He'd been living with it for a few weeks now. He'd be living with it for the rest of his life. "It was a lifetime ago," he said quietly. "A whole different lifetime."

Jordy stood behind him and threaded her arms around his waist as he steered the boat gently against the pilings. "I miss him, too. I'll help whatever way I can."

Don't leave me then.

Their last seventy-two hours in Wales had been one long marathon with the special CID guys, and via phone with a very pissed off Kuhn. Most of that time they'd spent apart.

Jordy had been taken in for thorough medical examination and she'd stayed to talk to Claire, the beaten woman from the photographs. The other woman, Judith Sumner, hadn't pulled through. Both women were single, lived in nearby areas, had friends and coworkers, but no family. Both belonged to a mail-order book club and had, over time, ordered all of Cai's books. Margaron had made her selections carefully.

Jordy and Cai, along with Claire, had helped to arrange Judith's funeral. Margaron's cause of death was a mystery. Results hadn't come back on the autopsy, but early reports said it looked like a heart attack, possibly a congenital defect of some kind. The agents never found proof that she was Isolde's granddaughter, nor did they find where she'd hidden her victims before their final rendezvous at the ruins. Dilys had predicted correctly though. Claire's memory was vague on her whereabouts during her captivity. Jordy and Cai stuck to their story and after repeated, separate accountings of every minute detail, the agents had closed the case.

Cai hadn't talked about the whole thing much with Jordy, both of them having exhaustively talked of nothing else to the CID. Jordy had seemed to begin to come to terms with her role in Margaron's death. Standing beside Claire as they lowered Judith's casket into the ground seemed to help her move a bit more quickly along that path.

They had been cleared to go home just a little over twenty-four hours ago. Dilys had stayed behind, claiming she wanted to visit some old friends. Cai had to wonder if she wasn't just postponing coming back to Crystal Key because of Alfred. He wondered if she wouldn't end up staying in Wales permanently. He couldn't blame her, but selfishly, he was hoping otherwise. He wasn't ready to be all alone. He wasn't sure he'd ever be ready.

He also was in no shape to make any further life-altering decisions. He knew Jordy's time was almost up and she'd have to return to Virginia.

But he had no idea how he was going to survive letting her go.

At the dock, Jordy handed Fred up to Cai, then their bags, then took his hand up. She looked at the house and felt equal parts anticipation and trepidation. She was surprised how much it felt like coming home. But home was Virginia, not Crystal Key. Cai was no longer tied here in order to care for his grandfather. She wondered what plans he might make with his new-found freedom. Or would he remain here, and stay as reclusive as Alfred had been? And did any of those plans include her?

She picked up her bags as Cai shouldered his and glanced up at him. The last few days had been rough. Hell, the last week had been no picnic. They hadn't done much more than fall asleep together and both of them had slept most of the flight home. He hadn't said anything to her about his expectations for the two of them, or where they would go from this point. Honestly, she didn't know either. She had work to finish here. Cai had said that much. He would honor Alfred's commission. He wanted the piece finished. Jordy was glad for that, and for the small reprieve that gave them both.

She had felt a bit hollow, but now that she was here, with the warm sun shining down on her, she felt the beginnings of rejuvenation. She had a little time before she had to be back in Virginia. Maybe they'd both find some answers by then.

They went in through the kitchen door. Cai paused, then flipped on the lights. Jordy hadn't missed the slight stiffening of his shoulders. She wanted to help, she wanted to smooth the way for him. "I guess we're eating pizza until Dilys comes back, huh?"

Cai smiled, but it didn't reach his eyes. "I hadn't thought about that. You figure she's put some sort of spell on the appliances so they'll only work for her?"

Jordy was surprised by the reference. He'd made no mention of what had really happened in Wales. It was as if, after repeating their story so many times for the agents, he'd come to believe it himself. Maybe, now that they were home, he'd deal with it. She kept the mood light. "I wouldn't put it past her. God knows what we'll find in her spice rack."

Cai just stood there, bags in his hands, staring as if he'd never seen the room before. And maybe he hadn't. Now it was his kitchen. His house. His gardens. He looked a little lost and her heart began to break.

"Why don't we go and unpack. I'm guessing we'll need an incantation to make the washing machine work, too." She paused by his side and gently touched his arm.

"It's all so different. I didn't think it would be. Or maybe I just needed it not to be."

"Give yourself some time, Cai. You just got home."

"Yeah." He shouldered the bags up a bit higher and motioned for her to go ahead of him. "Why don't we meet back down here. We'll figure something out for dinner."

She wanted to drop her bags and take him in her arms. She wanted to kiss him softly and stroke his face and tell him everything was going to be okay. She wanted to ravish him, take him hard and fast, right here on the floor, and obliterate the pain from those too soft gray eyes.

What she did was nod. "About thirty minutes? I could use a shower. Wash the airplane ride out of my hair." It was on the tip of her tongue to invite him to join her. If he'd so much as looked at her, she would have. But he only nodded vacantly, his thoughts still miles away. Or a few weeks in the past.

Balancing Fred in one hand and a bag on each shoulder, she went upstairs to her room.

DINNER THAT NIGHT was a quiet affair. Cai had thawed a couple of steaks and grilled them along with a few potatoes. Jordy thawed out some frozen vegetables, put them in the microwave, and heated a tray of dinner rolls. They ate out on the lanai.

She waited for Cai to begin a conversation, but he was lost in his thoughts. Almost finished with their meal, she couldn't stand the silence any longer. "It's hard to believe it was only a month or so ago that I met your grandfather. I remember thinking what a lovely place this was, so peaceful and beautiful."

Cai nodded.

Jordy swallowed a sigh. Maybe she was pushing for too much, too soon. "I was thinking I'd like to go out and check on the cottage this evening if that's okay with you. Make sure the clay hasn't dried out, that sort of thing."

"Sure, fine. I have some calls to make." He tossed his napkin on his plate and stood. "Let's just put these in the sink. I'll deal with them later."

He wasn't even looking at her. Jordy said nothing.

They carried their dishes in, then he headed to the hallway toward his office. She really felt like she was intruding, and maybe she was, but dammit, the very least he could do was talk to her. He'd already made it clear he expected her to stay and finish the dragon.

And he might want to pretend the whole thing hadn't happened, but when they'd joined hands on that Pearl, she'd known there was a bond between them that no other could match. And he had felt it too, dammit! She'd seen the look on his face when she'd come back, and she'd watched him risk his life to save her.

She was trying not to feel hurt, or abandoned, to be understanding of what was going through his mind. But she wished he'd turn to her for help, instead of sealing himself off like this. Maybe he just needed some time.

She wished she could believe that was all it was.

"Any idea how long you'll be?" she asked.

He stopped at the door. "An hour or two at least."

"Fine." But she was talking to his back.

IT WAS ALMOST midnight when she finally came back inside. She hadn't meant to stay out there so long, but she'd peeled back the plastic and been seduced into just doing one or two minor touches. That had led to one or two more, and before she knew it, she was in her zone, oblivious to the world. She was glad for it though. Not only had it kept her from brooding about Cai, but it had made her feel closer to Alfred.

Her satisfied smile faded when she noticed Cai's light still glowing from his office window. She'd been hoping to find him out on the deck, or on the dock. While she worked she'd also decided that she wasn't going to just sit back and let him make the calls. The days where she danced to someone else's tune were over.

When she got to the office door, she paused just before knocking. She heard the steady tapping of computer keys. Was he working or just clearing up business stuff that had accumulated while they'd been out of the country? He didn't talk much about his work, but she'd had the feeling that things hadn't been going all that smoothly. Not that she could blame him. Maybe she should leave him to his work. After all, she'd found solace in hers, it was likely his writing would provide the same thing for him.

She turned away just as the typing stopped. She heard a deep sigh and the chair creaking. Just as she was about to second guess her decision, the typing started again. With a sigh of her own, she walked toward her bedroom. She paused at his bedroom door and contemplated waiting for him there. They had slept together every night for several weeks now. But in Wales it hadn't been the same. It had been sleeping, and occasionally clinging to one another.

She wondered now if he still needed that bond, that reassurance.

She walked on to her own door and made the unsettling realization that *she* did. She didn't want to sleep alone. Ever again.

She closed the door behind her, fed Fred, stripped down, and slipped into bed.

CAI'S FINGERS FLEW over the keys. His conscious mind was well lost in the sorcerer's world he'd begun in *The Quest for the Dark Pearl.* He'd contemplated calling Eileen and asking if there was any way he could alter the title or get out of doing the remainder of the series. It was a painful remainder of something he'd rather not think about excessively. Alfred was gone, Dilys was on vacation, and the nightmare had come to an end. He didn't need to seek explanations for things that likely had none. It was better left forgotten, part of his past.

But he knew his commitment to the series of books would have to be honored. He hadn't called Eileen. Instead, he'd opened the file of the last chapter he'd been working on, and reread his work. He'd trashed half of it, then begun reworking what was left. Before long he was lost in his work. It felt so good to find that place again, that one place where everything else ceased to exist but the words on the page and the corresponding images in his head.

He gave into it willingly, with a sense of relief so profound, he didn't question it.

He worked well into the night, stopping to brew coffee in the pot he kept in his office, then kept on going. His eyes grew scratchy, his shoulders stiff, and his wrists numb, but he never stopped. If he stopped, he'd have to think. About Alfred, about what had really happened in Wales, about Dilys' defection. About Jordy and his feelings for her.

About what in the hell he was going to do with his life now that the only person he had to consider was himself.

He was still typing when the sun broke the horizon.

FORTY-THREE

FIVE DAYS PASSED, and five nights, and Jordy was still just as confused as when they'd stepped off the boat. She worked all day, Cai worked long into the night. They hadn't slept together once. Hell, they were lucky to do more than grunt at each other as they passed in the kitchen to grab something edible before heading to bed or back to work.

Jordy poured her frustration and pent-up emotions into her work, damning herself for returning to a routine she'd sworn she wouldn't fall into. But Cai had closed himself off, and after spending the first three days making excuses for him and herself, she'd finally been forced to admit the truth. She was scared.

If she confronted him like she wanted to and forced him to deal with all the issues left unresolved between them, she had the feeling he'd retreat even further away from her. So she told herself he just needed more time to find his way out of his grief, to come to terms with what he wanted. And she prayed like hell she was part of that. But as three days turned into four, and four into five, and the calendar told her she had very little time left before she had to go back to her apartment or lose it to another tenant, she knew she was going to have to conquer her fears and speak up soon. Or she was going to lose him anyway.

And soon was right now. The dragon was done.

She rolled her shoulders and stood. It had to dry and be fired, then she had to apply the finish, but the dragon existed now. She smiled, then pumped her fists.

"Thank you, Alfred. He's beautiful, isn't he?" She wouldn't have been in the least surprised if he'd answered her, but the air was silent. Still, she knew he approved. It was the best work she'd ever done.

She washed her hands and cleaned her tools and carefully put away a week's worth of clutter. She was done. Her work on Crystal Key was completed. Alfred had talked about other commissions, but she wouldn't allow Cai to honor them. Alfred had already done everything for her. He'd given her back her life. A life Cai apparently didn't want to be a part of.

She swallowed the pain and focused on the positive. After all, that's what she'd come down here to find. She'd have laughed at that if her throat hadn't been so tight.

Photos, she thought, forcing her mind to the task. She'd take photos of the dragon. She had done the same for many of her pieces, or Suzanne had, but she would use them, too. She would pull them together and create a portfolio, with the dragon as her centerpiece. She would go out, haunt the galleries in Richmond, and Washington, D.C., if she had to, hound anyone who'd listen to her. It only took one yes, one person who'd believe in her enough to commission one piece. And one piece would lead to another. It would take time, probably a long time, but she had plenty of that. Her own studio was a long way off. And she'd have to get a part-time job somewhere, something to keep her in macaroni and cheese and Fred his fish flakes.

She closed the cottage door and headed to the house. It

was now or never. There was nothing keeping her on Crystal Key. It was time for her to go home.

Unless he asked her to stay.

She opened the door to the house, terrified he wouldn't, terrified he would.

He wasn't in the kitchen and he wasn't in his bedroom. She didn't hear the shower either. She'd already been past his office. The door was open, the lights were off. She checked the dock, she even checked her own room. Empty.

"Where is he, Fred?"

Fred was too busy swallowing his flakes to respond. She smiled. Fred seemed to be a bit rounder now that all was right-side-up with his world. Fat and happy. "Some fish have all the luck."

She wandered out to the hallway. There was only one other place he could be.

CAI DIDN'T LOOK up when the door to Alfred's office opened. He was sitting behind Alfred's desk, in his chair, staring at his typewriter. He hadn't touched a thing. He wasn't certain when or if he would. Perhaps this was better left for Dilys. He still felt unwelcome here. Fifty years could pass, a hundred, and this would still be Alfred's domain—only his.

Jordy didn't wait for his invitation. She came in and quietly began looking at the framed photos and newspaper accounts that covered the opposite wall.

He found his attention drawn away from his memories, his fears, his grief, drawn instead to the woman in front of him. He'd been avoiding her. Avoiding making the decision of what came next. And she'd let him do it. She was probably hurt. Maybe angry as hell.

Or worse, she didn't care at all.

She'd seemed as easily caught up in her work as he had

been in his. Maybe he'd been hoping she'd make the decision for him. Maybe that was precisely why she was here now. He wasn't ready.

He wasn't ready to say good-bye to someone else he loved. It would rip him to pieces.

And yet he sat there, silent. Unable to open his mouth and tell her he loved her. Unable to ask her to change her plans, change her dreams, and stay here with him.

He told himself he was being unselfish. That because he truly loved her, he was letting her follow her dreams without the burden of his own. But he was a coward. He was hurting. He was confused. He was in love. A hell of a combination.

"Your grandfather accomplished more in his last eighty years than some men could in three lifetimes."

His *last* eighty years. Was she going to go there, then? Was she going to force a discussion of what had happened in that dank chamber in Wales? Already it seemed like some long-ago nightmare to him, surreal and fictional. Except the images that haunted him in his sleep, of Jordy strapped to that table, a glinting blade suspended over her abdomen, were all too real. In that nightmare, he didn't always make it in time. His indecision costing her life.

He didn't need a course in Jung or Freud to analyze the meaning of that one.

She turned abruptly and sat down in the wing-backed chair. "I finished the dragon."

If it were possible, he stilled further. "You what?"

"I'm finished." She grinned. It was cocky and bold and it made his entire body ache. "It's pretty damn good, too. It has to dry yet, and there are several more time-consuming stages, but the sculpting is done."

"How long will the rest take?" His palms were sweating.

"Several weeks at least, perhaps longer. I'm going to have to ship it to Virginia and have it fired there."

"Virginia." So this was it. This was what his indecision was going to cost him. Every last thing he had.

She nodded. "I'll want your approval first, of course, since you'll be the one making the final payment on it. And I'll need you to sign a few forms stating you won't mind if I use photos of the piece in the promotional literature I plan to put together."

"Promotional material?" The last part of his life was crumbling before his eyes and all he could do was parrot her like an idiot.

"Yes. I'm going to use photos of the dragon as the centerpiece of a portfolio I'm planning to put together as a showcase of my previous work. That way I can begin to solicit commissions right away, instead of working on actual pieces first, pieces that might not sell. If I get even one gallery or shop interested, it will be a start."

He was angry. No, he was mad as hell. In fact, he was furious. How dare she have plans? How dare she have been sitting out there in that cottage, blithely planning her entire future? A future that didn't include him.

Because you're a goddamn moronic coward, that's why.

"Jordy—"

Her eyes lit up and she shifted forward. "Yes?"

"I . . ." She'd made plans. She'd told him all along she was going home. It shouldn't be so goddamn shocking. It shouldn't be so shattering. And he had no right, not one single right, to ask her to change any of them. This was what she'd wanted. To return home strong and whole and ready to kick ass. "Congratulations. I know how much this means to you. I know Alfred would have prized that dragon. I—" He stood and reached out his hand. "I wish you the very best of luck. I know you're going to go back and show them all how tough and special you are." He should leave it at that, but he couldn't. "Personally, I don't think they deserve you or the art you create. They didn't stand by you when it counted. But I know it means a lot to you. You deserve all the success I know you're going to achieve."

Her brows gathered together. "What did you just say?" She stood and stalked to the opposite side of his desk and all but spit at his extended hand. "Are you really serious? You want to shake hands? Shake hands!" She slapped his hand away. "How dare you. How dare you be all polite and conciliatory."

"You made plans. They obviously didn't include me. I'm trying to do the right thing."

"The right thing? I made plans because you seemed to want a life by yourself. You shut me totally out. What the hell was I supposed to do?"

"What do you want me to do, Jordy? You've said all along you were going home."

"Oh, no, you're not getting off that easily."

Now he was mad. "Easy? You think letting you go is easy?"

"Well, it sure as hell seems to be." She took a shaky breath and her eyes grew suspiciously bright. "Let me ask you something. What in the hell happened in Wales, huh? Where is the man that held me all night long? Where is the man that made sweet, incredible love to me in that stone house? Where is the man who pretended to be a dark sorcerer to save my life?" She smacked the desk with both palms. "Where in the hell is the man I fell in love with? Where did he go?" Tears gathered in her eyes now and she dashed them angrily away. "I want that man back." She spun around and growled. "God, I hate it when I cry."

Cai was around the desk and pulling her into his arms before his heart could leave his throat.

She pounded on him and he let her.

"Don't let these tears fool you," she ground out between huge gulps of air. "I'm mad as hell and I'm not going to take this lying down. Do you hear me?"

"Perfectly." He gripped her chin and held it so she was forced to look at him. "I love you, Jordalyn Decker."

"Yeah, well, I know you're grieving, but I don't want to hear about— What did you just say?"

"No. It's your turn to repeat it first. I want to hear you say it when you're not screaming it at me."

"I've fallen in love with you," she said fiercely, defensively. Then reached up and gently stroked his face. "I love you, Malacai L'Baan."

"I love you, too."

She wiped her eyes. "But you were going to shake my hand and let me walk out of your life? You weren't going to even ask me if I'd stay?"

"You could have asked me to come with you." That stopped her.

"Would you have?"

"Would you stay here if I asked you to?"

"You just lost your grandfather. You have a whole new life, with only your own desires to limit your choices. I wasn't sure I fit in that picture."

"Exactly. You've planned your triumphant return to Warburg since you got here. How could I ask you to change that? But I can't say my motives were completely selfless. In fact, I'd have asked you in a heartbeat, completely and totally selfishly. But I was afraid you'd say no."

"Would you have come if I'd asked?"

"I would have followed you to the ends of the earth. I can write anywhere. Would you have stayed?"

She sobered and he hated the tiny thread of doubt that wove back into his heart. "Something you said, just before you insulted me with that handshake thing, jolted me."

"Which conciliatory polite thing would that be?"

She grinned, which relieved him greatly. "I'm serious. You said the people of Warburg hadn't stood by me when it counted and that they didn't deserve to benefit from all my hard work."

"I know it means a lot to you to go back there, but yes, I believe that."

"I think you make a lot of sense."

"I do? I mean, yes, I do. You should listen to me."

"Maybe you should tell me what you're thinking more often."

He bent down and kissed her soundly and deeply on the lips. "I promise I will, if you will."

"I really love you, Malacai L'Baan, that's what I think." She kissed him hard. "Now it's your turn."

It took him a moment to regroup. "Are you sure?"

Her eyebrows lifted at his provocative tone and she smiled, then frowned, then smiled again. "I think I am. Yes. Yes. I'm certain. Go ahead."

"Well . . . I think you should contact Eileen and get her to put together a list of possible agents. Not literary agents, but I'm sure she has some contacts in the art world in New York City. I say to hell with Warburg, you should shoot for the stars."

Obviously insulted, Jordy said, "That's what you were thinking? About calling Eileen?"

"Yeah. Why, what did you think I was thinking?"

"Well, I thought you were going to ask me to—"

"What?"

"Never mind."

"Say it. You have to say it."

"Fine. I thought you were going to ask me to marry you or something ridiculous like that and if you laugh at me I'm going to knee you."

"So, are you asking me then?"

"Asking you?"

"Yes. Are you asking me to marry you?"

She started to respond, then paused, calculating. "If I did, would you say yes?"

He grinned. "What do you think?"

She smacked his chest, then yanked his face down to hers. "I think you'd better say yes, then I think you'd better take me upstairs and make love to me until neither of us can think straight. Besides, sleeping alone sucks."

He scooped her up in his arms. "Jordy Decker, I like the way you think."

She laughed and threw her arms around his neck. "Is that a yes?"

"I think so."

EPILOGUE

Two years later . . .

Jordy stood and stretched, rubbing her lower back. She swore she was carrying this baby between her knees. She smiled at the piece she'd just finished. The bronze patina was perfect. Her agent, Leonore, was going to flip when she saw it. It would be the centerpiece of the show. But it wouldn't be for sale. This one was personal. This one was for Cai.

She rubbed her tummy and swallowed her trepidation. Her first New York show was still four months away, but with the baby due any day, she hadn't thought she'd finish in time. Eileen had picked a winner with Leonore. And this time, Jordy kept her hands in all avenues of her career and was enjoying it. But with the baby coming, she'd begun to worry how she'd handle it all. Her agent had been great, telling her to relax and enjoy nesting, that the pieces already done were enough.

"But wait until she sees you."

Just then a tight pain wrapped the muscles in her lower belly into a fist. She clutched the table for support. "What timing." She waited until it passed, trying to breathe like she and Cai had learned in class. Breathing, hell, this hurt.

Cai chose that moment to knock on the door. "Is it safe?"

She'd been snarling at him for weeks to keep out until she was finished. She couldn't believe she'd kept it a surprise, but she had. She straightened and took a deep breath. Her lower back still ached, but she pasted on a smile. "It's safe."

He walked in, then stopped dead. He stared, open-mouthed at the figure of a man astride a great winged horse. "It's incredible."

She walked over to him and slid her arms around his waist. "It's from a drawing I did of you right after we met. I think I knew even then that you would dominate my thoughts for the rest of my life. It's yours."

He took her face and kissed her hard. "I—I don't know what to say."

"Say you won't mind if I let Leonore use it as a centerpiece for the New York show. It won't be for sale."

"Done." He kissed her again, then looked back at the finished piece. "Is that how you saw me?"

She smiled. "It's how I still see you."

He smiled, but his brows furrowed. Then he snapped his fingers. "I almost forgot why I came out here. I just had a call from Dilys."

Jordy's smile grew wide and real. "Finally. I'd hoped to hear from her before the baby came."

"She's coming back. To help us."

Jordy's eyes widened. "Oh?"

"Yeah. Oh. I wasn't sure if we should jump for joy, or run screaming for the hills."

Jordy laughed and rubbed her tummy as the news sunk in. "I'm glad." And she was. "I'll be glad for the help and the company." Dilys had stayed in Wales as Cai had predicted. She'd come back for their wedding, then returned to her friends there. Jordy and Cai had traveled over to see her on the anniversary of Alfred's death. They'd all paid their respects. Then Cai had surprised Jordy with a visit to Alfred's artist friend Mara. She and Jordy had struck up a long-distance friendship and Mara planned to attend Jordy's opening in June. Cai and Jordy both ventured into the world a bit more these days. Cai even did book tours, more to demystify the man behind the books than because he truly enjoyed them. They both agreed that while they enjoyed their growing circle of friends, they mostly enjoyed being alone together on Crystal Key.

They had both found their balance.

Cai came over to her. "Are you really okay with it?" He rubbed her tummy and her lower back, as always knowing just where she needed his touch.

She leaned back into him, thinking how rich and full their lives had become. "Yeah, I am." She looked up. "You?"

He smiled dryly. "I think so."

Jordy wondered what else was going on behind those eyes of his. "You know, with Dilys coming back, maybe it's time we talked about . . . you know . . . it."

When Jordy had told Cai he was to become a father, they'd both sat in stunned silence for a time, each knowing what the other had immediately thought about. Jordy was intrigued by the possibilities. Unlike Cai, she often thought about the Dark Pearl and all of Alfred's stories. She'd taken to sitting in his office in the late afternoons and reading his books. She felt closer to him now than ever before. And she still missed him fiercely.

Cai had chosen to go on with his life, remembering Alfred in his own quiet ways. He was uncomfortable with that segment in their past and Jordy let him handle it his own way, as long as he didn't mind that she handled it her own way. Now Dilys was coming back . . . and the baby was on its way.

When he said nothing, she rubbed his hand reassuringly. "Maybe it will be a girl." But she knew differently. She'd had no tests run, but she knew. She suspected Cai did as well.

The next contraction hit before he could comment. She gripped a nearby table with one hand and Cai's hand with the other. "Maybe it's time to call the doctor."

Cai went pale. "It's time? Why didn't you tell me?"

She gritted her teeth through the contraction, then burst out in a laugh when it subsided. "I didn't think I was going to have to. He's going to tell you himself." She looked up at him and held on to this sober gaze. "He's going to be okay, Cai. We're going to love him so thoroughly and well, he'll be the best loved baby on the planet."

Cai's expression was fierce and his eyes glassed over. "Damn straight."

"And I'm glad Dilys is coming. Just in case."

Cai pulled her into his arms and hugged her as tightly as her swollen belly and aching back would allow. "I just want you happy. And I want a healthy baby. That's all."

"Then get the boat ready, or you're going to be greeting him on the floor on my studio."

JORDAN ALFRED L'BAAN didn't greet the world for another fourteen hours and seventeen minutes. Both mother and father were sweaty, exhausted, and exultant.

The doctor laid him on Jordy's stomach, swaddled in a blanket. Cai touched his fingers, Jordy trembled with overwhelming emotions. "Hello there, Mr. L'Baan. Open your eyes. Your mom wants to meet you."

"And your dad."

Cai had done extensive research when he'd learned he was to become a father and Jordy had read everything he'd found. She knew that babies' eyes were always dark blue and the true color came out over time.

So the nurses gasped, along with Mom and Dad, when Jordan finally opened his eyes. Two bright turquoise orbs stared back at them. Alfred's eyes.

We knew the moment we looked in his eyes.

Jordy hadn't forgotten Alfred's comment about his son's birth.

Cai gripped her hand hard. "Do you think it's really true?" he asked in hushed awe.

Jordan stared silently up at his parents.

His mother smiled. "I think we're going to find out."

ABOUT THE AUTHOR

Nationally bestselling author Donna Kauffman believes in keeping her feet on the ground, in touch with the tangible, the real. However, the endless possibilities of romance spark all sorts of intriguing ideas. She enjoys following those flights of fancy . . . even if they have her feet lifting off the terra firma every so often. In love, anything is possible.

Donna currently lives in Virginia with her husband and young sons. Her two Australian Terrors . . . er, Terriers, are also doing fine. She loves to hear from readers and can be contacted via her website at www.donnakauffman.com